MICHAEL JOSEPH

Published by the Penguin Group
Penguin Books Ltd, 80 Strand, London WC2R ORL, England
Penguin Group (USA) Inc., 375 Hudson Street, New York, New York 10014, USA
Penguin Group (Canada), 90 Eglinton Avenue East, Suite 700, Toronto, Ontario, Canada M4P 2Y3
(a division of Pearson Penguin Canada Inc.)
Penguin Ireland, 25 St Stephen's Green, Dublin 2, Ireland (a division of Penguin Books Ltd)
Penguin Group (Australia), 250 Camberwell Road, Camberwell, Victoria 3124, Australia
(a division of Pearson Australia Group Pty Ltd)
Penguin Books India Pvt Ltd, 11 Community Centre, Panchsheel Park, New Delhi – 110 017, India
Penguin Group (NZ), 67 Apollo Drive, Rosedale, Auckland 0632, New Zealand
(a division of Pearson New Zealand Ltd)
Penguin Books (South Africa) (Pty) Ltd, 24 Sturdee Avenue, Rosebank,
Johannesburg 2196, South Africa

Penguin Books Ltd, Registered Offices: 80 Strand, London WC2R ORL, England

www.penguin.com

First published in the United States of America by G. P. Putnam's Sons 2011
First published in Great Britain by Michael Joseph 2011

1

Printed in Great Britain by Clays Ltd, St Ives plc

A CIP catalogue record for this book is available from the British Library

HARDBACK ISBN: 978-0-718-15645-9
TRADE PAPERBACK ISBN: 978-0-718-15646-6

www.greenpenguin.co.uk

in Books is committed to a sustainable
for our business, our readers and our
. This book is made from paper certified
Forest Stewardship Council.

Devil's Gate

Clive Cussler
and Graham Brown

MICHAEL JOSEPH
an imprint of
PENGUIN BOOKS

Devil's Gate

Clive Cussler is the author or co-author of a great number of international bestsellers, including the famous Dirk Pitt® adventures, most recently *Crescent Dawn*; the NUMA® Files adventures; the *Oregon* Files, such as *The Jungle*; the Isaac Bell thrillers; and the Fargo novels, which began with *Spartan Gold*. His non-fiction works include *The Sea Hunters* and *The Sea Hunters II*; these describe the true adventures of the real NUMA, which, led by Cussler, searches for lost ships of historic significance. With his crew of volunteers, Cussler has discovered more than sixty ships, including the long-lost Confederate submarine *Hunley*. He lives in Arizona.

Graham Brown is the author of *Black Rain* and *Black Sun*. A pilot and an attorney, he lives in Arizona.

Find out more about the world of Clive Cussler by visiting www.clivecussler.co.uk
Visit the NUMA® website at www.numa.net

PROLOGUE

Santa Maria Airport, Azores island chain, 1951

HUDSON WALLACE STOOD ON THE RAMP just outside the terminal building on a cold, wet night. His leather jacket did little to keep out the chill as a mix of drizzle and fog shrouded the airport and the whole island around it.

Across from him, blue taxi lights glowed in stoic silence, doing little to warm the scene, while above a beam of white light swung through the fog followed moments later by a flash of green as the airport's beacon spun slowly and repetitively.

Hudson doubted anyone was up there to see it, not with the clouds so thick and low, but God help him if he were. Mountains surrounded the airport on three sides, and the island itself was just a speck on the map in the middle of the dark Atlantic. Even in 1951 finding such a spot was no easy task. And if someone could find Santa Maria though this soup, Hudson guessed he'd hit the peaks long before he saw the runway lights through the rain.

So getting to the island was one thing. Leaving was something else. Weather notwithstanding, Hudson wanted to go, couldn't wait to get moving, in fact. For reasons he knew too well it had become unsafe to stay. Despite that fact, and despite being the pilot and owner of the Lockheed Constellation parked on the ramp, he didn't have the final word.

With little to do but watch and wait, Hudson pulled a silver case from his coat pocket. He drew out a Dunhill cigarette and stuck it between his lips. Ignoring the "No Smoking" signs plastered every twenty feet, he cradled a Zippo lighter to his face and lit the Dunhill.

He was a hundred yards from the nearest plane or fuel line, and the whole airport was soaking wet. He figured the chances of causing a problem were just about nil. And the chances of anyone bothering to leave the warm, dry terminal building to come outside to complain? He figured they were even less than that.

After a deep, satisfying draw, Hudson exhaled.

The heather gray cloud of smoke faded as the door to the terminal opened behind him.

A man wearing ill-fitting clothing stepped out. His round face was partially hidden by a brown hat. His jacket and pants were made of coarse wool and looked like surplus leftovers from the Red Army winter catalog. Thin, fingerless gloves completed the appearance of a peasant traveler, but Hudson knew differently. This man, his passenger, would soon be wealthy. That is, if he could survive long enough to reach America.

"Is the weather going to clear?" the man said.

Another drag on the Dunhill. Another puff of smoke from Hudson before he answered.

"Nope," he said dejectedly. "Not today. Maybe not for a week."

Hudson's passenger was a Russian named Tarasov. He was a

refugee from the Soviet Union. His luggage consisted of two stainless steel trunks, heavy enough that they might have been filled with stones. Both of which sat locked and chained to the floor of Hudson's aircraft.

Hudson hadn't been told what was hidden in those trunks, but the newly formed Central Intelligence Agency was paying him a small fortune to get them and Tarasov into the U.S. He guessed they were paying the Russian a lot more than that to defect and bring the cases with him.

So far, so good. An American agent had managed to get Tarasov to Yugoslavia, another communist country, but under Tito there was no love of Stalin there. A hefty bribe had managed to get Hudson's plane into Sarajevo and out before anyone began asking questions.

Since then they'd traveled west, but word was out and one attempt on the man's life had left Tarasov limping with a bullet still in his leg.

Hudson's orders were to get him to the U.S. as quickly as possible, and keep it quiet on the way, but they never specified a route. A good thing too, because Hudson wouldn't have followed it.

So far, he'd avoided all European cities of note, traveling to the Azores instead, where he could refuel and then go nonstop to the States. It was a good plan, but he hadn't counted on the weather, or on Tarasov's fear of flying.

"They'll find us here sooner or later," Hudson said. He turned to his passenger. "They have agents everywhere, in every harbor and airport at least."

"But you said this was out of the way."

"Yeah," Hudson said. "And when they don't spot us at any place that's 'in the way,' they're gonna start looking elsewhere. Probably already have."

Hudson took another drag on the cigarette. He wasn't sure the Russians would check the Azores. But two Americans and a foreigner landing in what was essentially an international airliner—and then waiting around for three days without talking to anyone—was the kind of thing that might draw attention.

"At some point, you're going to have to decide what you're more afraid of," he said, nodding toward the plane sitting alone in the drizzle. "A little turbulence or a knife in the gut."

Tarasov looked up to the churning dark sky. He shrugged and held his hands out, palms up, like a man trying to show the world he had no money. "But we cannot fly like this," he said.

"Land," Hudson clarified. "We cannot *land* like this." He made a motion with his hand like a plane descending and flaring for landing.

"But we can sure as hell take off," he continued, raising his hand again. "And then we can head due west. No mountains that way. Nothing but ocean . . . and freedom."

Tarasov shook his head, but Hudson could see his resolve faltering.

"I checked the weather in New York," he said, lying once again. He'd done no such thing, not wanting anyone to guess his destination. "It's clear for the next forty-eight hours, but after that . . ."

Tarasov seemed to understand.

"We go now or we're stuck here for a week."

His passenger did not appear to like either choice. He looked at the ground and then out toward the big silver Constellation with its four massive piston engines and sleek triple tails. He stared into the rain and the cloak of the night beyond.

"You can get us through?"

Hudson flicked the cigarette to the ground and crushed it out with his boot. He had him. "I can get us through," he said.

Reluctantly, Tarasov nodded.

Hudson looked out toward the plane and made a winding motion with his hand. The sharp sound of the starter motor rang out and black smoke belched from the number 3 engine. The plugs fired and the big radial engine came to life. In moments, the huge propeller was spinning at fifteen hundred rpms, blasting rain and spray out behind the aircraft. Seconds later the number 1 engine sprang to life.

Hudson had hoped he would be able to convince their passenger to fly. He'd left Charlie Simpkins, his copilot, in the plane and told him to keep her primed to go.

"Come on," Hudson said.

Tarasov took a deep breath and then stepped away from the door. He began walking toward the waiting plane. Halfway there, a shot rang out. It echoed across the wet tarmac, and Tarasov lurched forward, arching his back and twisting to the side.

"No!" Hudson yelled.

He sprang forward, grabbing Tarasov, keeping the man on his feet and hustling him toward the plane. Another shot rang out. This one missed, skipping off the concrete to the right.

Tarasov stumbled.

"Come on!" Hudson shouted, trying to get him up.

The next bullet hit Hudson, catching him in the shoulder, spinning him around. He fell to the ground and rolled. The shell had knocked him downward like someone hitting him from above. He guessed the shot had come from the terminal's roof.

Wincing in pain, Hudson pulled a Colt .45 from his shoulder holster. He spun and aimed toward the roof of the building, firing blindly in what he guessed was the approximate direction of the sniper.

After blasting off four shots, Hudson thought he saw a shape duck behind the lip of the terminal's roof. He fired another shot in that direction and then grabbed Tarasov once again, pulling him backward toward the plane, dragging him across the ground like a sled, until they reached the stairs near the front of the aircraft.

"Get up," Hudson shouted, trying to haul him up.

"I . . . can't," Tarasov said.

"I'll help you," he said, lifting. "You just have to—"

As he pulled Tarasov to his feet another shot cracked, and the man sprawled to the ground face-first.

Hudson ducked behind the stairs and shouted toward the aircraft's open doors.

"Charlie!"

No response.

"Charlie! What's the word?"

"We're ready to go!" a voice yelled back.

Hudson heard the last of the engines winding up. He grabbed Tarasov and rolled him over. The man's body was limp like a rag doll's. The final shot had gone through his neck. His eyes stared lifelessly up and back.

"Damn," Hudson said.

Half the mission was blown, but they still had the steel trunks and whatever was in them. Even though the CIA was a secret organization, they had offices and an address. If he had to, Hudson would go find them and bang on the front door until someone took him in and paid him.

He turned and fired toward the terminal again. And in that moment he noticed the lights from a pair of cars racing toward him from the far end of the ramp. He didn't figure they were cavalry.

He dashed up the stairs and dove through the door as a bullet ricocheted off the Connie's smooth skin.

"Go!" he shouted.

"What about our passenger?"

"Too late for him."

As the copilot shoved the throttles forward Hudson slammed the door shut, wrenching the handle down just as the plane began to move. Over the droning sound of the engines he heard the crackle of glass breaking.

He turned to see Charlie Simpkins slumped over toward the center console, his seat belt holding him up.

"Charlie?"

The plane was on the move as Hudson ran forward. He dove into the cockpit as another shot hit and then another.

Staying on the floor, he reached up and slammed the throttles forward. As the engines roared he scrambled under the pilot's seat and pushed hard on the right rudder. The big plane began to pick up momentum, moving ponderously but gathering speed and turning.

Another rifle shot hit the sheet metal behind him and then two more. Hudson guessed he had turned far enough that the aircraft was pointing away from the terminal now. He climbed up into his seat and turned the plane out onto the runway.

At this point he had to go. There was nowhere safe back on that ramp. The plane was pointed in the right direction, and Hudson wasn't waiting for any clearance. He pushed the throttles to the firewall, and the big plane began to accelerate.

For a second or two he heard bullets punching holes in the aircraft's skin, but he soon was out of range, roaring down the runway and closing in on rotational velocity.

With the visibility as bad as it was and the shattered window on the left side, Hudson strained to see the red lights at the far end of the runway. They were coming up fast.

He popped the flaps down five degrees and waited until he was a hundred yards from the end of the asphalt before pulling back on the yoke. The Connie tilted its nose up, hesitated for a long, sickening second, and then leapt off the end of the runway, wheels whipping through the tall grass beyond the tarmac.

Climbing and turning to a westbound heading, Hudson raised the landing gear and then reached over to his copilot.

"Charlie?" he said, shaking him. "Charlie!"

Simpkins gave no reaction. Hudson checked for a pulse but didn't find one.

"Damn it," Hudson said to himself.

Another casualty. During the war a half a decade back, Hudson had lost too many friends to count, but there was always a reason for it. Here, he wasn't sure. Whatever was in those cases had better be worth the lives of two men.

He pushed Simpkins back up into his seat and concentrated on flying. The crosswind was bad, the turbulence worse, and gazing into a wall of dark gray mist as he climbed through the clouds was disorienting and dangerous.

With no horizon or anything thing else to judge the plane's orientation visually, the body's sensations could not be trusted. Many a pilot had flown his plane right into the ground in conditions like these. All the while thinking he was flying straight and level.

Many more had taken perfectly level planes and stalled and spun them because their bodies told them they were turning and falling. It was like being drunk and feeling the bed spin; you knew it wasn't happening, but you couldn't stop the sensation.

To avoid it, Hudson kept his eyes down, scanning the instruments and making sure the plane's wings stayed level. He kept the climb to a safe five-degree angle.

At two thousand feet and three miles out, the weather got worse. Turbulence shook the plane, violent up- and downdrafts threatening to rip it apart. Rain lashed the windshield and metal around him. The hundred-fifty-mile-an-hour slipstream kept most of it from pouring in through the shattered corner window, but some of the moisture sprayed around the cockpit, and the constant noise was like a freight train passing at full speed.

With the bullet holes and the broken window, Hudson couldn't pressurize the plane, but he could still climb to fourteen thousand feet or more without it becoming too cold to function. He reached behind his seat and touched a green bottle filled with pure oxygen; he would need that up higher.

Another wave of turbulence rocked the plane, but with the gear up and all four engines going Hudson figured he could power through the storm and out the other side.

The Constellation was one of the most advanced aircraft of the day. Designed by Lockheed with help from world-famous aviator Howard Hughes, it could cruise at 350 knots and travel three thousand miles without refueling. Had they picked Tarasov up a little farther west, Hudson would have gone for Newfoundland or Boston without stopping.

He turned to check his heading. He was crabbing to the north more than he intended. He went to correct the turn and felt a spell of dizziness. He leveled off, just as a warning light came on.

The generator in the number 1 engine was going, and the engine was running extremely rough. A moment later the number 2 engine began to cut out, and the main electrical warning light came on.

Hudson tried to concentrate. He felt light-headed and groggy as if he'd been drugged. He grabbed his shoulder where the bullet had hit him. The wound was painful, but he couldn't tell how much blood he was losing.

On the instrument panel in front of him, the artificial horizon—an instrument pilots use to keep wings level when they can't see outside—was tumbling. Beside it the directional gyro was tumbling.

Somehow the aircraft was failing simultaneously with Hudson's own body.

Hudson looked up at the old compass, the ancient instrument that was the pilot's last resort should everything mechanical go wrong. It showed him in a hard left turn. He tried to level off, but he banked too far in the other direction. The stall horn sounded because his airspeed had dropped, and an instant later the warning lights lit up all over his instrument panel. Just about everything that could flash was flashing. The stall horn blared in his ear. The gear warning sounded.

Lightning flared close enough to blind him, and he wondered if it had hit the plane.

He grabbed the radio, switched to a shortwave band the CIA had given him, and began to broadcast.

"Mayday, Mayday, Mayday," he said. "This is—"

The plane jerked to the right and then the left. The lightning snapped again, a million-volt spark going off right in front of his eyes. He felt a shock through the radio and dropped the microphone like a hot potato. It swung beneath the panel on its cord.

Hudson reached for the microphone. He missed. He leaned farther forward and tried again, stretching, and then grasping it with his fingertips. He pulled it back ready to broadcast again.

And then he looked up just in time to see clouds vanish and the black waters of the Atlantic filling the horizon and rushing up toward him.

Geneva, Switzerland, January 19, 2011

ALEXANDER COCHRANE WALKED ALONG the quiet streets of Geneva. It was well past midnight, on a dark winter evening. Snow drifted softly from above, adding to three inches that had fallen during the day, but there was no wind to speak of, and the night was hushed and peaceful.

Cochrane pulled his knit cap down, drew his heavy wool coat tighter around him, and thrust his hands deep into the coat's pockets. Switzerland in January. It was supposed to snow and often did, usually taking Cochrane by surprise.

The reason for that was that Cochrane spent his days three hundred feet underground in the tunnels and control room of a massive particle accelerator known as the Large Hadron Collider, or LHC. The LHC was run by the European Council for Nuclear Research, though it went by the acronym CERN as the French spelling used those initials (Conseil Européen pour la Recherche Nucléaire).

The temperature in the LHC's control room remained a perfect 68 degrees, the lighting was constant, and the background noise was an unchanging hum of generators and pulsing energy. A few hours spent down there felt no different than a few days, or a few weeks, as if time wasn't passing.

But of course it was, and it often stunned Cochrane how different the world appeared upon his return to the surface. He'd entered the building this morning under blue skies and a crisp, if distant, sun. Now the clouds hung thick, heavy and low, illuminated from beneath in an orange glow by the lights of Geneva. All around lay a three-inch blanket of snow that had not been present twelve hours before.

Cochrane walked through the field of white headed for the train station. The big shots at CERN—the physicists and other scientists—came and went in CERN-provided cars with drivers and heated seats.

Cochrane was not a physicist or particle theorist or any other designation of that nature. He was an educated man to be sure. He had a master's in electromagnetic theory, twenty years of experience in the energy-transfer business, and was well compensated. But the glory of CERN went to the physicists and the others looking for the building blocks of the universe. To them Cochrane was nothing more than a highly paid mechanic. They were bigger than him. Even the machine he worked on was bigger than him. In fact, it was bigger than anyone.

The Large Hadron Collider was the largest scientific instrument in the world. Its tunnels ran in a twenty-seven-kilometer circular track that extended outside the territory of Switzerland and into France. Cochrane had helped design and build the superconducting magnets that accelerated the particles inside the tunnels. And as an employee of CERN he kept them running.

When the LHC was powered up, it used an incredible amount of energy, most of that for Cochrane's magnets. After being chilled to 271 degrees below zero, those magnets could accelerate protons to nearly the speed of light. The particles in the LHC traveled so fast that they zipped around the twenty-seven kilometers eleven thousand times in a single second.

The only problem for Cochrane was that one magnet failure shut down the whole thing for days or even weeks at a time. He'd been particularly irked a few months back when a subcontractor installed a second-rate circuit board, which had promptly blown. Even now it boggled Cochrane's mind; a ten-billion-dollar machine done in because someone wanted to save a couple euros.

It had taken three weeks to repair the damage, every single day spent with higher-ups breathing down his neck. Somehow it was his fault. Then again, it was always his fault.

Even though things were going well now, the physicists and the CERN leadership seemed to regard the magnets as the weak link in the system. As a result, Cochrane was held on a short leash and seemed almost to live at the facility.

It made him angry for a moment, but then he shrugged. Soon enough it would be someone else's problem.

Cochrane continued through the snow to the train station. To some extent the snow was a plus. It would leave tracks. And he wanted there to be tracks tonight.

He climbed up onto the platform and checked the time. Five minutes till the next train. He was right on schedule. The platform was empty. In five minutes or less he'd be on his way to a new life, one he felt certain would be infinitely more rewarding than his current one.

A voice called out to him. "Alex?"

He turned and gazed down the platform. A man had come up the far stairway and was striding toward him, passing beneath the halogen lamps.

"I thought it was you," the man said, coming closer.

Cochrane recognized him as Philippe Revior, deputy head of security at the LHC. His throat tightened. He hoped nothing was wrong. Not tonight. Not this night.

Cochrane pulled out his phone to make sure he hadn't been summoned back. No messages. No calls. *What the hell was Revior doing here?*

"Philippe," Cochrane said as cheerfully as he could. "I thought you were prepping for tomorrow's run."

"We've done our work," Revior said. "The night crew can handle the rest."

Cochrane felt suddenly nervous. Despite the cold, he began to sweat. He felt Revior's arrival had to be more than coincidence. Had they found something? Did they know about him?

"Are you catching a train?" he asked.

"Of course," the security chief said. "Who drives in this?"

Who drives in this? Three inches of snow was a normal winter day in Geneva. Everyone drove in it.

As Revior moved closer, Cochrane's mind whirled. All he knew for sure was that he could not have the deputy head of security traveling with him. Not here, not now.

He thought of heading back to the LHC, claiming suddenly that he'd left something behind. He checked his watch. There was not enough time. He felt trapped.

"I'll ride with you," Revior said, producing a flask. "We can share a drink."

Cochrane looked down the tracks. He could hear the sound of the train coming. In the far distance he saw the glow from its lights.

"I, um . . . I . . ." Cochrane began.

Before he could finish he heard footsteps from behind, someone coming up the stairs. He turned and saw two men. They wore dark overcoats, open to the elements.

For a second Cochrane assumed them to be Philippe's men, members of security, or even the police, but the truth was laid bare in the look on Revior's face. He studied them suspiciously, a lifetime of evaluating threats no doubt telling him what Cochrane already knew, that these men were trouble.

Cochrane tried to think, tried to come up with some solution to avoid what was about to happen, but his thoughts formed like molasses in the cold. Before he could speak the men drew weapons, short-barreled automatics. One pointed at Cochrane and one at Philippe Revior.

"Did you think we would trust you?" the leader of the two men said to Cochrane.

"What is this?" Revior said.

"Shut up," the second man said, jabbing the gun toward Revior.

The leader of the two thugs grabbed Cochrane by the shoulder and yanked him closer. The situation was spiraling out of control.

"You're coming with us," the leader said. "We'll make sure you get off at the right stop."

As the second thug laughed and glanced toward Cochrane, Revior attacked, slamming a knee into the man's groin and tackling him.

Cochrane wasn't sure what to do, but when the leader turned to fire, Cochrane grabbed his arm, shoving it upward. The gun went off, the shot echoing through the dark.

With little choice but to fight, Cochrane pushed forward, bowling the bigger man over and scuffling with him on the ground.

A backhand to the face stunned him. A sharp elbow to the ribs sent him tumbling to the side.

As he came up he saw Revior head butting the second thug. After putting him out of action Revior charged and tackled the leader, who'd just thrown Cochrane off him. They struggled for the gun, exchanging several vicious blows.

A thundering sound began to fill the background as the approaching train rounded the curve a quarter mile from the station. Cochrane could already hear the brakes screeching as the steel wheels approached.

"Alex!" Revior yelled.

The assailant had flipped Revior over and was now trying to get the gun aimed at Revior's head. The old security specialist held the arm off with all he had, then pulled it close, a move that seemed to surprise the assailant.

He chomped down on the man's hand with his teeth, and the thug whipped his arm backward instinctively. The gun flew out of his grip and landed in the snow beside Cochrane.

"Shoot him!" Revior shouted, holding the assailant and trying to immobilize him.

The sound of the train thundered in Cochrane's ears. His heart pounded in his chest as he grabbed the gun.

"Shoot him!" Revior repeated.

Cochrane glanced down the track, he had only seconds. He had to choose. He targeted the assailant. And then he lowered his aim and fired.

Philippe Revior's head snapped backward, and a spray of blood whipped across the snow-covered platform.

Revior was dead, and the assailant in the gray coat wasted no time in dragging him back into the shadows, throwing him behind a bench, just as the approaching train passed a wall of trees at the end of the station.

Feeling as if he might throw up, Cochrane stuffed the gun into his waistband and covered it with his shirt.

"You should have backed off," Cochrane said.

"We couldn't," his would-be attacker replied. "No contingency for that."

The train was pulling into the platform, stirring up the snow and bringing a rush of wind all its own.

"This was supposed to look like a kidnapping," Cochrane shouted over the noise.

"And so it will," the man said. He swung a heavy right hand and struck Cochrane on the side of the head, knocking him to the ground, and then kicked him in the ribs.

The train stopped beside them as both assailants pulled Cochrane up and dragged him backward toward the stairs.

Cochrane felt dizzy as they hauled him off, disoriented and confused. He heard a pair of shots fired and a few shouts from passengers stepping off the almost empty train.

The next thing he knew, he was in the back of a sedan, staring out the window as they raced along the streets through the falling snow.

2

Eastern Atlantic, June 14, 2012

THE WATERS OF THE EASTERN ATLANTIC rolled with an easy swell as the *Kinjara Maru* steamed north for Gibraltar and the entrance to the Mediterranean. This ship made 8 knots, half its maximum speed but the most efficient pace in terms of burning fuel.

Captain Heinrich Nordegrun stood inside the vessel's air-conditioned bridge, his eyes on the radar screen. No weather to speak of and little traffic.

There were no ships ahead of them and only a single vessel behind them, ten miles off; a VLCC, or Very Large Crude Carrier, commonly called a supertanker. VLCCs were the largest ships afloat, larger than American aircraft carriers, too large to use the Panama or Suez canals, and often topping out at 500,000 tons when fully loaded. Though the vessel behind them must have been empty, based on the speed she was making.

Nordegrun had tried hailing the tanker earlier. He liked to know who else was out there, especially in questionable waters. Here, off the coast of West Africa, things were not as dicey as they could be on the other side of the continent, near Somalia. But it still paid to check in with other ships and find out what they knew or what they'd heard. The ship had not responded, but that was no real surprise. Some crews talked, others didn't.

Dismissing the tanker from his mind, Nordegrun glanced through the windows ahead of him. The open water and the calm night made for good sailing.

"Bring us to twelve knots," he said.

The helmsman, a Filipino man named Isagani Talan, answered. "Aye, sir."

Such was the state of the world's merchant marine that Nordegrun, a Norwegian citizen, captained a Bahamian-registered vessel, built in South Korea, owned by a Japanese company, and crewed mostly by Filipino sailors. To round out the worldly status of their voyage, they carried an African cargo of minerals bound for a factory in China.

An outsider might have thought it madness, but the only thing that mattered was that the players knew their jobs. Nordegrun had sailed with Talan for two years and trusted him implicitly.

The vibration in the ship changed as the engines answered the call. Nordegrun switched from the radarscope to a monitor that lay before him. It sat flat, resting on top of a block like the chart tables of old, but it was a modern high-definition touch screen. It currently displayed the waters around them and his ship's position, course, and speed.

All seemed well from a distance, but by tapping on the screen Nordegrun was able to zoom in and see that a southerly current had pushed them five hundred yards off course.

Nothing to worry about, Nordegrun thought, *but if perfection was possible, why not reach for it?*

"Two degrees to port," he said.

Talan was positioned ahead of Nordegrun on the bridge at the ship's control panel. It also looked nothing like the setup of a classic ship. Gone was the big wheel and the image of a man whirling it to one side or the other to change course. Gone was the telegraph, the heavy brass lever that signaled the engine room to change speed.

Instead Talan sat in a high, pedestal-like chair with a computer screen in front of him. The wheel was now a small steel hub, the throttle was a lever the size of a car's gearshift.

As Talan made his adjustments, electronic signals went to the rudder-control units and the engines in the stern of the ship. The course change was so slight that it couldn't be felt or noticed visually, but the captain could see it on the screen. It took several minutes, but the big ship swung back onto course and settled in on its new speed.

Satisfied, Nordegrun looked up.

"Keep us on that line," he said. "Since they've given us all this nice equipment, we might as well use it."

"Yes, sir," Talan said.

With the ship back on course, Nordegrun checked the chronometer. It was after ten p.m. local, the third watch was in place. Confident that the ship was in good hands, he glanced at the officer of the deck.

"She's all yours," he said.

Nordegrun turned to head below, checking the position of the tanker trailing them one last time. It had matched the *Kinjara Maru*'s course change and, oddly enough, had accelerated to 12 knots as well.

"Monkey see, monkey do," he mumbled as he walked for the door.

Stepping out through the door and heading aft, Nordegrun squinted into the gloom. He could make out the lights on the ship following them. A strange hue, he thought. They were a bluish white, like the high-intensity headlights on modern luxury sedans.

He'd never seen that on a ship before, even from a distance. All he could ever recall was the standard yellowish or plain white light that incandescent and fluorescent bulbs gave off. Then again, years back, no one thought they'd see a ship that was guided by a computer.

He stepped into the stairwell and shut the hatch. Clambering down the stairs toward his quarters, Nordegrun felt a spring in his step. Unlike earlier generations, he and his officers were allowed to bring family aboard. Nordegrun's wife of two years waited below, joining him for the first time at sea. She would go with him as far as Cairo, disembarking and flying home as the *Kinjara Maru* moved through the Suez Canal.

It would be a good week, he thought, a vacation without taking one. If he hurried, he had time to join her at the ship's mess.

As he reached the lower deck, the lights in the stairwell dimmed. He glanced up. The filaments in the incandescent bulb above the door looked like embers on the verge of going out. Higher up, the fluorescent tubes began flickering at an odd rate.

They returned to normal for a second, but there was no doubt in Nordegrun's mind that they had some type of generator issue. Aggravated, he turned to climb back up the stairs.

The lights dimmed again, then brightened until they were blazing white. The fluorescent tubes made a strange noise and then shattered simultaneously, raining glass down on him. On the wall, the incandescent bulb blew out in a loud pop, flashing the stairwell in electric blue and then plunging it into darkness.

Nordegrun held the rail, shocked and surprised. He'd never seen anything like it. He felt the ship begin to heel over as if she were turning hard. With no idea what was going on, he raced up the darkened stairway and ran forward. Lights were blowing all over the ship.

Nordegrun felt a spike of pain in his neck and jaw. Stress, he thought, the fight-or-flight reaction, as something went wrong with his vessel.

He burst into the bridge. "What the devil is happening?" he shouted.

Neither Talan nor the officer of the deck responded. Talan was busy shouting into the ship's intercom. The OOD was wrestling with the computer, desperately tapping the override keys as the ship continued to turn.

Nordegrun caught a glimpse of the rudder indicator full over to port. An instant later the screen flared and went blank. Sparks shot from another machine, and the pain in Nordegrun's head got suddenly worse.

At almost the same time, the officer of the deck fell to the ground, holding his head and grunting in pain.

"Talan," Nordegrun shouted. "Go below. Get to my wife."

The helmsman hesitated.

"Now!"

Talan left his post, Nordegrun grabbed the ship's radio and tried to transmit. He pressed the talk switch, but the radio let out a high-pitched squeal. He reached for another device but suddenly felt his chest burning.

Looking down, he saw the buttons on his coat glowing red. He grabbed one and pulled at it but it burned his hand. The noise in his head reached a crescendo, and Nordegrun fell to the ground. Even with his eyelids shut, he saw stars and flashes of light as if someone were pressing his eyes in with their thumbs.

A pop in his head sent blood running out his nose. Something in his sinuses had ruptured.

Nordegrun opened his eyes to see smoke filling the bridge. He crawled for the doorway. With blood streaming down his face, he pushed the hatch open and got partway outside. As he did, the noise in his head became a scream.

He fell to the deck, his face angled aft. Behind him what looked like electricity was arcing between the rail and superstructure. Farther off he saw the ship with the strange lights still trailing them. It remained ten miles off but now glowed a dozen times brighter as if it were covered in Saint Elmo's fire.

Nordegrun's mind was so far gone, he could do nothing but stare at it. And then his body stiffened in some type of convulsion, the pain spiked beyond anything he could have imagined, and Nordegrun screamed as his skin burst into flame.

Eastern Atlantic, June 15

AS DAWN BROKE OVER THE ATLANTIC, Kurt Austin stood near the bow of the NUMA vessel *Argo*, wiping sweat off his face with a towel. He'd just finished fifty laps around the main deck. Only, because the deck did not encircle the ship, he'd been forced to enter the superstructure at the end of every lap, race up two flights of stairs and across the main transom, then down two flights and back out to begin the next lap.

It would have been far easier to hit the exercise room, pound the treadmill for five miles and then climb on the StairMaster, but they were at sea, and to Austin the sea had always meant freedom; freedom to roam and explore the world, freedom from traffic and smog and the sometimes claustrophobic existence of modern urban life. Out here—with the promise of dawn on the horizon—he wasn't about to lock himself in a cramped windowless room for his morning workout even if it had air-conditioning.

Wearing black sweatpants and a faded gray T-shirt with the

NUMA logo on it, Kurt felt as good as he could remember. He stood just over six feet tall, with broad shoulders and curly silver-gray hair that looked almost platinum at times. He considered his eyes a shade of blue, but apparently they were an unusual shade, as many people—especially the women in his life—had tried to explain.

As he closed in on his fortieth birthday, Kurt had rededicated himself to working out. He'd always been in shape. A career in the Navy and several years as part of a clandestine CIA salvage team required it. But with the decade number on his age going to four, Kurt was determined to get in the best shape of his life, better than he'd been at thirty, better than he'd been at twenty.

It was a tall order. It took more work, left more aches and pains, and was slower in coming than when he'd been younger, but he was almost there.

Ten pounds lighter than he'd been a year before, benching, curling, and lifting more weight in the gym, he could feel the strength surging through his body like it had in his youth when he believed he could do anything.

It was needed too. A career at NUMA came with lots of physical punishment. Beyond the regular labor-intensive work of any salvage operation, he'd also been beat up, shot at, and half drowned on a regular basis. After a while the dings started to add up. A year ago he'd considered taking up a standing offer to go back to work for his father, who owned a prominent salvage company of his own. But that felt like leaving on someone else's terms, and if there was one thing Kurt Austin didn't do, it was follow any lead but his own.

He stared out at the horizon as it changed from a deep indigo to a pale grayish blue. The light was rising even though the sun had yet to show its face. He stretched and turned, trying to crack his back. Off the starboard beam, something caught his eye; a thin trail of smoke, drifting skyward.

He hadn't seen it during his run, the darkness had obscured it, but it was no illusion.

He squinted and stared, but in the predawn gloom he couldn't make out the source of the smoke. He took one last glance and then headed for the stairs.

Austin stepped onto the bridge to find Captain Robert Haynes, the *Argo*'s commanding officer, standing with the officer of the watch, plotting out their course to the Azores, where the NUMA team would participate in an X Prize–like race to crown the world's fastest two-man submarine.

The operation was a milk run. A pure research assignment given to Kurt and his partner, Joe Zavala, as a reward for all the heavy lifting they'd done on recent missions. Joe was already on Santa Maria Island making preparations and, as Kurt guessed, making friends, especially among the women. Kurt was looking forward to joining him, but before the minivacation could begin they would have to make a slight detour.

Haynes never lifted his eyes from the charts. "Done wearing out my decks?" he asked.

"For now," Kurt replied. "But we're going to need to change course to one-nine-zero."

The captain looked up briefly and then back down at the chart table. "I told you before, Kurt, you lose something over the side, you're going to have to swim for it if you want it back."

Kurt smiled briefly, but the situation was serious.

"There's a line of smoke off our starboard beam," Kurt said. "Someone's got a fire going, and I don't think it's a barbecue."

The captain stood straight, the joking look gone from his face. A fire at sea is an incredibly dangerous event. Ships are filled with pipes and conduits that carry flammable liquids like fuel and hydraulic fluid. They often carry dangerous and even explosive cargoes: oil, natural gas, coal, and chemicals, even metals like magnesium and aluminum that burn. And unlike a fire on land, there's really nowhere safe to run unless you abandon ship, the last option in any captain's handbook.

Kurt knew this, as did every man on the *Argo*. Captain Haynes didn't hesitate or even attempt to confirm the accuracy of Kurt's assessment. He turned to the helmsman.

"Take us around," he said. "Make your course one-nine-zero. Bring us to flank speed."

As the helmsman executed the order, the captain grabbed a pair of binoculars and headed out onto the starboard wing of the bridge. Kurt followed.

The *Argo* was fairly close to the equator, and at such latitudes the light grew quickly. Kurt could see the smoke plainly now, even without the binoculars. Thick and dark, it rose skyward in a narrow vertical column, thinning out only marginally on the way up and drifting slightly to the east.

"Looks like a cargo vessel," Captain Haynes said.

He handed the binoculars to Kurt.

Kurt trained them on the ship. She was a midsize vessel, not a containership but a bulk carrier. She appeared to be adrift.

"That's oil smoke," Kurt said. "The whole ship is shrouded in it, but it's thickest near the aft end."

"Engine-room fire," Haynes said. "Or a problem with one of the bunkers."

That would have been Kurt's guess as well.

"Did you pick up any distress calls?"

Captain Haynes shook his head. "Nothing. Just regular chatter on the radio."

Kurt wondered if the fire had taken out her electrical system. But even if it had, most ships carried backups, and every vessel of that size would have a few handheld transceivers, an emergency beacon, and even radios in the main lifeboats. To hear nothing from a 500-foot vessel burning and adrift seemed all but impossible.

By now the *Argo* had finished its turn and was heading dead at the stricken ship. Her speed was coming up, and Kurt could feel them surging through the water. The *Argo* could make 30 knots in calm seas. Kurt guessed the range at just over five miles, closer than he'd first thought. That was a good thing.

But ten minutes later, as he trained the binoculars on the super-structure and increased the magnification, he spotted several things that were less than good.

Flames were licking out through various hatches all along the deck, meaning the entire vessel was burning, not just the engine room. The ship was definitely listing to port and was down at the bow, meaning she was taking on water as well as burning. But worst of all, there were men on the decks who seemed to be dragging something toward the rail.

At first Kurt thought it was an injured crewman, but then they let go of the person, dropping him to the deck. The man tumbled as if he'd been shoved and then got up and began to run. He made three or four steps, only to fall forward suddenly onto his face.

Kurt snapped the binoculars to the right just to be sure. He could clearly see a man holding an assault rifle. Without a sound he saw the muzzle flash. One burst and then another.

Kurt turned back to the man who'd fallen. He lay utterly still now, facedown on the deck.

Pirates, Kurt thought. *Hijackers with assault rifles. The cargo vessel was in deeper trouble than he'd guessed.*

Kurt lowered the binoculars, fully aware that they were now heading toward more then a rescue.

"Captain," he said. "Our problems just multiplied."

4

ABOARD THE *KINJARA MARU,* Kristi Nordegrun struggled with the darkness. Her ears rang with a strange sound, and her head pounded as if she'd been drinking all night. She lay on the floor, her limbs stiff and folded under her in an awkward tangle.

Try as she might, she could not even remember how she'd gotten there, let alone what had happened. Based on the numbness in her legs, she guessed she had been in that position for a long time.

Unable to stand yet, Kristi propped herself up against the wall, fighting an unbalanced equilibrium.

She was in the deepest part of the crew's quarters, several flights below deck and near the center of the vessel. She'd come here because the mess was on this deck and she was going to meet her husband for a late meal before they retired for the night. She looked around but didn't see him. That concerned her.

If she had been knocked unconscious for some time, surely her husband would have found her. Then again, if the ship was in trouble, his first duty was as captain.

Kristi realized she could smell smoke. She couldn't remember an explosion, but the ship was definitely on fire. She remembered her husband telling her there were some waters of the world where terrorists planted mines. But it seemed not to concern him on this journey.

She tried again to stand, fell to the side, and knocked over a table upon which cans of soda stood. In the darkness she heard a strange sound, like marbles rolling around.

The noise moved away from her but continued until ending with several dull clunks. At that moment Kristi realized what had happened: the cans were rolling away from her, gathering speed until they hit the bulkhead.

Her equilibrium was definitely off, but so was the floor. The ship was tilting, listing. Panic gripped her. She knew now that the ship was sinking.

She crawled to the wall, bumped into it, and then followed it to the door. She pushed on the door. It moved a few inches and then hit something soft. She pushed again, leaning her shoulder into it and shoving it a few more inches. Trying to squeeze through, she realized the object blocking her way was the body of a man, lying against the door.

As she pushed, the man moved a fraction, rolling over and moaning.

"Who are you?" she said. "Are you hurt?"

"Mrs. Nordegrun," the man managed to say.

She recognized the voice, one of her husband's crew members from the bridge. A nice man, from the Philippines, her husband had said he'd be a good officer one day.

"Mr. Talan?"

He sat up. "Yes," he said. "Are you okay?"

"I have no balance," she said. "I think we're sinking."

"Something happened," he said. "We have to get off the ship."

"What about my husband?"

"He's on the bridge," Talan said. "He sent me for you. Can you make it to the stairs?"

"I can," she said. "Even if I have to crawl."

"Is better that way," he said, finding her hand and guiding her in the right direction.

"Yes," she agreed. "We need to stay underneath the smoke if we can."

Before getting married, Kristi had been a paramedic and then a trauma nurse. She'd been on the scene of many accidents and fires and even a building collapse. And despite her fear and confusion, her past training and experience were kicking in and taking over.

Together, they began crawling along the floor. Fifty feet on, they found another crewman, but they could not wake him.

Kristi feared the worst but had to be sure. She checked the man for a pulse.

"He's dead."

"How?" Talan asked.

She didn't know. In fact, she could find no marks on him, and his neck seemed uninjured.

"Perhaps the fumes?"

The smoke was thicker here, but it didn't seem dense enough to kill.

Kristi put the dead man's hand back on his chest, and the two crawled on. They reached the stairwell and pushed the door open. To Kristi's relief there was less smoke inside, and by holding on to the railing she could stand.

As they began to climb, a thin shaft of light shone down on them. In the hallway, some of the emergency lights were working while others were out, and at first Kristi guessed that this illumination came from an emergency light in the stairwell, but there was something odd about it. The light was whiter, more natural, and it seemed to dim and brighten sporadically.

Two levels up was a door with a tempered-glass window in it. Kristi guessed that the light was coming from there, but it made little sense to her. It had been dark when she'd gone to the ship's pantry. How could it be daylight?

She knew there had to be another explanation. She kept climbing, trying to keep up with Talan. As they reached the landing at the top, daylight streamed in from outside, obscured off and on by waves of smoke that drifted by.

"It's morning," she said, dumbfounded.

"We must have been unconscious for many hours," Talan said.

"And no one came to find us?" she asked, the fear in her heart stirring at the implications.

It didn't seem possible for so much time to have passed, or for nobody to have come looking for them in all those hours, but based on what she was seeing it had to be true.

She stepped forward and nearly lost her balance. Talan caught her and eased her to the bulkhead.

"Hold on," he said.

"I'm all right," she murmured.

Talan released her and went to the door, touching it as if testing it for heat. Kristi noticed the glass in the window was sagging and discolored like melted wax.

"It's okay," he said. "No fire now."

He pushed on the door and it squeaked open.

He stepped out and beckoned for her to follow. She stepped through and grabbed hold of the ship's rail.

As Talan looked toward the bow, trying to gauge the condition of the ship, a man appeared through the drifting smoke, twenty yards aft. He was large-framed, broad-shouldered, and wearing black. Kristi couldn't recall the crew wearing black.

The man turned to them, and she could see he held a machine gun of some kind.

She gasped. And out of instinct, perhaps, Talan pushed her to the ground just as machine-gun fire rang out. She watched helpless as his chest was riddled with bullets. He fell backward over the railing and into the sea.

Kristi lunged for the door and pulled on it, but before she could open it the man who'd appeared from the smoke was on her. He slammed it shut with a heavily booted foot.

"No you don't, love," he said with a distinctive snarl. "You're coming with me."

Kristi tried to squirm away, but he stretched out a big paw and grabbed her by the collar and then yanked her up to her feet.

KURT AUSTIN STOOD ON THE *Argo*'s bridgewing as the ship charged across the water. At 30 knots the bow was carving the ocean in two and blasting waves of spray up into the wind. Curtains of water spread out and fell, lacing the surface with patches of foam that were quickly left behind.

Kurt studied the stricken bulk carrier through the binoculars. He'd seen men going from hatch to hatch, dropping grenades or some kind of explosives into them one after another.

"That's damn strange," Kurt said. "Looks like they're scuttling the ship on purpose."

"You never know with pirates," Captain Haynes said.

"No," Kurt agreed, "but usually they're after money. Ransom money or the chance to sell the cargo on the black market. Can't do that if you've sent the ship to the bottom."

"Good point," Haynes said. "Maybe they're taking the crew."

Kurt took another look along the deck. The accommodations block sat at the tail end of the ship. The structure—which some sailors referred to as a "castle"—rose five stories from the deck like an apartment building.

It stood high and proud, but the flat foredeck of the ship was only just above the water, the tip of the bow no more than a foot or two from being awash. He could see little else through the fire and the smoke.

"I saw them shoot at least one poor soul," he said. "Maybe they had an important passenger aboard, the rest being expendable. Either way. I doubt they'll surrender."

"We've got three boats ready to go," Haynes told him. "The fast boat and our two tenders. You want in?"

Kurt put the binoculars down. "You didn't think I was going to stand around and watch, did you?"

"Then get down to the armory," the captain said. "They're fitting out a boarding party now."

————

ABOARD THE *KINJARA MARU,* the hulking leader of the "pirate" gang dragged Kristi Nordegrun across the deck. He was known by the name Andras, but his men sometimes called him "The Knife" because he loved to play with sharpened blades.

"Why are you doing this?" she asked. "Where's my husband?"

"Your husband?" he said.

"He's the ship's captain."

Andras shook his head. "Sorry, love, you may now consider yourself single again."

With that, she lunged at him, her hand slamming into his face. She might as well have punched a stone wall. He shook off the blow, threw her to the deck, and whipped out one of his favorite toys: a locking jackknife with a five-inch titanium blade. He locked the blade into place and held it toward her.

She shrank back.

"If you aggravate me, I'll carve you up with this," he said. "Understand?"

She nodded slowly, the fear plain as day in her eyes.

Truthfully, Andras didn't want to cut her, she would fetch more money with a clean face, but she didn't need to know that.

He whistled to his men. With the crew dead and the ship going down, the last part of a long job was done. It was time for the rats to leave the sinking ship.

They gathered round him and one of them, a scruffy-looking man with yellowish teeth and a fishhook scar on his upper lip, took special notice of Kristi. He dropped down, touching her hair.

"Nice," he said, rubbing her golden locks between his fingers.

At that moment, a heavy boot hit him in the side of the head.

"Get out of it," Andras said. "Find your own prize."

Wearing a new welt on his face and a look of shock, Fishhook scurried away like a scolded hound.

"What are you going to do with me?" Kristi asked with surprising force.

Andras smiled. He was going to have his way with her and then he was going to sell her on the black market. A nice little bonus to the money he'd been paid for this job. But she didn't need to know that either.

Ignoring her question, he put the blade away and dropped down beside her. Using a metal wire, he bound her hands, wrapping them several times before twisting the ends together. With a piece of cloth he gagged her. That would keep her quiet.

Before he could get her up, a voice shouted from above. "Ship approaching! Looks like a cutter or some type of frigate."

Andras snapped his head up. He tried to peer through the thick smoke. He couldn't see anything.

"Where, you damn fool?" he shouted. "Give us a direction."

"West-northwest," his man shouted.

Andras strained to see through the drifting cloud of soot and smoke. A large vessel approaching was bad news, but something far worse caught his eye; a thin white wake, close to the *Kinjara*'s hull.

He could see it in gaps between the smoke. It crossed toward the front of the ship, where it vanished in the dark clouds. He looked toward the bow, which was now awash in two feet of water.

A second later the oily haze parted, and a ribbed inflatable boat raced out of the smoke, gliding right up onto the bow. Two men lay prone on its forward section, aiming and firing M16 rifles.

Andras saw two of his men fall, and another was hit and hobbling. The others scrambled for cover as the fast boat beached itself on the deck near the *Kinjara*'s second cargo hatch.

Several men in fatigues piled out of the boat on either side as one of the shooters—a man with distinctively silver hair—aimed and fired with deadly accuracy.

Two more of The Knife's men went down before the shooter rolled off the attacking boat and took cover behind one of the open cargo hatches.

"Americans," Andras cursed. *Where the hell had they come from?*

5

IN AN INSTANT THE DECK of the freighter became a battleground. Bullets and shell casings flew in all directions. Andras moved quickly, grabbing Kristi and dragging her backward. He added the occasional burst to what had become a raging gun battle, but his plan was to do more than stand and fight.

As he pulled back, he saw the situation for what it was: a first strike. The Americans had stormed in, taking out a half dozen of his men, but they were now pinned down on the deck, caught in a sort of cross fire while the ship burned and slowly sank beneath them. He guessed they wouldn't have done that intentionally, unless they had backup coming.

The sound of a loudspeaker echoed from the approaching cutter.

"Throw down your weapons and surrender," an authoritative voice demanded.

While he had no intention of doing anything of the sort, Andras was keenly aware of the danger to himself. But then, he was a man who'd made his life knowing how to turn the tables.

He reached one of the loading cranes. Grabbing the hook that dangled from it, he slipped it under the wire he'd wrapped around Kristi's hands.

He threw the power switch and was rewarded with the sound of its hydraulic pump running. Before he sent her out, he ripped the gag off Kristi's mouth.

She looked at him.

"You're going to want to scream," he said, "trust me."

With that, he threw the lever and the crane sprang to life. It pulled her upward and began swinging her out over the battleground for all to see.

KURT AUSTIN CROUCHED BEHIND a steel hatch cover. His idea to race around the bow of the vessel and literally drive right up onto it had been a cunning move. With the smoke surrounding them and the *Argo* approaching from the opposite direction, Kurt and his men had taken the pirates by surprise, speeding onto the deck and hitting several of them immediately.

The one flaw in his plan had been the number of pirates. There were far more than he'd expected, more than a dozen, maybe close to twenty. Those who'd survived and taken cover now had him pinned down.

Sooner or later the other tenders from the *Argo* would arrive, giving them a numerical advantage, but until then it would be tough sledding.

The radio on his belt crackled, a call from one of the tenders. *"Kurt, we're approaching the stern, no resistance so far."*

He didn't have time to reply as shells started pinging off the hatch behind him. He ducked lower, trying to see where they were coming from. Before he could decide what to do next, he heard a female scream. He glanced skyward to see a woman, in her mid-thirties, dangling from the hook of a crane.

Seconds later, a voice bellowed above the din.

"Are we ready to stop this madness?" the voice shouted.

Kurt didn't look up, as that was a good way to get one's head blown off, but the guns around him went silent.

Kurt glanced at the young woman. Blood streamed down her arms and across her clothes.

"Now that I have your attention," the voice boomed, "you're going to let my men get off this stinking garbage scow of a ship or I'll blast this woman to shreds like a piñata."

Kurt glanced around, sweat and smoke burning his eyes. He noticed water beginning to swirl at his ankles, and several feet away it poured into one of the open cargo hatches.

The ship was settling fast. The bow was now completely sub-merged with only a few high points sticking out like dead trees in flooded field. Worse yet, as the water began filling the forward cargo holds the weight on the front section would increase rapidly.

In a few minutes the *Kinjara Maru*'s fate would change from a gentle settling to a nosedive into the abyss.

"I'm waiting!" the hidden speaker shouted.

"Kurt?" a voice asked over the radio. *"What do you want to do?"*

Kurt looked up at the woman again. "Hold your positions," he said into the radio.

"Well?" the unknown voice shouted, demanding an answer.

"Okay," Kurt yelled back. "Take your men and get out of here." He shouted to his men. "Hold your fire until they're clear."

Almost instantly Kurt heard movement, the pirates pulling back.

"Can anyone see him?" Kurt whispered into the radio. "He has to be up high."

Someone must have risked a look because a shot rang out. A grunt sounded over the radio.

"No peeking," the voice shouted.

"Damn," Kurt mumbled. He keyed the mike on his radio. "Who got hit?"

No response. Then someone said, "It's Foster."

Kurt shook his head angrily. "You hit one more of my men," he shouted to the unseen figure, "and I promise you'll die on this boat!"

"I'm sure," the hidden man replied, "that you'd like to believe that."

By now the water was lapping at Kurt's thighs. It felt like the tide coming in, only way too rapidly. The ship's equilibrium was changing. As the pitch increased, loose items began sliding down the deck toward him.

Kurt glanced up at the woman again. She had to be in tremendous pain. He wanted to shoot the scum who'd hung her up there, but he didn't dare risk a look for her tormentor.

Then the sound of large outboard motors starting echoed from over the starboard side of the ship. In a moment, the soft rumble turned to a fierce roar, and what looked like a stripped-down powerboat began racing off into the distance.

"Go," Kurt shouted.

His men sprang into action.

"Hawthorne's down," someone said.

"Get him up," Kurt shouted. "Get him and Foster into the boat."

"What about the search?"

"I doubt these guys left any survivors," he said. "Either way, you don't have time to look."

The ship had tilted ten degrees nose down, far enough for a length of chain to come sliding toward him like a great metallic snake.

Kurt dodged the chain. It hit the edge of the cargo hatch and poured itself into the cavernous space below, rattling ominously as the links slid over the edge until the chain released itself into oblivion.

"Get off the ship," Kurt ordered.

"What are you going to do?" one of his men asked.

"I'm going to get that woman."

6

AS THE *KINJARA MARU* FOUNDERED, Kurt Austin scrambled forward and up the sloping deck. The footing was treacherous where the deck had become coated with water, oil, and sludge. He pulled himself upward with anything he could grasp.

Reaching the ladder that led up to the crane, Kurt climbed it, catching sight of the pirates racing away to the south. Putting them out of his mind and hanging on to the railing, he reached the crane operator's hutch.

A strangely shaped folding knife with a black handle and a steel or titanium blade stood on its point, embedded into the crane operator's seat. A little present left behind by the thug who'd strung the woman up. Kurt grabbed it, folded it up, and slid it into a pocket.

Turning to the control panel, he checked for power. Thankfully, the lights on the panel remained illuminated.

"Hold on," he shouted to the woman, realizing even as he spoke that she wasn't *holding* anything at all, but guessing that "Hang in there" would have had a terrible ring to it.

Years in the salvage business had left Kurt very familiar with cranes. He grabbed for the control handle that would retract the crane back to his position. As he operated the lever he heard a whirring sound, and the crane jerked backward a few feet and then slammed to a halt. The poor woman swung back and forth like a pendulum, crying and screaming in pain. Seconds later a hydraulic warning light came on.

It was only then that Kurt noticed red liquid pouring down the side of the crane. He glanced and saw that the hydraulic line had been cut clean through. Now the little gift made sense to him. He could almost hear the thug laughing.

His headset crackled.

"Kurt, we're off the ship, but you should know that we can see the top of the rudder. The fantail of this thing is coming out of the water."

Kurt looked forward. The front quarter of the ship was submerged, debris floating everywhere. Time was running out fast.

With the crane dead, he had little choice. He dropped his rifle and began to climb out onto the crane's boom. It was a tricky crawl made worse by the grease, oil, and hydraulic fluid. Trying to keep the boom underneath him, he scooted forward.

From behind him, a group of steel barrels came tumbling down the deck. One of them hit something sharp, sparked, and then exploded. The blast knocked Kurt sideways. His feet slipped, and the weight of his boots threatened to drag him off the boom.

Ahead of him, the woman screamed, sobbing as she shouted out to him. "Please," she begged. "Please hurry."

Kurt was doing all he could just to hang on. He glanced back. Fire enveloped the hutch he had been standing in only moments before. Moving had been a lucky break, but not if it just postponed the inevitable.

He swung his legs to one side and then back the other way and up, catching the boom with one leg. A smaller secondary explosion echoed from below as the smell of kerosene enveloped him. Down through black smoke, Kurt could see flames licking across the water as the burning fuel spread, blasts of heat roasting him as he moved forward.

Another ten feet and he reached the spot where the woman was hooked. The wire wrapped around her wrists was slicing into her skin. Her arms were scarlet with flowing blood, and her face was pasty white.

He grabbed her by the arms and tried to pull her up, but he had no leverage. Swirling waves of heat rose up from the crackling fires below. The ship shuddered as something internal broke loose. One of the engines or even the cargo sliding around.

"Kurt, she's going," came the call over the radio. *"Any minute she's going."*

I'm aware of that, Kurt thought. He grabbed her arms again.

"Pull yourself up," he shouted.

"I can't," she cried. "My shoulder is out."

That didn't surprise Kurt. But it left him with only one choice.

He grabbed the knife from his pocket, flipped it open, and slid it under the wire that held the woman. Trying desperately not to cut her but knowing he didn't have much time, Kurt began to saw. The wire snapped all at once, and the young woman plunged toward the ocean.

Kurt pushed off and dropped in after her.

Smoke and fire passed him in an instant. He hit the water, and felt one leg strike something beneath it. When he came up, the woman was right in front of him, bravely trying to tread water with one arm.

Kurt grabbed her and splashed away from the flames of burning gas and oil. Quickly, he realized a much greater danger. The water was swirling around them. He felt it pulling at his feet like the undertow at the beach.

The ship was going down.

He looked aft. The fantail had risen up like the *Titanic*, the bow was beginning to plunge.

Grabbing the woman's good arm, he began to swim, pulling her along. When the ship went down, it would create a massive wave of suction dragging everything within a hundred-foot radius down with it. Both of them would be long drowned before it released their bodies back to the surface.

It was hopeless, but he swam hard anyway. And then the fast boat from the *Argo* suddenly raced in. It slid to a stop beside them.

The men rapidly hauled the woman in, literally yanking her out of the water, as Kurt pulled himself over the side. The engines roared again.

Kurt fell into the back of the boat. Looking up he saw the "castle"—the five-story structure that housed the crew's quarters and the bridge and the antenna masts—plunging toward them at a forty-five-degree angle, like a building falling out of the sky.

The fast boat leapt forward like a stallion as the pilot slammed the throttle home. Right out into daylight.

The castle crashed into the water no more than twenty feet behind them. A surge of foam hurled them along and then spat them out like a surfer ejecting from a massive breaker.

Seconds later the *Kinjara Maru* was gone.

As they sped away, heavy rumbling sounds rose up from the depths, along with surges of air and debris.

Kurt looked at the woman. She was covered in soot and oil, her shoulder was either broken or separated, her wrists were gashed by the wire that had cut into them, and her eyes were swollen and almost as red as the blood that soaked her clothes. Using her less injured hand, she placed pressure on the gash on her other wrist.

"We have a doctor aboard the ship," Kurt said. "He'll tend to your injuries as soon as we board."

She nodded. At least she was alive.

"To the *Argo*?" the helmsman asked.

Kurt nodded. "Unless you have somewhere else in mind?"

The helmsman shook his head. "No, sir," he said, and pointed the boat toward the *Argo*.

TEN MINUTES LATER, they were back on board the *Argo*. While the ship's doctor tended to the young woman and the away team stowed the fast boat, Kurt stepped onto the bridge.

The ship was already accelerating and changing course.

"You look like hell," Captain Haynes said. "Why aren't you in sick bay?"

"Because I'm not sick," Kurt replied.

The captain eyed Kurt strangely and then looked past him. "Somebody get this man a towel. He's dripping all over my bridge."

An ensign tossed him a towel, which Kurt used to dry his face and hair. "Can we catch them?" he asked.

Haynes glanced at the radar screen. "They're faster than us, doing forty knots. But a little boat like that didn't bring these boys all the way from Africa. I'll bet you a steak dinner they're heading for a mother ship somewhere."

Kurt nodded. Pirates had become more sophisticated in recent years. While most still operated from little hamlets along the coasts of poor Third World nations, some had larger vessels that took them out to sea. Mother ships, disguised as old freighters and such.

They hid their tricked-out speedboats inside and often used semi-legitimate voyages to disguise their true purpose. Kurt had heard from one authority that the pirates would be easy to catch if someone would just look for the freighters that constantly dropped off cargo without ever picking any up. But then the buyers were too smart to ask where goods came from when they were getting such great deals.

"Anything on radar?" Kurt asked.

"Nothing yet," Haynes said.

As dry as he was going to get, Kurt tossed the towel and picked up the captain's binoculars, gazing out toward the target.

The fleeing boat itself was hard to see, but the long white wake it left was a giant arrow pointing right to it. They were five miles off, and putting the *Argo* farther behind, but it would take hours for them to escape radar range, and by that time . . .

A flash caught Kurt by surprise, momentarily blinding him through the binoculars. Immediately following it, Kurt saw debris flying in all directions and an expanding cloud.

"What in the world . . ."

A few seconds later the sound reached them. A single low boom, like a massive firework had gone off. When the view cleared, the speedboat was gone; obliterated in a single, thundering explosion.

KURT AUSTIN HAD BEEN in the communications room of the *Argo* for
over an hour. The last forty minutes of that he'd been talking with
NUMA's director of operations, Dirk Pitt.

Kurt got along well with the Director, having known him when
Pitt was still doing fieldwork for NUMA. Considering the kind of
missions NUMA's Special Operations Team often ended up taking
on, it helped to have a boss who'd "been there and done that," as
Pitt had pretty much been everywhere and done everything.

Moving to the head office hadn't dulled Pitt's senses, even if it
did place him in the crosscurrents of the political world.

As the *Argo* patrolled a wide circle near where the *Kinjara Maru*
had gone down, Kurt explained what they knew and what they
didn't. Pitt asked questions. Some of which Kurt couldn't answer.

"The strangest part," he said, "is that they sank the ship deliberately instead of taking her for a prize. And they killed the crew. It
was more like a terrorist action than a pirate raid."

A flat-screen monitor on the wall displayed Pitt's rugged features. He seemed to clench his jaw while thinking.

"And you never found a mother ship?" he asked.

"We did a fifty-mile leg in the direction they were heading," Kurt said. "Then Captain Haynes took us on a dumbbell pattern south for five miles and back north for ten. Nothing on radar in any direction."

"Maybe their course was a false track. To draw you off until they put some distance between you and them," Pitt offered.

"We thought about that," Kurt said, considering a conversation with the captain as the search began to look fruitless. "Or they might have even had enough gas on board to get back to the coast. A drum or two lashed to the boat could explain the explosion."

"Still doesn't explain what they were doing on that ship," Pitt noted. "What about hostages?"

"Maybe," Kurt said. "But we have the captain's wife with us. They left her deliberately to hold us up. She said there was no one unusual on board. In fact, if anyone were to bring a ransom she seemed like the best candidate to me, but it wouldn't be that much."

On screen, Pitt looked away. He rubbed a hand over his chin for a second and then turned back to the screen.

"Any thoughts?" he asked finally.

Kurt offered a theory. "My dad and I did a lot of salvage work when I was younger," he began. "Boats go down for plenty of reasons, but people send 'em down for only two. Insurance money or to hide something on board. One time we found a guy shot in the head but still strapped into the seat of his boat. Turned out his partner shot him and sunk the boat, hoping to cover it up. Didn't count on the insurance company deciding they could salvage the wreck and get some money out of it."

Pitt nodded. "You think this is the same kind of thing?"

"Kill the crew, sink the ship," Kurt said. "Someone's trying to keep something quiet."

Pitt smiled. "This is why you make the big bucks, Kurt."

"I get big bucks?" Kurt said, laughing. "I'd hate to see what you're paying everybody else." ·

"It's a scandal," Pitt said. "But it's a heck of a lot more than the admiral paid me when I started."

Kurt laughed at the thought. Pitt had told him once that his first month's pay for NUMA wouldn't cover a broken arm, even though he'd risked his life half a dozen times in that month. Then again, neither of them did it for the money.

Kurt continued. "Kristi Nordegrun, the woman who survived, said she didn't know what happened, but the lights flickered and blew out, her head seemed to ring, and she lost her balance and consciousness. She believes it was at least eight hours before she woke up again. She still seems disoriented, she can't walk without holding on to something."

"What does that tell us?" Pitt asked.

"I don't know," Kurt said. "Maybe some kind of nerve agent or anesthetic gas was used. But it's just one more thing that screams 'more than pirates' to me."

Pitt took this in. "What do you want to do?"

"Go down there and poke around," Kurt said, "see what they're trying to hide from us."

Pitt glanced over at a map on his wall. An old-fashioned push-pin marked the *Argo*'s location. "Unless I have you in the wrong spot, there's three miles of water between you and the seafloor. You got any ROVs on board?"

"No," Kurt said. "Nothing that can go that deep. But Joe's got the *Barracuda* on Santa Maria. He could modify it, and we could be back here in a few days, a week at most."

Pitt nodded as if he were considering the thought, but Kurt sensed it was more in admiration of his gung ho attitude than in granting permission for the excursion.

"You earned some R and R," Pitt said. "Go on to the Azores. Contact me once you get there. In the meantime I'll think about it."

Kurt knew the tone in Pitt's voice. He wasn't a man to close off any possibilities, but he'd probably come up with his own idea long before Kurt called in.

"Will do," Kurt said.

The screen went blank, Pitt's face replaced by a NUMA logo.

In his heart, Kurt knew there was more to this incident than the obvious, but how much more was the question.

It could have been the "pirates" simply trying to cover their tracks. Maybe they'd taken cash or other valuables. Maybe they'd killed a few of the crew in the takeover and then decided to hide the incident by shooting the rest and scuttling the ship. But even that scenario left questions.

Why set the ship on fire? The smoke could and did give them away. It would have been easier to flood her and sink her without the explosions.

And what about the pirates themselves? Recent history had pirates all around the world, mostly locals from poor countries who saw the world's wealth passing them by in great ships and decided to grab a share for themselves. But the few men Kurt had seen on the *Kinjara Maru* did not look like your typical pirates. More like mercenaries.

He looked over at the folding knife now lying on the table beside him, a unique-looking and lethal piece. He remembered it sticking in the chair. It seemed like a taunt, a calling card and a slap in the face all at the same time.

Kurt thought about the arrogance of the man's words, and the voice itself. It hadn't been the voice of some poverty-stricken West African pirate. And stranger still, Kurt had the oddest feeling that he'd heard that voice somewhere before.

8

THE CONTINENT OF AFRICA sits at the oceanic crossroads. But despite this position, it has always been more of a roadblock to trade than a thoroughfare. Its sheer size and inhospitable habitats—from desert sands in the Sahara to the dark impenetrable jungles across its vast central region—made it impossible to cross profitably.

In the past, ships that wished to swap oceans were forced to sail on a ten-thousand-mile journey that took them around South Africa, into some of the most treacherous waters in the world and past a point wistfully named the Cape of Good Hope, though its original name was the more accurate *Cabo de Tormentas*: Cape of Storms.

The completion of the Suez Canal made the journey unnecessary, but did little to bring Africa into the modern world. Quite the contrary. Now ships had only to cut the corner, slip through the Suez, and they were soon on their way to the Middle East and its oil fields, Asia and its factories, Australia and its mines.

As world commerce boomed, Africa rotted like vegetables left unclaimed on the dock beneath the withering sun.

Inland could be found genocide, starvation, and disease, while along the African coasts lie some of the most lawless places in the world. Somalia is for all intents and purposes a land of anarchy; the Sudan is little better. Less well known but almost as forlorn are the West African countries of the Ivory Coast, Liberia, and Sierra Leone.

Liberia's troubles were well chronicled, as leader after leader fell amid scandal and corruption, and the country lurched toward anarchy and mayhem. The Ivory Coast was much the same.

And for much of its history, Sierra Leone had fared even worse. Not too long ago, the country had been considered a more dangerous place than Afghanistan and had a lower standard of living than Haiti and Ethiopia. In fact, Sierra Leone had once been so weak that a small group of South African mercenaries had all but taken it over.

The group, operating under the "invite" of the existing regime and calling themselves "Executive Outcomes," routed a much larger group of rebels who threatened to take over the mines. The nation's only real source of wealth at the time.

The mercenaries then proceeded to protect and control these assets, quadrupling production and taking a large cut for themselves in the process.

Into this world of instability came Djemma Garand. A native of Sierra Leone but trained by these South African mercenaries, Djemma rose to power in Sierra Leone's military, making important friends and ensuring that his units were trained, disciplined, and ready.

It took decades, but eventually the opportunity presented itself, and Djemma took power in a bloodless coup. In the years since, he had consolidated his position, raised the nation's standard of living, and earned the grudging approval of the West. At least his regime was stable, even if it wasn't democratic.

As if to show their approval they'd even stopped asking about the welfare and whereabouts of Nathaniel Garand, Djemma's brother and a robust voice for democracy, who had been rotting in one of the country's prisons for the last three years.

Djemma considered imprisoning his own brother both his darkest moment and also his finest. Personally, it sickened him, but the moment he'd given the order any fears he'd had about his own ability to do what was necessary for his country vanished. Places like Sierra Leone were not ready for democracy, but with a strong, unquestioned hand they might rise to that point someday.

Standing on the marble floors of his palace, Djemma looked like any other African dictator. He wore a military uniform with a pound of medals dangling from his chest. He shielded his eyes with expensive sunglasses and carried a riding crop, which he liked to slam on flat surfaces when he felt his point was being taken too lightly.

He'd seen the movie *Patton* several times and admired the general's way. He also found it interesting that Patton considered himself a reincarnation of the African Hannibal. For Hannibal's legend and his exploits held special interest to Djemma Garand.

In many ways the Carthaginian general was the last African to shake the world with his sword. He went over the Alps with an army and his elephants, ravaging the Roman Empire on its home soil for years, defeating legion after legion, and failing to bring it down only because he had no siege engines with which to attack the capital of Rome.

Since then, amid wars and coups and everything else that occurred on the African continent, the rest of the world only watched with disinterest. They worried about the flow of minerals and oil and precious metals, but even a temporary stoppage or civil war or more starvation had little effect on them.

After a little saber rattling, new dictators would eagerly agree to the same terms as the old. Most for them, and a few pennies for the poor. As long as business was conducted this way, what did the world have to worry about?

Seeing this, living it, breathing it, Djemma Garand intended his rule to be something more. Though he traveled in an armored Rolls-Royce, flanked by Humvees with machine guns, Djemma vowed to be more than a despot. He desired a legacy that would leave his people better off for all eternity.

But to do that would mean more than changing his country; it would require changing Sierra Leone's place in the world. And to do that he needed a weapon that could reach beyond African shores and shake that world, a modern version of Hannibal's elephants.

And that weapon was almost in his grasp.

Taking a seat behind an imposing mahogany desk, Djemma carefully placed his sunglasses on one corner and waited for the phone to buzz. Finally, a light illuminated.

Gently, without any rush, he lifted the receiver.

"Andras," he said quietly. "You'd better have good news."

"Some," the salty voice replied.

"That is not the kind of answer I expect from you," Djemma said. "Explain."

"Your weapon didn't work as advertised," Andras said. "Oh, it damaged the ship all right, but it did no better than last time. Took out the navigation and most of the controls, but she kept steaming under partial power, and half the crew survived, those trapped deep inside. This device of yours is not doing what you expect."

Djemma did not like the sound of that. Little else could so easily send him into a rage as to hear that his project, his own Weapon of Mass Destruction, had yet again failed to perform up to standards.

He covered the phone, snapped his fingers at an aide, and scribbled a name on a piece of paper.

"Bring him to me," he said, handing the scrap to the aide.

"How many of the crew lived?" he asked, returning his attention to the call.

"About half," Andras said.

"I trust they no longer survive."

"No," Andras said. "They're gone."

A slight hesitation in Andras's voice concerned Djemma, but he pressed forward. "What about the cargo?"

"Off-loaded and on its way to you," Andras insisted.

"And the ship?"

"Rusting on the bottom."

"Then what is it you're not telling me?" Djemma said, growing tired of having to pry information from his most highly paid asset.

Andras cleared his throat. "Someone tried to stop us. Americans. I would guess a SEAL team or two. Makes me think your secret has leaked out."

Djemma considered the possibility and then rejected it. If information had leaked, they would have been stopped before the attack commenced. More likely a simple rescue party with a few guns.

"Did you deal with them?"

"I escaped and covered our trail," Andras said. "There was noth-ing else I could do."

Djemma was not used to hearing that someone who'd tangled with The Knife had survived. "I hate to think you're going soft on me," he said.

"Not on your life. These men were tough. You'd better find out who they were."

Djemma nodded. For once they agreed.

"And what about your operation . . ." Andras said. "Python, is it? Will that still be going off?"

Operation Python was Djemma's masterstroke. If it succeeded, it would bring his country endless wealth, stability, and prosperity. And if it failed . . . Djemma didn't want to think about that pros-pect. But if his weapon did not work as planned, failure was a real possibility.

"It cannot be delayed much longer," Djemma said.

"Want me to come lend a hand?" Andras offered. His voice dripped with cynicism. He'd made it clear earlier that he thought Djemma was mad for attempting what he was about to do. Even madder for trusting his own army to do it. But Andras was an out-sider, he didn't know Djemma's troops the way their general and leader did.

Djemma smiled. By using Andras's services, he was making the man incredibly rich, but if there was a way to get even more wealth and power Djemma expected Andras would follow it. There was no filling his insatiable pockets.

"Where I grew up," Djemma said, "the old women had a saying. A snake in the garden is a good thing. It eats the rats that devour the crops. But a snake in the house is a danger. It will kill the master and eat the baby, and the house will ring with sorrow."

He paused and then clarified. "You will get your money, Andras, perhaps enough to buy a small country of your own. But if you ever set foot on the soil of Sierra Leone, I will have you killed and your bones scattered to the dogs in my courtyard."

Silence rang across the phone line, followed by soft laughter.

"The UN is wrong about you," Andras said. "You are ruthless. Africa could use more men like you, not less. But in the meantime, as long you keep paying, I'll keep working. Don't run out of money like the papers say you're about to. I would hate to extract my fees in less pleasant ways."

The two men understood each other. The Knife was not afraid of Djemma, even though he should be. He was not afraid of anything. This is why Djemma had chosen him.

"Get yourself to Santa Maria," he said. "I will give you further instructions once you arrive."

"What about the *Kinjara Maru*?" Andras asked. "What if someone goes to look at her?"

"I have plans to deal with that if it occurs," Djemma said.

Andras laughed again. "Plans for everything," he said sarcastically. "You make me laugh, Garand. Good luck with your mad plans, fearless leader. I will watch the papers and root for your side."

The phone clicked, the line went dead, and Djemma placed his receiver down on its cradle. He sipped water from a glass of fine crystal and looked up as the doors to his office opened.

The aide he'd sent running out came back in. Two of Djemma's personal guards followed, escorting a white man who looked less than happy to be present.

The guards and the aide left. The twelve-foot-tall doors closed with a thud. Djemma and the Caucasian man stood facing each other.

"Mr. Cochrane," Djemma said officiously. "Your weapon has failed . . . once again."

Alexander Cochrane stood like a scolded child might, staring with insolence at his would-be father. Djemma did not care. There would be success or there would be consequences.

ALEXANDER COCHRANE WALKED toward Djemma's desk with a sense of foreboding far beyond anything he could recall. For seventeen months, Cochrane had been toiling to construct a directed-energy weapon of incredible power.

This weapon would use superconducting magnets, like those Cochrane had designed for the Large Hadron Collider what seemed like several lifetimes ago. It would accelerate and fire various charged particles at almost the speed of light in a tight beam that could be rapidly "painted" over a target, destroying electronics, computers, and other circuitry.

If tuned correctly, the weapon could act like a giant microwave beam, heating organic matter, cooking its targets from the inside out, setting them afire, even if they took cover behind steel-and-concrete walls.

Through the skies, Cochrane's weapon could shoot down attacking aircraft at ranges of two hundred miles or more, or it could wipe out approaching armies by sweeping back and forth across the battlefield like a garden hose aimed at approaching ants.

At its ultimate level of development, Cochrane's weapon could destroy a city, not like an atomic bomb, not with fiery heat or ex-

plosive force, but with precision, cutting here and there like a sur-
geon's scalpel, turning one block after another into a wasteland.

It could kill the occupants or leave them alive, at Cochrane's—or
Djemma's—choosing. But even if tuned to destroy electronics and
systems only, it could render a city uninhabitable by destroying all
modern technology within it in a matter of seconds. Without computers, phones, an electrical grid, or running water, today's modern,
integrated city would become a land of anarchy or a ghost town
shortly after Cochrane—or Djemma—set his sights on it.

But to do all that, the weapon had to work, and so far the results
were inconclusive.

"I told you it needs more testing," Cochrane stammered.

"This was supposed to be the final test," Djemma said.

"What happened to the boat?"

"You mean the *ship*," Djemma corrected.

"Ship, boat," Cochrane said, "same thing to me,"

"Your lack of precision bothers me," Djemma replied, with an
undertone to his words. "A ninety-thousand-ton vessel is not a boat."

"What happened to the *ship*?" Cochrane asked, sick and tired of
Djemma's condescending attitude. The man acted as if he were
asking Cochrane to build a television set or assemble a computer
from prefabricated parts.

"The *Kinjara Maru* has gone down to . . . what do you Americans
call it? Ah, yes, Mr. Davy Jones's locker."

"And the cargo?" he asked. Nothing would improve without this
cargo.

"One hundred metric tons of titanium-doped YBCO," Djemma
said. "Removed as per your request."

Cochrane breathed a sigh of relief. "Well, that's good news."

"No!" Djemma snapped, slamming his riding crop on the desk. "Good news would have meant your promises to me were kept. Good news would have been to hear that your weapon worked as you said it would, completely disabling the ship and killing all the crew instantly. As it was, the ship continued under power, and there were survivors, who we had to deal with."

Cochrane had grown used to Djemma's moodiness but was stunned by the sudden anger. He jumped at the snap of the crop. Still, his self-confidence was not shaken.

"So what?" he said finally.

"So, our men were exposed," Djemma said. "A group of Americans tried to interfere. We have now attracted the wrong kind of attention. All thanks to you and *your lack of precision*."

Cochrane shifted in his chair. His sense of discomfort would have turned into outright fear were it not for one simple fact. Even though Djemma could have him killed with the snap of his fingers, he never would as long as he needed and wanted the weapon to work.

So far, Cochrane had covered his bases well, everything from insisting his disappearance be made to look like a kidnapping—so he could go back to the industrial world someday—to the way he'd gone about constructing Djemma's weapon.

He'd done all the development work himself, drawn up the plans and supervised the efforts on-site. He'd made himself so integral to the project that Djemma could do little to threaten him, unless he wished to abandon the hope of finishing it and possessing the final version of the weapon.

Remembering this, Cochrane spoke with renewed confidence.

"All systems take time to fine-tune," he insisted. "Do you think they build the supercolliders from scratch and then just flip the switch and watch them go? Of course not. There are months and months of tests and calibration before they run even the most basic experiment."

"You've had months," Djemma said pointedly. "And I don't want any more experiments. The next test will be full-scale."

"The weapon isn't ready," Cochrane insisted.

Djemma's glare rose to a new level of intensity. "It had better be," he warned. "Or you will burn alongside me when they come for us."

Cochrane paused. Djemma's words confused him. Why would they burn? All along, Djemma had insisted they would sell the weapon, not to one world power but to all of them. Let them point Cochrane's gun at one another's heads much as they'd pointed nuclear missiles at one another for fifty years. They would never use it, and both Cochrane and Djemma would be rich. There was no danger in that. And no need to rush.

"What are you talking about?" he asked.

"I have something else in mind from what I told you," Djemma said. "Forgive me for deceiving such an honorable man."

The sarcasm in Djemma's voice showed how he really viewed Cochrane, and despite the lure of wealth and even clandestine fame, Cochrane suddenly felt worse than he ever had at CERN.

Djemma pulled a file and leafed through it. "You come to my country with your careful plans," he said. "Plans to have your cake and eat it too. To build a Weapon of Mass Destruction, deposit millions in Bahamian and Swiss banks, and then flee back to the high life, no doubt spinning tales of your great hardship and daring escape."

"We had a deal."

"Deals change, Cochrane," the African leader said. "And you made it easy for me."

He pulled a photo from the file and slid it across the desk to Cochrane. The main part of the photo was a police shot of Philippe Revior lying dead in the snow. A smaller inset in the upper right-hand corner showed a handgun laid out on a white cloth. The gun looked terribly familiar to Cochrane.

"You are a murderer, Mr. Cochrane."

Cochrane squirmed.

"Do not be shy," Djemma insisted, "this is true. It is only by the poor placement of security cameras that the world doesn't know this already. If you attempt to leave, or to cross me or continue to drag your feet, I will be sure the story gets out. For proof, I have the gun with your fingerprints all over it."

Cochrane's face tightened in a look of disgust. He was trapped and he knew it. Whatever Djemma had in mind, Cochrane would have to make it work or his life would be forfeited in the bargain.

After stewing in silence for a moment, Cochrane finally spoke. "You know I wouldn't cross you. It's worth too much to me to finish."

"And yet you fail."

"Only on your timetable."

Djemma shook his head. "It cannot be changed."

Cochrane was afraid of that. It meant he would have to own up to the truth. "Fine," he said. "I will do what I can. But there are only two ways to get the weapon more power. Either we need better materials or, if you want it done more quickly, I'll need some help."

Djemma smiled and even began to laugh, as if it brought him

great joy to have pried this confession out of Cochrane. "You finally admit it," he said. "You have promised more than you can
deliver. You are in over your head."

"It's not like that," Cochrane insisted. "The system is—"

"You've had a year and a half and every dollar you've asked for,"
Djemma growled. "Dollars that could have brought food and housing to my people."

Cochrane looked around. The palace was immense, and built of
imported stone and marble. Gold-plated fixtures sprouted from
every bathroom. *What about those dollars?*

"It's an incredibly complex machine," Cochrane said. "To get it
right may require assistance."

Djemma looked down at Cochrane, his eyes burning holes in
Cochrane's mind much the way the weapon was supposed to.

"I know this already," the African leader said. "Go back to your
work. You will get your materials and your help. This much I
promise you."

Santa Maria Island, the Azores, June 17

THE INHABITANTS OF VILA DO PORTO spotted the sleek lines of the NUMA vessel *Argo* just after noon local time. Because the *Argo* had originally been built for the Coast Guard and designed for rescue work, law enforcement, and interdiction, her profile was that of a small warship: long, lean, angular.

Two hundred fifty years prior, the appearance of such a ship, or the equivalent type in its day, would have been studied cautiously from the streets and the watchtowers of the Forte de São Brás.

Built in the sixteenth century, with cannon mounted high on sturdy walls of stone and mortar, the fort was now a Portuguese naval depot, housing personnel and local authorities, though few vessels from their navy visited the island regularly.

As the *Argo* dropped anchor outside the harbor, Kurt Austin considered the act of piracy he'd recently witnessed and the fact that such acts were on the rise worldwide. He doubted such forts would be needed again, but he wondered when the nations of the world would grow angry enough to band together and begin fighting piracy on an international level.

From what he'd heard, the sinking of the *Kinjara Maru* had sent shock waves around the maritime community, and tough talk was growing. That was a good step, but something in Kurt's mind told him the talk would fade before any real action occurred, and the situation would remain unsatisfactory and unchanged.

Whatever the outcome, another thought had dominated Kurt's mind, even as he'd repeated his story in conversations with Interpol, with the *Kinjara Maru*'s insurers, and with several maritime antipiracy associations.

They steered all questions toward the notion of piracy and seemed to ignore Kurt's point that pirates didn't sink ships they could steal or kill crew members they could ransom.

His thoughts were acknowledged, and then, it seemed to him, filed away and most likely forgotten. But Kurt didn't forget them any more than he could forget the sight of crewmen being gunned down as they tried to flee, or Kristi Nordegrun's strange story about the lights flickering, a screaming noise inside her head, and blacking out until daylight came.

Something more was going on here. Whether the world wanted to acknowledge it or not, Kurt had a bad feeling they would be forced to in time.

With the *Argo* standing down, Captain Haynes gave most of the crew shore leave. They would be here for two weeks while Kurt and Joe finished their testing and competed in the Submarine Race. During that time a skeleton crew would remain aboard the *Argo*, with a different group rotating on and off every few days.

The captain's last words of advice to the crew was to keep their noses clean and stay out of trouble, as the islanders were known to be pleasant but not the kind to put up with rowdy outsiders, having detained many, including the crew of none other than Christopher Columbus himself.

As Austin stepped off the *Argo*'s tender in the shadow of the Forte de São Brás, he wondered what that reputation might mean for his good friend Joe Zavala. Joe was a solid citizen, but he tended to immerse himself in the social scene wherever he went, and while Joe wasn't a troublemaker, he liked mischief and he loved his fun.

When Kurt arrived at the shop where the *Barracuda* was being prepared, Joe was nowhere to be found. A security guard laughed when asked about him.

"You're just in time to see him fight," the guard said. "Over at the rec center, if he hasn't been knocked out by now."

Kurt took this news suspiciously, got directions to the recreation center, and double-timed it over there.

Stepping inside, Kurt found his way to a large gymnasium from which the sounds of an excited crowd were flowing.

He opened the door to find a crowd of two or three hundred sitting on bleachers arranged around a boxing ring. It wasn't exactly Madison Square Garden, but the place was packed.

At the sound of the bell, the crowd rose and cheered and stamped their feet until the building shook. Kurt heard the scuffling sounds of feet on canvas and then the *thwap-thump* of fists in padded gloves exchanging blows.

He made his way down the aisle and got a glimpse of the action in the ring. He saw Joe Zavala in red trunks. His friend's short black hair was all but hidden under the protective headgear he wore. But as Joe shuffled back and forth, moving lightly on his feet, his rugged, rangy frame and his tanned, well-muscled arms and shoulders glistened with the sheen of sweat.

Across from Joe, in black trunks and headgear, Kurt saw a larger man. In fact, he looked like some version of the Norse god Thor. At least six-foot-four, with blond hair, blue eyes, and a chiseled physique, Joe's opponent moved with far less grace but threw punches like bolts of thunder.

Joe dodged one, ducked another, and then backpedaled away. For a moment he looked a little bit like middleweight champion Oscar De La Hoya—a comparison that would have made Joe proud. Then he stepped in, landed a few punches that seemed to have no effect, and suddenly looked less like the middleweight superstar as a thundering right hand from Thor caught him in the side of the head.

The crowd gasped, especially a line of women in the front row. Joe stumbled away, grabbed the ropes in front of the women, adjusted his headgear, and smiled. Then he turned and kept moving until the bell rang again.

By the time Joe reached his corner, Kurt was already there.

Joe's trainer gave him water and hit him with the smelling salts.

Between deep breaths and a few more sips of water, Joe spoke. "About time you showed up."

"Yeah," Kurt said. "Looks like you're wearing him down," he added. "If he keeps hitting you in the head like that, his arms are gonna get tired."

Joe swished the water around in his mouth, spat some out, and then looked over at Kurt. "I got him right where I want him."

Kurt nodded, finding that doubtful. Joe had boxed in high school, college, and the Navy, but that was a long time ago.

"At least you have some fans," Kurt said, nodding toward the front row, which included a group ranging in age from a college girl with a flower in her hair to several women that might have been Joe's match in years to a pair of older women who were way overdressed and too well made-up for such an event.

"Let me guess," Kurt said. "You're fighting to defend their collective honor."

"Nothing like that," Joe said, as his trainer dunked Joe's mouth guard and then stuffed it back in his mouth. "I ram ober sombone's cow."

The bell pinged, and Joe stood, clapped his gloves together, and went back out to do battle.

Joe's words had been muffled by the mouth guard, but it sounded to Kurt like he'd said *I ran over someone's cow*.

This round went quickly, with Joe dodging the thunderbolts and then landing a few jabs on Thor's midsection. He might as well have been punching a stone wall. When Joe made it back, he was noticeably winded.

"You ran over a cow?" Kurt asked.

"Actually, I just bumped into him," Joe said breathing hard.

"Was it the God of Thunder's cow?" Kurt asked, nodding toward Joe's opponent.

"No," Joe said. "One of the ranchers here."

Kurt did not feel the fog of confusion lifting. "How does that turn into a boxing match?"

"There are rules here," Joe said, "but no fences. The cows wander everywhere, out onto the roads and everything. If you hit a cow at night, it's the cow's fault. But if you hit a cow in the day, it's your fault. I bumped into one at dusk. Apparently, that's, ah . . . *una zona gris*: a gray area."

"So you have to fight to the death in a cage match?" Kurt said, joking.

"Does this look like a fight to the death?" Joe asked.

"Well . . ."

"The guy whose cow I hit owns the gym. The Scandinavian guy over there moved here and became the local amateur champ a year ago. The islanders like him but would rather see someone else as champ, someone who looks more like them."

Kurt smiled. With his Latin background, Joe looked far more like the islanders than Thor did.

The bell rang again, and Joe answered it, stepping up and trying to get inside the Scandinavian man's long reach. It was dangerous work, but aside from a few glancing blows Joe seemed to be holding his own, and the Scandinavian seemed to be slowing.

Joe sat down again, and Kurt changed the subject.

"I need to talk to you about the *Barracuda*," he said.

"What about it?"

"Can it dive to sixteen thousand feet?"

Joe shook his head. "It's not a bathysphere, Kurt. It's designed for speed."

"But could you modify it to do the job?"

"Yeah," Joe said. "By putting it inside a bathysphere."

Kurt went silent. Joe was a genius with machines. Still, he could work only within the laws of physics.

Joe rinsed his mouth and spat.

"Okay, I'll bite," he said. "What's on the bottom of the Atlantic that you want to take a look at?"

"You heard about what happened the other day?"

Joe nodded. "A ship almost fell on your head."

"It did," Kurt said. "I'd like to get a better look at it now that it's all safe and sound on the bottom."

The bell rang, and Joe stood, his eyes on Kurt. He seemed to be thinking. "There might be a way," he said, a gleam shining in his eyes.

By that moment, Joe had lingered too long. The God of Thunder had roamed across the ring.

"Look out," Joe's cornerman shouted.

Joe turned and ducked, covering up, as the haymaker glanced off his raised arm. He stepped back into the ropes, protecting himself, as the other fighter fired blows at him, left and right.

Suddenly, Kurt felt horrible for his friend, as what was supposed to be a friendly match looked more like a one-sided beating. Partly his fault for distracting Joe. If it had been a wrestling match, he'd have grabbed a folding chair and slammed it over Thor's shoulders. But he guessed that wouldn't do for Queensbury rules.

Thor's gloves made a heavy thumping sound as they slammed into Joe's arms, ribs, and head.

"Rope-a-dope," Kurt shouted, throwing out the only boxing advice he could think of.

His voice was drowned out by the roar of the crowd. Meanwhile, Joe's cheerleaders gasped. The older women looked away as if they couldn't watch.

With little room to maneuver, Joe continued to cover up, unable to even open his arms and clinch the other fighter. Kurt looked at the clock. This was the last round, but there was over a minute to go.

It didn't look like Joe would make the bell. Then a moment presented itself. As the Scandinavian wound up to deliver another hammer blow, he opened himself up.

At that very instant, Joe dropped his shoulder and fired an uppercut. It caught Thor on the chin and snapped his head backward. From the look of things, Thor hadn't expected anything but defense from Joe at that point. Kurt saw the man's eyes roll as he stumbled backward.

Joe stepped forward and fired a heavy right, sending Thor to the canvas.

The crowd oohed in surprise. Joe's cheerleaders shrieked with pleasure, like young girls watching the Beatles step off an airplane. The ref began to count.

The Scandinavian fighter rolled onto his hands and knees by "Four," while Joe danced around the ring like Sugar Ray Leonard. By "Six," Thor was using the ropes to help himself up, and Joe looked a little less happy about things. By "Eight," Thor was standing, looking clearheaded and glaring across the ring. Joe's face had turned decidedly sour.

The ref grabbed Thor's gloves and looked ready to send him back into the fight.

And then the bell rang.

The round was over, the fight was over. It was ruled a draw. Nobody was happy but everybody cheered.

FIFTEEN MINUTES LATER, with his debt to society paid, a few autographs signed, and at least one new phone number in his pocket, Joe

Zavala sat with Kurt, ripping the tape off his hands and then pressing an ice bag to his eye.

"That'll teach you to run over people's cows," Kurt said, using a pair of scissors to help Joe with the tape.

"Next time I fight," Joe said, "you sit in the back row. Or, better yet, find something else to do."

"What are you talking about?" Kurt asked. "I thought that went well."

Joe had to laugh. Kurt was as good and loyal a friend as Joe had ever known, but he did have a penchant for glossing over the downside of things. "I've always wondered about your definition of 'well.'"

With the tape off, Joe moved the bag of ice to the back of his neck as Kurt explained what had happened aboard the *Kinjara Maru*.

It sounded as odd to him as it had seemed to Kurt. "Sixth sense going off?" he asked.

"Three alarms," Kurt said.

"Funny thing," Joe said, "I hear the same sound in my head right now. But I think it's for a different reason."

Kurt laughed. "All I want is a look," he insisted. "Do you think the *Barracuda* can get us there?"

"There might be a way to do it," Joe replied. "But only as an ROV. I wouldn't trust the mods to keep anyone safe at that depth. Plus, there would be no room for us anyway."

Kurt smiled. "What are you thinking?"

"We could build a small outer hull and encase the *Barracuda* inside it," he began.

As Joe spoke he could see the design in his head, could feel the shape beneath his hands. He designed things intuitively. He did the math just to back up what he already knew.

"We fill that compartment with a noncompressing liquid, or hyperpressurize it with nitrogen gas. Then we flood the interior of the *Barracuda* itself or pressurize it to several atmospheres as well, and the three-stage gradient should help balance out the forces. Neither the outer hull nor the inner hull would have to handle all the pressure."

"What about the instrumentation and the controls?" Kurt asked.

Joe shrugged. "Not a problem," he said. "Everything we put inside is waterproofed and designed for a high-pressure environment."

"Sounds good," Kurt said.

He looked pleased. Joe knew he would be. And so he dropped the bomb.

"There is one minor problem."

Kurt's gaze narrowed. "What's that?"

"Dirk called me before you got here."

"And?"

"He gave me orders not to let you talk me into anything reckless."

"Reckless?"

"He knows us too well," Joe said, guessing it took one adventurous, even "reckless," mind to know the workings of another.

Kurt nodded, smiling a bit. "That he does. On the other hand, 'reckless' gives us a lot of leeway."

"Sometimes you scare me," Joe said. "Just putting that on the record."

"Draw up the plans," Kurt said. "The race is in two days. After that, we're on our own."

Joe smiled, liking the challenge. And while he feared the wrath of Dirk Pitt if they lost NUMA's million-dollar *Barracuda*, he was pretty certain that he and Kurt had built up enough markers to cover it if they did.

Besides, if the stories he'd been told were true, Dirk had lost a few of Admiral Sandecker's more expensive toys over the years. How angry could he really get?

AS HE STRODE THROUGH THE PASSAGEWAY of the NUMA vessel *Matador*, Paul Trout had to duck each time he came to a bulkhead and its watertight door. While anyone over six feet had to crouch at the bulkheads or risk a nasty whack of the head, Paul was six-foot-eight in bare feet, with wide shoulders and long limbs. He all but had to contort himself to make it through unscathed.

An avid fisherman who preferred the outdoors, Paul was simply not designed for the tight quarters found inside a modern vessel. Naturally, he spent much of his time in one ship or another, twisting himself into small machinery-filled compartments, bending his spine like a pretzel to fit into submersibles, or even just walking the inner passageways of the ship.

On another day he would have detoured outside onto the main deck before walking the length of the ship, but the *Matador* was currently operating off the Falkland Islands in the South Atlantic. It was winter in the Southern Hemisphere, and both the wind and sea were up already.

Climbing through another hatch, Paul reached a more spacious compartment. He peered inside. The dimly lit room was quiet, with most of the light coming from glowing dials, backlit keyboards, and a trio of high-definition, flat-screen monitors.

A pair of scruffy-looking researchers sat in front of the outboard monitors, while in between them, on a plate of backlit glass marked with a grid, stood a shapely woman with hands outstretched as if she were balancing on a tightrope. A visor covered her eyes and held her wine red hair like a band, while strange-looking gauntlets with wires running from them encased her hands. On her feet a set of high-tech boots sprouted wires of their own, all of which ran to a large computer a few feet behind her.

Paul smiled to himself as he watched his wife, Gamay. She looked like a robotic ballerina. She moved her head to the right, and the picture on the monitors moved similarly, bright lights illuminating a smooth, sediment-covered surface with a jagged hole in what had once been the hull of a British naval vessel.

"Gentlemen," she said, "there's the entry point of the Exocet missile that sank your proud ship."

"It doesn't look all that bad, really," one of the men said, his English accent as thick as his beard.

The *Sheffield* was the first major British casualty of the Falklands War, hit by a French-made missile that didn't detonate but still ignited fires that raged throughout the ship.

She survived for six days after the attack before sinking during an attempt to tow her to port.

"Bloody French," the other Englishman said. "Probably just getting back at us for Waterloo and Trafalgar."

The bearded man laughed. "Actually, they went to great lengths to tell us the weaknesses of these missiles, and that helped us stop them, but I'd have preferred if they'd been a wee bit more cautious about who they sold them to in the first place."

He pointed to the opening. "Can you take it inside?"

"Sure," Gamay said.

She moved her right hand and closed her fingers on an invisible control knob. A second later the sediment stirred up a bit, and the camera began to move closer to the gaping wound on the ship's hull.

Paul glanced at one of the displays on the wall. In a visual depiction reminiscent of a First Person Shooter video game, he saw what Gamay saw in her visor: a control panel and various gauges measuring depth, pressure, temperature, and both horizontal and vertical orientation.

He also saw a second screen that displayed a view from several feet behind the vessel she was piloting. Again it looked like a video game on the screen, as a small, almost human-shaped robotic figure moved forward toward the shattered hull plating.

"Detaching umbilical," Gamay said.

Much smaller than a standard ROV, and shaped more like a person than an undersea vessel, the figure was known by the incredibly awkward name Robotic Advanced Person-shaped Underwater Zero-connection Explorer. Because the acronym shortened to RAPUNZE, the test team had taken to calling the little figure *Rapunzel*. And this moment, when it disconnected from all surface connectivity, was considered *Rapunzel* "letting down her hair."

Under normal circumstances, *Rapunzel* could release the mile-long umbilical cord that kept her connected to the *Matador* and operate on her own in environments where cords, wires, and anything else trailing could be a hazard. Powered by batteries that would last three hours untethered, she was propelled by an impeller located in what would have been her belly. Fully gimballed, it could be rotated three hundred sixty degrees in any direction, allowing her to move up, down, sideways, backward, or any combination in between.

Because she was human shaped, she could bend and move into places a normal ROV could not go. She could even shrink, retracting her arms and legs so that she took up no more space than a beach ball with a light and video camera on top.

By using the virtual reality setup and force-feedback boots and gloves, the designers made it possible to operate *Rapunzel* as if a human were down there doing the work herself. It was expected this would be a huge boon to the salvage world, keeping divers out of dangerous wrecks and allowing exploration into wrecks long considered too dangerous or too deep to get at.

Exploring the *Sheffield* was to be *Rapunzel's* coming-out party, but something was wrong. A red warning light flashed repeatedly on one of the keyboards and also in the virtual cockpit. The umbilical would not disconnect.

"Let me try this again," Gamay said, resetting the sequence.

Paul stepped in quietly. "Don't mean to interrupt," he said, "but I'm afraid *Rapunzel* has to come back home for dinner."

"Is that my wonderful husband out there?" Gamay said, still fiddling with imaginary controls.

"It is. We have a storm brewing up," Paul explained, his northeastern accent turning the word *storm* into something that sounded more like "stahm." "We need to batten down the ship and head north before it turns into a full-blown gale."

Gamay's shoulders slumped a bit. It didn't matter anyway, the umbilical would not release, and they couldn't send *Rapunzel* inside the ship with the cords still attached. She pressed some other switches. An icon labeled "Auto Return" popped up on screen, and Gamay's virtual hand reached out and touched it.

Rapunzel began to pull away from the *Sheffield* and then ascend through the depths. The LEDs on Gamay's gloves and boots went dark. She took off her visor and blinked at Paul. She stepped toward him and almost lost her balance.

Paul caught her. "You all right?"

"It's a little disorienting to come out," she said. She blinked a few more times as if trying to refocus on the real world, then smiled at him.

He smiled back, still wondering how he'd been lucky enough to find someone so pretty and perfect for him.

"How was it?" he asked.

"Just like being down there," she said. "Except I'm not wet and cold, and I can go have lunch with you while *Rapunzel* makes the fifteen-minute journey back up from the bottom."

She reached over and kissed him.

"Umm-hmm," one of the Englishman coughed.

"Sorry," she said, turning back to them. "I'd say *Rapunzel* is going to be a huge plus for us. We'll get the bugs worked out while the storm hits and then drop her down and try it again."

"Actually," Paul said, "we won't. At least, not until October."

"Weather getting too rough for you, old boy?" the Englishman asked. "When I was a kid, we'd go through this kind of chop in a motor launch."

Paul had no doubt the man was telling the truth—he was a twenty-five-year vet of the RN before he'd retired a decade ago. He'd been on the *Sheffield* when it had taken that lethal hit.

"I guess it is," Paul said, going with the thought. "We're heading north. Once we're through the storm, a helicopter will be coming in to pick you guys up. I guess it's back to England from there. I'll be sure they have tea on board."

"Ha," the bearded man said. "Very good of you."

The two Englishmen stood. "I guess we saw what we came to see. Would love an invite when you come back."

"Of course," Gamay said. They shook her hand and moved off, making their way down the hall far more easily than Paul had come up minutes before.

Gamay eyed them. "Leaving a site because of a storm that will blow over in a few days?" she said suspiciously.

"Seemed a good excuse to give our guests," Paul replied.

"What gives?" she asked. "And don't lie to me, you'll sleep alone tonight."

"You know that tanker that went down the other day? Kurt was there when it happened, even rescued the captain's wife."

"Of course," she said. "Trouble finds him."

Paul laughed. Trouble did have a way of looking Kurt Austin up and coming to visit. Paul and Gamay had often been part of whatever followed. Seemed like this would be no exception.

"Well, there's more to the sinking than the press has been told," he explained.

"Like?"

"Pirates killing the crew and deliberately scuttling the ship," Paul said.

"Doesn't sound right, does it?" Gamay said.

"Nope," he said. "Not to Kurt or Dirk, or even the insurance company. With their permission, Dirk has asked us to take *Rapunzel* over and take a look."

Gamay took her robotic gloves off and sat down to undo her boots. "Sounds simple enough," she said. "Why do you look concerned?"

"Because Dirk told me to be concerned," Paul said. "He figures someone went to great lengths to hide whatever happened on that ship. And that being the case, whoever *they* are, they might get a little upset with the likes of us poking around."

She reached out and took his hand.

"Do you think you can get *Rapunzel* inside a sunken ship?" he asked.

"Would have liked to finish the test," she said, "but yes, I think we can get her inside."

12

AS IT RACED THROUGH THE WATER a hundred feet below the surface, the *Barracuda* looked more like a manta ray with stubby wings than a submarine—or even a barracuda, for that matter. About half the size of a compact car, her wedge-shaped snout narrowed, both horizontally and vertically, with a slightly bulbous expansion at the very tip.

This was a hydrodynamic feature that got the water moving smoothly around and over the vessel, reducing the drag and increasing both her ability to accelerate and her top-end speed.

In addition, her stainless steel skin was covered in microscopic V-shaped grooves, too small to be seen from a distance except as a sort of haze on the finish. The grooves were similar to the coatings used on the hulls of racing yachts, and they too added speed by reducing the drag.

Because she was eventually expected to do salvage work, an enclosed bay in the root of each wing held assorted equipment: cutting torches, grappling claws, and other tools. In truth, the *Barracuda* had been designed more like a stealth fighter than a submarine. The question was, could she fly like one?

With Kurt and Joe sitting in tandem, Kurt at the controls and Joe just behind him monitoring all the systems, the *Barracuda* surged through the water at 34 knots. Joe insisted she could make 45, but that would rapidly drain the battery. To make two laps around the race's fifty-mile course, 34 would be the best they could do.

"Coming up on a depth change," Joe mentioned.

The race was not just a horizontal affair, where the submarines could run at top speed and come home. It required maneuvers to be fulfilled: depth changes, course changes, even a section that required them to weave through a group of pylons, charge forward to a certain point and then back out, before turning around and racing off to the next buoy.

The competition itself was a three-stage process, with a hundred-thousand-dollar prize being offered to the winner of each stage and a cool ten million to the overall victor.

"Can you believe these guys are offering ten million to the winner?" Joe said excitedly.

"You realize NUMA gets that money if we win," Kurt replied.

"Don't depress me," Joe said. "I'm dreaming. Gonna get a ranch in Midland and a truck the size of a small earthmover."

Kurt laughed. For a moment, he considered what he might do with ten million dollars, and then he realized he would probably do exactly what he was doing right now. Work for NUMA. See the world. Sometimes save an ocean or two.

"Again, who put up the money?"

"African Offshore Corporation," Joe said. "They're big into continental-shelf drilling."

Kurt nodded. The supposed point of the whole competition was to develop submersibles that could be used to operate quickly, safely, and independently at depths of up to a thousand feet. Kurt guessed that publicity had more to do with it than anything else.

Still, even if he wouldn't get the money, Kurt liked to win.

"In fifteen seconds, begin descent to two hundred fifty feet," Joe said.

Kurt put his hand to a keypad, typed in 2-5-0, and held his finger over the "Enter" button. Either Kurt or Joe could change the depth manually if they wanted, but the computer was more precise.

"Three . . . two . . . one . . . mark."

Kurt hit "Enter," and they heard the sound of a small pump as it pushed oil from the rear into a forward chamber of the sub. This caused the nose to grow heavier and pitch down. With no need to take on water, to angle dive planes, or to adjust power, the *Barracuda* continued at flank speed, descending, and actually accelerating as it dove.

Around them the light began to fade, the color changing from a bright aquamarine to a darker blue. Up above, it was a beautiful sunny day, with high pressure all around.

"How we doing?" Kurt asked.

"Four miles to the outer marker," Joe said.

"What about the other contestants?"

It was a timed race, the subs having left at ten-minute intervals to keep them apart, but Kurt and Joe had already passed one vessel. Somewhere up ahead they would catch another competitor.

"We could ram them if they get in our way," Joe said.

"This isn't NASCAR," Kurt replied. "I'm thinking that would be some kind of points deduction."

As Kurt kept the *Barracuda* precisely online, he heard Joe tapping keys behind him.

"According to the telemetry," Joe said, "the XP-4 is a half mile ahead. We should see his taillights in about ten minutes."

That sounded good to Kurt. The next depth change was in seven minutes. They would come up to one hundred fifty feet, cruise over a ridge, and race along near the top of an underwater mesa—a flat plain that had once been an underwater lava field.

"Easier and more fun to pass people when they can see you go by," he said.

Seven minutes later, Kurt put the *Barracuda* into a climb, they zoomed up over the ridge and leveled off at one hundred fifty feet. A moment later the radio crackled.

". . . experiencing elec— . . .—blems . . . batteries . . . system malfunc— . . ."

The garbled low-frequency signal was hard to make out. But it rang alarm bells in Kurt's mind.

"You get that?"

"I couldn't make it out," Joe said. "Someone's having problems though."

Kurt grew quiet. All the subs had been equipped with a low-frequency radio that, theoretically, could reach floating buoys along the race path and be retransmitted to the referee and safety vessels stationed along the route. But the signal was so weak, Kurt couldn't tell who was transmitting.

"Did he say electrical problems?"

"I think so," Joe said.

"Call him out," Kurt said.

A moment later Joe was on the radio. "Vessel reporting problems. Your transmission garbled. Please repeat."

The seconds ticked by with no response. Kurt's sense of danger rose. To make the submarines fast, most had been built with somewhat experimental technology. Some even used lithium ion batteries that, in rare circumstances, could catch fire. Others used experimental electrical motors and even hulls of thin polymers.

"Vessel reporting problems," Joe said again. "This is *Barracuda*. Please repeat your message. We will relay to the surface."

Up ahead, Kurt saw a trail of bubbles. It had to be the wake of the XP-4. He'd forgotten all about it and was now driving right up its tailpipe. He banked the *Barracuda* to the left and then noticed something odd: the trail of bubbles arced down and to the right. It didn't make any sense, unless . . .

"It's the XP-4," he said. "It's got to be."

"Are you sure?"

"Check the GPS."

Kurt waited while Joe switched screens. "We're right on top of him."

"But I don't see him anywhere," Kurt said.

Joe went right back to the radio. "XP-4, do you read?" Joe said. "Are you reporting trouble?"

A brief burst of static came over the radio and then nothing.

"We'll lose if we turn," Joe said.

Kurt had considered that. The rules were strict.

"Forget the race," Kurt said, and he banked the *Barracuda* into a wide right turn, slowing her pace and manually taking over depth control. Throwing on the *Barracuda*'s lights, he searched for the trail of bubbles.

"What's the XP-4 made of?" he asked. Joe knew the other competitors far better than he did.

"She's stainless steel like us," Joe said.

"Maybe we could use the magnetometer to help find her. A thousand pounds of steel ought to get us a reading from this distance."

Kurt spotted what he thought was the line of bubbles. He turned to follow the curving, descending trail. Behind him Joe booted up the magnetometer.

"Something's wrong," Joe said, fiddling with the controls.

"What's the problem?"

"See for yourself."

Joe pressed a switch, and the central screen on Kurt's display panel changed. The lines of azimuth and magnetic density should have been a relatively clear display, but the various lines were spiking and dropping, and the directional indicator was pivoting like a compass needle just spinning in circles.

"What the heck's wrong with it?" Kurt mumbled.

"Don't know."

The radio buzzed with static again and this time a voice cut through it.

". . . continued problems . . . smoke in cabin . . . possible electrical fire . . . shutting down all systems . . . please—"

The transmission ended abruptly, and it chilled Kurt's blood.

He looked through the curved Plexiglas windshield of the *Barracuda*, slowing the small submarine even further. As the speed bled off, he pitched the nose over until they were angled almost straight down.

Dropping slowly through the water, he scanned the bottom. At one hundred fifty feet, light from the surface still filters through, but the surrounding color is a pure dark blue, and the visibility is limited to somewhere around fifty feet.

Increasing that visibility were the *Barracuda*'s lights. Since seawater scatters and absorbs longer wavelengths of light rapidly, Joe had installed special bulbs that burned in a bright yellow-green part of the visible spectrum. The lights helped cut through the gloom, and as the *Barracuda* approached the bottom Kurt spotted what looked like a gouge in the sandy sediment.

He turned to follow it.

"There," Joe said.

Up ahead, a tubular steel shape that looked more like a traditional submarine lay on its side. The designation "XP-4" could be seen, painted in large black letters.

Kurt circled around it until he reached a spot from which the canopy could be viewed. Bubbles were pouring slowly from the tail end of the sub, but the cockpit seemed intact.

He shut the lights off and tried to hover alongside, though the current was making it difficult.

"Signal them."

As Kurt struggled to keep the *Barracuda* in position, Joe grabbed a penlight, aimed it out the window at the XP-4, and tapped out a message in Morse code.

Kurt could see some movement inside, and then a message came back.

"All . . . elec . . . pwr . . . out," Joe said, translating.

Kurt felt them drifting again and tapped the thruster.

"They have to have oxygen," Kurt said, reviewing in his mind the safety rules the event's organizers had put in place. "Can they pop the canopy?"

Joe flashed the light on and off, putting the message through. The response dashed those hopes.

"Canopy . . . elec . . . trapped."

"Who ever heard of making your canopy electric?" Kurt mumbled. Then he looked back at Joe.

"Ours has a manual release," Joe assured him.

"Just checking."

Joe smiled. "Can we tow them out?"

"Looks like we'll have to," Kurt said. "Use the hook."

Behind him, Joe activated the controls for the grappling system, and a panel on the right wing of the *Barracuda* opened. A folded metallic apparatus emerged. Once it was locked into place, it unfolded into a long metallic arm with a claw on the end.

Even as the claw extended, Kurt realized they were drifting away from the XP-4.

"Get me closer," Joe said.

Kurt nudged the thrusters again, and the *Barracuda* angled toward the rear section of the XP-4 to a point where a handle extended from its hull. On the surface, the XP-4's mother ship would lock onto this handle with a crane to hoist the sub out of the water. Kurt and Joe would try to do the same down below.

"Maybe this could help our salvage grade," Joe said.

"Just grab the sub," Kurt said.

The claw extended and missed. Kurt adjusted their position, and Joe tried again and missed again.

"Something's wrong," Joe said.

"Yeah, your aim," Kurt said.

"Or your driving," Joe said.

Kurt didn't want to hear that, but it was true. And yet each time he adjusted for the current, the *Barracuda* seemed to get pulled off-line again. He glanced outside at the sediment in an attempt to get the best read on the current.

"Ah, Kurt . . . ?" Joe said.

Kurt ignored him. Something definitely *was* wrong. Unless his eyes had been damaged somehow, the *Barracuda* was drifting in the opposite direction of the current. And, strangely enough, the XP-4 was moving as well, albeit at a slower rate as she was dragging along the bottom.

"Kurt," Joe said with more urgency.

"What?"

"Look behind us."

Kurt turned the sub a few degrees and craned his neck around. The sandy bottom gave way to darkness. They were drifting toward a cliff of sorts. On the charts it appeared as a deep circular depression with a rise in the middle: the caldera of a volcano that had once been active here thousands of years before.

Thoughts of the damaged XP-4 tumbling down the edge of that caldera with two men trapped inside were enough to make Kurt forget about the strange movements of both subs. All he wanted to do was grab the XP-4 and get out of there.

He pressed forward until they were nose to nose with the other sub. Joe stabbed at the small handle with the grappling claw but could not catch it. Sediment began to stir up around them as Kurt goosed the thrusters.

They'd reached the point where the ground had started sloping away.

Whatever was going on, they were being dragged toward the caldera. Kurt used main power, blocking the XP-4, pumping the throttle, in an attempt to hold them back.

The XP-4 began to swing, pivoting against the nose of the *Barracuda*. It was being pulled past her. The caldera yawned behind them.

"It's now or never, Joe."

Joe grunted as he worked the controls. The arm extended, and the claw locked on.

"Got him," Joe said.

The XP-4 had reached the edge and was tumbling; Kurt had no choice but to let the *Barracuda* fall with it for a moment. If he gunned the throttle, the arm would bend and snap under the load.

They slipped off the edge, drifting backward and out into the dark. Kurt turned the nose of the *Barracuda* away from the XP-4. The grappling claw pivoted until it was pointing to the rear, and the two subs fell sideways as Kurt brought the main thruster slowly up to power.

Slowly, the *Barracuda* pulled the XP-4 away from the caldera's wall and began to level off. Both vessels were still sinking, still being strangely drawn toward the center of the volcano.

The *Barracuda* began to accelerate, with the XP-4's torpedo-shaped body trailing behind them. As long as Kurt towed them and didn't twist or bend the arm, he was fairly confident it would hold.

"We're still descending," Joe said.

Kurt was aware of that but couldn't explain it.

"Maybe they took on some water," he guessed. He added more power until the thruster was almost fully on. The descent slowed, and they began to pick up speed, speed they would need to climb.

A shape loomed up ahead, a hundred-foot column of rock that rose up from the center of the caldera like a chimney. If he had to guess, Kurt would have said it was the volcanic plug that cooled and hardened when this particular vent for the earth's heat had gone dormant. Problem was, it lay directly in their path.

"Should I blow the tanks?" Joe asked.

"No, we'll lose them," Kurt said. He went to full power and

slowly pulled the nose up. They were approaching the tower of rock awfully fast.

"Come on," Kurt urged.

It felt as if the tower of rock was drawing them in like a black hole. And with the weight they were towing, they seemed almost incapable of rising at anything more than the slowest of speeds.

"Climb, damn it," Kurt grunted.

They were heading right into it, like a plane flying into a cliff. All light from the surface was cut off by the shadow of the rock. They were rising but not fast enough. It looked like they were going to hit it head-on.

"Come on," Kurt said.

"Kurt?" Joe said, his hand over the ballast control.

"Come on, you—"

Suddenly, they saw light again, and at the last second they rose up over the tower. Kurt leveled off, allowing their speed to increase.

"Think we scraped the paint," Kurt said.

Behind him, Joe breathed a sigh of relief. "Look at the magneto-meter," he said.

Kurt didn't really hear him.

"It's pointing dead aft, right at that tower of rock. This is some kind of high-intensity magnetic field," Joe said.

At any other time, Kurt would have found that interesting, but ahead of him, lit up by the blazing yellow-green lights, he gazed upon a sight he found hard to believe.

The mast of a great ship sprouted from the ocean floor like a single limbless tree. Beyond it lay a smaller fishing vessel, and just to the left of that was what might have once been the hull of a tramp steamer.

"Joe, do you see this?" he asked.

As Joe angled for a better view, Kurt took the *Barracuda* right over the three vessels. As he did, they spotted several more. Cargo vessels that looked like the old Liberty ships, rusting hulks covered in a thin layer of algae and sediment. All around them, boxy containers lay strewn about as if they'd been dumped over the side of some ship at random.

He saw the wing of a small aircraft, and four or five more unrecognizable objects that appeared to be man-made.

"What is this place?" Kurt wondered aloud.

"It's like some kind of ship graveyard," Joe said.

"What are they all doing here?"

Joe shook his head. "I have no idea."

They passed over the wrecks, and the ocean bottom slowly returned to normal, mostly sediment and silt, with plant life and bits of coral here and there.

Wanting to go back but realizing they had a more important rendezvous with the surface, Kurt put the *Barracuda* into a nose-up climb once again. Slowly, the seafloor began to recede.

Then, just before their lights lost contact, Kurt saw something else: the fuselage of a large aircraft, half buried in the silt. Its long, narrow cabin swooped back in graceful flowing lines until it ended in a distinctive triple tail.

Kurt knew that plane. When he was younger, he and his father had built a model of it, which Kurt and a friend had blown to pieces with fireworks they'd found.

The aircraft with the sweeping lines and the triple tail was unique. It was the beautiful Lockheed Constellation.

New York City, June 19

THE NEW YORK OFFICES of the Shokara Shipping Company occupied several floors of a modern glass-and-steel structure in midtown Manhattan. An international operator of a hundred seventeen merchant vessels, Shokara kept track of its ships from a control room on the forty-sixth floor, wined and dined potential clients on the forty-seventh, and handled its accounting on the forty-eighth. The forty-ninth floor was reserved for VIPs and corporate executives, and was usually empty except for the cleaning crews, who kept the feng shui–designed space immaculate.

This week, however, was vastly different. Shokara's president and CEO, Haruto Takagawa, was in residence. As a result, both the level of activity and the level of security had increased many times over.

Takagawa had originally planned to spend a month in New York, enjoying Broadway, the nightlife, and the marvelous museums of the city. At the same time, he would meet with various stockbrokers and members of the Securities and Exchange Commission. By the end of the month he hoped to be announcing Shokara's listing on

the New York Stock Exchange, a private offering to raise more capital and a new subsidiary, Shokara New York, which would begin to
handle shipping from the U.S. to Europe and back.

And while those tasks still loomed on his schedule, Takagawa
had spent most of the past week dealing with the aftermath of a
pirate attack and the sinking of one of his ships, the *Kinjara Maru*.

The situation was doubly tricky for Takagawa, first because it
came at a terrible time, right before the planned corporate moves,
and second because the ship itself had been listed as operating out
of Singapore for Australia, not out of Africa headed for Hong
Kong. That fact had the insurance company claiming the policy was
void, as ships off the African coast were hijacked far more often
than ships traveling from Asia to Perth or Sydney.

And while those two thorns irritated his side, they would be inconsequential in the long run. A deal would be struck with the
insurance company, once they'd weaseled a percent or two off the
price, and in a few days no one in New York would care about his
sunken ship any more intensely than they cared about a truck that
had a flat tire. These things happened.

What did matter was the demands from the buyer in China
that they be reimbursed for the cargo that was lost. This was tricky
for many reasons, but mostly because of the nature of the cargo
itself.

As a Japanese conglomerate, Shokara operated under Japanese
law, but in trying to open a U.S.-based subsidiary, Takagawa was
expected to comply with American rules. Those rules prohibited
the transfer of certain technologies to other countries, and some of
the materials on board the *Kinjara Maru* might well fit that category.

At this particular moment in time, he couldn't afford for that information to come out. If it did, or if the right people caught wind of the truth and got angry, Takagawa's time in New York might add up to nothing more than an expensive vacation.

Just when things seemed to be settling down, his intercom buzzed.

"Mr. Takagawa," his secretary announced. "There are two men in the ground-floor lobby who would like to meet with you."

Takagawa didn't bother asking if they had an appointment, they would have been allowed up if that were the case.

"Who are they?"

"Their credentials indicate they are on staff with an American organization known as the National Underwater Maritime Agency," she said. "They want to talk to you about the *Kinjara Maru*."

NUMA. Takagawa knew the Agency well, and not just because chance had allowed some of its agents to spot the piracy on one of his ships and attempt to intervene. He knew all about NUMA from an incident that had occurred more than a decade ago.

Unlike others in the Japanese shipping world, he had a great fondness for the men and women of NUMA. It made his answer that much harder.

"Tell them I cannot speak on this subject," he said.

Silence returned for a moment, and Takagawa reached over to one side. He flipped on a monitor and pressed a button that allowed him to see the front desk in the lobby.

Two young men in suits stood there, appearing bright-eyed and eager. They looked more like Ivy League lawyers or accountants than the intrepid men he'd once dealt with. Then again, there could be only one reason they wanted to talk to him about the *Kinjara Maru*. So why not send lawyers?

The secretary's voice returned. "They say they're willing to wait all day if they have to, but they must speak with you."

"They can wait until the end of time," he said, "but I will not talk to them. Have security escort them out of the building."

He switched off the video monitor and went back to his work. NUMA could be a problem for him. Takagawa had found they could be a problem for anyone if they wanted to be.

14

Eastern Atlantic, June 20

TWENTY-FOUR HOURS AFTER THE DISCOVERY of the marine graveyard, Kurt Austin stood by the *Argo*'s port railing. The ship was holding station near the subsurface caldera that had nearly swallowed the XP-4, along with Kurt, Joe, and the *Barracuda*.

As Kurt stared out across the water, the midafternoon sun was starting to fall. It gave the light a warm bronze hue as the shadows stretched out and the air grew more humid. Beneath this pleasant light, the sea appeared calm and glassy, almost oily in complexion, as if the warm sun had lulled it to sleep like a tiger on the African savanna.

Standing there, Kurt reflected on the strange turn of events. Upon reporting the discovery, Kurt and Joe had been publicly thanked by the Portuguese authorities. And then, in private, they'd been scolded, and immediately ordered not to disturb or take anything from the site or even return to it, as if they were vandals or thieves of some kind.

All kinds of orders came down. Officially, the Portuguese insisted these precautions were for safety reasons. In a way, Kurt could understand that. The fluctuating magnetic properties around the rock formations made subsurface navigation difficult. At times, when the magnetic field was peaking, steel-hulled submersibles, including the *Barracuda*, were literally drawn toward it as if being reeled in by a cable. Fighting that pull became harder the closer one got to the tower.

On one run, Kurt had found himself in a position where the current and the magnetic pull were acting in the same direction. God help him if he bumped it, he'd thought.

Shortly after Kurt's experience, a second sub reported electrical problems. And even days after their exposure, the driver and navigator from the XP-4 continued to complain of headaches and strange issues with their vision. All of which added to the mystery of the place and the conspiracy theories already swirling.

As for the Portuguese government, it had no reason to quash the stories. They might even lead to a bonanza in tourist dollars, something every small island could use.

In some ways, that influx was already beginning. The morning after the discovery, only the *Argo* had been present. Today, three other tenders had joined it, and if the scuttlebutt was to be believed, there would be ten ships out here the next day, all of them filled with tourists waiting to get a look at the now infamous "Underwater Graveyard."

Tours of the site were being touted, with press releases going out, and a grainy YouTube video already capturing over a million hits.

In a few days, Kurt guessed he'd be looking at a free-for-all, something like trying to snorkel with a thousand other tourists, with their bright bathing suits and Styrofoam noodles, and yet imagining you were getting a "real life" aquatic experience.

As he pondered this, footsteps approached him from behind. Kurt turned to see Joe Zavala, carrying a frosty tall-necked bottle of beer in each hand.

"Bohemia," Joe said, handing him one. "Best beer in Mexico."

Kurt took the bottle and tipped it back, savoring the icy taste on such a hot, humid day.

"Where'd you scrounge this up?" Kurt asked.

"From the captain's private stock," Joe said. "Supposed to be for our victory celebration."

"And the captain let you get your paws on it early?" Kurt asked. Joe nodded.

"That's a bad sign," Kurt replied. "Are we to be shot at sundown?"

"Nah," Joe said. "But we have now been officially kicked out of the competition."

Kurt had to laugh. Rules were rules, but stopping to rescue a competitor seemed like a good reason to make an exception.

"So how's it feel to lose ten million dollars?" Joe asked.

Kurt thought about that. Their chances of winning had been excellent. He took another swig from the bottle and leaned back against the rail. "Suddenly," he said, "I'm very happy that NUMA would have gotten the money anyway."

Joe laughed, and both men turned at the sound of a helicopter approaching. They watched a gray Mk 95 Super Lynx cruise in from the east, taking a straight line toward the *Argo*. As it drew closer, the red-and-green insignia of the Portuguese Navy could be clearly seen on its flank.

It slowed to a hover above the fantail and then began to descend toward the helipad.

A crewman popped out of a hatch near where Kurt and Joe stood just as the helicopter was touching down.

"Cap'n wants you guys in his ready room," the crewman said.

The timing seemed suspicious.

"Did he say why?" Kurt asked.

The crewman hesitated, looking uncomfortable. "Something to do with our new arrivals, sir."

The crewman held the door for them, apparently unable or unwilling to say any more.

Joe looked at Kurt. "Now you've done it."

Kurt's eyebrows went up. "What makes you think this is my fault?"

"Because it always is," Joe said.

The crewman shifted his weight nervously, then mumbled, "The cap'n said don't be late."

Kurt nodded and began moving forward. "I told you the cold beer was a bad sign."

He stepped inside.

Joe followed. "At least we're on our own ship," he said. "They can't make us walk the plank on our own ship . . . right?"

The door closed behind them, and Kurt guessed they were about to find out.

MINUTES LATER, Kurt, Joe, and Captain Haynes sat in chairs around a small conference table. Like everything else on a ship the size of the *Argo*, this ready room was compact and efficient. But with seven men piled inside, including two high-ranking representatives of the Portuguese Navy and the governor of the Azores Islands chain, it felt a little claustrophobic.

Captain Haynes turned their way.

"Gentlemen, this is Rear Admiral Alexandre Sienna of the Portuguese Navy. He's been put in charge of this discovery."

Hands were shook, pleasantries exchanged, and then Admiral Sienna got down to it.

"My government believes you men have found something of great scientific importance," the admiral began. "For this, Portugal thanks you."

Reversal number three, Kurt thought. And probably all for nothing.

"Without samples, we don't know what's been found," Kurt began. "But it's probably just a massive chunk of magnetized iron alloy. I'll admit, it's a lot of specialized rock in one place, but this is an old volcano. It might be unusual, but—"

"I promise you, Señor Austin, this is more than unusual," the admiral said. "Perhaps you have seen the aircraft flying overhead, several times a day?"

Kurt recalled the flybys; Portuguese P-3 Orions. He'd assumed they were keeping an eye on the *Argo* and the other vessels, as if a few naval personnel from the Forte de São Brás coming on board hadn't been enough.

The admiral continued. "We have been using sophisticated instruments to study the magnetism. What we have learned so far will astound you. The magnetic force in this area is in constant flux. At one point, it would be enough to lift several hundred tons; an hour later, it's barely stronger than the standard background level of the earth's magnetism. And yet several hours further on, the field is more powerful than ever."

That did astound Kurt, and perhaps it explained why maneuvering around the tower of volcanic rock was so tricky. And yet, from what he knew, ferrous, or iron-based, magnetism did not fluctuate much. That was why stones could be mined, put to use as magnets, and allowed to sit. Some magnets risked demagnetization, but certainly nothing like what the admiral was describing.

"What are you suggesting?" Kurt asked.

"We will have to study the properties to be sure," the admiral said. "But my scientists tell me you may have discovered a naturally occurring "—he paused as if looking for the right word—"conductive material. And that under specific geological conditions, perhaps related to underground magma movements or even fluctuations in the earth's magnetic field, this tower of rock and metal becomes vigorously charged. As such, it exerts incredible magnetic force on objects around it."

"Vigorous," Joe added. "I like that. It all but pulled us in during one of those *vigorous* fluctuations."

"Yes," the admiral said. "That seems to be what it does. The experts we have spoken with think this magnetic structure may have pulled in all the ships and other objects you see resting in that caldera."

Kurt's eyes went wide. He felt as if they were rapidly entering UFO and Amelia Earhart territory.

"Are you kidding me?" he said. "We made it out of there towing the XP-4 along with us. I saw cargo ships down there, and at least two aircraft. You're telling me you think this thing drew them in like some kind of siren from Greek mythology?"

The admiral looked shocked by Kurt's boldness. Captain Haynes looked just as appalled.

Joe leaned over. "Remember the plank," he whispered. "Walking it. Swimming with *los tiburones*."

Kurt took a breath. "My apologies, Admiral. It's just that this is something of great scientific interest, and, from the looks of things, it's being turned into an amusement park. We should research it. At least, someone should, even if it's not us. But it gets a lot harder to do any real science when the claims get so astronomical."

"Yes," the admiral said, looking disappointed. "Perhaps you are right, but, I assure you, the electromagnetic forces we have already measured are, in fact . . . astronomical."

Kurt felt as if the admiral was waiting for him, maybe even baiting him, but he couldn't help but bite. "What are you getting at?"

"Do you know what a superconductor is?"

"The basics," Kurt said, not actually sure that he knew the basics. "They're materials that conduct electricity without any resistance. I always hear that they're going to end up being used in magnetically levitated trains and things like that someday."

Captain Haynes took over for the moment, and Kurt got the distinct feeling the two men had already discussed the subject, perhaps not alone.

"Superconductors do all that and more," Haynes began. "Their properties make them perfect for *any* electronic application. From operating a computer to powering a magnetically levitated train to electrical motors for cars that get the equivalent of five hundred miles per gallon. According to one study, replacing the U.S. electrical grid with superconducting wires would reduce the amount of power needed to light the country by forty percent. You could immediately shut down five hundred coal-burning power plants at least."

"Didn't know you were such an expert, Captain."

"I wasn't three hours ago," the captain replied. "Been talking with the admiral here and the folks back at NUMA all day."

"I see," Kurt said. "So these superconductors might do something for global warming. Especially if extrapolated to the rest of the world. What's the holdup?"

"Most superconductors only work at incredibly low temperatures," the captain explained. "Usually one has to chill them with liquid nitrogen or something similar to create the superconducting effect."

"I'm guessing that isn't going to work for the grid," Kurt said.

"It doesn't work for any standard application," Captain Haynes explained.

"So why are we talking about it?"

Admiral Sienna took over. "Because, Senhor Austin, what you and your friend may have discovered is a superconducting alloy that works at almost room temperature."

Now it made sense. No samples. No close approaches. The Portuguese sailors that had been placed on the *Argo*, the patrol boat that had shadowed the site since they returned.

"If that's what we have down there," Captain Haynes explained, "it could be worth hundreds of billions once it is analyzed and synthesized and mass-produced."

That made sense to Kurt, but even a superconductor had to have a source of power. "So where does the juice come from?" he asked.

"This is a former volcanic archipelago," Admiral Sienna reminded everyone. "You must realize, there could be a trillion metric tons of magma oozing around underneath the caldera—some of which may be comprised of liquid metal—and such movement can create a magnetic field of its own. Our experts assure us that it's possible for such forces to be quite large."

"And you're thinking the magnetism pulled these ships and airplanes to the bottom of the sea?" Kurt asked.

"In truth, we don't know," the admiral said. "These waters have quite a reputation, similar to your Bermuda Triangle. We don't know what has occurred here, but the theory we're going with is that the ships and containers and aircraft you see went down in the waters to the northwest of the caldera. There is a strong current that funnels along a diagonal route between two low chains of submerged mountains. As the funnel tightens, the strength of the current increases, right up until it drops over the edge of the caldera."

Everything they'd seen on the bottom—the sunken ships, the aircraft, the containers and other junk—all of it lay on the northwest side of the rock tower.

"So you're saying, add the current and the magnetism together and you have enough power to pull the junk in?"

The admiral nodded, and Kurt found himself thinking that it might almost make sense. "So what do you want from us?"

"Well," Admiral Sienna said, "we are in a rather difficult situation. These waters are disputed between my country and Spain. They have been contested since the time of Columbus, over five hundred years. Since the caldera is more than twelve miles from the closest Azorean landmass, it falls into this disputed zone. For the most part, fishing and other things are regulated under a patchwork of different agreements. We even have one that covers the discovery of any oil."

Kurt did not like where this was heading.

"But there is nothing to cover underwater mining or the discovery of new alloys," the admiral added.

"So you're arguing over it already," he said.

"We are . . . discussing," the admiral said. "But my nation is inclined to send one of its finest warships—the *Corte Real,* a Vasco da Gama–class frigate—to this very spot. The Spanish want to send a ship of their own. Perhaps not as nice or as impressive, but a presence nevertheless. You see where this will go."

"Okay, so we'll clear out," Kurt said. "Let me know when you've figured out the details. I'm sure you'll be able to reach me at the retirement home by then."

The admiral looked upset.

"Tiburones," Joe reminded him under his breath.

"Yes," the admiral said, "it will probably devolve into some type of litigation. Unless . . ."

Kurt took a deep breath. "Unless what?"

"Unless a neutral organization of world renown would be willing to watch over the site and coordinate preliminary research while we discuss the details amongst ourselves."

Kurt looked at Captain Haynes, who nodded. "I already ran it by the Director. He's in agreement."

"There are many parties who want to see this site," the admiral said. "Already I have a stack of petitions from scientists who want to come and study it. But rules must be established and followed. If you would help us put them in place . . ."

Kurt turned to Haynes. "Captain, that's up to you and Dirk. Not us. We do what we're told."

"You are the discoverers," Admiral Sienna said. "And you are well known for other things you have found, including the statue the *Navigator*, and for your part in learning the truth about the blue medusa and stopping the plague that threatened the world last year. It would be good for you to be here. All sides would respect your presence."

"You want us to be administrators," Kurt said, unable to hide his disdain for this plan.

"The other officers and I will handle the paperwork and logistics," Captain Haynes said. "You and Joe will be on point, keeping everyone in line out there."

"You want us to be the disciplinarians?" Kurt asked.

The captain smiled. "Turnabout, if ever I've seen it."

Kurt glanced at the map on the wall. Five hundred miles to the east of their position, the Trouts were getting ready to dive on the *Kinjara Maru*. Her sinking continued to monopolize his thoughts during any downtime, and with his and Joe's early exit from the contest, he'd hoped to return and take part in that dive. It seemed events would not allow it.

They were stuck here, he knew that. And if that was the case, he figured it was better to be running the show and dishing out the red tape than trying to cut through it.

He turned to Joe. "Mr. Zavala?"

"You know I'm always at your back," Joe said.

If Joe was in and Captain Haynes was on board, at least Kurt knew he wasn't going it alone. "All right," he said. "I'm game."

15

Moscow, Russia, June 21

KATARINA LUSKAYA CLIMBED THE STEPS fronting the Science Ministry's building after returning from lunch in one of Moscow's magnificent parks. On a sunny June day, it was 82 degrees, not very humid at all, and absolutely beautiful in the great city.

It seemed hard to believe that in three months the first snows would be falling, and, six weeks after that, it would be twenty below and dangerous to walk around outside.

Savor it while you can, she told herself.

Fit and athletic, Katarina had a warm smile but a relatively plain look about her. Her short mahogany hair was cut in an attractive style that angled along her chin line. At times, her bangs fell across her face, hiding her eyes. She was not the kind of woman who would stir up attention by walking into a room, but after being there for a while she might have a crowd around her, drawn to her energy and laughter and spirit over the perhaps more superficial charms of others.

Thirty-one years old, Katarina had just recently completed her doctorate in advanced energy systems and was now a full-fledged member of the Science Directorate. Her unit was charged with figuring out what Russia should do if it ever ran out of oil and natural gas. Current estimates had that occurring in fifty to a hundred years, so every member of the team knew their work was not exactly aimed at a pressing need.

In a way, that made it better. No one bothered them, no one interfered. They were one of the few groups in the Science Directorate allowed to practice unadulterated research, done for no other reason than for the sake of the science itself.

Katarina enjoyed that. She did not build weapons. She did not pollute the sky or the water or the land. She did not work for a corporation that would take what she had done, earn billions from it, and give little back.

There was freedom in such a setup, a sense of purity. And yet, if she were honest, she felt restless more often than not. Enough so that on such a gorgeous day, she didn't relish going back to work.

That feeling multiplied the instant she reached her office.

She stepped inside to find a pair of men in dark suits waiting. One, with a broad face, flattened nose, and a sharply defined case of five o'clock shadow, lingered by the far wall. He stood like a statue, with his hands clasped in front of him. The other man, bald and squat, sat at her desk.

"Sit down," the Bald Man said.

"Who are you?" she asked. "What are you doing in my—"

"We are from the State," the Bald Man said ominously.

That was never a good thing to hear.

Reluctantly, Katarina sat across from him, finding it odd to be on this side of her own desk.

"You are Katarina Luskaya," the Bald Man said, and then pointed to the flat-nosed man standing by the wall. "He is Major Sergei Komarov."

Katarina waited, but the Bald Man didn't give his own name. A disconnected fear began to grow inside her. Even in today's Russia, a visit from the State could go very badly.

And yet, try as she might, Katarina could think of no reason for the government to be offended with her. She wasn't political in any real way. She wasn't a criminal. She did her job and paid her taxes. Years prior, she had even waved the Russian banner as a skater at the Winter Olympics. And while she hadn't won, she had performed admirably, finishing fourth, even with a partially torn ligament in her knee.

"What do you want?" she said. "I've done nothing wrong."

"Your brother was a paratrooper," the Bald Man said, ignoring her question.

"Yes," she said. "He died two years ago."

"Unfortunate," she was told. "He was a loyal soldier. He did what his country asked him to do."

She noticed the words came respectfully.

The man leaned forward, steepling his fingers together and looking into her eyes. "We know that you are loyal also," he said. "And we want you to do something for your country."

His first statement eased her fears a little while the second raised them back up. "I'm just a scientist, and I'm junior here. What can I possibly do besides my work?"

"Something that your background, athleticism, and small amount of fame will be an asset in performing."

The Bald Man slid a folder across the desk. It rested in front of her, but Katarina kept her hands to the side.

"You are a scuba diver," the Bald Man said. "In the Black Sea, every summer."

This was true. It was a hobby. "Yes," she said.

"Then you will do fine," he said. He nodded toward the folder. "Open it."

She looked inside. She saw photos of a group of islands, some ships, and a few news clippings. She realized she was looking at a collection of information on the strange discovery in the Azores. Her group had already been talking about it.

"We want you to go there," the Bald Man said.

She pictured the beaches, the sun, the simple pleasures of an island vacation. *Suddenly, working for the State didn't sound so bad.*

"You want me to investigate this discovery?"

"Yes," he said unconvincingly. "At least, you should appear to be doing that."

Her nerves returned. "What am I really to be doing?"

"Look at the final page."

Katarina leafed through the loose papers and found the last one. On it, she saw several black-and-white photos. One was of a weather-beaten older man. The photo itself looked ancient, like one she had of her grandmother, the color slightly off, the clothing poorly constructed and course. A second photo showed two stainless steel trunks. The third showed a propeller-driven aircraft. She noticed the distinctive triple tail.

"The man is Vladimir Tarasov," the Bald Man said. "He was once a soldier in the Red Army. He fought against the Tsar and in the Great Struggle, but he betrayed us in 1951."

"What did he do?" she asked. In the photo, he looked like a broken-down farmer who'd spent too many years in the field. He seemed harmless.

"He tried to defect, taking with him property that belonged to the peoples of the Soviet Union. Properties that now rightly belong to Russia."

"What kind of property?" she asked, and then, based on the cold stares she received, immediately wished she hadn't.

The Bald Man pursed his lips, but to her surprise he then spoke. "Of course you know the story of Anastasia Nikolayevna," he said.

"Anastasia?" she asked. "The daughter of Tsar Nicholas?"

"Yes," the Bald Man said. "When Nicholas II was killed for his crimes against the people, the entire family shared his fate; his wife; his son, Alexei; his daughters, Olga, Tatiana, Maria, and also Anastasia. Four others died with them."

Katarina felt as if she were in a dream.

"For a century, there have been those who claim that Anastasia survived," he said.

She knew this. It would have been hard not to. "I remember hearing about a woman who claimed to be her years ago."

"Yes," the Bald Man said dismissively. "Some German woman suffering delusion or outright madness. But she has not been alone, there have been dozens of claims. Perhaps because of what really happened during the executions."

The Bald Man's statement begged a question that Katarina would not ask: What did happen?

The Bald Man continued to explain anyway. "At the time, those who had carried out the orders were afraid the Romanov supporters would find out before they had a chance to solidify power. So stories were circulated that the Tsar's family had been moved to a safer location to keep them from the mobs that were forming. Orders were given to bury the dead in separate locations so that no one would suspect what had occurred. The bodies of Anastasia and her brother Alexei were taken away. Their remains were recently discovered and their identities confirmed by DNA evidence."

"But what does this have to do with an American plane in the middle of the ocean?"

"At the time of their executions, the Romanovs were still under the delusion they could bribe their way to freedom. They were moved into a room, lined up, and shot at point-blank range. Incredibly, some of them survived the initial volley, and even a second round of shooting."

Katarina knew this part of the story. "They had jewels sewn into their clothes, along with small plates of melted gold," she said.

Major Komarov leaned forward and added, "A very expensive bulletproof vest."

"*Da,*" the Bald Man said. "They were eventually killed with shots to the head and bayonets, but naturally the guards were in shock. No one knew where this treasure had come from since it was believed all the Tsar's wealth had been confiscated. A search was begun, and a manservant who was allowed to live led the soldiers to trunks filled with jewels and coin. But before these items reached the Bolsheviks, they vanished. Thirty years later, a defector who had been one of those soldiers dug them up from a hiding place and tried to take them to America."

Now she understood. "Tarasov."

The Bald Man nodded. "The Americans would have been happy to take him, but they would not do it officially unless he could make it to America," he said. "They sent a man named Hudson Wallace, a freelance agent of theirs, to pick him up. The aircraft was his. Tarasov boarded it in Sarajevo and was flown out overnight."

"What does this have to do with the discovery in the Azores?"

The Bald Man grinned, and his round face wrinkled like a hound dog's. "Wallace could not fly from Sarajevo to the United States in a single leg," he said. "He didn't have the range."

"He went to the Azores," she said.

"While most of our agents foolishly watched the skies over Paris, Madrid, and London, one of my more prescient forerunners guessed that Wallace would choose a less obvious location to refuel. Somewhere friendly and out of the way. He sent a message to our agents in Santa Maria. Hudson's big silver plane landed several hours later. When Wallace and Tarasov tried to escape, our agents shot them, killing Tarasov. Unfortunately, the American managed to reach his aircraft and fly away, out into a storm."

"Unfortunate," Major Komarov added.

"Very," the Bald Man agreed.

"Wallace didn't make it to the United States," he continued. "Or Newfoundland or Canada. He lasted precisely nine minutes before radioing a 'Mayday' and then crashing into the Atlantic. Miraculously, he survived. He was rescued a week later by Portuguese fishermen, and he told a strange story about electromagnetic interference, all his instruments failing, and a sudden loss of electrical power. A story we, naturally, did not believe."

"You don't think he crashed?"

The man across from her smiled, no doubt pleased by her curiosity.

"For years we thought it was a lie," he said. "Either his lie or the CIA's. The United States did not look for the plane, and our own search turned up nothing. It seemed a good cover story to brush the entire situation under the rug. But now we feel differently."

She cocked her head to the side.

"Look at the bottom photo, Ms. Luskaya."

She turned her attention back to the page. She saw a murky, somewhat blurred image. For a moment she couldn't figure out what she was looking at. And then it hit her: three metallic fins sticking up out of the sediment. Connected to them she saw what had to be the fuselage of a plane.

"That is Hudson Wallace's plane," the Bald Man from the State informed her. "It appears to be mostly intact."

"Amazing," she said, looking up.

"Quite," he replied. "And we want you to go there. You will pretend you've come to study the strange magnetism these Americans claim to have found. And when you get the chance, investigate this aircraft. If the trunks are still inside—or you can locate them nearby—then you are to recover them and bring them back home to Russia."

In a weird way it was flattering. Her country needed her for a mission of some sort. But why did they need *her*?

"May I ask why you don't send a professional agent?"

"You are a known member of the scientific establishment," the

Bald Man said. "You have been overseas many times before, your activities have always been legitimate. By sending you instead of an agent with a cover, we vastly reduce the possibility of suspicions being raised."

"What if I don't want to go?" she asked cautiously.

The Bald Man narrowed his gaze and stared at her. Over her shoulder, she felt the presence of Major Komarov just as strongly. It no longer felt as if they were asking. That shouldn't have been a surprise. The State rarely made requests.

"We can be barbarians at times, Ms. Luskaya," the Bald Man said. "But in this case there is no need. You want to go. You want to test yourself. I can see it in your eyes."

She looked down at the photos once more. A strange mix of fear and excitement coursed through her. The feeling was so similar to the adrenaline rush she'd felt before competitions that it scared her. She was quite sure saying no was not an option, but it didn't matter.

The Bald Man from the State was right: She wanted to go.

Eastern Atlantic, June 22

AFTER ARRIVING ON STATION THE DAY BEFORE, the NUMA vessel *Matador* had set up shop and begun "mowing the lawn": a search pattern that allowed them to scan the ocean floor in strips, one ten-mile leg to the northeast and another ten-mile leg to the southwest, and then back again. With fairly precise information as to where the *Kinjara Maru* went down and good records on the currents in the area, they were able to find the ship in less than twelve hours.

Once found, the *Kinjara Maru* and her debris field had been mapped by a pair of deep diving ROVs. With the information and photographs plugged into a computer and a three-dimensional model of the ship created, the crew of the *Matador* were able to examine the ship and come up with a game plan for actually exploring it before they even went down.

It was the perfect mission for *Rapunzel*, with one particular problem.

"Didn't anyone bring an extension cord?" Paul Trout grumbled.

"We weren't expecting to go deep-sea fishing," Gamay said in her best calming voice. She knew her husband well enough to know that he was slow to anger but hard to rope back in once he got there.

"The deepwater kit is on its way out," she added. "It'll be here the day after tomorrow, but in the meantime . . ."

"Dirk still wants us to take a look at it," he said.

She nodded. "The ship is resting halfway down a pretty steep slope. Dirk wants us to pull some samples before she goes any deeper."

Both of them knew what that meant. Despite the danger, they would have to go down in the deepwater submersible.

"We can connect *Rapunzel* to the submersible and operate her free of the tethers once we're down there."

"I'm going with you," Paul said.

"You barely fit," she replied.

"So it'll be a little cramped," he said. "I like being in close quarters with you."

THREE HOURS LATER, Paul and Gamay were hovering over the wreck in a bathyscaphe-type submersible named the *Grouper*. *Rapunzel* was attached to the outer hull and charging her batteries. They were lying on their stomachs side by side, like kids riding their sled. Paul piloted the *Grouper* while Gamay readied *Rapunzel* for her sortie.

The temperature in the *Grouper* was a cool 48 degrees as the deepwater currents surrounding them dropped to a few degrees above freezing. Between the cramped quarters and the cold, Paul's entire body ached.

"Feels like Maine in November," he said into the intercom.

"At least it's not raining," Gamay said. "We start getting rain in here, we have a big problem."

Paul looked around. The *Grouper* was the sturdiest of all NUMA's deep-sea vehicles. It had been to twenty-four thousand feet, sixteen was a walk in the park.

"We'll be all right," he said.

"I know," Gamay said. "It does make me wonder about our luck though."

They were approaching the hull of the sunken vessel. He slowed them to a crawl.

"How so?"

"Somewhere, Kurt and Joe are sitting on a beach, basking in the sun and their newfound fame and probably ogling pretty women all around them."

"I'm ogling one right now," Paul said. "And when we're done here, I actually get to kiss you."

"Promise?" she said, lightheartedly. "I'll make it worth your while."

A cough on the intercom reminded him that others were listening in and monitoring everything in the sub.

Suddenly, Paul did not know how to respond. He felt a nervous flush rush across his face, an effect Gamay always managed to have on him.

"Paul, your heart rate is rising," a voice said over the comm.

"Umm, we're at the wreck site now," he said, all very official. "Traveling along the port side."

"Better get into my gear," Gamay said.

Paul brought the *Grouper* up and over the *Kinjara Maru*'s deck. The big ship was tilted hard over on one side, leaning into the slope. Her massive hatches were yawning wide, fish swimming here and there, but the vessel had yet to be claimed by the sea.

In a way it felt odd to Paul. Most of the wrecks they explored were old, covered in sediment, barnacles, and sea life. The *Kinjara Maru* looked as if she didn't belong, all brightly painted and scarred only where the fires had burned her.

"All of her cargo hatches are open," Paul said.

"Kurt said the pirates were firebombing the holds," Gamay replied.

"No need to open all of them," Paul said.

"Could they have been looking for something?"

In some ways that made sense to Paul, although what a group of pirates in speedboats could be looking for on a bulk cargo ship was beyond him.

"Maybe they just wanted her to go down faster," he said. "As soon as the forward hatch started taking on water the ship was a goner."

"Back to hiding something," Gamay said.

So far, the ship's owners and the insurance company had been uncooperative. They seemed loath to disclose the ship's manifest or even confirm the type of cargo on board. An odd situation, to say the least.

"We get anything from the company yet?" Paul asked

"Negative," the controller said. "Nothing but silence."

"You know, technically this ship is a wreck," he said. "We salvage it, and the cargo is ours."

"I don't think Dirk is going to approve the budget for that," Gamay said. "But there's nothing to stop us poking around. Let's find an opening and see if we can get *Rapunzel* inside."

Paul brought the *Grouper* toward the aft end of the big ship. The crew's quarters and the bridge lay there, partially torn open, as the crushing impact with the seafloor had ripped away a third of the structure.

"It looks like a cross section," Paul said.

"That might be good for us," Gamay said. "Nothing like easy access."

Again Paul blushed, not sure Gamay even realized her double entendre. He brought the *Grouper* to a hover twenty feet away from what was left of the bridge. Moments later, *Rapunzel* was in the water and moving toward the gaping hole where a part of the wall had once been.

With the autopilot keeping the *Grouper* in position, Paul turned to his wife. She lay flat in the aft section of the sub. The familiar visor covered her head, the wired gauntlets and boots on her hands and feet. The rest of her was clad in skintight neoprene.

"How is it?" he asked.

"Feels weird to be lying down," she said. "I'm used to doing it standing up."

The intercom buzzed. "Paul, your heart rate is jumping again. Are you all right?"

"I'm fine," he replied tersely, then covered the intercom.

"Honey, can you just watch what you say until we get back up topside?"

She laughed, and Paul knew full well that she was teasing him. There was little she liked more than to poke holes in his reserved New England attitude. It was one of the reasons he loved her so much.

"Sorry," she said with a sly smile.

Paul looked outside and watched the little mechanical figure move toward the shattered bridge and then disappear inside. On a smart phone–sized monitor he watched what Gamay saw in the visor: the view through *Rapunzel*'s eyes as she traveled deeper into the ship. In a corner of the bridge they discovered something.

"Is that a body?" Paul asked.

"Looks like it," she said.

"What happened to him?"

Rapunzel moved closer.

"Looks like he's been burned," Gamay said. "Except . . ."

The cameras on *Rapunzel* panned around the room. The walls were clean and smooth, the gray paint unmarred. Even the chair beside the man looked undamaged.

"No sign of fire," Paul said.

"As gross as this sounds," she said, "I'm going to get a sample."

Rapunzel moved in, extended a little drill with a vacuum tube attached. The drill hit the man's thigh and began to turn, drawing out a two-inch core. The vacuum system pulled it into a sealed container.

"I'm taking her deeper into the ship."

With Gamay occupied controlling *Rapunzel*, and the autopilot keeping the *Grouper* on station, Paul had little to do.

Boredom at sixteen thousand feet. It was worse than being trapped on an airliner.

The intercom buzzed. "Paul, we're picking up a sonar contact."

Now his heart had a different reason to race. "What kind?"

"Unknown," the controller said. "West of you and very faint. But moving fast."

"Mechanical or natural?" Paul asked.

"Unknown . . ." the controller began, then, "It's small . . ."

Paul and Gamay could only wait in silence. Paul imagined the sonar operator staring at the screen, listening to the earphones and trying to place the nature of the target.

"Damn it," the controller said. "It's a torpedo. Two of them, heading your way."

Paul grabbed the *Grouper*'s thrust controller, switching off the autopilot.

"Get *Rapunzel* back," he said.

Gamay began to move, gesturing quickly as she turned the little remote explorer around.

"Move, Paul," the controller urged. "They're closing fast."

Forgetting *Rapunzel*, Paul threw the *Grouper* into reverse, backing away from the wreck and then turning the small sub around.

"I can get her out of there," Gamay said.

"We don't have time."

Paul pushed the throttle to full and blew out some of the ballast. The *Grouper* began to rise and accelerate, but she was nothing like the *Barracuda*. Seven knots was her maximum.

Suddenly, the controller's voice broke in a panic. "The targets are above you, Paul. You're climbing right into them."

Paul went back to a dive, thinking it would have been nice to have known that a few minutes ago. "Where are they coming from?"

"Don't know," came the reply. "Head south. Toward the bow. That will take you away from their track. "

Paul put the *Grouper* in a turn. Unable to see or track the targets, he had to rely on the controller.

"Keep moving," the voice on the intercom said. "You have ten seconds."

There was no way the *Grouper* could avoid a torpedo that had locked onto it; their only hope was to confuse it with clutter. Paul decided to pop up, taking the *Grouper* over the deck, hugging the *Kinjara Maru* as closely as possible.

A resounding clang told him he'd hit something protruding. The reverberation was loud but inconsequential, and Paul didn't dare separate from the larger ship.

"Three seconds, two . . . one . . ."

"Paul?" Gamay called. She was scared, he could hear it. There was nothing he could do about it.

A high-pitched whining sound raced overhead as the first torpedo passed. Another followed moments later, heading off into the distance. The torpedoes had missed. And as Paul listened he couldn't hear them coming back.

Paul breathed a sigh of relief, but he had to be sure. "Are they turning?"

"No," the controller said. "They're continuing on. Straight and true."

Paul sighed with relief, his shoulders visibly slumping. And then a pair of reverberating explosions rocked the depths of the Atlantic.

The shock wave slammed the *Grouper*. Paul hit his head and felt the craft tilt. Gamay slid into him, and the submersible banged into one of the *Kinjara Maru*'s crane booms.

Another explosion followed, more distant but still strongly felt. The *Grouper* shuddered and then steadied as the shocks passed on.

"Are we okay?" Gamay shouted, pulling off the visor.

Paul glanced around, he saw no leaks. Time to get to the surface.

"Where on earth did those come from?" Paul shouted.

"Sorry," the controller said. "The first two masked them. This isn't exactly a Seawolf-class sonar array we've got going here."

Paul understood that the setup was designed to find small objects and map the seafloor, not track fast-moving torpedoes at great depths. Time to upgrade, he thought

"Any more of them?" he asked over the comm.

The controller was silent for a moment, as if he were checking and rechecking. "No," the man said finally. "But we are picking up a vibration. It sounds like . . ."

The controller's words trailed off, an act that concerned Paul. *A vibration. What did he mean?*

As Paul waited for clarification he began to feel something. Where his hand rested on the control panel he could feel a tremor of some kind. At first it was subtle, but then the *Grouper* began to shake and slide to the side as if some force or current was pushing it out of position. In seconds the tremor became a deep rumbling, like a freight train approaching.

"What is that?" he asked.

"We're reading a massive signal up here. I've never seen anything like it. All kinds of movement."

"Where?"

"Everywhere," the voice said, sounding panicked.

There was a terrible pause as the rumbling increased and then their controller spoke again.

"Good Lord!" the controller shouted. "There's an avalanche coming your way."

THE RUMBLING IN THE DEPTHS shook the *Grouper*. Sliding rock and sediment from the slope that the *Kinjara Maru* sat on was tumbling down at an accelerating pace, released by the exploding torpedoes.

As the avalanche came on, it forced the water out of its way, creating its own current and stirring up the sediment. Clouds of silt engulfed them, lit up by the submersible's lights. The world outside the view port became a swirl of brown and gray.

"Get us out of here," Gamay shouted.

Paul intended to do just that, but whatever vessel had fired the torpedoes at them was probably still waiting out there. And, in all honesty, being blown to bits seemed just as ghastly as getting buried alive.

He flipped the ballast switch and dumped the rest of the iron that held them down. He pushed the throttle back to full and angled the nose of the *Grouper* upward, but the *Grouper* was too underpowered to overcome such a current, and it banged against the *Kinjara Maru*'s hull once again.

Gamay put her hand on his arm as they began to rise. Then suddenly they were yanked to a stop.

"We're caught on something," Gamay said, craning her head around, desperately trying to see what it might be.

Paul threw the motor into reverse, backed up for a few feet, and then went forward at a different angle. Same result: a steady acceleration followed by sudden stop that twisted the *Grouper* around like a dog being yanked backward on its leash.

Through the dust and silt Paul could see items tumbling across the deck and bits of the *Kinjara*'s superstructure being torn away. The rumbling sound reached a deafening pitch.

A wave of thicker sediment hit the sub, and all went dark. Something metallic snapped, and then the *Grouper* started to tumble.

Gamay's visor and a couple of other items slid to one side and then toppled over and up the wall and then onto the ceiling. Paul held on but saw his wife was unable to brace herself. She hit the side wall and then banged against the ceiling two feet above them and then came back down.

He realized they'd rolled over, becoming momentarily inverted. He reached out, pulling Gamay to him.

"Hold on to me," he shouted.

She wrapped her arms around him as they continued to bang and twist at the mercy of the current and the landslide. Something slammed against the view port for a second, racing out of the murky water, hitting it hard, and then being swept away. The lights failed, and the wrenching sound of something being torn off the outside of the *Grouper* ended with a snap.

And then it stopped.

The rumbling sound continued for another minute or so, dissipating into the distance like a herd of buffalo had stampeded past.

Paul held his breath. Amazingly, incredibly, they were still alive.

In the darkness, he felt his wife breathing hard. His own heart pounded, and his body prickled with adrenaline. Neither of them said a word, as if the mere sound of their voices might set off another landslide. But after a full minute of silence, and no further sounds of danger, Paul felt his wife move.

She looked up at him through the dim illumination of the emergency lighting, She appeared as surprised to be alive as he was.

"Any leaks?" she asked.

He looked around. "Nothing up here."

She eased off him. "When we get home, I'm finding out who built this thing and I'm buying him a bottle of scotch."

He laughed. "A bottle of scotch? I might put his kids through college if he has any."

She laughed too.

As Gamay moved back, Paul eased over to the control panel. They were obviously resting at an odd angle, maybe forty-five degrees nose down, and rolled over thirty degrees or so.

"The main power is out," he said. "But the batteries look fine."

"See if you can get them back online," she said, pulling on the headset that their tumble had ripped off.

Paul went through the restart, got most of the systems back online, and then rerouted the lights through the backup line. The lights came back on. "Let's see if we can—"

He stopped midsentence. Gamay was staring past him, a hollow look in her eyes. He turned.

Packed sediment had pressed itself against the glass of the view port. It looked almost like a sand painting, with a few swirls and striations.

"We're buried," Gamay whispered. "That's why it got so quiet all of a sudden. We're buried alive."

KURT FOUND THE FIRST SEVENTY-TWO HOURS as chaperone of the sea to be twice as bad as he'd expected. No, he thought, that was an understatement, it was at least three times as bad as he'd feared.

Every group of researchers wanted special treatment, every group seemed to question the rules and his decisions, even his authority.

A team from Iceland insisted that an experiment by one of the Italian groups would interfere with the baseline data they were trying to collect. A Spanish group had been caught trying to plant a flag on the tower of rock in strict contravention of the agreed-to plan. And while Kurt found their boldness somewhat endearing, the Portuguese were ready to duke it out over the incident. He half expected pistols at dawn, the way they spoke.

Meanwhile, the Chinese were complaining about the presence of *three* Japanese teams, to which the Japanese responded that the Chinese didn't need anyone there as they would just steal all the data in a cyberattack once it was downloaded anyway.

Dealing with enough squabbling to make the UN jealous was not the only problem. Along with Joe and the rest of the *Argo*'s crew, Kurt also had to act as lifeguard.

Most of the science teams had only rudimentary training in the ways of the sea, either on the surface or below. Two of the teams had already collided head-on. Their small boats suffered only minor damage, but it was enough to send them back to Santa Maria for repairs.

Others had issues diving. One team narced itself by using the wrong mixture, and two of the *Argo*'s rescue divers had to corral them before they lost consciousness. Another member of a different team had to be forced to take a decompression stop he didn't think necessary, and a French scientist almost drowned when an inexperienced divemaster put too much weight on the man's belt and he sank to the bottom like a stone.

In full gear, Kurt and Joe dove down and rescued the scientist, only to surface and find another team with an engine fire aboard their rented vessel. It was enough to make Kurt wish they'd never found the damn tower in the first place.

As the sun began to head over the yardarm, the day's madness seemed to be winding down. Most of the smaller boats were heading back in toward Santa Maria. Kurt guessed the bars would fill up quickly, and stories would be tossed around, growing more extravagant with each telling. Or perhaps not. He wasn't really sure what scientists did with their spare time. Maybe they would plot against one another all night and come out in the morning ready to cause him and Joe more headaches.

Either way he was already regretting his decision to play umpire when he stepped out onto the *Argo*'s starboard bridgewing and spotted a 50-foot black-hulled trawler he hadn't seen before.

"You recognize that one?" he asked Joe.

Joe squinted off into the distance. "Wasn't here this morning."

"I didn't think so," Kurt replied. "Get the Zodiac ready."

FIVE MINUTES LATER, Kurt, Joe, and two men from the *Argo*'s crew were skipping across the light swells, headed for the trawler. They reached it and circled it once.

"You see anyone on board?" Kurt asked.

Joe shook his head.

"You know," Joe said, "technically, this boat's outside the exclusivity zone."

"Come again?" Kurt said.

"We're three-quarters of a mile from the tower," Joe said. "The exclusive zone is a mile in diameter. Technically, this boat's outside that. We're only supposed to have authority over vessels, divers, and submersibles inside that radius."

Kurt looked at Joe oddly. "Who made that rule?"

"I did."

"When did you start becoming a bureaucrat?"

Zavala shrugged, a wry smile on his face. "You put me at the big desk and tell me to take charge, these kind of things are going to happen."

Kurt almost laughed. Governor Joe.

"Well, if you're in charge, let's widen that circle."

"We need a quorum," Joe said.

"Did that boxer hit you harder than I thought?" Kurt asked.

Joe shook his head and looked at the crewmen. "All in favor of enlarging the observation zone say aye."

Kurt and the other two crewmen said aye simultaneously.

"The rule is duly changed," Joe said.

Kurt tried hard not to laugh. "Great. Now get us aboard that boat."

On board the trawler they found maps, diving gear, and some type of paper with Cyrillic lettering on it.

"It's Russian," Kurt said. "We have any Russian teams registered?"

Joe shook his head. "We got papers from their Science Ministry requesting information, but no one signed up."

"Looks like they came anyway."

Kurt moved to the rear of the small boat. A long anchor had been thrown out. There was no flag up, but Kurt was pretty sure a diver had gone down that chain. He noticed a pair of shoes by the dive ladder.

"Only one pair of shoes," he noted.

"Someone went down alone," Joe guessed.

Diving alone was crazy enough; leaving no one on the boat up above was even crazier. A little wind, a little change in the current, or the arrival of an opportunistic pirate or two, and you could surface to find yourself lost and alone in the ocean.

"Look at this," the *Argo*'s crewman said, pointing to a video screen.

Kurt turned. On the monitor was a murky scene being broadcast from an underwater camera.

"Could it be live?" Kurt asked.

"It looks that way," the crewman said, examining the setup.

Kurt studied the screen. The dark water and swirling sediment were obvious as the camera maneuvered in what looked to be a confined space. He saw metallic walls and equipment.

"Whoever it is, they've gone inside one of the wrecks," Joe said.

"Unbelievable," Kurt said. Short of antagonizing a group of sharks, wreck diving was about the most dangerous thing you could do underwater. He could not believe someone would try it alone.

"This person is far too stupid to be in our exclusivity zone."

Joe laughed and nodded.

Kurt pointed to a second set of tanks. "Are those charged?"

Joe checked the gauge. "Yep."

"I'm going down," Kurt said.

A minute later Kurt was in the water, breathing the compressed air and kicking with long strokes as he made his way down the chain. Approaching the bottom, he saw a pinpoint of light and angled toward it.

Whoever it was, they'd gone into the downed Constellation. Considering that the middle of the plane was broken open like a cracked egg, that didn't seem so reckless. But the movements of the camera had seemed odd, and as he stared at the shaking beam of light he wondered if the diver was in some kind of trouble.

Kicking harder, he made it to aircraft's triple tail. The cone of light from inside the fuselage continued moving in a random pattern.

He swam to the break in the aircraft's skin. The light was coming from the forward section. The random movements made Kurt think it might be floating loose. He feared he was about to find a dead diver, one who'd run out of oxygen but whose light, probably attached to his arm by a lanyard, still had battery power and was floating around above him like a helium balloon on a string.

He eased inside, working his way around tangled insulation and bent sheet metal. Clouds of sediment wafted from the front of the plane, and the oddly moving beam pierced the darkness, faded, and then came through again.

Kurt swam toward it. Emerging through the cloud of silt, he found a diver digging voraciously, twisting and pulling frantically. The flashlight was attached to the diver's belt.

He reached out and put a hand on the diver's shoulder. The figure spun, swinging a knife toward him.

Kurt saw the blade flash in the reflected light. He blocked the diver's arm and then twisted it, dislodging the knife. Bubbles from both regulators filled the cabin. Combined with the swirling sediment and the waving light, they made it difficult to see.

The knife tumbled through the water and disappeared. Kurt held the diver's right arm in a wristlock. His other arm shot forward, grabbing the diver by the neck. He was about to rip the diver's mask off—a classic underwater fighting technique—when he saw that the diver was a young woman, and her eyes were filled with panic and fear.

He released her and held up a hand with his fingers spread. *Calm down.*

The woman nodded but remained rigid. She motioned toward her feet.

Kurt looked down. Somehow she'd gotten her leg caught between a twisted part of the fuselage and some equipment. A jagged cut in the sheet metal marked her attempts to saw through the metal with her knife. It didn't look like she'd gotten very far.

Kurt had a better idea. He sank down, wedged his back to the skin of the fuselage, and placed both feet on the attached equipment box. With all the strength in his back and legs, he pushed against the metal box. He expected it to snap and break loose, but instead it bent just enough.

The woman pulled her foot out and immediately began rubbing her ankle. When she looked up, Kurt put his index finger and thumb together, making a circle—the universal OK symbol. *Are you okay?*

She nodded.

Next he brought his two index fingers together parallel and then looked at her questioningly.

She shook her head. Apparently, she wasn't diving with a buddy. Just as he thought.

He pointed at her sharply and then made the thumbs-up signal.

She hesitated and then nodded reluctantly. Grabbing her light, she began to swim out of the aircraft. Kurt took a last look around and then followed.

After a decompression stop for her, they broke the surface together a few yards from her boat. She swam to it and climbed in first. Kurt followed.

Joe and one of the *Argo*'s crewmen remained aboard to welcome them.

The woman removed her mask, pulled back the head covering on her wet suit, and shook out her hair. She didn't look happy to have boarders. Kurt didn't care.

"You must be out of your mind to make a dive like that on your own."

"I've been diving alone for ten years," she said.

"Yeah," he said. "You spend a lot of time exploring sunken wrecks?"

She grabbed a towel, dried her face, and then looked back at him defensively. "Who are you to be telling me what to do? And what are you doing on my boat anyway?"

Joe puffed up his chest, about to launch into an explanation. Kurt beat him to it. "Our job is to make sure you scientists don't drown or infringe on the rules we set up. You seem to be doing both, so we came to check you out," he said. "This boat isn't even registered as part of the study. You want to tell us the reason?"

"I don't have to register with you," she said smugly. "I'm outside your official zone. Outside of your jurisdiction, as you Americans like to say."

Kurt glanced at Joe. "Not anymore," he said, turning back to the woman. "We enlarged it."

"We even had a vote and everything," Joe added.

She looked from Kurt to Joe and then back again. "Typical American arrogance," she said. "Changing the rules to suit you whenever the need arises."

Kurt could almost understand that sentiment, except she was missing an important fact. He grabbed the pressure gauge on her tank and turned it over. As he suspected, she was well into her reserve air.

"Typical Russian stubbornness," he replied. "Getting angry at the people who just saved your life."

He showed her the gauge.

"You had less than five minutes of air left."

Her eyes focused on the gauge, and Kurt let it drop. She reached out and took it in her hand, studying it for a long moment.

"You should be glad we're so arrogant," he said.

She let the gauge go gently and looked up. He could see her jaw clench, though he wasn't sure if it was out of embarrassment or anger. "You're right," she said finally, taking a more subdued tone. "I am . . . appreciative. I was just . . ."

She stopped and focused on Kurt, and whatever she was about to say she replaced it with a simple "Thank you."

"You're welcome," Kurt said.

He noticed a change in her demeanor, even a hint of a smile on her face. "You are the ones in charge here?" she asked.

"Unfortunately," Kurt replied.

"I'm Katarina Luskaya," she said. "I'm here on behalf of my country. I would like to talk to you about this discovery."

"You can register with the liaison officer in the—"

"I was thinking more like talking tonight," she said, focused on Kurt. "Perhaps over dinner?"

Joe rolled his eyes. "Here we go. The Austin charm in full effect."

Kurt was too busy for this. "You've seen too many movies, Ms. Luskaya. There's not much I can tell you anyway."

She stood up, unzipping the top half of her suit, exposing a bikini top that accentuated her curves and an athlete's midrift.

"Perhaps there's something I can tell you," she said. "Since you are in charge, I have some information you might be interested in."

"You're serious?"

"Very," she said. "And, besides, we all have to eat. Why should we do it alone?"

"So we're all going?" Joe asked.

Kurt cut his eyes at Joe.

"Maybe not," Joe said. "Lots of paperwork to do anyhow."

Kurt doubted the woman had any information of value, but he admired her blatant attempt to get him alone and no doubt see what information he might have.

It suddenly dawned on Kurt that if there was even the slightest chance that something important could be learned from Ms. Luskaya, well, then it really was his duty to find out.

"You're staying in Santa Maria?" he guessed.

She nodded, and Kurt turned to Joe.

"I trust you guys can make it back to the *Argo* on your own?"

"And if we can't?" Joe said.

"Then signal for help," Kurt said, smiling.

Joe nodded reluctantly and motioned toward the Zodiac. The *Argo*'s crewmen climbed aboard and Joe followed, muttering something about "shirking responsibilities" as he went.

Kurt looked at the young woman. "Do you have a car in town?"

She smiled. "Mmm-hmm," she said. "And I know just the place to take you."

ANDRAS, THE KNIFE, stood at a pay phone overlooking the harbor at Vila do Porto. He felt as if he'd gone back in time, using such a phone to make a call. He could hardly remember seeing one over the last few years. But despite its vacation destination status, the Azores were not quite up to speed in the technology department. Many of the island's inhabitants were less than wealthy and often did not have landlines or mobile phones, so the pay phones still sprouted in many places.

For Andras, that meant the chance to make an untraceable call, one the U.S. government or Interpol could not tap into as its digital signal flew through space and bounced off a satellite somewhere. To listen to this conversation they would have to break into a heavy trunk line buried under Azorean soil and stretching across the floor of the Atlantic to North Africa, where it made landfall.

This was not impossible—in fact, the Americans had famously done just that to a Russian trunk line during the cold war—but unlikely, considering no one had a strategic reason to care what conversations were going on between the Azorean islanders and their families and friends on the mainland.

And that was a pleasing thought to Andras, because recent discoveries had raised the specter of danger for him.

He dialed and waited for what seemed like hours. Finally, he was connected to an operator in Sierra Leone and then to an office in Djemma's palace. Eventually an aide put the President for Life on the line.

"Why are you calling me?" Djemma said. He sounded like he was in a tunnel somewhere—apparently there were drawbacks to using old landline technology.

"I have news," he said. "Some good, some bad."

"Begin, and be quick."

"You were right. At least twenty scientific groups have shown up, with others on their way. This magnetic phenomenon seems to be drawing great interest."

"Of course it is," Djemma said. "Why else do you think I sent you there?"

"It's not only scientific interest. There are some military personnel here as well."

Djemma did not sound concerned. "That is to be expected. You will have no issues with them if you do as planned."

"Maybe," Andras said. "But here's the real problem. The Americans who almost caught us on the *Kinjara Maru* are here. I've seen their ship in the harbor. Now it anchors over the magnetic tower. According to the Portuguese, they've been put in charge of the entire study. I'm sure there's a military angle to it."

Djemma laughed. "You continue to make your enemies bigger than they really are, perhaps to add glory to your name when you knock them down, but it smacks of paranoia."

"What are you talking about?" Andras asked.

"You were not attacked by U.S. Navy SEALs or Special Forces, my friend. These men from NUMA are oceanographers and divers. They find wrecks and salvage ships and take pictures of sea life. Honestly, I'd have thought you could handle them. I wouldn't let it get out that they bested you so easily, it may reduce your ability to charge such outrageous fees."

Djemma laughed as he spoke, and Andras felt his blood beginning to boil.

"Are you worried about facing them again?" Djemma asked, needling him.

"Listen to me," Andras said, growing furious. And then he paused as a sight he could hardly believe came walking right up the dock toward him. The same silver-haired American who'd interfered with him on the *Kinjara Maru*, walking with a dark-haired woman he recognized as the Russian scientist he'd been told about. As they drew closer, Andras recognized the man in a more concrete way.

"Well I'll be," he whispered to himself.

"What?" Djemma said. "What are you talking about?"

Shrinking back into the kiosk that held the pay phone and turning away, Andras ignored them as they passed on the far side of the street.

"Andras," Djemma said. "What the hell is going on?"

Andras returned to his phone call, calculating a new play. "This NUMA is not as toothless as you might think," he said. "My concern is that they will interfere again. One of their members in particular. It would be best if I take them out."

"Don't antagonize them," Djemma warned. "You'll only draw attention to us at the wrong time. We are very close to making our move."

"Don't worry," Andras said. "It'll go off without a hitch, I promise you."

"I'm not paying you for revenge," Djemma said.

Andras laughed. "Don't worry," he said. "This one's on the house."

Before Djemma could reply, Andras slammed the heavy plastic receiver back onto its metal cradle. The sound it made and the sensation left him grinning maniacally, so much more satisfying than pressing a red button on a cell phone.

GAMAY TROUT TRIED HER BEST TO REMAIN CALM, to control her breathing and her emotions. Beside her, Paul continued a useless attempt to raise the *Matador* on the underwater transceiver.

"*Matador*, this is *Grouper*. Do you copy?"

No response.

"*Matador*, this is *Grouper* . . ."

He'd been at it for thirty minutes. What else could he do? Their only hope was for the *Matador* to send down the ROVs and try to dig them out. That is, if they could be found and if they weren't under a hundred feet of sediment.

So Paul continued to try. Matador, *this is* Grouper. Matador, *please respond.* And each time he spoke the words, the sound grated on her nerves like some form of Chinese water torture.

There had been no response for thirty minutes. There would be no response in the next thirty, or the next thirty thousand, if he tried. Either the antenna had been torn off in the landslide or they were buried too deep for any signal to get out.

Taking another calming breath, she rubbed his shoulders.

"They might be able to hear us," Paul told her. "Even if we can't hear them."

She nodded, twisted herself around in the other direction, and checked on their air status. They had nineteen hours of air left. Nineteen hours of waiting to die. In a manner she'd never felt before, Gamay was suddenly aware of how tight the confines of the *Grouper* were. It was a coffin. A tomb.

A wave of claustrophobia swept over her so powerfully that she began to shake, began to wish they'd been killed in the landslide or that she could just open the hatch and let the water pour in and crush them. It was irrational, it was panic, but it was astoundingly real to her.

"Matador, *this is* Grouper . . . *Do you read?*"

She held herself together, fighting back tears that were threatening to break through.

Uncomfortable sitting with her head bowed in the cramped vehicle, she lay down and closed her eyes, resting her face against the cold metal of the floor like one might rest on the tiles of the bathroom after a heavy night of drinking.

It calmed her nerves a bit, at least until she opened her eyes and noticed something she hadn't seen before: a drop of water trickling down the side of the metal plating. Any hope of it being condensation was erased as another drop quickly followed, and then another.

Drip . . . Drip . . . Drip . . .

Perhaps they wouldn't have nineteen hours after all.

"Matador, *this is* Grouper . . ."

There was no point in telling Paul. He would know soon enough, and there was nothing they could do about it anyway. At 16,000 feet, the pressure outside was almost 6,800 pounds per square inch. The slow little drips would quickly become faster drips as the water forced the plates apart, and at some point it would start spraying, blasting them with a jet of ice-cold water powerful enough to cut a person in half. And then it would all be over.

Gamay glanced around the cabin for other leaks. She saw none, but something new caught her eye: light emanating from the tiny screens in her virtual reality visor.

She grabbed it. The screens were still functioning. She saw a metallic wall and sediment floating around. The particles swirled and caught the light.

"*Rapunzel* survived," she said quietly.

"What was that?" Paul asked.

"This is a live shot," she said. "*Rapunzel*'s still functioning."

Gamay pulled the visor on and then her gloves. It took a moment to orient herself, but she quickly realized that *Rapunzel* was floating freely. She had the little robot do a 360-degree turn. Open water beckoned through the same gaping hole that *Rapunzel* had used to enter the ship.

"I'm bringing her out."

"How are we still in contact with her?" Paul asked.

"Her umbilical cables are eight feet long where they hit the *Grouper*. They must be sticking out of the sediment."

"That means we're not buried too deep," Paul said. "Maybe she can dig us out."

Gamay maneuvered *Rapunzel* out of the ship, while Paul began to watch the monitor on his control panel.

"Take her up," he said. "We need a bird's-eye view."

Gamay nodded and had *Rapunzel* ascend. She rose vertically for a hundred feet, high enough to get a better view but still close enough that her lights and her low-light camera could make out the ship and the seafloor.

The avalanche had changed everything. The *Kinjara Maru* now rested on her side like a toy that'd been knocked over. The bow was almost buried in sediment, and the ground underneath was flatter and smoother. Gamay guessed that the avalanche had moved the ship a hundred yards or so.

"Any idea where we are?" she asked.

"We were headed to the bow," he said. "No idea what happened after the landslide hit."

Gamay guided *Rapunzel* toward the bow of the ship and then out over the field of sediment. After ten minutes of up-and-back passes, neither she nor Paul had seen any sign of themselves.

In some corner of her mind, the oddness of the situation struck Gamay. How strange, she thought, to be consciously looking for yourself with no idea where you might be.

After another pass she asked. "You see anything?"

"Nothing."

The cables that were signaling *Rapunzel* and receiving her signal had to be sticking out, but a foot or two of cable would be hard to spot on a seafloor now littered with debris.

Still lying on her back, Gamay started *Rapunzel* on another pass. As she did, the touch of icy water reached her elbow. She lifted the visor for a second. A small pool was forming beside her, maybe two tablespoons' worth. The drip was coming faster.

She pulled the visor back down. They had to hurry.

"Maybe if you were closer to the seafloor," Paul said.

It would increase the resolution but narrow the field of view, the difference between looking for a contact lens that had fallen out of your eye from a standing position or crawling around on the floor, scanning the tile inch by inch. She didn't think they had that much time.

"I'm taking her higher," she said.

"But we can barely see as it is."

"Blow some of the air," she said.

Paul did not immediately answer.

"I don't know," Paul said. "Even if they didn't hear us, the *Matador* knows were in trouble. They'll have ROVs down here pretty soon."

"It will help us," she said.

Still, he hesitated.

"Even if they send ROVs, they're going to need to know where we are," she said.

"Okay," he said finally, perhaps responding to the desperation in her voice, perhaps realizing that she was right.

"Get *Rapunzel* to whatever depth you think is best," he added. "Tell me when, and I'll vent the cylinder we've been drawing off of. It's half empty."

Gamay guided *Rapunzel* back out over the sunken freighter's bow and let her rise to the very brink of visibility. It gave them the widest field of view.

"Ready," she said.

Paul turned a lever and locked it. With his other hand he reached over and pressed the emergency vent switch. There was a hiss of air through the lines, the sound of bubbles exploding and then turbulent water churning. It lasted for about fifteen seconds and then slowly waned. The silence that followed was eerie.

"Do you see anything?" he asked.

Gamay was guiding *Rapunzel* forward, turning her head left and right, looking for what should have been a telltale rush of bubbles catching the light. It should have been easy to see and unmistakable, but neither she nor Paul caught it.

"It has to be there."

"I don't see anything," Paul said

"Vent another bottle," she said.

He shook his head. "Two cylinders is a quarter of our air."

"It's not going to matter," she said.

"Of course it matters. If we're buried, it's going to take a while for them to dig us out. I don't want to suffocate while they're still digging."

For the first time she heard real stress in his voice. So far, he'd been business as usual. The strong, silent Paul she knew. Perhaps that was for her. Perhaps he was as afraid as she was. She had to tell him the truth.

"We're leaking back here," she said.

Silence first, and then, "Leaking?"

She nodded.

"How bad?"

"Not bad yet," she said. "But we're not going to last long enough to worry about the air."

He stared at her for a moment and then finally nodded his agreement. "Tell me when."

She pulled the visor back down and brought *Rapunzel* back to the bow of the freighter. This time, she picked the port side to scan.

"Okay," she said.

Paul turned the lever on cylinder number 2, locked it, and vented the second air tank. The turbulent sound of escaping air shook the *Grouper* again, and Gamay strained her eyes looking for any sign of it. She turned, stared, and turned again.

Nothing. Nothing in any direction.

A new fear crept in. What if they weren't near the bow at all? What if the avalanche had swung the *Kinjara Maru* around or taken them so far from the ship that they'd be virtually impossible to find? The freighter could even be sitting on top of them at this point.

The view screens in front of her eyes flickered and shook. For a second she feared that they were about to lose the video feed. But then the screens stabilized except for one area near the very top. Something was distorting the camera's picture.

She hoped it wasn't a crack in the glass, which would be as fatal to *Rapunzel* as the leak in the *Grouper*'s side would soon be to them. But the camera continued to operate, and Gamay realized the distortion wasn't a crack. It was caused by something else: a bubble that had been caught on the lens.

She played back the video of the flicker and slowed it down. Sure enough, it was a rush of bubbles passing by *Rapunzel*. She rotated the small ROV to look straight down. There, almost directly below, sat the oblong shape of the *Grouper*. Not buried, as they'd suspected, but planted facedown in the silt, with metal debris from the *Kinjara Maru* piled on top.

Paul saw it too. "Have I mentioned how much I love my wife?" he said excitedly.

"I love you too," she said, already guiding *Rapunzel* down toward them.

"Does *Rapunzel* have a cutting torch?"

She nodded, and as the small robotic machine reached them Gamay snapped the acetylene torch on and began slicing through one of the metal beams that had landed on top of the *Grouper*.

The torch burned through the beam in two minutes flat. It broke in half and fell away with a resounding clang. The *Grouper*, now at full upward buoyancy, shifted as the weight was released.

It felt as if the little sub was trying to float free. But something still held them.

"You see the cables near our tail?" Paul asked. "We're tangled in them."

Gamay saw the cables, maneuvered *Rapunzel* one more time, and brought the torch to bear. This section of debris was lighter but more cumbersome. As *Rapunzel*'s torch cut through each length of steel cable, she had to pull them away to keep them from entangling the *Grouper* again.

As the last section of cable was dragged away, the *Grouper* twisted and began to rise. Sliding through the rest of the loose debris, it moved upward.

Inside, it sounded like metal garbage cans being knocked about in the middle of the night. But as the last clang died away and strands of cable slid off them with a scraping sound, they were free.

"We're ascending," Paul shouted.

Gamay put *Rapunzel* into auto surface mode and flipped her visor up.

To see water streaming past the view port instead of a pile of sand and silt was beautiful. To feel the vertical acceleration as the little sub rose was intoxicating.

She took a deep breath, relaxed for a second, and then heard a crack, like a plate of glass had been snapped in two. She turned her head.

The trickle of water forcing its way in had suddenly become a steady stream.

THE RESTAURANT WAS NAMED ESCARPA, which was a way of saying "cliff top" in Portuguese. The name fit, as the low, wide building made of mortar and native stone sat high up in the hills above Santa Maria, three-quarters of the way to the top of the Pico Alto. An eight-mile drive on a twisting mountain road had brought Kurt and Katarina to its doorstep.

On the way, they'd passed open fields, tremendous views, and even an outfit that rented hang gliders and ultralights to tourists. Only a dozen times during the ride had Katarina put the wheels of her small rented Focus onto the gravel during a turn. And if Kurt was honest, only three of those times seemed likely to end in certain death, as the guardrails, which had been intermittent the whole way up, were nowhere to be seen.

But having watched the young woman shift and break and mash the gas pedal at just the right moments, Kurt had decided she was an excellent driver. She'd obviously been trained, and so he figured she was just trying to test his nerve.

He chose not to react, lazily opening the sunroof and then commenting on how incredible the valley looked with nothing standing between them and a trip down into it.

"Enjoying the drive?" she'd asked.

"Immensely," he'd said. "Just don't hit any cows."

Having gotten no reaction out of him only seemed to make her drive harder. And Kurt could barely contain his laughter.

Now at a table, watching the sun drop over the island and into the ocean, they had an opportunity to order. She deferred to him and he chose the island specialty: *Bacalhau à Gomes de Sá*, Portuguese salt cod with potato casserole, along with fresh, locally grown vegetables.

Kurt took a look at the wine list. Despite several excellent French and Spanish choices, he believed a local dish was best accompanied by a local wine. The Azores had produced wine since the sixteenth century, some of it known to be very good. From what he'd been told, most of the grapes were still picked by hand. He felt it a shame to let such work go to waste.

"We'll take a bottle of the Terras de Lava," he said, picking a white to go with the fish.

Across from him, Katarina nodded her approval. "I get to choose dessert," she insisted, smiling like a trader who'd just gotten the best part of the deal.

He smiled back. "Sounds fair."

Guessing he would be finishing that dessert before he learned her secret, he chose a different subject.

"So you're here on behalf of your government," he said.

She seemed a little prickly about that. "You say that like it's a bad thing. As if you're not here on behalf of your government."

"Actually, I'm not," he said. "Joe and I were here for a competition. We just stuck around at the request of the Portuguese and Spanish governments. To keep the peace between them."

"Quite a distinction," she said, taking a bite from one of the appetizers. "I believe the last time they got in an argument it took the Pope drawing a line across the world to settle it."

Kurt had to laugh. "Unfortunately, we have no such powers."

The wine came. He tasted it and nodded his approval.

"Why did they send you here?" he asked.

"I thought you'd be more discreet," she said.

"Not my strong suit."

"I work for the Science Directorate," she explained. "Of course they're interested in this discovery. A dozen wrecks believed to be dragged down to the depths by the powerful magnetism of this rock. Who wouldn't be?"

That made sense, even if some of her other actions didn't.

"No one's suggesting they were dragged to the bottom by the magnetism," he said. "Only that during and after their sinkings, the current and the magnetism combined to slowly draw them in."

"Yes," she said. "I know. But isn't it more romantic to imagine this place like the sirens of Greek mythology?"

"More romantic," he said. "But less accurate."

The gleam of adventure shone from her eyes. "Are you sure? After all, this part of the ocean has claimed an inordinate number of ships and planes over the years."

Before he could interject she began a list. "In 1880, the HMS *Atalanta* went down in these waters. The survivors reported waves of dizziness and sickness and seeing bizarre things. These sights were later called hallucinations and attributed to a shipboard epidemic of yellow fever. But as it was 1880, and the diagnosis was made well after the fact, no one really knows.

"In 1938, a freighter named the *Anglo-Australian* and its crew vanished within sight of the island chain. No wreckage was ever found. In 1948, an airliner known as the *Star Tiger* disappeared after taking off from here. There was no Mayday or distress call issued. No wreckage was ever found. In 1968, after having unexplained radio troubles, one of your submarines, the USS *Scorpion*, vanished not far from here. As I understand it, the wreckage suggested she exploded from within."

Kurt knew some of the stories. The fact was the *Star Tiger* disappeared well to the west of the Azores, perhaps a thousand miles from here, and the *Scorpion* was believed to have suffered a catastrophic failure at depth. There were some in the Navy that insisted she'd been rammed or hit by a Russian torpedo in retaliation for the accidental ramming of a Russian sub in the Pacific. He decided not to relay that theory.

"This place is much like the Bermuda Triangle," she said. "Can't we let it be mystical for just a moment?"

"Sure," he said. "But you should know, U.S. Coast Guard studies have found no significant difference in the rate of ships and planes disappearing in the Bermuda Triangle than anywhere else on the seas. The oceans of this world are dangerous places wherever you decide to go."

Looking disappointed again, she took a sip of wine. "You know, they're calling it the Devil's Gate."

"Who is?"

"The other scientists," she said. "Maybe the press."

That was the first he'd heard of it. "I haven't seen any press, not since the first day," he said. "And I'm not sure I understand the reference."

"The wreckage down there," she said. "It lies in a wedge-shaped slice, narrowing from the west to the east and pointing toward the tower. At the closest end is a narrow gap through which the current accelerates and then spills over into the deeper waters. At the far end, the presumed entry point, there's a wider gap between two distinctive raised sections of rock that look something like pillars."

"And that's the gate," he said.

She nodded. "'Wide is the gate and broad is the road that leads to destruction,'" she said. "That's from Matthew. Chapter seven, verse thirteen. The theory I've heard tossed around is that the ships and planes and other wreckage have been dragged through the wide and crooked gate and cannot get through the straight and narrow. A graveyard of the damned: the Devil's Gate."

Kurt had to admit it sounded far more exciting than North Central Atlantic Magnetic Anomaly, or whatever it had officially been named.

"The ships check in but they don't check out," he said.

"Exactly," she said, smiling at him.

"None of which explains why you were diving on a wrecked aircraft at the entrance to that gate," he said.

"No," she agreed, not attempting to defend her actions or even offer a reason for them. "Nor does it explain why an aircraft made of aluminum—a nonferrous, nonmagnetic metal—would be drawn in by this decidedly magnetic anomaly."

She had a point, one that hadn't dawned on Kurt before. As her words sunk in, she took another sip of the wine.

"Very good wine," she said. "Would you excuse me? I'm just going to freshen up."

Freshen up? After trying on three different outfits, she'd spent half an hour in the bathroom of her hotel room fixing her hair and makeup. How much fresher could she get?

Kurt stood politely as she walked away. The truth was, she looked fantastic in a simple black cocktail dress and red high-heeled shoes. Especially in contrast to his somewhat disheveled state. He was still in the clothes he'd been wearing this morning, with a change into dive gear, a quick change back, and no shower in between.

He watched her leave, thought about what she'd just said, and took the opportunity to grab his phone and send a text to Joe.

He typed furiously.

I need anything you can find about this Katarina Luskaya. Why she's here. Who she's worked for in the past. And anything about that old plane she was diving on. I need it quick.

A text came back from Joe seconds later.

I must be a mind reader. Already on it. Here are a few links. FYI: the plane was listed as lost out of Santa Maria in 1951. There's a Civil Aeronautics Board file and a crash report. There's also a CIA stub on it, but I can't get access to any of the data.

A CIA stub. Kurt guessed he shouldn't have been surprised. He started looking over the links Joe had sent, dividing his attention between the entrance to the restrooms and the phone.

IN THE LADIES' ROOM, Katarina lingered in front of the mirror, hovering over a marble sink. She wasn't looking at her makeup or her hair or anything besides her own phone.

"Come on," she urged as the download proceeded sluggishly.

Finally, the screen changed, and a bio of sorts on Kurt Austin appeared. It held more than she expected, more than she had time to read. She scanned the main points, texted a reply to Command saying she'd received it, and slid the phone back into her purse.

A quick check of her hair told her it was as good as it would get, and she turned and walked out.

KURT GLANCED TOWARD THE RESTROOMS, then back at his phone, then back toward the restrooms. He saw the door swing open, read one more line, and stuffed the phone back into his pocket.

He stood and pulled out her chair as she arrived.

"You look so much fresher," he said, smiling.

"Thank you," she replied. "Sometimes it's hard to feel pretty enough."

Kurt sensed some unintentional truth in what she'd said. He pinned it on a lifetime of competing in a sport that was judged as opposed to one where you scored or you didn't. Too much subjectivity had a way of making people uncertain of themselves.

"You look stunning," he said. "In fact, everyone here is wondering why you're having dinner with a scruffy guy like me."

She smiled, and Kurt detected a slight blush.

By now the sun had disappeared. They made small talk till the entrées came, and then, after another glass of wine, Kurt decided to reopen the earlier conversation.

"I have a question," he said. "Why did you dive on that plane alone? You had two sets of tanks on board. Don't you have a partner?"

"That's two questions," she said, again smiling. "I came to Santa Maria with another representative of the government. But he is not part of the Science Directorate. The assignment is my own," she added. "The tanks came with the boat."

Kurt guessed that other representative would be a handler of sorts, to watch over her, to keep her both in line and out of trouble.

"Your turn," he said, taking another bite of the fish.

"I think I might like this game," she said, then fired away. "You seemed awfully angry when we came up," she said. "What made you so mad? Was it my violation of your precious 'exclusivity zone' or the fact that I never registered in the first place?"

"Neither," he said. "I don't like to see people get hurt. You could have been killed down there in that wreck. Another five minutes and you would have been."

"So Kurt Austin is a man who cares?"

"Absolutely," he said, offering an intentionally warm smile.

"Is that why you're in the salvage business?"

"I don't follow you."

"Any fool can blow up a boat and send it to the bottom," she said. "But it takes skill and dedication and far greater risks to bring one back up again. I can see you doing it for exactly those reasons: because it's harder *and* because it's better. And because you like saving things."

Kurt had never thought of it quite that way, but there was some truth in what she'd said. The world was full of men destroying things and throwing them away. He took pride in restoring old things instead of tossing them out.

"I suppose I should thank you," she added. "I'm guessing you dove down to salvage me."

He hadn't been sure she was in trouble when he'd gone in the water, but he'd been glad to pull her out alive instead of dead. He considered her motivation for taking such a risk in the first place.

"And you're a competitor," he said, taking his turn at amateur analysis.

"It has plusses and minuses," she said.

"National competitions, world championships, the Olympics," he said. "You've spent your whole life trying to prove to coaches and judges and the audience that you're worthy of their scores, that you even belong in the arena in the first place. Despite a partially torn ligament, you nearly got the bronze in Torino."

"I nearly won the gold," she corrected him. "I fell on the last jump. I finished the program on one foot."

"As I recall you couldn't walk for a couple of months afterward," he said, a fact he'd just read on Joe's update. "But the point stands. A different skater would have backed down, saved her leg for another day."

"Sometimes you don't get another day," she said.

"Is that what drove you on?"

She pursed her lips, studying him and twirling her fork in her angel-hair pasta. Finally, she spoke. "I wasn't supposed to medal," she said. "They almost gave my spot to another skater. Most likely, I would never get another shot."

"You had something to prove," he replied.

She nodded.

"And this whole thing—an assignment outside your laboratory—I'm guessing this is new to you," he said. "You must have people back home to impress, maybe you feel you have something to prove to them. Or you might not get another shot."

"Maybe," she admitted.

"Nothing wrong with that," he said. "We all want our bosses to be impressed. But there are places on this earth where you don't take chances. The inside of a wrecked aircraft a hundred forty feet below the surface is one of them."

"Haven't you ever wanted to show someone they were wrong about you?"

Kurt paused, and then spoke a half-truth. "I try not to worry about what other people think about me."

"So you have no one to prove anything to?" she asked.

"I didn't say that," he replied.

"So there is someone," she said. "Tell me who. Is it a woman? Is there a Mrs. Austin, or future Mrs. Austin, waiting for you back home?"

Kurt shook his head. "I wouldn't be here if there was."

"So who is it?"

Kurt chuckled. The conversation had certainly turned. "Tell me the secret you're holding, and I'll give you the answer."

She looked disappointed again. "I suppose dinner ends as soon as I give you that?"

Kurt didn't want it to end, but then again . . . "Depends on the secret," he said.

She picked up her fork as if she could stall him just a little longer and then she put it down dejectedly.

"Yesterday you rescued a French diver," she said.

"That's right," he said. "The guy had a hundred pounds of weight on his belt. Where you were reckless, he was just an idiot."

"Maybe not," she said.

"What do you mean?"

"It was a setup," she said. "While you and your partner were pulling him out of the water, another member of the French team was drilling a four-foot core sample out of the side of that rock. They've been bragging about it already."

Kurt felt an instant burst of anger. He exhaled sharply and then grabbed his napkin and threw it on the table.

"You were right," he said. "Time to go."

"Damn," she said.

He stood, left a handful of bills on the table, and took her by the hand. They headed for the exit.

"But what about your secret?" she said.

"Later," he said.

With Katarina in tow, Kurt pushed the door open and stepped through. Something moved in the shadows. An object swung toward him from the right. He tensed himself in the instant he had, and then a bat or a club or a pipe of some kind slammed him in the gut.

Despite his strength, the blow jarred Kurt and knocked the wind out of him. He doubled over and crumpled to his knees.

PAUL AND GAMAY were rising fast in the *Grouper*. With all the ballast dumped on the bottom of the ocean, the sub's nose pointed upward, and, the electric motor churning at full power, they rose at nearly three hundred feet a minute.

As the depth decreased, the pressure decreased. But twenty minutes into the climb they were still ten thousand feet below the surface, and the steady flow of water was increasing.

"The weakest part of the hull is the flange," Paul shouted, noticing that the water was flowing in where the two sections of the submarine had been joined together like lengths of pipe.

"We have clamps, we can help seal it," Gamay shouted back.

Paul reached over to the wall and tore down a Velcro-latched covering. Behind it was a set of tools that the sub's designers thought might be useful to its occupants. Included in that package were four clamps. Large, sturdy, and designed to fit the particulars of the *Grouper*, they were not that much different from a standard screw clamp that one might have on a workbench at home except they worked on a ratchet system like a jack used to lift up a car. Apparently, whoever had designed the boat realized the flange between the two halves of the sub was the weakest part.

Paul ripped down one of the clamps and handed it to Gamay; he was too big to turn around and get back there to help her.

"You'll find a spot on the flange with a notch in it, like the notch under a car for the jack. Slip the clamp on there. Once you get it locked, give it everything you've got to wrench it down. Then I'll hand you another one."

She nodded and took the clamp. Running her hand along the flange, she located the notch, lined the clamp up, and began to tighten it.

"Should I leave a little play, like when we do the lug nuts on the tires?" she asked.

"No," he said. "Slam that sucker down as hard as you can."

As Gamay worked, Paul sensed the *Grouper* rolling a bit. He glanced back at the control panel. They were still angled up at thirty-five degrees, but the sub was yawing to the right. He figured one of the control fins had been damaged and bent. He corrected their alignment and glanced back at Gamay.

He could see the strain on her face as she worked to get one final click on the first clamp.

"How are we doing?"

She slammed the handle home. "I think that one's done."

He looked over at the leak. It hadn't stopped. If anything, it was a little worse. Looking past her, he could see water pooling at the tail end of the sub, maybe a gallon or two.

He grabbed another clamp as they passed nine thousand feet. "Here," he said. "Hit the other side of the leak next."

KURT AUSTIN FELL in what seemed like slow motion to him.

He'd seen the pipe coming his way. And from the corner of his eye he'd caught sight of a burly man swinging it like an amateur ball player, using a big wide arc, a slower swing than it could have been.

He'd been able to react fast enough to flinch and harden his body against the blow, but not enough to dodge it.

As he doubled over, most of his mind focused on the intense pain across his abdomen, with just enough left over to hear Katarina scream and to realize the next blow would likely cave his head in.

Even as his knees hit the ground he flew into action.

He saw legs and lunged for them, pushing hard off the ground and driving his shoulder into the man's knee.

The joint hyperextended backward and gave out with a sickening snap. The thug let out a shout and fell backward. Kurt climbed onto him and slammed his fist into the man's face, exploding his nose in a spray of blood.

A second shot shattered a cheekbone or an eye socket, and the man's head snapped sideways, unmoving.

Whether he was dead or just unconscious, Kurt didn't know or honestly care. He had bigger things to deal with, mainly a second thug that had jumped on his back and now had him in a sleeper hold.

"Get out of here," he shouted in a raspy tone to Katarina.

He tried to pull the man's arm loose, a natural reaction that was impossible to accomplish under the best of circumstances. In this case, with his abs screaming from the impact of the pipe, Kurt had no power or leverage, and the man knew it.

The arms tightened, cutting off the blood supply to Kurt's brain.

Gasping for air, Kurt rolled and tried to slam the man against a van parked beside them. He pushed back and felt the impact. He did it again, but far weaker this time, and the man didn't let go.

He groped around for a weapon of any kind, a rock or a stick. Then suddenly he heard a dull thud, and the man's grip weakened. Kurt sucked in a breath of air as a second thud followed, and the man sloughed off him like a dead vine falling from a tree.

He tried to turn but couldn't, tried to stand but couldn't do that either. He could only squat there on the parking lot's black surface. He felt hands grasping his arm, small hands but with a firm grip. They pulled him up, helping him to his feet.

"Put your arm over me," Katarina said.

He threw his arm over her shoulder despite the pain it caused him. Leaning on her, they hobbled across the parking lot and made it to the small car. He just about fell into the passenger seat as she ran around to the driver's side.

She opened the door, tossed the pipe she'd grabbed from the first assailant into the back, and climbed into the driver's seat

The small engine came to life with a quick turn of the key, and seconds later they were speeding out of the parking lot onto the twisting mountain road.

Unseen by either of them, two Audis snapped on their headlights and turned to follow.

GAMAY HAD WRENCHED the third clamp into place and tightened it down with all the strength in her lithe body. Breathing hard, with the muscles in her arms burning, she glanced at the seam through which the water was forcing itself. The leak had slowed back to a trickle for a while but had now increased again and was becoming a continuous flow.

"Give me the last one," she shouted to Paul. She hoped it would make a difference. She hoped that four clamps, a couple hundred extra pounds of force holding the seam together, would be enough to offset the thousands of pounds of pressure trying to force its way inside the *Grouper*.

"Here," Paul said as he handed her the last of the clamps.

She found the fourth notch and slotted the clamp into place. "What's our depth?"

"Four thousand feet," he said.

She began pumping the lever. The arms on the clamp closed on the flange and locked, each additional pump getting harder until she could barely move the lever.

She let out a primal grunt as she gave the last push everything she had.

"That's all I can do," she said, falling back exhausted.

The leak had slowed, not quite to a trickle, but it no longer looked like someone had turned on a faucet and let it run.

"What's our rate of climb?" she asked.

"We're down to two hundred feet per minute," Paul said.

"Slower?" she said. "Why are we moving slower? Are we losing rpms?"

"No," Paul said. "We're gaining weight."

He nodded toward the tail end of the sub, and she turned. At least thirty gallons of water had pooled in the *Grouper*'s tail. Thirty gallons, two hundred sixty pounds of added weight, and rising.

Gamay now realized they weren't just in a race against the hull splitting open, they were in a race against time. Even with the reduced leak the *Grouper* would slowly take on water and continue to get heavier. Survival or destruction would be determined by the balance between how much water was coming in and how fast they could continue to rise. If they didn't get to the surface soon, they'd reach a point where the *Grouper*'s buoyancy was overridden by the added weight. At that moment, their long slow climb would turn into an even longer and slower descent, one from which there would be no escape.

THE TIRES OF THE RENTAL CAR squealed on the macadam of the mountain road. Kurt looked behind them. Two sets of lights had suddenly appeared and were getting closer at every turn.

"We should have gone back into the restaurant," she said.

He'd considered that, but there were only ten or so people in the building, and maybe a pair of cooks in the back. Not enough to really make it a secure location, and too many lives to endanger.

"Keep going," he said. "We're dead if they catch us up here. The best thing we can do is get to the city. We can find the police down there."

Katarina kept her foot on the gas, whipping the car through the turns as she'd done on the way up the hill. It kept them ahead. But two long straightaways allowed the larger, more powerful Audis to catch them.

Another series of hairpins gave them some breathing room, but if Kurt remembered it right, the longest straight section was coming up.

"Do you have a weapon?" he asked.

Katarina shook her head.

Unfortunately, neither did he. The Azores had strict policies regarding guns and such. Perhaps that was a good thing. Otherwise, the thug at the top of the hill might have had a Lugar or a Glock instead of a pipe.

Still, it led to problems here and now.

"We're coming up on another straight bit," she said.

They rounded the curve, and Katarina stomped on the gas, but the Audis all but leapt toward them, moving up fast in the rearview.

Suddenly, the window shattered on Kurt's side, and the sound of bullets punching holes in the sheet metal rang out. Kurt ducked down. So much for the no-gun policy.

Katarina began swerving back and forth, trying to keep the pursuers off them. As she did, Kurt spotted something sliding around in the backseat: the pipe he'd been hit with.

He grabbed it, glanced in the side mirror, and had an idea. The lead Audi was just a few feet back on his side.

"Hit the brakes," he shouted.

"What?"

"Just do it."

Katarina shifted her weight, gripped the wheel, and slammed her foot on the brake pedal. As she did, Kurt threw open his door.

The rental car's tires dug into the asphalt, screeching, streaming white smoke. The Audi's driver was taken by surprise; he hit his brakes late, took the rental car's door clean off, and then rumbled over it.

Shocked and confused, he didn't notice Kurt leaning out of the car, holding on to the garment handle above the door and swinging the pipe with a backhand like Rafael Nadal's.

The blow smashed in the windshield. A thick spiderweb of

cracks spread out over the driver's half, completely blocking the view. The Audi swerved away and then came back as if it would ram them.

Kurt swung again, this time a forehand coming in from the side. It took out the driver's window, catching the driver in the side of the head. The Audi swerved hard this time, dropping back and moving toward the cliff, then swerving rapidly to the right. It hammered the rocky slope on that side of the road, flipped, and tumbled. It slid on its caved-in roof, shedding parts and glass for a hundred yards, but avoided going off the cliff.

"That's gonna leave a mark," Kurt said.

The second Audi cut around the first one and began to accelerate. Kurt doubted the same plan would work twice. He looked ahead. Two more sets of lights were coming up the hill. They could have been locals or tourists, but they stayed abreast of each other, like one car trying to pass another and never actually making it. He was pretty sure what that meant.

"They're trying to corral us," he said over the wind that was pouring through the missing doorway.

For a moment he saw trepidation flicker across Katarina's face, and then the young agent who had something to prove stood on the gas pedal and gripped the wheel like a madwoman. The little Focus shot forward as Katarina flipped her high beams on for good measure.

"I'm not stopping," she shouted.

Kurt didn't doubt that, but as he glanced ahead he guessed the drivers of the cars charging up toward them had no plans of stopping either.

FOR TEN SOLID MINUTES the *Grouper* continued to climb, but ever more slowly.

"We're passing a thousand," Paul said.

A thousand feet, she thought. That sounded so much better than sixteen thousand or ten or five, but it was still deeper than many steel-hulled submarines were able to go. She remembered a ride she'd taken with the Navy years ago on a Los Angeles–class attack submarine that was about to be retired. At seven hundred feet the side had dented in with a resounding clang. As she nearly jumped out of her skin, the captain and crew laughed heartily.

"This is our test depth, ma'am," the captain had said. *"That dent shows up every time."*

Apparently, it was an inside joke played on all guests, but it scared the heck out of her, and the fact that she and Paul were still three hundred feet deeper than that meant one thousand feet could be just as deadly as sixteen thousand.

"Nine hundred," Paul said, calling out the depth again.

"What's our rate?" she asked.

"Two-fifty," he said. "Give or take."

Less than four minutes to the surface, less than four minutes to life.

Something snapped off the outside of the hull, and the *Grouper* started to shake.

"I think we lost the rudder," Paul said.

"Can you control it?"

"I can try to vector the thrust," he said, his hands working the two joysticks on the panel furiously.

She glanced to the rear. At least eighty gallons of water had filled the sub. The icy liquid had already reached her feet, causing her to pull them up toward her body.

A minute went by, and they began closing in on five hundred feet. A strange creaking sound reverberated through the hull, like a house settling or metal bending. It came and went and then came again.

"What is that?" she said. It was coming from above her head.

She looked up. The clamp on the top of the flange was quivering, the creaking sound coming from the hull above it.

She looked aft. The tail end of the sub was filled with water. A hundred gallons or more. Eight hundred pounds more than the front. All that extra weight twisted and pulled and bent the sub at the already weakened seam, trying to crack it in half like breaking a stick in the middle.

They had to level out before it ripped them apart. Had to spread the weight evenly even if it meant just climbing due to their buoyancy.

"Paul," she said.

"Two hundred," he called out.

"We have to level out," she said.

"What?"

The hull groaned louder. She saw the upper clamp slip.

"Paul!" She lunged forward as the clamp shot away from the notch. It hit her in the back of the leg, and she screamed.

Her voice was drowned out by the sound of the second clamp being flung from its moorings and the furious dissonance of water gushing into the sub like it was blasting from a high-pressure fire hose.

HALFWAY DOWN the twisting mountain road to Vila do Porto, the game of chicken was on. Katarina kept her foot down on the accelerator. The cars coming up at them seemed undaunted. If anything, they'd accelerated also, and continued to charge shoulder to shoulder, their headlights blazing.

Kurt put a hand up to block the glare, trying to save some of his night vision. He glanced in the mirror; the single car behind them was closing in. He wondered if everyone had gone insane.

He flicked his eyes forward again, caught sight of a road sign and an arrow. It read "Hang Gliders—Ultralights."

He grabbed the wheel, yanked the car to the right.

"What are you doing?" Katarina shouted.

They skidded onto a gravel road, turned sideways for a moment, and then straightened, as Katrina spun the wheel madly in one direction and then the other.

Behind them the sound of screeching tires pierced the night. A slight crunch followed, not the massive impact Kurt was hoping for but a happy sound nonetheless.

"Keep going," he said.

"We don't know where this goes."

"Does it matter?"

Of course it didn't. And moments later the lights swung onto the dirt road far behind them, so there was no way to turn back even if it did.

"Up ahead," Kurt said. "Head for the cliff."

"Are you crazy?" she shouted. "I can barely keep us straight as it is."

"Exactly."

They rumbled along the gravel-strewn road. A massive cloud of dust billowed out behind them, not enough to block out the light completely but enough to obscure everything. He could imagine the Audi's driver, blinded, getting pinged with rocks, sliding this way and that, as he tried to keep up.

Sometimes extra horsepower and bigger tires were bad. With standing water and gravel, this was the case exactly. At a high-enough speed, the Audi would become uncontrollable—it would literally begin to float on the tumbling rocks and pebbles underneath its tires—but the little Focus, with its skinny tires, dug right through the gravel down to the more solid ground.

"Let him get a little closer," Kurt said, scanning the terrain up ahead.

She nodded. She seemed as if she knew what he was thinking.

"Now punch it and turn."

She slammed the gas pedal down, spinning up more dust and rocks and pulling away from the Audi. But the Audi driver must have mashed his pedal as well because his car now surged toward them.

"I said turn," Kurt yelled.

She threw the wheel over, but the Focus skidded, and Kurt realized he'd overplayed their hand. He grabbed Katarina by the shoulder, pulled her into the passenger seat, and then dove out of the car through the open section where the door had once been, dragging her with him as he went.

They tumbled and rolled on the grass beside the road. The Audi shot by, missing them by a foot or two. The Focus disappeared off the cliff, and the Audi's brake lights lit up.

"Too late," Kurt said.

The Audi skidded through the dust cloud and then vanished, going over the edge at twenty miles an hour or so.

It was eerily silent for three seconds, and then twin explosions boomed through the night one right after the other.

The gritty air swirled around them. For a second it seemed as if they were alone.

"They're gone," Katarina said.

Kurt nodded and then glanced down the dirt road. White light could be seen filtering through the settling dust, moving toward them. Two cars remained.

"They're headed this way," Kurt said.

He took Katarina by the hand and led her back away from the road. "Come on," he said. "We can't run, but we can still hide."

PAUL PULLED GAMAY toward the cockpit of the *Grouper*. She was clutching her leg as if she'd been injured.

"I'm okay," she said.

Behind her, the sub was filling with water.

He turned to look at the depth gauge. 150. 140.

The needle continued to turn, but it moved slower and slower. Despite the props turning at full rpm, despite all the ballast being gone, the *Grouper* struggled to ascend. 135.

The gurgling water was filling the sub. It had reached the halfway point and was rapidly climbing toward them. Paul turned back to the controls. He angled the *Grouper* straight up, trying to maximize the vertical component of the propeller's thrust. It gave them a slight kick, but as the water began to swirl around his legs he could feel their momentum failing.

The needle touched 130, went just below it, and then stopped.

The *Grouper* was standing on its tail now, the propeller straining to keep it going. It wasn't going to be enough.

The water churned around Paul's waist, Gamay clung to him tightly.

"Time to go," he said.

Gamay was struggling to keep her head above water as the sea filled the little submersible like a bottle.

"Take a breath," he said, pulling her up, feeling her shiver in the chill of the water. "Take three deep breaths," he corrected. "Hold the last one. Remember to exhale as you ascend."

He saw her doing as he'd said, tilting her head back to suck in one last breath as the water covered her face. He managed to inhale once more, and then he went under. In a few seconds he'd reached the hatch. With the pressure now equal inside and out, the hatch opened easily.

He pushed it back and helped Gamay escape. As soon as she was free he shoved her upward, and she began kicking for the surface.

The *Grouper* was already dropping. Paul had to get himself free. He pushed off as the hull of the submarine slid out from under him. He kicked for the surface, trying to use smooth, long strokes.

The neoprene suits helped; they were buoyant. Without weight belts, they were almost as buoyant as life preservers. The desire to live helped. And the fact that they'd been at depth breathing compressed air helped. He exhaled slightly as he surged upward, hoping that Gamay remembered to do the same. Otherwise, the compressed, pressurized air would expand in the chest and explode the lungs like an overinflated balloon.

A minute into his ascent, Paul could feel his lungs burning. He continued to kick hard and smooth. Around him, he could see nothing but a watery void. Far below, a fading pinprick of light marked the *Grouper* as it plunged back into the depths.

Thirty seconds later he exhaled a little more, the pressure on his chest building. He could see light above but no sign of Gamay. At two minutes his muscles were screaming for oxygen, his head was pounding, and his strength waning.

He continued to kick, but ever more slowly. He could feel his muscles beginning to spasm, his body shaking, convulsing.

The spasms passed. The surface shimmered above, but Paul could no longer tell how far away it was. The light faded. The shimmering blue he could see narrowed to a small spot as his arms and legs became too heavy to move.

All movement stopped. His head lolled to the side, the light vanished, and Paul Trout's last thought was *Where's . . . my . . . wife?*

THE DUST AND THE DARKNESS gave cover as Kurt led Katarina across a grassy field on the cliff side. The approaching cars moved slowly, picking their way along the gravel road. Both cars had front-end damage, and one of them had only a single working headlight. The little game of chicken had worked out in Austin's favor, both damaging the vehicles and delaying them.

As they approached, Kurt imagined the drivers wondering where their comrades had gone to. Or, for that matter, where their prey had gotten to and how they'd escaped in the underpowered little rental car.

Lying flat in the grass, Kurt waited for the cars to pass. Once they had, he and Katarina resumed their move across the grass, arriving at a cyclone fence.

Kurt looked through the fence. A small hangarlike building stood dark and quiet on the other side. A sign read "Ultralight Charters $50 Per Half Hour."

"Climb over," he said to Katarina. "Quietly."

She put her hands on the top of the fence, stuck her toes into one of the diamond-shaped spaces, and scaled up and over in two quick steps. Kurt was glad to be on the run with an athlete.

He followed, dropping down quietly beside her.

"Where are your shoes?" he asked.

"You mean my expensive Italian stilettos?"

"Yeah. Your shoes."

"They kind of fell off when you threw me out of the moving car."

He noticed her dress was torn, and she had bleeding abrasions on her bare elbow and forearm. His own knee and shoulder were bleeding as well, and he could feel the small particles of gravel that had been ground into the palms of his hands. Still, it was better than being dead.

"I'll buy you a new pair if we get out of this alive," he said. "Keep moving."

They sprinted across the grass and ducked behind a large ex-posed tank like one might see at a propane filling station. From the smell, Kurt knew it contained AvGas, 100 octane fuel for small propeller-driven aircraft like the ultralights.

Hidden behind this tank, Kurt watched the two remaining Audis crawl toward the cliff. They stopped near the spot where the cars had gone over, leaving their remaining lights on. Two men got out of each car. One of them carried a flashlight; the other three car-ried short-barreled assault weapons of some type.

"Let's get out of here," Katarina whispered.

"Don't move," he said. "They can't see us here. I don't want them to hear us either."

The men with the guns moved toward the edge of the cliff and peered over. A fire must have been burning down below because the smoke and dust were lit up, turning the men into silhouettes.

"Looks like they went over," one man said.

Kurt couldn't hear the initial reply, but then the man with the flashlight moved to the edge.

"Get me a scope," the man with the flashlight said. When the order was not followed rapidly enough, he barked louder. "Come on, we don't have all night."

As the man spoke, Kurt recognized the voice as belonging to the thug on the *Kinjara Maru*.

"So you're not dead," Kurt mumbled. He'd thought there was something suspicious about the explosion on the water that took the hijackers' boat. It had seemed a little too convenient. A little too perfect of an ending for what appeared to be a sophisticated operation.

"You know these people?" Katarina asked.

"I know that man's voice," Kurt said. "He was part of a hijacking that took place a week ago. We thought he'd blown himself up by accident. But obviously it was a trick meant to make us think he did."

"So these men are after you?" she said.

He turned to her. "You didn't think they were after you, did you?"

She seemed offended. "They could have been. I'm a very important member of the Russian scientific establishment. I'm quite certain they'd get more ransom money for kidnapping me than they would for you."

Kurt smiled and fought back a laugh. She was probably right about that. "Didn't mean to offend you," he said.

She seemed to accept that, and Kurt turned back toward the thugs at the cliff's edge. They were perfectly backlit in the smoke. If he'd had a rifle, he could have taken them all right now, knocking them down one after the other like ducks in an arcade. But all he had was the metal pipe and the knife that the thug now hunting them had left behind on the *Kinjara Maru.*

Kurt watched as the man stepped to the edge with a scope in his hand. He stared through it for a long moment and then changed angles a bit. Kurt guessed he was now looking at the second car.

"They're dead," one of the other thugs said. "All of them."

"Don't be so sure," the lead man said.

"That's a long way down," the thug replied. "No one's going to survive that."

The lead man turned and pushed his subordinate back against the car in a menacing fashion. A pretty ballsy move, considering he was the only one without a weapon. Obviously these men did not question him.

"You're right," the leader said. "No one could have survived such a fall. Unless they didn't take it."

He slapped the night vision scope in the man's hand. "There are no bodies in or around that car," he said.

"Damn," Kurt whispered. Where their biggest problem had seemed like a long walk back to civilization, they now had a much more pressing issue: these thugs would not leave the plateau until they'd found him and Katarina or until police units came—perhaps half an hour away or more.

He doubted they could hide that long.

As the lead thug turned and began spraying his light across the grassy field, Kurt ducked back down behind the fuel tank. When the beam of light pointed off in another direction, Kurt grabbed Katarina's hand again. "Hope you're not afraid of heights."

They scrambled across the open space and made it to the dark hangar. After quietly forcing the lock with the pipe, they slipped inside.

"What are we going to do?" Katarina asked.

"You got fifty dollars?" he said, sneaking over to one of the ultralights and unscrewing the gas cap.

"Not on me," she said. "Why?"

"We'll have to leave an IOU," he said, grabbing a helmet and handing it to her.

"We're going to fly out of here?" she guessed.

He nodded.

She smiled so broadly, he swore it lit up the room. "I always wanted to try one of these things," she said.

He checked the tank to make sure it held some fuel. Seeing it was half full, he screwed the cap back on, moved to the hangar door, and began pushing it open slowly.

OUTSIDE NEAR THE CLIFF, Andras and his men were fanning out. Andras had grabbed a Glock 9mm that he now held in his left hand, and the flashlight was in his right. One of his men was making his way along the edge of the cliff, another going in the opposite direction.

Andras guessed his quarry had moved inland. It opened up the terrain and would force him and his men to consider many more hiding places. It would be the better tactic, he thought. And having encountered this man from NUMA once, Andras knew that, if anything, he was very smart.

It would make it all the sweeter when he killed him.

His light played across the ground. Had Andras feared they were armed, he would have been walking in the dark using the night vision scope. But his targets had shown no weaponry during the chase except for a lead pipe and their own wits, so he knew he could safely proceed.

He was rewarded when something caught the light: a woman's shoe, dusty in places, but the red patent leather was unmistakable. Ten feet away, he saw another one. He whistled to his men, and as they gathered he shone the light around, spotting the cyclone fence and the building beyond.

"Surround the building," he said. "They're inside."

His men dashed to the fence and began to climb. As they did, a sound like a lawn mower starting spilt the quiet of the night.

Andras hopped the fence and shone his flashlight toward the building just in time to see one of the ultralights come rumbling out and begin accelerating across the grass.

"Shoot them," he ordered.

Two of his men dropped down and opened fire as the buzzing ultralight sped away. In a moment, it exploded, and flames engulfed the nylon wing.

Too easy, he thought. And he was right.

AS THE FIRST ULTRALIGHT began to zoom across the grass, Kurt and Katarina climbed into a second one and started it up. Kurt hoped the noise and movement of the first one would mask their departure in the other direction.

He sent the decoy to the right and seconds later turned his own craft to the left. Even as he pushed the throttle he heard the gunfire.

A moment later he saw a flash cross the grassy plain that served as the ultralight's runway. Just enough light to see by.

He gunned the throttle, realizing the time for stealth had ended. The little fifty-horsepower engine buzzed like a swarm of angry bees, and the small wooden prop spun up to full rpms in a second.

The gangly craft sped forward, accelerating down the grass strip and lifting off in a hundred feet or so. Kurt turned out toward the cliff, trying to put the hangar between him and the men with the guns. He heard a few sporadic shots and then nothing. By then he and Katarina were gone, out over the cliff, accelerating into the darkness and heading for the lights of Vila do Porto.

ON THE GRASSY RUNWAY, Andras realized his mistake. They'd been had by a stroke of misdirection. He turned just in time to see the other ultralight take off. He fired at it and then ran to the hangar with his men.

Inside was a whole fleet of the flying contraptions. Four of them looked to be in working condition.

"Get in," he shouted to his men. "We'll shoot them down from the air."

As his other men climbed into a second aircraft, Andras went to hop into the front seat of the lead craft and stopped. A familiar object stood vertically on its point, stabbed straight down into the ultralight's padded seat.

Andras recognized the matte-black finish, the folding titanium blade, and the holes in the handle. It was the knife he'd plunged into the crane operator's seat on the *Kinjara Maru* after cutting the hydraulic lines.

So the man from NUMA had taken it and kept it. And now he'd returned it. There had to be a reason. Clearly, he was showing Andras that he knew who was after him, but Andras suspected something more.

He stepped out of the ultralight, looking for danger.

"Don't start them," he ordered as one of his men reached for a key.

Andras moved to the engine of the machine he'd been about to pilot. He checked the hydraulic lines and the fuel lines, thinking those would be poetic targets for his adversary to strike—and probably deadly, had he or his men started the aircraft in the confines of the barnlike hangar. He found nothing wrong with the exposed sections of the tubing and saw no liquids dripping onto the floor below.

He looked up.

The wings had huge cuts in them, long, clean slices that were not easily seen. From the look of it, they'd been carefully made to avoid leaving the nylon in obvious dangling strips. The damage might not have been enough to keep the craft on the ground, but Andras had no doubt that, once airborne, the fabric would have frayed in the airstream, shredding in minutes. Had they taken off, he guessed, they would have discovered it shortly after making it out over the cliffs.

"We should check the others," one of his men suggested.

Andras allowed them to do so, but he knew there was little point. They would all be the same.

He pursed his lips, disappointed, but sensing something new in his heart: admiration. The kind of thrill a hunter feels when he realizes his prey might be bigger, stronger, more fierce and intelligent than expected. Such a thought never brought anger, only a greater exhilaration. So far, he'd given this man from NUMA some grudging respect, but he'd still underestimated him. A mistake he wouldn't make again.

"It's been a long time since I faced such a challenge," he whispered to himself. "I'm going to enjoy killing you."

Continental shelf, off the coast of Sierra Leone, June 23

DJEMMA GARAND SAT in the passenger cabin of an EC155 Eurocopter. The sleek modern design included a ducted tail rotor, an all-glass instrument panel, and a leather-clad interior stitched by the same company that did the seats on custom Rolls-Royces.

It was fast, relatively quiet inside, and the epitome of luxury for any self-respecting billionaire or dictator of a small country.

For the most part, Djemma hated it. He preferred boating or going by car to any place he needed to be. His days in the field had shown him firsthand how vulnerable small helicopters were to ground fire. An RPG exploding nearby could bring down many rotary aircraft, let alone a direct hit. Small-arms fire could do the same.

But more than an actual attack, Djemma felt it was too easy for small planes and helicopters to have unexplained accidents, accidents that seemed to plague the leaders of small war-torn nations at a rate completely out of proportion to the amount of time they spent traveling.

Air crashes usually had no witnesses, especially over mountainous or jungle terrain. Without a forensic team to sift through the debris, there was almost no way to tell if a craft came down on its own, had been hit by a missile or gunfire, or had been blown to pieces by a saboteur's bomb.

Normally, Djemma wouldn't travel in them. But in this case he'd made an exception. He'd done so because speed was of the essence, because events and even trusted allies seemed to be conspiring against him, because if the lid blew off his plan he had to know if his weapon was ready.

The EC155 crossed the shoreline and headed out into the Atlantic. Ten miles off the coast, four little dots appeared on the horizon. As the helicopter grew closer, they resolved into sharper forms: huge offshore oil rigs, set up in a perfect square, with several miles between them. At least a dozen boats patrolled the waters around the rigs, and huge barges with equipment sat moored to one of them.

"Take us down to number three," Djemma ordered.

The pilot complied, and a few minutes later Djemma was removing his headset and stepping out of the gleaming red-and-white helicopter and striding across the platform.

The rig's superintendant and his senior staff waited in a formal line.

"My President," the superintendant said. "It is an honor to have you—"

"Spare me," Djemma said. "And take me to Cochrane."

"Right away."

Djemma followed the man across the helipad toward the main block of the oil rig. They stepped inside, passing an area filled with coolant pipes, thick with condensation and frost, and then into a climate-controlled area filled with computer screens and flat-panel displays.

On the most prominent centrally mounted screen, a strangely shaped design appeared. It looked like the schematic of a racetrack or a rail yard. It could best be described as an elongated oval connected to a wider circle, off of which two dozen straight lines stretched, fanning out like tangents.

Small data marks, unreadable from any distance, seemed to indicate conditions within each section defined by the tangents. The sections were also color-coded. Djemma noticed that most were illuminated in green. This pleased him.

"All sections of the loop have power?"

"Yes, President," the superintendant replied. "We activated them this morning. Currently we are only operating at test levels, but Cochrane confirmed that we are within specs."

"Excellent," Djemma said. "Where is he now?"

"In one of the targeting tunnels," the super said. "He is overseeing the final phase of construction."

"Show me," Djemma ordered.

They crossed the climate-controlled room and arrived at an elevator barely large enough for two men. It took them down through the rig and beneath it in a clear Plexiglas tube like those used at amusement parks and places like SeaWorld.

Brilliant light shimmered and danced through the water. Schools of fish swam everywhere, as they often did near oil rigs and other man-made structures. Below them, a scar crossed the ocean floor in a long line from east to west.

The line appeared straight only because the curve was so gradual; but had the ocean been drained, it would have been easy to see from space that this line matched exactly the circular design displayed inside the control room. At the far end, men in hard-shell dive suits and small submarines no larger than a family car worked on filling in the last section.

Farther off, at the very limits of underwater vision, Djemma spotted another submarine, lying on its side. This was no small vessel but a giant, its hull cut open like a whale that had been gutted. Unlike the other things he saw, this sight angered him.

The elevator car approached the sandy bottom and then went beneath the seafloor, continuing in the tube in the dark another forty feet before stopping. The darkness was banished when the doors opened to a concrete hall lit by fluorescent lights.

The superintendant stepped out, and Djemma followed him. He noticed that the hall was not square but built in an oval shape, a design like the arches of ancient Roman aqueducts, that helped the tunnel support the outside pressure of rock and water. He also noticed something else.

"It's wet in here," he said, noticing pools of water on the floor and wet spots on the walls.

"Until it finishes curing, the concrete is porous," the super said. "We have treated it and buried it forty feet beneath the seafloor, but we still have seepage. It'll clear up in a month or so."

Djemma hoped he was right. He continued on through the tunnel until he reached an intersection point.

A ladder led down.

Djemma climbed down and came out in a different type of tunnel. This one was perfectly circular in cross section, wide enough to drive a small car through, and lined with power conduits and cooling tubes like those seen above. Pinpoint LED lighting and shiny metallic rectangles on three sides ran as far as the eye could see.

In the other direction, he spied Cochrane.

"You are almost done," Djemma said. "This pleases me more than you know."

"The construction is almost done," Cochrane said. "We still have to test it. And if you think you're going to get me the kind of power you keep demanding, you'd better have something up your sleeve. Because, as it stands, I can only get you sixty percent of what you require."

"I no longer am surprised or grow angry at your failures," Djemma said. "I've grown used to them. Have you heard of this Devil's Gate near the Azores?"

"I don't get a lot of news down here," Cochrane said. "But, yeah, I heard of it. Some type of naturally occurring superconductor."

"That is the report," Djemma said. "I have men there. I believe that will be the answer."

Cochrane put down some type of fiber-optic testing device he was working with and wiped the sweat from his forehead. "I'm not sure you understand," he said. "We just worked in three hundred tons of material your sub brought us from the freighter. We don't have space for anything else."

"Space," Djemma said. "Interesting that you should use that word. Because I am worried about space and what can be seen from it."

"What are you talking about now?" Cochrane asked.

"The Russian submarine that we took the reactors from. You were told to have it dismantled and dispersed by now. I don't want anyone spotting it from a satellite."

"It's on its side, fifty feet down, covered in netting," Cochrane said. "And they're not looking for it," he insisted. "The Russians sold it. They don't care what happens to it. And the only submarines the Americans care about are the ones carrying ballistic missiles out there in the depths. Only you and Comrade Gorshkov know where this one went to, and even Gorshkov doesn't know what you're doing with it."

"Finish the dismantling," Djemma ordered. "And don't question me again or I'll dismantle you . . . piece by painful piece."

Cochrane rubbed a hand across his face. "We have eleven construction subs and forty hard suits, not enough to do both jobs. So you choose. Do you want the target lines finished or do you want that rusting hulk of a submarine recycled?"

Djemma fought to control his anger. What he wanted was both, and a designer less insolent and more competent than Cochrane. But between the reports from Andras, the Americans snooping around the *Kinjara Maru*, and the increasingly pointed questions coming from the World Bank and his other creditors, Djemma didn't have time for both.

He decided the carcass of a submarine could remain. Once he took action, it wouldn't matter if the world knew about it or not. That would be the least of their concerns.

"Finish the target lines and the emitters," he said. "Washington, London, Moscow, Beijing. Those four must be ready in one week or we will be vulnerable."

He waited for Cochrane's next battery of complaints and excuses as to why he couldn't comply, but for the first time in ages none came forth.

"They'll be ready," Cochrane said. "I promise you."

26

Eastern Atlantic, June 23

GAMAY TROUT SAT in a small chair in the *Matador*'s sick bay with a blanket around her shoulders and a piping hot cup of decaf in front of her. The ship's doctor wouldn't allow her the real thing for at least twenty-four hours. She wasn't drinking it, only using it to warm her hands, so what did it matter? Truthfully, nothing mattered to her now, nothing except the man who lay in front of her, unmoving, on the hospital bed.

The crew of the *Matador* had plucked her out of the water within five minutes of her surfacing. But with the darkening skies and growing swell, she had never seen Paul surface.

Twenty minutes later, after two agonizingly slow passes, a lookout had spotted Paul, floating faceup. He made no attempt to signal and was only afloat because the wet suit gave him positive buoyancy.

They'd brought him down to sick bay, where she was being treated for mild hypothermia and oxygen deprivation. Immediately, they'd pulled a sheet between the two of them, but she could hear them working feverishly. Someone had called out "No pulse," and then the doctor said something about "cardiogenic shock."

At that point she'd grabbed for the curtain and pulled it back. Her husband looked like a ghost, and she'd turned away and begun to cry.

Three hours later, she was up and about and functioning something like her normal self. Paul remained unconscious, covered in blankets, with an IV of warmed fluids dripping into his arm and a mask delivering pure oxygen to his nose and mouth. His eyes remained closed, and he hadn't as much as twitched in over an hour.

Watching him lie there in such utter stillness, Gamay had to keep checking his heart monitor just to remind herself that he was alive.

She squeezed his hand; it felt like wet clay. She couldn't remember his hands being anything but warm, even on the coldest New England winter days.

"Come back to me," she whispered. "Don't leave me here, Paul. Please don't leave."

The door behind her opened, and the ship's doctor, Hobson Smith, came in. Almost tall enough to require ducking as he came through the door, Smith had a gray Fu Manchu mustache, sharp eyes, and a relaxed, almost fatherly style. No one on board knew how old he was, but if NUMA had any mandatory retirement age Hobson Smith would have been well past it. And the ship all the poorer for it. His presence was like that of a loving uncle.

"No change?" he said as if he were asking her.

"He hasn't moved," she said. "His heart rate is—"

"His heart rate is strong," Smith said, taking over for her. "His pulse is good. The oxygen level in his blood is getting better also."

"But he's still unconscious," she said, unable to use the word *coma*.

"Yes," Dr. Smith said. "For now. Paul is strong. Give him a chance to heal."

She knew he was right, she understood that his vitals were improving, but she needed him to wake up, to smile at her and say something eminently dorky and endearing.

Smith pulled up a chair and sat beside her.

"Arm out," he said.

She extended her arm, and the doctor put a cuff around her bicep and then pumped it up to take her blood pressure. Next he checked her pulse.

"Just as I thought," he said.

"What?"

"Your own vitals aren't great," he said. "You're making yourself sicker, worrying about him."

She exhaled. She hadn't eaten or even had much to drink since she'd been back up on her feet. But didn't think she could keep anything down.

"I just don't understand," she said. "How did I end up surfacing so much quicker than he did?"

Dr. Smith studied her for a moment as if thinking about the question. "You said he gave you a push?"

She nodded. "After the *Grouper* flooded he opened the hatch, pulled me through, and gave me a shove upward. I extended my legs and pushed off his hands like a springboard, but I figured he was right behind me."

She took a breath, trying to fight back the emotion. "The sub was dropping at that point. Maybe he got pulled down with it. Maybe he had to fight to get free of the suction before he could start moving upward."

"I'm sure that played a part," Smith said. "On top of that, he's denser, heavier in muscle and bone. And don't take this the wrong way, but men on average have a lower body fat percentage than women. Add to that the fact that you were both wearing about the same amount of neoprene, and your buoyancy level would have been much higher than his. Even if he hadn't pushed you, you would have ascended faster and reached the surface before him."

She looked back at her husband, thinking of all the dives they'd been on, all the training.

"Besides," Dr. Smith added, "Paul always said you were the strongest swimmer he knew. All the more reason to marry you and make you a true Trout."

She smiled, remembering Paul making that joke a hundred times during the reception. She could barely stand to hear him say it by the end, and now she just wished he'd wake up so he could tell it again.

"He should have just gone first," she said, the words creaking from her throat like a rusty hinge.

Dr. Smith shook his head. "No man in his right mind would go first and leave his wife behind," he said. "Not a man like Paul anyway."

"And what if he leaves me now?" she said, as scared as she'd ever been in her life. "I don't know how to do this alone."

"I believe in my heart you won't have to," Smith said. "But you need to get your mind off of this and start thinking about something else. For your own good."

"And just what would you have me think about?" she said, a little sharper than she wanted to.

Dr. Smith scratched behind his ear and stood. He took Paul's hand from hers and placed it gently back on his chest, then he took her by the hand and walked her to the next room: the ship's laboratory.

"There was another survivor from the wreck whom you've forgotten about," he said with a twinkle in his eye. "Her name's *Rapunzel*."

Gamay had forgotten all about the little robot. And even though *Rapunzel* was an inanimate object, she couldn't help but feel glad that the robot had survived and been recovered. After all, *Rapunzel* had saved their lives.

"They picked her up," Gamay said.

"Uh-huh," Smith said. "And she brought with her three samples."

Gamay narrowed her gaze at the doctor. "Three?"

"A tissue sample you drilled from one of the crewmen," Smith said, switching on a recessed fluorescent light that flickered to life and illuminated a workbench.

"I remember that," she said. "Can't recall taking any other samples."

"Can't you?" With a product demonstrator's wave of the hand, he directed her attention to another bench. A length of steel cable lay on a flat surface.

"Still in *Rapunzel*'s grasp when she hit the surface," Smith said.

The cable that had held them down, she thought. She remembered cutting through it with *Rapunzel*'s acetylene torch, and then putting *Rapunzel* into a climb. She'd never directed *Rapunzel* to drop the cable.

"And what's the third?" she asked.

"A piece of plastic wedged into part of *Rapunzel*'s frame. A broken triangular-shaped piece, probably became embedded when she was in the freighter getting knocked about."

Dr. Smith walked over to the cable. Gamay followed. He pointed out several blackened marks.

"What do you suppose those are?"

She leaned closer. Touching the black spots, she could feel a different texture when compared to the rest of the cable, almost as if the metal had been lying on something hot enough to begin melting it.

"They remind me of spot welds," she said.

"I thought so as well," he said. "But I've never heard of someone spot-welding a cable before, and it certainly wasn't attached to anything."

"Maybe the cutting torch," she suggested.

"I checked the video," he said. "*Rapunzel* cut the cord in one quick move. She held the cable in place with her claw and burned through it with her torch. This section, two feet to the left, was never touched."

Gamay looked up, intrigued, at least, a bit. "Maybe after Paul is feeling better we can—"

"Gamay," Dr. Smith said. "We need you to do this."

"I'm not exactly up for it," she said.

"Director Pitt talked with the captain this morning," Smith said. "He wants you looking at this. He knows it's tough sledding for you right now, but someone's gone to great lengths to keep us from finding out what happened on that ship, and he wants to know why. These are the only leads we have."

"He ordered you to make me look at this?" she said, surprised.

Dr. Smith nodded. "You know Dirk. When there's a job to be done ..."

For the first time she could remember, she was actually angry with Dirk Pitt. But, deep inside, she knew he was right. The only hope of finding the people who'd harmed Paul began with figuring out who might want that ship on the bottom and why.

"Fine," she said, attempting to put her feelings aside. "Where do we start?"

He led her over to the microscopes. "Take a look at the plastic samples."

She set herself over the first microscope and peered into the eyepiece, blinking until everything became clear.

"Those are shavings from the plastic," Dr. Smith said.

"Why are they different colors?" she asked.

"Two different types of plastic. We think it came from some type of storage case. The darker plastic is much harder and denser, the lighter-colored piece is also a lighter grade of material."

She studied them both. Oddly, the darker plastic seemed to be deformed. The color was swirled in places; there were distortions in the material itself.

"It looks like the darker plastic melted," she said. "But the lighter plastic doesn't seem to have been affected."

"My thoughts exactly," he said.

"That seems backward," she said, looking up. "Lighter plastic should have a lower melting point, and even at the same temperature would have less ability to absorb heat without deforming because there is less material to act as a heat sink."

"You are very good at this, Mrs. Trout," he said. "Sure you don't want to work in the lab?"

"After what just happened," she said, "I might never leave it."

He smiled, crinkles forming around his eyes.

"You're saving the tissue sample for last," she noted.

"Because it's the most interesting," he said.

She slid over. "May I?"

"By all means."

She squinted into the microscope, increased the magnification once, and then once again. She found herself looking at cellular structures, but something was wrong.

"What happened here?"

"You tell me, my marine biology expert," Dr. Smith said.

She moved the focal point, scanning along the sample. "The cells on the right-hand side are skin cells," she said. "For the most part, they look normal. But the cells on the left—"

"You took a two-inch core out of the man's thigh. The cells on the right are surface cells. Those on the left are the deeper muscle cells."

"Yes. They look odd. Almost as if they've exploded from the inside."

"They have," Dr. Smith said. "The deeper you go, the more damage you see. The highest level of epidermal tissue shows no damage at all."

"Could it be a chemical burn?" she asked, unable to take her eyes off the ruined cells. "Maybe something that soaked in and then reacted."

"There's no residue present," Smith said. "And any chemical strong enough to do that would wreak havoc with the epidermis on its way in. You ever get strong bleach on your hands?"

"Good point," she said. "But what else could do this?"

"What could do *all* of this?" he said. "That's the question we have to ask ourselves."

She sat up and turned to face him. "One cause. Three events."

"If you can think of one thing that would fit the bill . . ." he said.

Her mind began to churn, not in hopeless, powerless circles, as it had while she sat over Paul, but in forward motion. She could almost feel the synapses waking up and firing, like lights going on one by one in a dark office tower.

"It looks like thermal damage," she said. "But high heat or fire would damage the surface layer of the epidermis the most."

"Exactly," he said. "That's the whole reason we have an epidermal layer of dead skin cells. As thin and weak as it is, it's basically a shell designed to keep moisture in and other things out."

She turned back to the microscope and glanced at the cells one more time. She thought about the plastic slivers under the other scope to her side. *What could possibly deform thick, heavy plastic without melting thinner lighter plastic, cause carbon deposits on metal as if it had been arc-welded, and destroy human tissue from the inside out?*

Gamay looked up from the microscope again. "Mrs. Nordegrun told Kurt she'd seen things in her head."

Smith scanned through the notes. "She told Kurt that she'd seen stars in front of her eyes right before she went down. She said, 'I don't want to sound crazy, but it looked like miniature fireworks going off in front of my eyes. I thought I was seeing something, but when I closed my eyes tight they were still there.'"

"I once read about astronauts experiencing something similar," Gamay said. "On a shuttle mission a few years ago, they saw sparks or shooting-star patterns even when they closed their eyes."

Smith sat up a little straighter. "Do you remember the cause?"

She thought back. "They were in orbit during a solar flare event. Despite the shielding on the crew's quarters, some of the high-energy rays made it through. As these rays impact the cones and rods in the eye, they trigger neurological responses that register as starbursts in front of their eyes."

"Not a hallucination?"

"No," she said. "They're actually seeing these things the same way I see you right now. Cones and rods transmitting a signal to the mind."

Dr. Smith listened and nodded thoughtfully. He stood up, walked over to the microscope, and took another peek at the tissue sample himself.

"When I was in the Air Force, probably before you were born, I remember a young man who walked in front of one of our Phantom jets during the middle of a radar test. He was just a kid, an enlisted guy a month out of basic. Nobody saw him coming. Unfortunately for him, that particular jet was what we called a Wild Weasel, designed to emit powerful radar bursts and flood the enemy screens with so much signal that they couldn't pick out our planes from the mess on their screens."

"What happened?"

"He let out a shout, fell to his knees, and then flat on the floor," Smith said. "The chief shut the radar off, and we dragged the kid to the infirmary, but he was already dead. Strangely, his skin was not hot to the touch. Turned out he'd fried from the inside out. As horrible as it sounds, he'd basically been cooked like a meal in a microwave. I was just a medic at the time, but I remember looking at his tissue under a microscope. It looked an awful lot like this."

Gamay took a breath, trying to put away the horror of what she'd just been told and focus on the scientific evidence.

"And the metal looks as if it's been arc-welded," she said.

He nodded.

"High-energy discharges can cause the resistance in the air to break down and electrical energy to jump the gaps," she said. "I've spent enough time with Kurt and Joe to know that that's exactly what arc welding is."

"Man-made lightning," Smith said. "That's why fuel and ordnance have to be handled in certain ways on base. Even a static-electric charge can ignite petroleum fumes."

"The marks on that cable look like a lot more than a static discharge," she said.

He nodded again, a sober look settled on his face. She guessed the doctor had a theory of what had happened. She guessed it would match what she was about to suggest.

"The lights blew," she said. "The equipment failed, even the emergency beacon. Otherwise, someone would have heard a distress signal. The captain's wife saw stars, and the poor crewmen on the upper levels were cooked from the inside out."

She looked him straight in the eye. "That ship was hit with some type of massive electromagnetic burst. It would have to be of ultra-high intensity to do the damage we've seen."

"A thousand radar emitters turned on to full power wouldn't do what we've seen," the doctor said.

"Then it's something more powerful," she said.

Dr. Smith nodded, looking grave. "Has to be."

She paused, trying not to let her thoughts run away with her.

"Do we even want to consider that it might be naturally occurring?" she asked, thinking about the anomaly Kurt and Joe were investigating a few hundred miles to the east.

"And the pirates just happened upon the stricken ship in the right place at the right time? And then someone accidentally tried to kill you and Paul for investigating it?"

Of course not, she thought. "Then it has to be a weapon," she said. "Something powerful enough to fry a five-hundred-foot vessel without any warning."

Smith offered a sad smile. "I concur," he said. "As if the world doesn't have enough to worry about."

She sensed it was she who was concurring with him, but it didn't matter.

"I have to talk to Dirk," she said.

Dr. Smith nodded. "Of course," he said. "I'll keep an eye on Paul."

Washington, D.C., June 23

THE VIEW FROM DIRK PITT'S OFFICE on the twenty-ninth floor of the NUMA headquarters building included much of Washington, D.C. From the generous rectangular window he could watch over a section of the shimmering Potomac, the Lincoln and Washington monuments, and the Capitol building, all of which stood lit up in brilliant white for the evening.

Despite the view, Dirk's attention was directed elsewhere, toward the monitor of his computer, on which a three-way teleconference was proceeding.

In one corner, the smiling face of Hiram Yaeger, NUMA's resident computer genius. Yaeger looked as if he'd just come off the road on a Harley; he wore a leather vest and had his long graying hair pulled back into a ponytail.

In the other corner of Pitt's screen, a drawn and waifish version of Gamay Trout gazed up at him. Her deep red hair was also pulled back, but out of necessity rather than style. Occasionally, as she spoke, a stray lock worked itself loose and fell in front of her eyes.

She would diligently push it back behind her ear or keep talking as if she didn't notice.

Despite her obvious pain, and eyes Pitt had never seen so dark, she seemed to be holding it together. Certainly she'd helped them take a big step forward in solving the mystery of what happened to the *Kinjara Maru*.

As she explained a theory she and the *Matador*'s doctor had come up with, Pitt had to admire her tenacity and devotion to duty. Such qualities were in abundance at NUMA, but they always shone the brightest under the darkest circumstances.

While Pitt listened and asked what he thought were pertinent questions, Yaeger took notes and mostly grunted the occasional "Uh-huh" and "Okay."

When Gamay was done speaking, Pitt turned to Yaeger. "Can you run a simulation on what she described?"

"I think so," Yaeger said. "Gonna be a shot in the dark, to some extent, but I could put you in the ballpark."

"Ballpark's not good enough, Hiram. I want box seats down the third baseline."

"Sure," Yaeger said, drawing the word out slowly. "But the closest I can come is telling you what kind of power might be needed and how this *might have* accomplished it. So you might be on the third baseline, but you're still gonna be up in the nosebleeds unless we get more data."

"You start working," Pitt said. "I'll bet you a case of imported beer that we'll get more data before you're done with your first run-through."

"Canadian?" Hiram said.

"Or German. Winner picks."

"Okay," Yaeger said. "I'll take that action."

His portion of the screen went blank, and Dirk turned to Gamay. "I'm not going to ask how you're holding up," he said. "Just want you to know I'm proud of you."

She nodded. "Thanks," she said. "And thank you for ordering me to study the samples. It helped me . . . helped me get back to being me."

Pitt was confused. "I never gave any order like that," he said.

"But the doctor . . ." she began. A smile creased her face for the first time.

"Doctor's orders," Pitt guessed.

"Apparently, part of my treatment," she said.

"Hobson's a crafty old guy," Pitt said, thinking warmly of the doctor. "And he's smart. If someone out there has developed a weapon like this, our best defense may be to find it and neutralize it before it gets used again. Thanks to you two, we have a chance."

"What help can we expect?" she asked.

"I've already talked to the admiral," Pitt said. "The Vice President, I mean. He's going to take what we've found directly to the President and Joint Chiefs. I'm sure they're going to be pretty damn interested, but as for getting involved . . . We've got to find them something tangible to get involved in. Right now, this is just a ghost that came to visit and left a mark. We have to put a body with that ghost, something they can deal with. You've given us the first step."

The rebellious strand of hair fell down across her face again, and Gamay dutifully tucked it back behind her ear. "Dr. Smith and I theorized that the crew might have been killed because of what they saw. In other words, having survived the electromagnetic burst, they had to be killed, and the ship scuttled, to keep things quiet."

"It's reasonable," Pitt said. "Dead men tell no tales."

"I know," she said. "But I was thinking there has to be something more. I mean, they fired torpedoes at us. We have to assume they could have done the same to the freighter when she was afloat."

Pitt considered this. Sometimes you learned more by what wasn't done than what was. "Would have been easier than boarding the ship."

"And quicker," she said.

"Yeah," Pitt said, "that it would. So why didn't they?"

"And why hit this particular ship in the first place?"

Another good question. He guessed there could be only one reason. One answer to both.

"There was something they wanted on that ship," he said. "Something they had to get before it went down. And whatever that something was, whoever was behind this didn't want the world to know it had gone missing."

On the screen, Gamay nodded. "That's the conclusion I reached too."

It explained a few things. The CEO of Shokara was an old friend of Dirk's—more of an old acquaintance, actually, in the sense that Dirk had once saved his life—but for a man who'd often insisted he'd do anything Dirk or NUMA ever needed, Haruto Takagawa had suddenly become very hard to reach.

Shortly after the freighter went down, Pitt had left a message for the man. But, so far, he hadn't received a call back. Perhaps that was understandable, considering the circumstances, but it was at least a yellow flag.

A few days later, just to cover all the bases, Pitt had sent a pair of NUMA's eager young associates to Takagawa's New York offices to get the type of information the Coast Guard would have required if the ship had gone down in U.S. waters. Primarily, the ship's manifest.

The two young men had been stymied in Takagawa's lobby, made to wait for hours and then all but tossed out on their ears. It felt like a slap in the face to Pitt, enough to get his considerable anger up and running. So far, he'd been too busy to press the issue. But now it seemed paramount.

"We need to know what the *Kinjara Maru* was carrying," Gamay said.

Pitt nodded. He knew what he had to do. He knew there was only one way to find out the truth.

28

Eastern Atlantic, June 24

A POUNDING ON HIS CABIN DOOR woke Joe Zavala. He sat straight up, almost ran for the door as if general quarters had sounded, and then remembered he wasn't in the Navy anymore.

The pounding returned. "Captain wants you on the bridge, Zavala," a voice shouted.

"Tell him I'll be right there," Joe said, grabbing his pants and pulling them on.

He heard footsteps as the messenger ran off. Only then did he sense that the *Argo* was in motion, not turning or making steerage or sitting at anchor near the anomaly but charging through the water as if racing something.

Joe pulled a shirt over his head, stuffed his bare feet into sneakers that he never untied, and then ran out the door.

A minute later, he was on the bridge. The *Argo* was indeed moving at flank speed, the bow rising and dropping as it rode the increasing swells.

"Captain," Joe said, reporting for duty even though he wasn't technically one of the crew.

"Where in God's green earth or Poseidon's blue water is Austin?" Captain Haynes barked.

Still a little groggy, Joe offered up his honest thoughts. "Probably waking up to something a lot nicer than I just woke up to."

"What are you talking about?"

"He's on a date," Joe said.

"A date?" Haynes shook his head. "How does a guy get a date out here in the middle of the ocean?"

Joe scratched his head. "That's a good question," he said. "I wish I could figure it out because, honestly, it gets kind of lonely when—"

"Zavala!" the captain shouted. "Wake up, man. This is not a dream. I need your full attention. Who is Austin out with?"

For a second, Joe wondered if it was a dream. The captain was acting weird. Kurt was a grown man, and Joe had reported Kurt's disposition to the officer of the watch upon returning from the Zodiac.

"He's with the Russian scientist he rescued from one of the wrecks," Joe said. "She told him she had some secret information that he might find interesting."

"What time was he planning on coming back?"

"Well," Joe said, "I guess that would kind of depend on how the date went . . . sir."

The captain cut his eyes at Joe and Joe burst out laughing.

"I'm sorry," Joe said, "but you sound like my pop back when my brother took the family car without asking and stayed out way past curfew. What's the big deal?"

The captain explained about the attack on the *Grouper*, Paul Trout's condition, and NUMA's theory that some type of electromagnetic weapon had been used on the *Kinjara Maru*. He made a point of explaining that whoever attacked the *Grouper* had used torpedoes.

"What are they doing now?" Joe asked.

"They're headed due west at full speed," the captain said. "Sometime tomorrow they'll be in range of a Navy guided-missile frigate. At that point they should be safe, and Paul will be transferred to a hospital ship."

"What about us? Is that why we're heading in?"

"The Director feels it's too dangerous to sit out here alone," the captain said. "If someone's targeting those with knowledge, we, and Austin, could be next. He's going to contact the Spanish and Portuguese admirals tomorrow and get us some backup. But until then, he wants us docked and all hands accounted for. And that's why I'm concerned. Because Kurt hasn't answered his damn phone all night."

"Have we contacted the local police?"

"Yes," the captain said. "We've made them aware of who Kurt is, what he looks like, and the fact that we're trying to find him. And they've made us aware of a fight, gunfire, and a vehicular chase that ended in two cars going off a cliff on a normally peaceful island. A man fitting Kurt's description was involved, but no body matching his has been recovered."

Thank God, Joe thought. He gazed through the *Argo*'s forward windows. The lights of Santa Maria were visible up ahead.

"We'll reach port in twenty minutes. I want you to come up with a plan to find him," the captain said. "I don't care if you use the phone or some flares or you rent a damn plane to fly around trailing a banner that reads 'Kurt Austin, Call NUMA.' You just find him before anything else goes wrong."

Joe nodded. He would start with the Russian scientist. Hopefully, someone at one of the hotels would recognize her.

AS THE *ARGO* was racing shoreward, Kurt and Katarina were descending toward the lights of Vila do Porto themselves. The sensation was rather unlike any Kurt could remember.

The open cockpit was designed for daytime use in warm weather. There were no lights to see the limited instrument panel by. In addition, though the small craft never made more than 50 knots, the damp mountain air blowing over them at fifty miles an hour was enough to chill them to the bone.

In daylight conditions Kurt would have brought them down to a lower altitude as rapidly as possible, but night flying presented a different challenge. Piloting such a craft through the mountains in the dark was like walking through an unfamiliar room without any lights on, only hitting the furniture here would hurt far worse than a stubbed toe.

At one point, he spotted the lights of a car on the twisting road down below. He angled toward them, knowing that the road cut through the mountain passes. Following the car, staying far above and well behind it, he was able to follow the road itself. But, perhaps not surprisingly, the car turned out to be faster than the flying lawn mower he was commanding.

As the car's lights became too faint to see, another set of lights came into view: the comparatively bright streets of Vila do Porto. He angled toward them, knowing that if he could keep them in sight no mountain could rise up and smite them from the sky.

Katarina noticed them too. "Are we almost there?" she said. Her teeth were chattering.

She sat behind him in the two-seat machine. Kurt remembered the simple black dress she had on. Not exactly made for 50-knot winds and 40-degree temperatures.

"You're cold," he said.

"Freezing to death," she insisted.

She had to be turning blue by now. "I thought you Russians were used to the cold."

"Yes, and we know how to dress for it, with layers and fur hats. You don't have one hiding up there for me, do you?"

He had to laugh, imagining her with a giant fur hat on.

"Lean forward," he said. "Press against me and put your arms around me."

"I thought you'd never ask," she said.

In an instant he felt her pressed against him, her arms wrapped around his chest. It was a lot warmer and nicer that way.

They continued on, buzzed their way through the last of the mountain passes, and watched as Vila do Porto spread out before them. The town had fifty thousand inhabitants, or thereabouts, but it looked like Metropolis at that moment.

"Where are we going to land?" Katarina asked.

Kurt had been thinking about that the whole way down. The ultralight only needed a two-hundred-foot strip to land and stop in.

In the daylight there might have been fifty places to put down safely, but at night everything that wasn't lit up looked the same. Thinking he was descending toward a flat field or patch of open ground, he could easily have them ramming a telephone pole, or a house, or a stand of trees.

They had to land somewhere lighted to be safe. The only problem was, most lighted areas had power lines strewn around them. Then Kurt spotted a sight that looked as glorious to him as the runway lights at JFK International. A soccer field, lit for a night game and open to the sky.

A hundred twenty yards of smooth, flat grass without any power lines crossing it or obstructions in the way. It was perfect. He angled toward it, descending slightly. There was a crosswind coming off the Atlantic, and Kurt had to crab the little plane sideways at a thirty-degree angle to keep them from getting blown inland.

At five hundred feet, he could see a crowd around the perimeter but no players on the field. Katarina pressed into him tighter.

"I need my arms back," he said.

"Sorry," she said. "Don't like flying. Especially takeoffs and landings."

"Don't worry," he said. "This one's going to be a breeze."

Within a minute of saying that, Kurt wished he'd kept his mouth shut. He saw players taking the field, either it was the start of the game or halftime had just ended.

He and Katarina were a hundred feet up, three hundred feet from the end of the grass. They had to hear him. Of course hearing a plane flying around didn't exactly make one run for cover. He guessed that would change in a few seconds.

The engine began to sputter and cough.

"We're almost out of fuel," he said.

"Just land, already," she shouted back.

He continued on, wishing the damn thing had a horn. "Too bad I don't have my vuvuzela," he shouted.

He could see the players shaking hands, the referee standing in the center with his foot on the ball about to blow the whistle. The engine sputtered again, and Kurt put the nose down to pick up speed. The prop sped up again, and he saw the players look his way. The crowd turned as well.

He zoomed over the crowd. A flagpole or something he hadn't seen hit the right wing. The frame bent, the right side dropped, and Kurt overcorrected back to the left.

Players began running for the sidelines as the sputtering craft descended into the lighted area.

They hit the grass and bounced. The ultralight almost nosed over, but Kurt corrected and planted the wheels firmly in the middle of the field, right at the fifty-yard line.

He reached for the brake, pulled it, and felt the small plane skid across the wet grass. One last player dove out of the way, and the ultralight slammed into the goal at the far end of the field.

The net wrapped around them, the propeller died, and the little plane stopped.

Kurt looked up and back. The crowd, the players, the ref, everyone, just stared in an incredible silence. They looked at him and Katarina, and then at one another, and then finally at the ref. He did nothing for a second, then slowly raised one arm, blew his whistle, and yelled, "Goooooaaaaaallll!"

The crowd shouted in unison, raising their arms as if it were a triumph, as if it were an overtime goal to win the World Cup for tiny Vila do Porto, and in moments the players were reaching for Katarina and Kurt, laughing and clapping, as they freed the plane from the net and dragged it back out onto the field.

The players helped Katarina climb out, admiring her form as they did. The ref helped Kurt. And then they were escorted off the field to the sidelines.

Kurt explained to someone a version of what had happened, promised to pay for any damages, and insisted that the ultralight rental outfit would come for its plane tomorrow.

As the soccer game began again, he and Katarina made their way out to the street. Somewhere near the field there had to be a cab waiting or bus they could take. A microvan pulled up with some kind of sign on it.

"We need to go to the harbor," Kurt said.

"I can take you," the driver said.

Kurt opened the door. Katarina went to climb in but paused.

"That was really quite incredible," she said, gazing into his eyes.

They'd almost been killed three times, her rental car had been sent off a cliff and turned into a burning hulk, and she was still almost blue from the cold, but her eyes sparkled as if he'd just shown her the time of her life. He had to admire that.

He reached out, pulled her to him, and kissed her on the lips. They kissed for a few seconds longer, her arms wrapping around him from the front this time, until the driver coughed lightly.

They parted.

"Was that to warm me up?" she asked.

He smiled. "Did it work?"

"Better than you know," she said, turning and climbing into the taxi. He got in after her, and the little bubble van moved off toward the harbor.

"You know," she said, "we're only a mile or so from the house where the French team is staying."

"Really," he said, remembering what she'd told him earlier. "Do you have the address?"

"It's right on the beach at Praia Formosa. The most luxurious rental in town."

That sounded like the French way to him.

"Driver," Kurt said. "Take us to Praia Formosa."

29

New York City, June 24

THE AVENUES OF MANHATTAN bustled with traffic and energy on a warm summer night. The people were out in droves, crowds on foot, others in cars and cabs and even carriages taking romantic rides around Central Park. It was twenty minutes after dusk, and the city that never sleeps was just getting started.

Dirk Pitt rode in a taxi headed for a five-star restaurant. As he cruised down Park Avenue, the orange reflection of the streetlights traveled methodically up the polished yellow surface of the car's hood. One after another, they passed, steady and slow like silent heartbeats. He imagined Paul Trout's heartbeat, prayed it was remaining strong, and thought of Gamay, watching over him, trying to will her husband back to consciousness.

He had come to meet with Takagawa face-to-face, but, assuming he'd be denied entry at the reception desk, Dirk decided to seek out his old acquaintance somewhere other than the office. He'd procured information as to where Takagawa would be dining this night and decided to surprise him on neutral ground.

The restaurant was called Miyako, a place known for local celebrities and ballplayers who brought their supermodel dates in late at night. Miyako served traditional Japanese fare in an ultramodern, upscale environment. Twenty-dollar martinis and shots of sake flowed like water, while traditional delicacies, such as poisonous puffer fish, sea cucumber intestines, and *uni*—otherwise known as sea urchin—filled out the menu.

Haruto Takagawa was expected to be dining there with his son, Ren, several ranking members of Shokara Shipping's executive staff, and at least two hedge fund managers looking to invest in Shokara's latest venture.

Dirk knew they'd be in a private room in the back, but he wasn't expecting they'd welcome him to join them. Just in case, he'd brought along a little reminder of Takagawa's debt.

The taxi pulled up to the curb in front of Miyako, and Dirk stepped out.

He paid the driver, and included a generous tip, and then strode into the restaurant's foyer, eyeing the room. A high wall with water cascading down it divided the main dining area from the private rooms in the rear. Dirk stepped forward just as an officious-looking man came around the corner. He stepped in front of Dirk, looking at him suspiciously.

"Excuse me," the man said. "We seat only those with reservations. And you must wear proper dress."

Dirk was wearing black slacks with a crease like a razor blade, an eight-hundred-dollar dinner jacket, and a two-hundred-dollar button-down shirt open at the collar.

"You must wear a tie to dine here," the man explained.

"I'm not here to eat," Dirk said, pushing past the man.

Leaving the host behind, Dirk crossed the room. In a town filled with politicians, power brokers, and celebrities, Dirk Pitt was an unknown, but he cut a striking figure as he moved.

At least a dozen of the patrons turned from their important conversations to watch him pass. If asked, they might have said he had an aura about him, one that drew their attention, a purpose in his step that carried conviction, determination, and confidence without arrogance or conceit. Or they might have said nothing. But they watched him walk until he disappeared behind the wall of trickling water.

Dirk Pitt stepped into the private dining room, and the conversation died. His arrival was abrupt and unexpected. It jarred the room, just as he'd hoped it would.

One by one the diners looked at him, Takagawa raising his eyes last. He sat at the far end of the table, and the look on his face suggested he was gazing upon the specter of Death. The other members of the group were stunned, but closer to anger than anything else.

One of the hedge fund managers stood, his five-thousand-dollar suit making Dirk's look as if it had come off the rack.

"Whoever you are, you're in the wrong place," he said, walking toward Dirk and reaching a hand toward him as if to usher him out of the room.

Dirk never even looked at the man, but he spoke in a tone that was almost a growl. "You put that hand on me and you'll never use it to count money again."

The hedge fund manager looked as if he'd been slapped in the face, but he stepped back and said nothing.

Takagawa's son Ren stood next. "I'm calling security," he said to his father.

Takagawa did not respond to his son's actions; he just stared at Dirk as if in a trance. Dirk guessed it was time to snap him out of it.

He tossed an eight-inch length of metal toward him. It rattled as it hit the table, and some of the other diners jumped back as if it might spring to life and attack them. It stopped in front of Takagawa.

Shokara's CEO reached out and took the metal shard in his hands. A nameplate, bent and twisted and blackened with soot. It read "Minoru." Smaller numbers beneath the name listed tonnage.

The son's call had gone through. "Security, this is Ren, I have a—"

Takagawa reached out and put a hand on his son's arm, stopping him midsentence.

"Put the phone down, my son," he said.

"But this man could be a threat," Ren said. "He disrespects you."

"No," Takagawa said wearily. "I have disrespected him. He is right to come here and find me. I am only ashamed, like an insect hiding underneath a stone."

Over Ren's phone, a voice. *"Ren, this is the security team. Do you need something? We're right outside."*

Ren looked at his father, who stared once more at the piece of metal.

"If not for this man," Takagawa said, "I would have burned to death thirty years ago when my ship went down. I would never have seen your face. Your mother gave birth to you while I was at sea, and there were no pictures yet."

Takagawa studied the carbon-charred metal placard. He'd given it to Dirk in thanks for saving his life and others on the crew. He looked at his right hand. Poking out from beneath the cuff was an area of burned and scarred skin, which Dirk knew ran halfway up Takagawa's arm.

"Is everything okay?"

Ren brought the phone up to his mouth. "Yes," he said finally. "A false alarm."

He hung up. Glared at Pitt for a moment, took a breath, and nodded in a bow of respect. "I apologize," he said.

"A son defending his father is nothing to apologize for," Dirk said.

Ren Takagawa stood back and pulled out his chair, offering the seat beside his father to Dirk.

"Arigato," Dirk said, sitting down.

The hedge fund managers and the other members of the party still appeared confused.

"This is highly irregular," one of them said.

"Please leave us," Takagawa said gravely. "We have something more important than business to discuss."

"Look, Haruto," one of them began. "I don't know what this is—"

A glance from Takagawa stopped him, and then one by one the group stood and left, some of them muttering under their breaths as they went.

"I'll talk to them," Ren said. He followed them out, and the two old acquaintances were left alone.

"I'm sorry it had to be this way," Dirk said.

"You have nothing to be sorry for," Takagawa replied.

"You know what I want," Dirk said.

Takagawa nodded.

"Then why didn't you just give it to my people?"

For the first time, the wizened old man looked into Dirk's eyes.

"They came for the manifest," he said. "I could have given it to them. But I would not do it because it would have misled you. And I was not willing to lie to you."

"So you gave them nothing," Dirk said.

Takagawa nodded. "There seemed to me some honor in not being overtly deceptive. If I said nothing, I have not lied. At least you would know to be concerned. But to tell you a falsehood after what you have done for me . . . I could not do such a thing and face you."

"Why not just tell me the truth?" Dirk asked.

"My position in Shokara is not absolute," Takagawa said. "Always there is palace intrigue to be dealt with. To tell you the truth would offend others. Perhaps even expose Shokara to liability. Or sanctions by your government."

Pitt didn't blink. He needed answers. At this point the cost to Shokara Shipping did not concern him.

"Haruto," Dirk said, "three of my people were injured trying to stop the hijacking of your ship. Two more have been attacked since we began investigating, and one of them is now in a coma while his wife prays for him to come back to her. So forgive me for being blunt, but I don't care what kind of problems it brings. If you're the man I think you are, then you know it's time to speak."

Takagawa looked at the twisted metal nameplate in front of him and then into Dirk's eyes. He stared long and hard before speaking. "Perhaps you have saved me twice," he whispered.

With that, he reached for a briefcase at his feet and lifted it up to the table. He laid it flat, popped the latches, and opened it. Reaching inside, he pulled out a folder, which he handed to Dirk.

"This is the information you seek," he said.

"What am I going to find in here?" Dirk asked.

"The truth."

"Which is?"

"The cargo on the *Kinjara Maru* was bound for Hong Kong. Most of it was standard bulk materials, but included in the mix and not listed on the manifest were three hundred tons of titanium-doped YBCO."

"What's YBCO?" Pitt asked.

"Yttrium, barium, copper, oxide," Takagawa explained. "It's an intricate crystalline compound that acts as a high-temperature superconductor. A newer, more advanced version has been developed that can be doped with titanium and iron peptides: the Ti version. It's by far the strongest superconductor ever created."

"Strongest?" Pitt asked. "What do you mean?"

"I wouldn't be able to explain it," Takagawa said. "I'm just an old ship's captain. But you must have people who will understand. The information I have on it is in there."

Pitt would get the information to Hiram Yaeger as soon as he returned to the office. "Why were you afraid to tell me that?" Pitt asked.

"Because it's not a naturally occurring compound," Takagawa said. "It's created in a lab. The Ti version is patented by an American corporation, and, more important, it's listed as a restricted technology. Transfer to other nations, including China, is illegal. By allowing it onto our ship, Shokara is in violation of this law."

Now Pitt began to understand. With economic tensions between the U.S. and China always simmering, and claims, mostly substantiated, that the Chinese government and its corporations preferred espionage and theft to honest development, neither the Chinese nor the U.S. government would be happy to hear that this compound had been shipped to Hong Kong. But with both countries needing each other, the most likely candidate to be punished and made a scapegoat would be the shipper: Shokara.

"Why would you be involved in something like this?" Pitt asked. "This country has been phenomenally good to you."

"I was not aware of it until after the *Kinjara Maru* went down," Takagawa said.

Dirk believed that. He sensed the heavy heart and the weight of dishonor that Takagawa felt.

"I believe someone boarded that ship to steal something," Pitt said. "It sounds like this YBCO was the most likely target."

"It is worth more than its weight in gold," Takagawa said.

"Do you know anything about the people who hit your ship?" Pitt asked. "Any rumors even?"

Takagawa shook his head.

There had to be something. "Where did you load the compound?"

"Freetown," Takagawa said. "Sierra Leone."

Dirk had been in Freetown ten years back when NUMA had consulted on a project to deepen the navigation channel. Though the country was still a shambles, Freetown was still one of the busiest ports in West Africa at the time.

From what he'd heard, things had improved quite a bit under the autocratic leadership of its president, Djemma Garand, but it wasn't exactly a hub of high-tech activity.

"Could it have come from there?" he asked.

Takagawa shook his head. "Sierra Leone has mines and mineral wealth, but, as I said, YBCO doesn't come from the ground."

"So Freetown was a transfer point," Pitt said.

"It happens this way," Takagawa said. "The loophole. You transfer to a country that is legally allowed to take the material and they send it to a third party without violating any of their own national laws. And then that third party sends it to Russia or China or Pakistan."

"Do you have any idea who the buyer is?" Dirk asked.

"They will deny it, but it's in there," Takagawa said. "Certainly it does not matter now. They did not receive what they paid for."

Dirk's mind was working overtime, playing catch-up. "What about the seller?"

Takagawa shook his head. "Not known to me."

Dirk didn't like the picture that was forming. "I need a favor," he said respectfully.

"I can give you no more."

Pitt stared at him. "Many of your crew died in flames, Haruto."

Takagawa closed his eyes as if in pain. His left hand went unconsciously to his right wrist and the scars. "Are you chasing them?" he asked.

"I'm about to start," Dirk said.

"Then I will give you all I can find."

Pitt stood and bowed his head slightly. "Thank you," he said. "I promise it will go no further."

Takagawa nodded but seemed unable to look directly at Dirk. Finally, Pitt turned to go.

"I was wondering," Takagawa said, "do you still have such wonderful cars? I collect them now myself."

Pitt stopped and turned back. "Yes, I still have them, and a few more."

"What one did you drive here tonight?" Takagawa asked, smiling just a bit, no doubt remembering how he and Pitt had discussed cars as a way to stay calm during their escape from the inferno thirty years back.

Pitt shook his head. "I took a cab."

Takagawa seemed disappointed. "A pity."

"But the other day," Pitt said, "I took my Duesenberg roadster out for a spin."

Takagawa's face brightened, as if the thought of Pitt at the controls of the luxurious automobile warmed his heart somehow.

"Friday," Takagawa said.

Dirk nodded. "It was a nice day for a drive."

KURT AUSTIN SLID THE DOOR of the microvan open and stepped out onto the street fronting Praia Formosa. The night was quiet; he could hear the waves breaking on the beach just beyond. He offered a hand to Katarina, helped her through the door, and paid the driver.

"Do you want to earn another fare?" he asked.

"Sure," the driver said, his round face lighting up.

"Go around the block," Kurt said, "and wait down the end with your lights off and watch for us."

In his hand Kurt held out a hundred-dollar bill. He ripped it in half and gave one piece to the driver.

"How long do you want me to wait?" the driver asked.

"Until we come back out here," Kurt said.

The driver nodded, put the vehicle in drive, and began to move away.

"You sure we're not putting him in danger?" Katarina asked.

Kurt was pretty certain they'd lost whatever tails had tracked them to the restaurant. "He's in no danger," Kurt said confidently. "Neither are we, unless the French team wants to fight about the core sample they've taken."

"Not the French way," she said.

"Which house?" he asked, noticing several villas along the stretch of sand.

"This way," she said. She turned and began walking, stepping off the rough pavement and onto the grass. Kurt guessed that felt better on her bare feet.

"We have to get you some shoes," he said.

"Or get rid of yours, and we'll go for a walk on the beach," she said, smiling at him.

That sounded like more fun than waking up a group of scientists and accusing them of stealing.

They arrived in front of a yellow-painted villa.

"This is the one," she said.

Kurt knocked. And then knocked again. They waited.

No answer.

The place was dark. Even the outside lights were off.

"You sure this is it?" Kurt asked.

"They had a party here last night," she said. "Everyone came."

Kurt knocked again, banging harder, not at all concerned that he might be waking the neighbors. As he pounded the door something strange happened. The outside light, which was off, flickered on for an instant with each strike of his fist.

"What the . . ."

He stopped hammering the door and turned his attention to the light. Reaching into the sconce, his hands found the bulb. It was loose. He twisted it and it came on. Two more turns sealed it tightly.

"Doing some maintenance?" Katarina said.

Kurt held up a hand, and she went quiet. He crouched down and studied the doorjamb. Gouges and scrapes around the lock told him more bad news.

"What's wrong?"

"Somebody forced the lock," he said. "They unscrewed the bulb so no one would see them working it. Old thief's trick."

Kurt tested the door. It was certainly locked now.

He headed for the side of the house. Katarina followed.

"Stay here," he said.

"Not a chance," she replied.

He didn't have time to argue. He snuck past a hedge of tropical bougainvillea and moved toward the rear of the house. A sundeck beckoned. Kurt hopped up onto it and moved to a sliding glass door.

Nothing but darkness inside.

It took all of three seconds to pop the door up off its tracks and slide it open.

"Did you used to be a burglar?" Katarina whispered.

"Gifts from a misspent youth," he whispered back. "Now, please stay here."

"What if someone starts to choke you again?" she asked "And I'm not there to save you?"

Kurt guessed he wasn't going to live that moment down. He snuck inside the house with Katarina right behind him. Right away he could tell something was wrong. The place was a shambles.

Katarina winced suddenly, made a slight noise, and dropped down to her hands and knees.

Kurt dropped down next to her. Aside from the two of them, nothing in the house was moving. "What's wrong?"

"Glass," she said, pulling a sliver out of her foot.

"Give me two minutes," Kurt said.

This time, she nodded and held her position.

Kurt moved quickly, exploring the rest of the villa, and then returned with a grim look on his face.

Back in the living room, he switched the lights on. The place looked as if it had been hit by a tornado; couches overturned, cabinets open, and items strewn about. A glass table lamp had been shattered, and shards of glass littered the floor.

"We need to call the police," Kurt said. He looked for the phone, spotted a pair of flip-flops by the door, and handed them to Katarina.

"Put these on."

As she slipped her feet into the sandals, Kurt located the phone and picked up the receiver.

No dial tone. He found the wall jack and realized the phone had been ripped out of it. The jack looked damaged. They'd have to find another one to plug it into. He headed for the kitchen.

"What happened here?" Katarina asked.

"The French habit of talking too much got the best of them," Kurt said. He'd found another phone jack near the sink. He plugged the cord in, got a tone, and began dialing.

As he waited for someone to pick up, he noticed an open drawer. Silverware and other utensils had spilled onto the floor, including a vicious-looking carving knife. It looked like the French had fought back.

With his attention diverted, Kurt didn't notice Katarina beginning to wander about. When he looked up, she was standing near the doorway to another room, reaching in as if to turn the light on.

"Don't," Kurt said.

Too late. The switch flicked, and the room lit up.

Katarina gasped and turned away. Kurt put the phone down and grabbed her, as she looked as if she might faint.

She glanced back in the room and then buried her face in his chest. "They're dead," she said.

"I'm sorry," he said. "I didn't want you to see that."

The entire French team had been murdered. Four bodies lay in the room, thrown disrespectfully against the wall like discarded junk. Bullet holes riddled one of the men, another looked as if he'd been strangled, based on the marks around his neck. The others were harder to see, and Kurt hadn't gone that close. But even from the doorway Kurt recognized the man he'd plucked from the depths with too much weight on his belt.

In Kurt's arms Katarina trembled, a hand over her mouth, her eyes closed tight. Kurt turned her away and led her to the living room. He righted the couch and sat her down.

"I have to call the police," he said.

She nodded, unable to speak.

As Kurt moved back to the open kitchen he kept an eye on Katarina. It was true men had already died that night, but they'd been men intent on killing or harming both him and her. And they'd gone off a cliff hidden in a car, all but unseen. This was different.

These men were fellow scientists. Katarina had apparently shared drinks with them on at least one occasion.

"How could the police not know already?" she asked.

"It probably happened quickly," Kurt said, hoping for the dead men's sake it had. "The assailants probably had suppressors on their weapons and took these men by surprise."

"But why?" she asked. "Why would anyone—"

"They had the core sample," Kurt said. "From what I understand it could be extremely valuable, that's why we're here while the Spanish and Portuguese figure out who owns it and in what percentages.

These guys were bold enough to take that sample illegally but stupid enough to talk about it."

"Too much wine," she said. "Men like to brag when they've had too much wine."

The police finally answered and promised to send both investigators and the coroner. While he waited, Kurt searched in vain for the core sample. He found a long rectangular box filled with foam in a room with other equipment. It lay open and turned over. He guessed the sample had been inside.

An hour of discussion with the police followed, and then Kurt and Katarina were allowed to leave.

"What will you do now?" Katarina asked.

"I have to get in touch with my ship," Kurt said, raising his eyes toward the harbor and finding himself surprised at what he saw.

"I have a radio set on my boat," she said. "You could use that."

"I don't think we'll need it."

She looked up.

"That's my ship right there," he said. "The one all lit up like a Christmas tree."

As Kurt wondered what the *Argo* was doing in port with every available light blazing he began looking around, hoping he and Katarina could bum a ride from one of the cops. All of a sudden a tiny van came zooming up.

Kurt recognized the driver's round, smiling face. "I thought the police would never let you go," he said. "Ready?"

Kurt figured a two-hour wait was more than enough to earn a hundred dollars. He fished the other half of the C-note out of his pocket and handed it over.

"Ready," he said.

WHILE KATARINA WAITED on the *Argo*'s bridge, Kurt Austin sat in the conference room with Captain Haynes and Joe Zavala. He spent ten minutes relaying the events he and Katarina had endured that night, concluding with the grisly discovery at the French team's beach house.

In response, Captain Haynes told him of the attack on the *Grouper*, Paul's near drowning, and his current condition. He and Joe then took turns explaining what they knew of Gamay's theory that the *Kinjara Maru* had been hit with some type of directed-energy weapon.

"Are we talking about something like the SDI program?" Kurt asked, referring to the Strategic Defense Initiative. "Something that could shoot down missiles?"

"Could be," the captain said. "The thing is, we don't really know. But it's possible."

"And why hit some random freighter in the middle of the Atlantic?" Kurt asked.

Before anyone could answer, the intercom light flashed, and the communications officer spoke.

"Incoming call for you, Captain. It's Director Pitt."

"Put him on speaker," the captain said.

The speaker crackled for a second and then the sound of Dirk Pitt's voice came over it. "I know it's late there, gentlemen, but I understand everyone is still up."

"We've been discussing the events," Haynes said.

"I just posed a question that's been on my mind since this started," Kurt said. "Why target a bulk carrier in the middle of the Atlantic? That goes for simple piracy or this electromagnetic weapon we're now talking about."

"I think I have the answer to that," Dirk said. "Hiram Yaeger is doing a study to figure out the power requirements and capabilities of such a weapon right now, but when I asked him what someone would need to create such a weapon his short answer was 'More.'"

"More?" Kurt said. "More what?"

"More everything," Dirk replied. "More energy, more materials, more money. *More* than it might be easy to get one's hands on. In this case, the *Kinjara Maru* was likely targeted for a shipment of titanium-doped YBCO. It's a highly advanced, hellaciously expensive compound used to make incredibly powerful superconducting magnets."

"And those magnets can be used in making energy weapons," Kurt guessed. "Just like the one Gamay thinks hit the ship."

"Exactly," Pitt said. "Basically, these superconducting magnets are essential to any high-intensity energy projects. Normal magnets create too much heat at high energy levels, but superconductors pass the energy through without creating any resistance at all."

Joe spoke up. "Sounds like someone has adapted that technology for a military purpose."

"Yaeger agrees with you," Pitt said. "And Gamay's tests on the samples from the *Kinjara Maru* are all but unequivocal."

"Any idea who's behind it?" Kurt asked.

"Not yet," Pitt said. "Could be a terrorist group, or some rogue nation or faction. Last year we fought with the Chinese Triad over a bioweapon, so I guess anything's possible."

"What about a money trail?" Kurt said. "If this stuff is so expensive, there has to be some record of its purchase."

"We're looking into it," Pitt said. "So far, we've been able to identify massive purchases of various superconducting materials spread around through several dozen companies that now appear to be dummies. It's as if someone was trying to corner the market on the more powerful superconducting materials."

Kurt looked at Joe and then the captain. Pitt continued to speak.

"The problem is, all the odd purchases lead to front companies, which in turn are operating as subsidiaries of other shell corporations. The funds come from unidentified sources, and the front closes up shop immediately after completing the deal. It makes for a hard path to follow. On the surface, it all seems legit. People get paid as they're supposed to, no red flags go up. No one's the wiser, at least until now."

Kurt said, "If they're cornering the market, why did they need to steal anything?"

"Titanium-doped YBCO is the most powerful superconductor made," Pitt said. "It can operate effectively in field strengths of up to nine hundred teslas."

"Aside from an excellent nineties rock group," Joe asked, "what exactly is a tesla?"

"It's a unit of power designed to measure magnetic field strengths," Pitt said. "I can't exactly tell you what nine hundred teslas means in numbers, but by comparison the superconductors used in levitating trains in Japan become overloaded at four teslas. So if four teslas can lift a train, nine hundred teslas can lift two hundred twenty-five of them."

Captain Haynes exhaled slowly. "Arms race," he said. "If you're building a weapon, you might as well have the most powerful version you can find."

Something still didn't make sense to Kurt. "If all this was so clandestine, how'd the pirates know this YBCO was on the ship?"

"Despite all the secrecy," Pitt said, "there were still three parties who knew about it."

"The buyer, the seller, and the shipper," Kurt said.

"And of the three of them," Pitt said, "who had any reason to sink that ship and make the material disappear?"

"The seller," Kurt said, realizing what Pitt was getting at. "So they get a good price, make all the arrangements to turn this super-conducting material over to the Chinese, and then they raid the ship and take it back."

"Pretty damn devious," Haynes said. "Are we sure we're not barking up the wrong tree?"

"I have the manifest of the *Kinjara Maru*," Pitt said. "Along with the captain's log and the loadmaster's notes, which are transmitted to Shokara's headquarters electronically when their ships leave port. I'd read them to you, but I'm driving, so here's the gist of it. I think you'll understand when I'm done."

Pitt continued. "The ship docked in Freetown, Sierra Leone, three days before it went down. It picked up a standard bulk cargo of various ores bound for China and then received orders to hold in port for two days, awaiting one more delivery."

"The YBCO," Kurt guessed.

"Right," Pitt said. "But when the shipment finally arrived, there were several things odd enough about it for the captain to note them in the log. First, the load was put aboard the ship by a group of men who were not regular dockworkers. A mixed group of white and black men did most of the loading. The captain remarked that they 'resembled a military or paramilitary unit.'"

"I've heard rumors of mercenaries taking over mines out there and running them for a profit," Kurt said.

"Only, YBCO isn't mined," Pitt said. "Beyond that, the leader of this group insisted that the YBCO absolutely had to be stored separately from the other ores in a specific temperature-controlled hold. A request that seemed odd enough to the loadmaster to risk an argument with these military men. An argument he lost."

"Why would they do that?" Joe asked. "Does temperature affect it?"

"No," Pitt said. "But the *Kinjara Maru* has only one small temperature-controlled hold."

"Making the material easy to find and off-load," Kurt said.

"That's what it sounds like," Pitt said.

"So the seller is also the pirate," Captain Haynes summarized.

"And the pirate has the energy weapon," Kurt added. "Which means the people who sold this YBCO—the same people who boarded the ship—are also the ones building the weapon out of it. So they must be the ones cornering the market."

"Makes you wonder what they're up to," the captain said.

"Exactly," Pitt said. "Whoever these people are, they need so much material for whatever they're doing that they're willing to anger the Chinese and risk exposure to get their hands on every ounce they can. Including some they've already sold."

"Maybe that explains why they're here on Santa Maria," Kurt said. "I've tangled with one of them already, same guy we argued with as the *KM* went down. Now, I don't know who took the core sample and murdered the French team, but one will get you ten it's all linked together."

"But we saw their boat explode," Captain Haynes said. "We even found a few bodies."

"A few sacrificial pawns," Kurt said. "The others probably went over the side before the explosion. Left the suckers behind."

"But we never spotted any other vessels in range to pick them up, or even a helicopter," the captain said. "And they certainly didn't swim to Africa."

"No," Kurt said. "But Paul and Gamay were attacked underneath the water. That means these people undoubtedly have a submarine of some kind."

"So there was a mother ship," the captain said. "Terrorists with a submarine. What's the world coming to?"

"Much like space," Pitt said, "the depths below are no longer just the domain of the world's nations. We know of half a dozen Chinese subs that were supposed to go to the scrapyard and vanished instead. There are also other models out there for sale, and private builds as well."

"Not to mention the Russian Typhoon-class subs that were turned into cargo haulers," Kurt said. "We dealt with one of them last year."

"And at least one of those is still unaccounted for," Pitt added.

"Wonderful," the captain said facetiously.

"So these thugs have a submarine," Kurt noted. "Maybe a Typhoon-class boat converted into a cargo carrier. They have some type of lethal electromagnetic weapon that fries you before you even know something's happening and they're willing to risk exposure and the wrath of the Chinese to get more material. And right now the tower of rock we believe to be a naturally occurring superconductor is sitting out there, unattended and all by its lonesome."

"The table *is* set," Pitt said. "You think they're going to show up for dinner?"

"Like St. Julien Perlmutter at an all-you-can-eat buffet," Kurt said.

Haynes nodded. "Makes sense. They've effectively chased us from the scene by showing their ability to attack."

"And they know that," Kurt said, guessing they'd seen the *Argo* come into port just as he had.

"A Portuguese frigate with ASW capabilities will be on scene tomorrow afternoon," Pitt said.

"I'm guessing they know or expect that too," Kurt said. "That gives them twelve hours to act."

Silence descended on them as everyone considered the implications.

"Those Typhoons *were* converted to cargo carriers," Dirk noted. "Able to haul fifteen thousand tons where their missile bays used to be."

"And if thirty tons of YBCO is worth sinking a ship over," Kurt said, "how likely is it that an outfit interested in 'more' is going to pass up a free haul like this?"

The silence returned. Even over the speaker all that could be heard was a quiet background of white noise.

"*If* they have a Typhoon," Pitt said, "all they would have to do is carve sections out of the wall and drop them in the missile bay like it's the back of a dump truck. But let's be clear. We don't know that they have one."

Kurt nodded, accepting that, and Joe glanced over at him, raising his eyebrows.

"Even if we did know what they had," Joe said, "what exactly are *we* going to do about it?"

Kurt considered Joe's words. A Typhoon armed with torpedoes and crewed by mercenaries was far beyond the *Argo*'s capability to deal with.

"Joe's right," the captain said. "We can't risk the ship. Until the naval forces come into range, we have no choice but to give these people wide berth, whatever they're up to."

Kurt knew they were right, but it felt like giving up to him, like quitting. There had to be a way to stop them. He glanced through the window in the conference room's door, focusing on Katarina. She sat quietly on the bridge, a NUMA windbreaker over her shoulders, sipping a cup of coffee and talking to a crewman as she waited. A thought came to him.

"What if we don't try to stop them?" he said. "What if we get out there, hide in among the wrecks, and lie in wait for them. Then if they do show up, we find a good moment and attach a transmitter to their hull. That way, we can track them to wherever their base is and let the big boys deal with the rest."

The captain and Joe seemed to like the plan. Pitt remained silent.

"Director?" the captain said.

"Sounds like a huge risk," Dirk said. "Easier to get some ASW patrols from shore-based aircraft."

"All that'll do is scare them off," Kurt said. "This way, we find out who they are and where they're from."

"And how do you plan on getting out there without tipping your hand?" Pitt asked. "They'll expect something the moment you leave port."

Kurt smiled and glanced at Joe. "We'll take the *Barracuda*," he said.

32

Santa Maria Island, Vila do Porto, June 24

AFTER CONCLUDING THEIR PLANNING SESSION in the conference room, Kurt, Joe, and the captain broke away to handle different tasks. Joe went to the *Argo*'s machine shop to get working on a transmitter that would be powerful enough to hang onto the back of a submarine making 25 knots and also small enough to go unnoticed. He promised a miracle within the hour.

The captain ordered the *Argo* darkened to a normal state and then made contact with the Vila do Porto police. He requested two cars be sent out and parked at the dockside with their lights flashing. He assumed that would help keep any trouble away and also distract anyone who was watching while the *Barracuda* was quietly slipped into the water.

Meanwhile, Kurt walked Katarina to the end of the dock, waiting for a car to arrive.

"Your chaperone," he said, avoiding the word *handler*.

"I'm not a spy," she insisted, "but it seems all my life I've had someone watching me."

"How do you deal with it?" Kurt asked.

"I'm used to it," she said. "But you can't imagine how hard it was to go on a date in Torino."

He had to laugh. "And this guy?"

"Sergei," she said. "Major Sergei Komarov."

Sounded like a good strong KGB/FSB enforcer. For the first time in his life Kurt felt glad about that.

"Stay close to Sergei," he said. "Keep your doors locked. I'm pretty sure these people have bigger fish to fry right now, but you never know. They know you've seen them, even if it was from a distance and in low light."

"I will," she said.

"Want to tell me why you were diving on that Constellation?"

She smiled, shook her head. "The major might not like that."

"Well, maybe tomorrow or the next day," he said.

The sad look returned to her eyes. "If I'm right, we'll be leaving in the morning. I might not see you again."

"Don't count on that," Kurt said. "I've always wanted to see Russia as a tourist. Maybe even come in the winter and get one of those giant fur hats."

"Come see me," she said, "I promise you won't need a hat to keep you warm."

The car arrived.

Sergei got out and stood by the door. Katarina gave Kurt a long kiss and then climbed in.

Thirty minutes later it was all a memory as Kurt and Joe raced through the ink-black Atlantic waters in the *Barracuda*, making their way to the tower of magnetic rock. They reached it in just under two hours, approaching the area with caution.

"I'm not hearing anything on the sonar array," Joe said.

"If they were on-site already, it would probably sound like a working gravel pit," Kurt said. "At least if they're planning on getting any large amount of material out."

"We should be in visual range," Kurt said. "Flip on the lights."

Joe switched them on, and the long, thin beams of yellowish light sprayed out over the underwater landscape. Once again, Kurt marveled at the sight of ship carcasses littering the seafloor. He'd once been fortunate enough to dive on Truk Lagoon, site of a World War II battle where the U.S. Navy had sunk sixty Japanese ships and downed over two hundred aircraft. The wrecks were more spread out than this Devil's Gate, but it was the closest thing he could think of to what he was seeing now.

"Let's set down beside the wreck of that old Liberty ship," Joe said. "From there we'll be almost invisible."

Kurt looked down at the diagram of where the wrecks lay. With an expert hand he glided the *Barracuda* to a spot of sand right beside the great ship. Putting down, he had the odd feeling of being a guppy in a fish tank, settling in beside the ubiquitous sunken ship with a great hole in the side.

"Cut the lights," he said.

Joe hit a few switches, and the *Barracuda* went instantly and absolutely dark.

Kurt held up his hand to test the old adage about not being able to see your hand in front of your face. Down here, at least, with daylight yet to break, it was true.

"How much air do we have?" he asked.

"Just under ten hours," Joe said.

"Well," Kurt said, trying to get comfortable, "nothing to do now but wait."

———

FOUR HOURS LATER Kurt felt a tap on the shoulder from Joe. They'd decided to sleep in two-hour shifts. Kurt hoped Joe's tap meant their guests had arrived.

"Something happening?" he asked, straightening and banging his head on the canopy and then his knee on the panel in front of him.

"Yeah," Joe said. "The sun's coming up."

Kurt looked up. A smidgen of light could be seen filtering in from above. And while it was still dark enough down below that the only light he could see came from the glowing phosphors on his dive watch, he noticed the time was almost seven a.m. It had to be plenty bright up top.

He tried to stretch again, but it was no use. "Next time you design a sub, try including a little headroom."

"Absolutely," Joe said.

"This is worse than an economy flight to Australia."

"At least they serve food on those," Joe said, "even if it's just peanuts."

"Yeah," Kurt said, thinking they could have planned better. Honestly, he hadn't thought they'd need to. His biggest fear was that they would have arrived and found the killers already at work, which would have made their job either a lot harder or impossible.

"I don't get this," he said. "I would have thought they'd use every minute to mine what they could. You hear anything on the hydrophones?"

"Nope," Joe said.

"You sure?"

"I've had these headphones on so long, I think they've melded with my brain," Joe said. "But nothing's going on out there except a few fish swimming around and mating."

"You can actually hear them mating?" Kurt asked.

"Just the groovy music in the background," Joe said, "but I know what they're doing."

Too much time sitting alone, listening to the sounds of the sea, had obviously warped his friend's brain. He rubbed his eyes and blinked repeatedly. *Too much time,* he thought.

"They're not coming," he said. "Turn on the lights."

"You sure?"

"At this point they'd barely have time to mine anything before they'd have to move out," he said. "So much for my big idea."

Joe started with the running lights and the low-level dash illumination.

Once their eyes adjusted to the presence of the minor lights, Joe flicked on the main exterior lights, and the area right around them lit up in the familiar yellow-green.

"Nothing's changed," Kurt said, half expecting the tower of magnetic rock to have disappeared out from under their noses. It still loomed in the distance like a monolith.

Kurt looked to the right, gazing at the dark shadow of the Liberty ship they'd sidled up to. A gaping wound below the waterline seemed to have been the fatal blow to this particular vessel. For a second he wondered if it had gone down in World War II like the ships he'd seen in Truk. Couldn't have been that old, there was only a modicum of sea growth on the ship. No more than a couple years' worth, if that.

He looked the other way out across the seafloor to where the next-closest wrecks lay. The first was a small plane, or at least what had once been a twin-engine Cessna. He remembered what Katarina had said about the triple-tailed Constellation being made of aluminum, a nonferrous metal that would not be affected by magnetism. It lay out on the very fringe of the area, but the remnants of this plane were in close. Why? he thought.

He looked at another of the sunken vessels that lay beyond the wrecked aircraft. It was a trawler, maybe 90 feet in length. Standard multinet fishing boat. He couldn't see it clearly from where they were, but he remembered gliding over it at one point in the initial survey. And, now that he thought about it, that trawler also wore little in the way of growth, even less than the Liberty vessel they'd parked next to.

He wondered if the magnetism was affecting the rate of growth. Some ships of the day used low-level electric charges to inhibit algae growth on their hulls. Maybe this was a similar effect.

He turned back to the ship that loomed beside them, his eyes focusing on the gaping wound in its side. And then it hit him.

"I'm an idiot," Kurt said suddenly. "I'm an absolute idiot."

"What are you talking about?" Joe asked.

"How could we be so stupid?" Kurt mumbled, still lost in his own thoughts.

"Well, we've had a lot of practice," Joe said.

"You know what else we've had a lot of practice doing?" Kurt said. "Hauling ships up from the depths. And also sending them to the bottom."

He turned, trying to look back at Joe. "How many ships have you scuttled as part of the reef-building program?"

"At least fifty," Joe said, "if you count all of the past ten years."

"I've been there half the time," Kurt said. "And how do we sink them?"

"We set charges below the waterline," Joe said. "Blow holes in them. How else?"

"Look at the damage on this ship," he said.

The *Barracuda* already had its main lights on, but Joe activated a secondary light that was directional. He aimed it at the hole in the Liberty ship's side. It left no doubt.

"The steel plates are blown outward," Joe said.

"Someone scuttled this ship," Kurt said.

"It could have been an internal explosion," Joe said. "You never know what she was carrying. Besides, that's a much bigger hole than any of us would have made."

"That's because you want the ship to settle slowly and securely, landing bottom down so it can form a nice reef. But if you were trying to sink something quickly and not have anyone see it, this might be the way."

Kurt powered up the impeller, and the *Barracuda* lifted off the seafloor. He guided them across the mouth of this Devil's Gate toward the trawler. There they found the same type of damage. A large outward blast had sunk the ship. A third freighter was the same.

"None of these ships have more than a year's sea growth on them," Kurt said. "The only thing that did was that Constellation out there. This place hasn't been collecting ships for ages. These all went down at the same time."

"How could we not have seen this?" Joe asked.

"We were too busy with the scientists," Kurt said. "Everyone was obsessing over that tower of rock, and, aside from Katarina, no one did more than a cursory examination of these ships."

As they settled in front of the gaping wound in the third ship, Kurt racked his tired brain to put it together. "This whole thing is a hoax."

"Sure seems that way," Joe added. "But why? What's the point? Who could even pull such a thing off?"

Kurt guessed they both knew the answer to that last question but not the reasons behind it.

He went over the events in his mind again, desperately looking for a connection. He felt something ominous approaching, like a storm he couldn't outrun. There seemed little of value anyone could get out of such a hoax.

If the same people who'd attacked the *Kinjara Maru* were in on this, how did it help them? It didn't get them any materials. It couldn't really bring them any more money. In fact, it had to have cost a small fortune to set up the hoax to begin with.

"Some terrorist groups are big on publicity," he said.

"There are more effective ways to get it than this," Joe said.

He was right. So far, aside from a few low-level reporters, Kurt hadn't seen any great flood of interest.

In fact, after the initial announcement, few in the outside world seemed to care what they'd found. The only people who'd shown up in droves and stuck around were the experts in magnetism and superconduction.

Kurt gasped as he realized the truth. "The scientists," he said. "That's what they're after."

It took the briefest instant for Joe to agree.

Apparently, the group that needed more of everything had included know-how on their shopping list. If Kurt was right, they'd baited a trap to bring experts from all over the world here. He only hoped they hadn't snapped it shut yet.

Kurt grabbed the controls and gunned the throttle. As soon as they were moving again, he angled the nose of the *Barracuda* upward, and they began accelerating and climbing toward the gray light filtering in from above. They had to get to the surface and send a message to the *Argo*.

The science teams needed to be warned.

33

SEVERAL HOURS EARLIER, shortly after Kurt and Joe had first set-tled in on the seafloor beside the Liberty ship, Katarina Luskaya was packing her suitcase under the watchful eye of Major Sergei Komarov.

With everything that had happened, the high command had de-cided to abandon the mission for now.

"You became romantically involved with the American," he said, sounding as if he disapproved.

"Not as involved as I would have liked," she said brashly.

"This is not what we sent you here for," he reminded her.

She'd almost forgotten that, so much had gone on. "He was in charge of the dive area," she said. "I thought it would be better if he took a liking to me. That's what I see in all the old movies, you know."

The major eyed her suspiciously and then smiled just a bit, a slight crease appearing in his permanent five o'clock shadow. "That is a good answer," he said. "Whether it is true or not, you are learning."

She offered a sheepish grin in return and went back to packing as a knock at the door sounded. The major wasn't so bad. More like a big brother than Big Brother.

He went to answer the door, putting one hand inside his jacket where his Makarov pistol rested.

OUTSIDE IN THE HALLWAY, two men stood at the door. A short man with dark hair held what looked like a small monocular, his taller partner held what looked like a length of pipe, though it had frost on its curved top and some type of heavy electrical battery pack on one side.

The shorter man placed the monocular on the peephole in the door. "Movement," he said, looking into the scope. "It's the male. Three seconds."

He stepped away from the door, and the man with the pipe moved in, holding one end of it against the door chest-high.

"Yes," the deep Russian voice of Major Komarov said through the door. "What is it?"

"Now," the shorter man said.

The pipe man pressed a button. A split second of buzzing and then a sudden thud, and splinters frayed out around the end of the pipe where it was pressed against the door. It was a mini rail gun powered by superconducting magnets and carrying a two-pound sharpened metal spike as a projectile. At the press of a button it instantly accelerated the spike to 100 miles per hour, more than enough to fire it through the door and the Russian major.

The pipe man stepped back and delivered a kick to the door. The jamb snapped, and what remained of the door swung open.

———————

KATARINA LUSKAYA HEARD an odd sound and looked up. Slivers of wood were flying through the room. The major stumbled backward, clutching his stomach, a short spearlike piece of metal sticking out from his abdomen. Blood soaked his white shirt. He hit the ground without a word.

Katarina reacted slowly at first, but then she moved with all the speed in her body. She lunged toward the major as she heard the door being kicked in. Landing beside him, she grabbed for the weapon in his coat. She pulled it from its holster, thumbed desperately for the safety, and turned toward the door.

A boot slammed into her face, snapping her head to the side, before she could fire. She tumbled, lost her grip on the pistol, and felt someone on top of her an instant later.

Already stunned from the blow, she struggled only an instant before a rag soaked with chloroform was pressed to her face. She felt her hands go numb, and then nothing but darkness.

34

AS THE *BARRACUDA* raced for the surface, Kurt could hardly contain the anger he felt at being so foolish. He'd jumped to conclusions early on, assuming he and the *Argo* were the targets of these madmen even though in hindsight it was obvious that they held little real value.

He and Joe had to get a call off. They had to reach the surface so the shortwave radio could be used to contact the *Argo* thirty miles away in the harbor at Santa Maria.

He thought of the dead French scientists, wondered why they hadn't been taken, and then remembered that it seemed as if they'd put up a hell of a struggle. He guessed all of the scientists would face the same choice, fight or surrender. Most would give in; some would die.

He wondered what would happen to Katarina. He hoped she and her "chaperone" from the State were already at the airport and boarding a plane.

"Forty feet," Joe called out.

Kurt eased back on the throttle just a tad. Crashing the surface at full speed was a good way to catch air, and possibly even flip the sub.

He leveled out and they broke the surface.

"Make the call," he said.

He didn't have to give the order. He could hear Joe flipping the switches and the sound of the surface antenna extending.

"*Argo*, this is *Barracuda*," Joe said. "Please come in. We have an urgent transmission to complete."

While both of them waited, Kurt held the *Barracuda* steady. She was designed to fly underwater, but she rode less well on the surface.

"*Argo*, this is *Barracuda*."

The next voice they heard was Captain Haynes's, which was a surprise in and of itself, although Kurt could understand him waiting up all night worrying about the dangerous operation Kurt and Joe believed they were attempting.

"Joe, this is the captain," Haynes said. "Listen, there's a problem here. We've tried to—"

A sharp crack rang out, and the cockpit canopy was suddenly covered with dimples and pits. A shadow crossed toward them from the left. Another crack sounded, and Kurt realized it was a shotgun blast. This time, he saw a gaping hole appear in the left wing.

He gunned the engine and turned hard to the right.

Looking over, he saw a powerboat bearing down on them.

It looked like it was about to cut them in half. He had no choice. He pushed the nose down, and they went under. Water poured in through tiny holes in the canopy. The boat crossed over them, passing with a roar and a loud bang that jerked the *Barracuda* sideways.

Kurt looked to the right, seeing that the winglet that acted as a rudder had been torn off the right side. He felt water pooling at his feet, and noticed how sluggish the sleek little sub had already become.

He pulled back on the stick, and the *Barracuda* turned upward, breaking the surface and skipping across a wave before coming back down.

"Be quick," he said to Joe.

"Captain, are you there?" Joe said.

He could see the speedboat turning back toward them on a wide curve to the right. Out beyond it he saw another powerboat racing in to join the fight. He didn't know what they were going to do to escape, but he knew they had to finish the call. He heard Joe keying the mike, but there was no feedback, no static.

"*Argo*, this is *Barracuda*," Joe said. "The scientists are the target. Repeat, the scientists are the target."

Kurt heard a click as Joe let go of the transmit switch. They waited.

"No answer," Joe said.

Kurt turned his head, ready to order Joe to try again, when he saw the tail end of the *Barracuda*. The high-frequency antenna was gone. The sheet metal looked as if it had been chewed up by the prop of the passing boat.

"I got nothing," Joe said.

The powerboats were racing toward them again, in a staggered formation. The *Barracuda* had no hope of outrunning them. And the only other radio on board was the underwater transceiver, which had a max range of about a mile.

"Use the speed tape," Kurt said. "Plug over these holes."

As Kurt angled away from the approaching boats and slammed the throttle to the firewall, Joe thrashed around in his seat.

In a moment he'd retrieved the tape from a small compartment and was ripping short lengths from the roll and trying to seal up the holes in the canopy caused by the pellets from the shotgun blast.

"Here they come," Kurt said.

"You know this won't hold at depth," Joe said.

"I'll try to stay near the surface," Kurt said.

He heard the ripping and slapping of the speed tape, the roar of the approaching boats, and the muted boom of another shotgun blast. This time, the spray of pellets missed, splashing a foamy hole in the wave beside them.

"Dive," Joe said.

Kurt pushed the nose down. The water swirled over the canopy, and the *Barracuda* tucked in underneath the waves, leveling off at ten feet. Plenty of water was still seeping in, but it wasn't spraying like before, and Joe continued to peel and slap on the tape.

As soon as he was finished, he grabbed what looked like a tube of toothpaste but was actually an epoxy resin hardener. Ammonia-like fumes filled the cockpit as Joe smeared the resin all over the tape. The hardener would react with other resins in the speed tape and harden the patches in under a minute.

Eight feet under, Kurt watched as one wake and then another flashed across the top of them. He immediately turned left, a direction the *Barracuda* seemed to favor after the damage they'd suffered.

"You see any other holes?" Joe asked.

Kurt looked around. The patches and smeared resin made it look like someone had sprayed graffiti over half the cockpit. The fumes had his head pounding and eyes burning already. But the water was no longer pouring in. And as the patches hardened it would almost cease.

"Good work, Joe," he said.

"Not my most aesthetically pleasing job," Joe said, "but it's not meant to be patched while submerging under fire."

"Looks like art to me," Kurt said, straining to see past the mess and locate the powerboats he knew had to be approaching.

"In a future life I'm going to work on a NASCAR pit crew," Joe said.

"Let's just work on extending our current lives a little bit," Kurt said. "Can you think of any way to contact the *Argo*?"

Silence reigned as both of them racked their brains. Kurt certainly couldn't.

"The data link," Joe said. "We can e-mail them."

"E-mail?"

"Not exactly, but we can send them a data message. It goes up to a satellite and then comes down. As long as someone sees the telemetry equipment go on, they'll get it."

Kurt wondered how likely that was, picturing the screens on the telemetry unit coming on and no one there to see them. Certainly there was no reason for anyone to be monitoring them right now.

"Anything else?"

"Either that or we paddle all the way back to Santa Maria and use semaphores," Joe said.

"That's what I thought," Kurt said. "Key up the telemetry system, let me know when you're ready."

"We'll need thirty seconds on the surface for the satellite to lock."

"I don't think we'll have that long," Kurt said. As if to prove the point, he saw one of the wakes coming back toward them, not racing this time but rather matching their speed and then paralleling their course. The second wake did the same on the other side and to the rear.

Kurt turned hard to the left, back toward the undersea graveyard. The boats followed.

"They can see us, Kemo Sabe," Joe said.

"We're like a dying fish leaving a trail of blood," Kurt said, thinking of the bubbles the sub was probably venting.

A strange concussive sound reached them, and Kurt saw spray patterns in the water above and ahead. He guessed their pursuers were shooting into the water with the shotguns. Not a real danger, but one more sign of an impossible situation.

Maybe if they went deeper.

He put the nose down a few degrees.

The depth meter read 15 and then 20 and then—

Crack!

One of the taped sections broke away, and a new spray of water came in.

As Joe slammed the section back into place and began taping it over, Kurt brought the sub back up, leveling off at ten feet. He changed course again but to no avail.

"They're probably wearing those Maui Jim sunglasses," Joe said. "You know, the ones that let you see fish in the water."

Kurt felt like a fish in a barrel. Or a whale being hunted from above by a couple of harpoon boats. Sooner or later they had to surface, if not to send the message, just to survive.

Despite Joe's efforts, the *Barracuda* was slowly taking on water, not just from the buckshot holes in the windshield but from the damage in other places. Compartments normally sealed against water were now filling with it.

And, like whales, Kurt and Joe were faced with pursuers above that were faster, bigger, and well armed. At this point they had to do little more than follow Kurt and Joe in the *Barracuda* and wait for them to come up for air.

A flash lit the sea ahead and to the right. A concussion wave shook the sub even as Kurt turned hard left. A few moments later a second flash went off directly in front of them. Kurt actually saw the water expand, contract, and then crash into the nose of the *Barracuda*.

"Grenades," he said.

Cracks were beginning to appear in the canopy. Tiny almost invisible lines were spidering out from behind Joe's tape job as the Plexiglas weakened and began to fail.

When another explosion shook them, Kurt knew they didn't have much time. "Get your message ready," he said.

"We won't last ten seconds up there."

"We will if we surrender," Kurt replied, realizing that once Joe hit "Enter," there would be no visible sign of the data message being sent, and they could stand there with their hands up, hoping not to be shot as a distraction.

Joe said nothing, but Kurt heard him tapping away at the keyboard. "Ready," Joe said.

Kurt pointed the nose toward the surface, hoping they wouldn't get machine-gunned on sight. Just as they breached the surface, he cut the throttles.

The *Barracuda* slowed instantly, and the pursuing boats passed them.

"Now," he said.

Joe hit the "Enter" key as Kurt pressed the canopy switch and the cockpit rose.

"Come on," Joe was muttering. *"Rápido, por favor."*

Kurt stood, hands raised high in surrender, as the boats circled back toward him.

The *Barracuda* rocked back and forth on the waves, and the powerboats pulled up next to them. A half mile off Kurt saw a larger boat headed their way too.

"We surrender," Kurt said.

Two men with shotguns pointed their weapons at him.

An almost inaudible beep chirped from the rear of the cockpit, and Joe stood up as well.

"Message sent," he whispered.

Kurt nodded almost imperceptibly. Whatever happened now, whatever fate held for them, at least they'd sent their warning. He only hoped it was in time.

Across from him, one of the men put his weapon down and threw them a line. In a moment the *Barracuda* was tied up to the larger of the two powerboats, and Kurt and Joe were standing on board it with their wrists chained in proper cuffs.

Apparently, their foes had come prepared.

The larger boat approached, a 60-foot motor yacht of a design Kurt had never seen, it appeared far more utilitarian than anything he could remember in that class. It almost looked like a military vessel done up to pass as a pleasure craft.

It sidled up next to them, and Kurt saw a man in jungle fatigues standing at the bow, gazing down at him. It was the same man he'd seen the night before and also on the *Kinjara Maru*. The grin of a conqueror beamed from his face, and he jumped down onto the deck of the powerboat before the yacht had even bumped up against it.

He strode toward Kurt and Joe in their defenseless positions, looking ready to inflict pain. Kurt stared him down the whole way, never blinking or looking away. "Andras," he said through gritted teeth.

"Friend of yours?" Joe asked.

Before Kurt could answer, the man hauled off and slugged him in the jaw, sending Kurt crashing to the deck.

Kurt looked up, blood dripping from his mouth, his lip split open.

"Sorry," Joe said. "Forget I asked."

35

TWO MEN GRABBED THE CHAIN on Kurt's cuffs and yanked him back up to his feet. "I want you to see something," Andras said. He motioned for the motor yacht to pull forward. A brief spurt of power did the trick, and as its motor died once again the two boats knocked together. On the aft deck of the larger vessel, a mixed group of thirty or more men and women sat in cuffs and shackles with their backs to the far rail.

As painful as the split lip and wounded pride were, this sight caused a far deeper agony. Kurt recognized them as members of the various science teams sent to study the magnetism. Katarina sat among them, a dark bruise covering the right side of her face.

Her eyes rose up to meet his gaze and then looked back down at the deck, sad and forlorn, as if she'd failed somehow.

Kurt spat a mix of blood and saliva onto the deck. "What are you up to, Andras?" he said. "What is this all about?"

"I'm flattered that you recognize me at last," Andras said. "Of course a little insulted that it took so long. I thought I would have made a bigger impression all those years ago. Then again," he said, "I didn't recognize you either. But you didn't have silver hair when I knew you. I'd like to think I caused some of that."

Kurt felt his body tense, his instincts urging him to thrash and fight. The despair of the scientists, the purple bruise on Katarina's face, the arrogance that oozed from Andras's mouth like sewer water: all of it tested his control.

If he could have busted his chains, he would have lunged for Andras and fought him to the death right there and then, but cuffed and disadvantaged he could do little by antagonizing the man except act as a punching bag.

Andras walked around him in a wide circle, pontificating. Kurt had forgotten how much the man loved to talk.

"Once I heard of this NUMA," Andras said, "I should have guessed you were involved. It just sounds so Kurt Austin to me. All upstanding and forthright. I'll bet you say the Pledge of Allegiance to your flag every morning, and you probably all have patches and jackets and matching key chains."

"Yeah," Kurt said through his teeth. "Maybe I'll bring you some of our swag when this is over and you're serving a hundred years in solitary."

"Solitary?" Andras said. "How cruel. At least when I commit you to the sea, I won't be sending you down alone." He leaned closer. "And just to be clear, when this is over, you will be fish food and I will be a king."

Andras smiled, and Kurt found something odd in the words and the way Andras had whispered them to him alone.

As a chill of fear crept over him, Kurt wondered what malice Andras would visit upon them now. He prayed it wouldn't include Katarina. Despite those prayers, Andras hopped back onto the motor yacht and walked right toward her. He crouched down, put a hand on her bruised face, and then stood.

"Put Mr. Austin back in his little submarine," he ordered.

Three men came over to Kurt, two white, one black. They heaved him off his feet and literally threw him into the *Barracuda*.

"Mathias," Andras ordered, speaking to the African man, "chain him to the lift bar."

Kurt stared at the bar. It resembled a towel rack, mounted on the *Barracuda*'s hull just outside the cockpit. It was a hard point on the hull, the strongest spot on the entire submersible. Welded directly to the frame and made of carbon steel, the lift bar was designed to hold the entire submarine's weight when she was pulled from the water by the *Argo*'s crane.

It was not a spot Kurt wanted to be handcuffed to.

Mathias took a key from around his neck and undid Kurt's handcuffs. Immediately, Kurt swung an elbow, catching one of the white men in the mouth. Almost instantly the other white man slammed Kurt in the back of the head, crashing his skull against the frame of the cockpit.

Kurt felt a moment of dizziness. When his head cleared, he felt his arms draped over the outside of the *Barracuda*'s hull, even though his body was mostly in the cockpit. His cuffs had been undone and recuffed around the lift bar.

"And the other one," Andras said.

Joe was thrown in next to Kurt and given the same treatment. And while they sat there helpless, Andras grabbed a shotgun.

"Slugs," he demanded.

A box was handed to him, and he began filling the weapon with the solid projectiles. When it was fully loaded, he pumped it and walked around to the rear of the submarine. He fired two quick blasts into the impeller and then a third into the starboard wing.

The *Barracuda*'s hollow wing began to take on water. Andras raised the weapon and blew a hole in the port wing.

Kurt could not remember feeling so desperate. He knew they were about to go under, a horrible death awaiting them, and his mind grasped for a way to cheat it.

"You think drowning us ends this?" he shouted. "We know about you. Our whole organization knows."

Joe said nothing. Kurt could hear him breathing fast and deep, trying to pump his lungs full of air. Kurt knew he should be doing the same, but he couldn't help himself. He wasn't going out quietly.

As the water filled the *Barracuda*'s wings, Kurt frantically tried to shout something that might make Andras call a halt to the proceedings. If he could just convince him they were valuable enough to spare, even if it was just for a while, it would give them a chance.

"We know about your submarine," he shouted.

Andras raised an eyebrow. "Do you, now?" he said. "That's more than I thought you knew. But, at any rate, it's not mine."

Feeling the slightest bit of traction, Kurt pressed. "We know what you're up to. We know about the energy weapon."

This seemed to hit closer to the mark. Something in Andras seemed to stir, and his eyes began to light up. He stepped closer.

"Yes," he said. "That's the spirit. I knew you wouldn't give up."

It seemed as if he'd realized Kurt's desperate gambit and was taking great delight in being part of it.

"Come on, what else?" he shouted

Kurt didn't respond right away, and Andras grabbed Mathias and yanked the key and its rope from around the man's neck.

"Come on, now," he shouted sarcastically, "You're Kurt Austin of NUMA! Surely you can do better than that. Give me some more. Give me something that will make you matter."

Katarina stood and rushed forward as best she could. What she had in mind, Kurt didn't know—and most likely she didn't either—but she didn't get far. One of the armed men grabbed her and yanked her back, flinging her to the deck, and Kurt's blood burned even hotter.

"Time's running out, Austin," their tormentor said. He brought out the knife that he and Austin had already traded twice and flipped open the titanium blade. He locked it into place and tied the key's lanyard through one of the holes on the handle.

The *Barracuda*'s wings were awash now; any second the cockpit would start filling. There were precious few seconds left.

"We know about the superconductor," Kurt said, hating himself for being led along. "We know who sold it to you," he lied. "We know it was loaded on the *Kinjara Maru* in Freetown."

Andras looked down as if thinking. He glanced briefly at Mathias and then turned back to Kurt, smiling maniacally.

"Good enough," he said, moving forward with the knife in his hand. "Good enough for half anyway."

He leaned toward the *Barracuda*, raised his arm, and plunged the knife into the thin skin of her outer hull. The knife punched though and lodged tight, just out of Kurt's reach.

"Unfortunately, half won't save you both."

The water poured into the cockpit and swirled up around Kurt's knees. They were going down.

He glanced at Joe. "Whatever happens," he said, "follow my lead."

Joe nodded as Kurt filled his lungs, breathing deep and fast, as the *Barracuda* began to roll and pitch nose down.

The water churned, the nose of the sub disappeared, and the rest followed, dragging him and Joe under. The last sound Kurt heard clearly was Katarina screaming his name.

ON BOARD THE MOTOR YACHT, Katarina fell forward as the *Barracuda* went under. She stared at the swirling waters where the small sub had been moments before.

"No," she cried in a cracking whisper. "No."

She lowered her eyes and lay facedown on the deck, shoulders shaking as she sobbed.

Andras stared at her. "Now, that's a pitiful sight."

He walked toward her and crouched down. He put his fingers under her chin and lifted her face until she was looking in his eyes.

"Don't worry," he said. "I have far more pleasant plans for you."

She spat toward his face, but he stepped easily out of the way. "Why do you all try the same tricks?" he asked. He stood back, and kicked her for good measure.

Stepping away, he turned to the pilothouse. "Start the engines."

As the diesels rumbled to life beneath the deck, Mathias, the key master, came toward him. Mathias was not one of Andras's men; Djemma had put him aboard, perhaps to watch Andras.

"You gave them the key," Mathias said. "What if they escape?"

Andras laughed. "I almost hope that they do. It would make

things more interesting," he said. "But they won't," he added. "At least, not both of them."

"Why?"

"Because people have to pay for their crimes, and death is not much of a punishment." Andras glared at the key master with fury in his eyes. He felt a particular mix of hatred and respect for Kurt Austin. He had suffered his own pain at Austin's hands once upon a time.

Satisfied that Mathias had been put in his place, Andras turned toward the bow.

Mathias grabbed his arm, turning him. "I will inform Djemma. He will not find this so amusing."

Andras's eyes narrowed to slits. "It wasn't done for amusement."

"Then for what? I see no purpose to it."

"There is purpose in everything I do," Andras assured him. "This, for example."

In the blink of an eye, Andras raised a tiny pistol and fired it. The report was no louder than a cap gun. There was no shouting, no wailing in pain, or even much reaction on the part of Mathias. Only a suddenly limp appearance to his face as a tiny hole appeared in the center of his forehead. He stumbled back, cross-eyed and shaking, but not dead, not yet.

As the key master backed into the railing, Andras pulled the trigger again. Mathias tumbled backward, falling overboard and splashing noisily in the water.

He disappeared for a second and then bobbed to the surface, supported by the gray life jacket he wore. A trickle of crimson blood flowed from two small holes in his head, but he didn't move or even tremble.

Andras put the pistol away, raised the shotgun for all to see, and bellowed at the top of his lungs, "Anyone else have a problem with authority?" He looked around from face to face.

No one spoke, and Andras glanced at the boat's pilot.

"Let's go," he said.

The engines roared, and the motor yacht moved off. The two powerboats quickly joined it, and the three vessels raced off to the north, trailing long wakes out behind them.

THIRTY FEET BELOW THE SURFACE and dropping, Kurt held his breath as he and Joe rode the *Barracuda* down. As the pressure grew in his ears and the light from above started to fade, Kurt tried to calm himself. A plan was forming in his head, but first he had to fight off the natural reaction of fear and panic, knowing those things would kill him as quickly as anything else.

Without goggles, everything around them was a hazy blur, but it was a yellow-green blur, which meant that the *Barracuda's* lights were still on. And that meant the shotgun blasts hadn't taken out her electrical system. And even though she was full of water, Joe had given her instruments and controls that were waterproof up to great depths.

If he was right about their location, the seafloor would catch them near a depth of a hundred twenty feet, and then Kurt would take his shot at turning that floor into something other than a receptive grave.

It wouldn't be easy, but they had a fighting chance. In fact, the way Kurt figured things, their odds were almost even. It really all depended on just how the *Barracuda* landed.

He pinned his eyes open even though the salt water stung and burned them. With the sub's nose pointed down, the forward lights began to illuminate the seafloor ten seconds before they hit. Kurt saw light-colored silt with a few dark outcroppings that he assumed were volcanic rock.

It rose up at them faster than Kurt expected. He braced himself and was slammed forward as the nose of the little sub thumped the floor like a giant lawn dart.

The impact jarred him, but he kept his wits and immediately went into action.

With his hands still cuffed to the *Barracuda*'s lift bar, Kurt swung the rest of his body outside the sub, kicking and pulling. In seconds he saw Joe doing the same thing, following his lead as promised.

Their only hope was to create an air pocket to breathe in while the rest of the plan materialized. And the only way they could do that was to get the *Barracuda* over on its back and get the oxygen flowing from the sub's compressed-air tanks.

Then the inner section of the cockpit would act like an over-turned bucket and fill with air for him and Joe to breathe.

The only problem was, even though the *Barracuda* had hit nose down, the sub's weight heavily favored its lower half, where the main systems rested: the engine, the batteries, the impeller. And though the sub had hit the ocean floor almost vertically on its nose, it was already trying to fall backward.

The only force keeping it from settling keel down came from Kurt and Joe's efforts, but they would wane in less than a minute.

Kurt kicked hard and yanked and pulled. He could feel his lungs burning already. If they could just get the sub a few inches past vertical, the weight would become their ally.

Straining with everything he had, Kurt's feet found the silty ground and dug in. His left foot slipped through the muck and then jammed against a jagged rock, giving him some leverage.

This time as he pulled, the tail of the sub moved and began to fall toward him. He pulled again, getting both feet onto the rock's surface and leaning all his weight into it.

Finally, the nose slipped backward and the tail fell toward them, and Kurt had to duck inside to avoid getting hit by the wing. The sub settled slightly askew, and propped up at a thirty-degree angle by the ruined canopy.

It wasn't perfect, but it was good enough to rule phase one of his plan a success. But with his lungs screaming and his head pounding, he and Joe had precious seconds to get the air flowing or it would all be for nothing.

Neither he nor Joe could possibly reach the switch with their cuffed hands, but their feet were a possibility. Kurt stretched for the panel, pointing his toe and pressing near the oxygen switch time and again.

Each time nothing happened, and he felt his movements getting weaker and less coordinated. He fought the urge to open his mouth and inhale. He fought the shakes and tried one more time. He must have hit the light switch because everything went dark for a second and then lit up again.

By now his legs and arms felt as if they were made of lead, and he couldn't get them to do what he wanted them to do. His mind began to work against him as his subconscious whispered *Give up*.

The thought made him angry, and he willed himself to make one more attempt, tensing what was left of his muscles. Before he could move, a sudden rush of bubbles came pouring into the cockpit.

Kurt could see only the turbulence at first, but as the bubbles began to fill the upside-down cockpit he saw an air pocket forming above him in what would have been the foot well had the sub been right side up. He twisted his body, stretched his neck, and pushed his face into the rapidly forming sanctuary.

Exhaling a huge cloud of carbon dioxide, he sucked at the air. He coughed and sputtered as he breathed in some water, but he didn't care, he kept gulping. The air was life, another chance to roll the dice instead of dialing up a big fat seven on the bottom of the ocean.

As the bubble filled with air, he blinked away the salt water and looked around. The smiling face of Joe Zavala was next to him.

"What happened?" Kurt asked, realizing he had never actually taken his last shot at getting the air on.

Joe smiled and contorted his body, bringing a foot up out of the water. It was bare. No shoe, no sock. He wriggled his toes.

"Just like turning the tap off in the bathtub," he said.

Kurt felt a laugh trying to break through. He didn't have enough air for it yet, but the feeling was grand.

"I couldn't hit the switch," Kurt said. "I was blacking out."

"You must have been short on air," Joe said. "Long rambling conversations with lunatics on the surface will do that to you."

Kurt nodded. Next time he'd just keep his mouth shut and breathe through his nose. With the *Barracuda*'s air starting to feed into his body, he felt his strength returning.

"Never thought I'd owe my life to your gorilla-like feet," he said. "Good work."

Joe laughed, then turned serious. "The vents are full open, and the system is trying to compensate for the bleed-off. That'll keep us in this little oasis for a while, but the supply won't last. Maybe twenty minutes before it's exhausted."

Kurt looked around. The *Barracuda* rested at an odd angle, and while Kurt and Joe were able to keep their heads and shoulders in the air pocket without too much trouble their hands were still cuffed outside, and the bubbles were streaming out of an upturned corner of the cockpit.

Kurt took a breath, ducked his head down, and swung it outside. He looked around in the muted green light. There, dangling just beyond his reach, was the key, and the knife that Andras had stabbed into the *Barracuda*'s hull.

He had no idea why Andras would give them such a chance— maybe just to taunt them, maybe for some other sick reason—but Kurt didn't care at this point. He swung around, kicked his shoes and socks off just as Joe had, and stretched for the lanyard.

He touched it but couldn't grasp it on his first attempt.

He ducked his head back inside for another breath and then tried again. This time, he caught the lanyard with his toes and tangled it up around his foot. Then he brought up his other foot and kicked the knife firmly but with control.

It moved but didn't break loose. A second kick jarred it free, and Kurt reeled it in, gripping the length of thin twine as forcefully as his toes could.

He ducked his head back into the cockpit, reveled in another deep breath, and brought his foot to the surface.

Joe laughed. "I make you an honorary King Kong."

"I'll take it," Kurt replied. "But neither one of us is going to undo these cuffs with our feet."

Kurt took another breath, ducked his head back outside again, and swung around. With great effort he bent his knee and twisted his hip. It was awkward, but in a moment he'd brought his foot up beside their hands and the lift bar.

He felt the edge of the knife first and then the twine of the lanyard. He grabbed it and held tight.

Shifting his head back inside, he took another breath. He had the key in his hand. They were one step closer.

"Are you free?" Joe asked.

"Not yet," Kurt said. "I'm not exactly up to speed on playing Houdini. But it's only a matter of time."

Unable to see his hands from inside the cockpit, he had to go by feel. He reminded himself to be careful; above all else he could not afford to drop the key like some bungling idiot in a bad movie.

He slowed his breathing a bit and felt for the keyhole on the cuffs. Despite the cold water that was rapidly numbing his fingers, he could feel an indentation. He angled the key, jiggled it a bit, and slid it into place. It turned, and the cuff on his left hand clicked.

His left hand was free. He slid it out and was then able to slide the loose cuffs under the lift bar and bring them back into the cockpit.

"Voilà!" he said, raising his hands like an amateur magician for Joe to see.

"Beautiful," Joe said.

"And for your next trick?" Joe asked.

"I will release the amateur cochampion of the greater southern Azorean islands boxing league."

Joe laughed. "Make it quick, my hands are getting numb."

Kurt nodded. The water temperature around them was probably no more than 60 degrees. Hypothermia would set in fairly soon.

He ducked outside, went to work on Joe's cuffs, and found there was a problem. He jiggled and forced the key in, but it wouldn't turn. He tried again, but had no better luck. Pulling the key out, he surfaced back in the air pocket.

"I'm still locked up," Joe said.

"I know," Kurt said, studying the key. "Hold on."

He took a deep breath, went back into the water, and tried again. This time, he tried both cuffs but to no avail. The key could be forced in, but it didn't slide in smoothly and it wouldn't turn a millimeter once it was in.

Suddenly, he remembered Andras telling Kurt his answers were "good enough for half."

It hadn't made sense at the time, but now it did. He'd given them one key. It matched Kurt's handcuffs but not Joe's. That was exactly the man Kurt remembered, never content just to defeat his foes but almost needing to torture those he'd vanquished, to cause pain before landing the killing blow.

Whatever other reasons Andras might have had for giving Kurt a chance to escape, this twisted little game had to be part of it. He could imagine Andras watching the scene play out in his mind and snickering.

Like some malevolent deity in Greek mythology, he'd granted Kurt a chance at life, but Kurt could only accept that gift at the expense of leaving his best friend to die.

No way on earth Kurt was going to let that happen. He went back inside, popping up once again.

"I think you're misunderstanding the concept here," Joe said. "When you come back in, I'm supposed to be free."

"We have a problem," Kurt said. "The key doesn't fit."

Joe stared at the key and then at Kurt. "The guy used a different key on mine. I saw it. The cuffs are different."

Kurt stuffed the key in his pocket and began looking around in the cockpit for a tool to break Joe loose. He found a pair of screwdrivers, a set of Allen wrenches, and some other instruments—all of them miniaturized out of necessity to fit in the tiny cockpit of the sub.

"Anything in here that we could use for leverage?" he asked. Joe had built the sub. He'd know it far better than Kurt.

"Not really," Joe said.

"What about the lift bar?" Kurt asked, referencing what Joe was cuffed to. "Can we remove it or release it somehow?"

Joe shook his head. "Not without taking half the sheet metal off first."

"Can we break it?" Kurt asked, though he already knew the answer.

"It's the hardest point on the sub," Joe said, beginning to shiver from the cold water. "It's welded right to the frame. It's designed to support the sub's entire weight when lifted out of the water."

The two men stared at each other.

"You can't get me free," Joe said, voicing a dreaded realization.

"There's got to be a way," Kurt mumbled, thinking, and trying to fight what was becoming a mind-numbing cold.

"Not with anything we have on board," Joe said. "You should go. Don't stay down here and drown with me."

"Why? So you could come back and haunt me?" Kurt said, trying to keep Joe's spirits up. "No thanks."

"Maybe there's a boat on the surface or a helicopter," Joe said.
"Maybe someone got our message."

Kurt thought about that. It seemed unlikely. And if Joe was right
about how long the air supply would last on full blast, Kurt doubted
they had more than fifteen minutes or so to wait. Not enough time
for someone to get to them even if he could call for help.

He needed a different answer, a third way between leaving Joe
to drown and dying down there alongside him. What he needed was
a hacksaw or a blowtorch to cut through the lift bar or, better yet,
through the chains on Joe's cuffs.

And then it dawned on him. He didn't need a full-on blowtorch,
just something that burned hot and sharp. He remembered the
green tank he'd seen in the Constellation's cockpit when he'd rescued Katarina. Green tank meant pure oxygen. Pure oxygen burned
hot and sharp. Modulated just right, that could be his cutting torch.

He flipped open a small compartment door. Inside were the
Barracuda's emergency supplies. Two diver's masks, sets of fins, and
two small air tanks; ones he now wished contained one hundred
percent oxygen but were filled with standard air.

Twenty-one percent oxygen and seventy-eight percent nitrogen
didn't burn, but at least it could be breathed.

He pulled them out.

Behind the tanks he found a packet of flares and an emergency
locator transmitter, an ELT. An uninflated two-man raft completed
the kit. Enough to save them if they could get free.

Kurt took one air tank and strapped it to Joe's arm like a blood pressure cuff. He turned the valve and put the regulator up by Joe's mouth.

"Breathe through your nose until the air in the *Barracuda* runs out, then start drawing on this," he said.

Joe nodded. "Where are you going?" he asked. "Are you going to the surface?"

Kurt was pulling on a pair of small swim fins.

"Hell no," he said. "I'm going to the hardware store to get us a cutting torch."

Joe's gaze narrowed. "Have you lost your mind?"

"Years ago," Kurt said, pulling the mask down. He strapped the emergency air bottle to his own arm and turned the valve. "But that doesn't mean I'm crazy."

He took a test breath off of the yellow tank's regulator.

Joe's eyebrows went up. "You're serious?"

Kurt nodded.

"I hope it's not too far away, then," Joe added.

Kurt hoped not as well. He knew roughly where they were when they'd been captured. He thought he could make it.

He put the regulator in his mouth and ducked his face into the water to look for one more thing that he'd need to pull it off. He found it and then submerged.

"Hurry back," Joe said, but Kurt was already moving.

IF JOE HAD SAID ANYTHING ELSE, Kurt didn't hear him. He dropped down out of the *Barracuda* like a man swimming from the mouth of a cave and began kicking forward with powerful strokes.

The fins weren't full-sized, but they helped immensely, and with the mask on he could see clearly. But he still had to make a guess as to his whereabouts. He took out a piece of equipment he'd grabbed from the dash of the *Barracuda*: the magnetic compass.

It was just a dial in a sealed ball half filled with kerosene. As long as it hadn't cracked or broken, it would still perform its only function. And that was to point toward the most powerful magnetic source around. Normally, that would be the north magnetic pole. But in this case Kurt guessed it would point toward the magnetic tower of rock.

Though he was quite certain the whole thing was a fraud of some kind, the magnetism emanating from the tower was real. Whether it was being generated by some type of device implanted within the rock that sent out an electromagnetic current or was just a result of highly charged minerals being positioned in the right place, he couldn't say.

He lit one of the flares and held the compass out. It spun and dipped and slowly came onto a heading. The speed with which it centered told him it was reacting to something very strong, and he felt certain that it was pointing toward the tower.

Knowing he and Joe had been traveling basically to the east before they'd been caught, he triangulated in his head a direction to swim and lit out for the Constellation.

Five minutes later he came upon one of the ships in the graveyard. Two minutes after that he spotted the triple tails of the old aircraft. He pumped his legs hard, knowing both that time was running short and that he needed to keep as active as possible to delay the onset of hypothermia.

He ducked through the gaping hole in the aircraft's side, swam forward surrounded by the bubbles he was exhaling, and made it to the cockpit.

A skeletal form sat in the copilot's seat, still strapped in and stripped of everything organic. Only the plastic of the life vest, a pair of rusted dog tags, and the nylon-and-metal seat belt holding him in remained. Another few years and even the bones would be gone.

As he looked at the form for the second time, he realized that this plane's presence had been part of what threw him. Part of what blinded him to the hoax.

The skeleton in the copilot's seat, the CIA records of its secret mission, its departure from Santa Maria and its subsequent crash nine minutes later, all these things had lent some official credence to the mystery.

Putting the thought out of his mind, he reached down and released the clasp holding the oxygen tank to the floor. Picking it up, he studied the valve for signs of corrosion or decay. While there was some growth on the ring around the bottle's neck, there didn't appear to be much damage. He only hoped the thick steel tank still contained its pure cargo.

JOE ZAVALA REMAINED TRAPPED in the inverted hull of the *Barracuda*. His head and shoulders protruded into the cockpit and its lifesaving air pocket. His arms remained drawn awkwardly across his body, bent at the elbows and protruding out from under the cockpit's rim. He could no longer feel his hands or his feet. But he could still think, and he realized that running the air full blast was a mistake.

The excess was merely pumping itself out over the side before it could be used.

He managed to stretch his leg once again and use his toes, numb as they were, to jab at the switch.

The jet of air bubbles ceased. The cabin of the cockpit grew deathly quiet, and Joe continued to breathe slowly and count the seconds until Kurt returned with whatever he had in mind.

It was only a question of time, he told himself. Kurt would return no matter what. Joe knew his friend would never give him up until there was literally no other way. He just hoped that whatever Kurt had in mind worked and worked quickly.

As he waited in the silence, Joe found counting to be utterly tedious as a method of passing time. In fact, he'd honestly begun to believe it actually slowed time down somehow.

He decided to sing instead, both as a way to fight the silence to keep himself alert and as a way to take his mind off the fear and freezing sensation that was creeping through his body.

At first he considered singing something related to warmth, but somehow belting out the Supremes' version of "Heat Wave," or a similar tune, seemed like it would make things worse in this frigid environment.

Instead he settled on another song, one that seemed more appropriate. It took a second to bring the words together, but then he was ready.

"We all live in a yellow submarine . . ." he began.

Even Joe would have admitted it was more talking than singing at this point, but it was something to do. And it gave him some ideas.

"Note to self," he said. "Paint next submarine yellow. And include a heater that works underwater, even if the whole cockpit floods. And missiles, definitely missiles."

With that note filed away, Joe continued, singing louder with each chorus. He was on the third chorus, really beginning to get the hang of it, finding the acoustics of the inverted *Barracuda* to be most pleasing to the ear, when he realized he was getting delirious. The air was growing stale.

He stretched out his leg and banged it against the control panel. His feet were so numb, he could only feel the impact higher up on his calf, but he knew he was in the right area. He tapped and tapped again, continuing his awkward attempts, until the air jets came back on.

At the sound of the bubbles racing through, pouring into the cockpit, he rejoiced and began singing once again.

And then, mid-verse, Kurt Austin surfaced through the foam and bubbles, rudely interrupting his performance.

Kurt spat his own regulator out and lifted his mask. "Well, you're having a lot more fun than I expected."

"Practicing for *American Idol*," Joe managed. His teeth had begun chattering. "What do you think?"

"You may not be going to Hollywood, but I think we can get you out of this sub."

Kurt held up a green tank of some kind. "One hundred percent oxygen," he said. "I'm going to cut you loose."

Joe tried to smile. *The sooner, the better,* was all he could think.

Kurt was already working, jabbing at the barnacles on the tank's valve with a screwdriver. He managed to get it partially cleared, then stopped.

He showed the pinhole to Joe. "You think that's enough?"

"Test it."

Kurt worked the valve handle for a good minute, even banging it on the frame of the cockpit, until it would move. Finally, it gave. A few bits of debris blasted out of the valve's opening. Kurt held it underwater. Bubbles poured out in a narrow jet.

Kurt grabbed another flare from the survival kit and ripped a length of aluminum trim off the control panel. The thin strip of metal would be needed in his project. He looked at Joe. "It's gonna be hot," he said.

"That doesn't sound so bad," Joe said. Unlike Kurt, he hadn't moved for a good twenty minutes, and sitting still in 60-degree waters without a wet suit was enough to bring on hypothermia. He was getting close to that point.

"I'll be careful," Kurt said, pulling his mask back down.

"Kurt," Joe said very seriously. "I'm not dying down here. If you have to take my hand off, do it. I can't feel it anyway."

"And deprive the boxing world of your pugilistic skills?" he said. "Perish the thought."

"Kurt, I'm just saying—"

"Why don't you go back to singing," Kurt said. He held up the bottle, "I'm making a little request: 'Light My Fire' by the Doors."

With that, Kurt put his regulator back into his mouth and submerged.

Joe knew Kurt would do his best, but he also knew Kurt would do as he'd asked if necessary. And to save Joe from thinking about it, he wouldn't tell him in advance.

To take his mind off it, he did as Kurt had suggested . . . almost. This time, he'd give it everything he had, really belting it out.

"We all live in a yellow submarine . . ."

OUTSIDE THE *BARRACUDA,* Kurt heard Joe's warbling voice and was secretly glad to be out beyond the confines of the sub. Still, it made him smile.

He got up beside the lift bar. Joe's hands were curled up into balls from the cold. He pulled Joe's right hand as far from the left as he could. He then lit the new flare and held up the strip of aluminum.

He pressed the pointed end of the strip into the narrow links of the hardened steel chain that held Joe's hands together. Then he brought the oxygen bottle awkwardly to bear and turned the valve.

The jet of bubbles burst forth once again. He directed it toward the aluminum strip and Joe's chains and the burning tip of the flare. Immediately, what looked like a jet of fire burst forth.

It was awkward work. Kurt felt like he needed three hands, but by holding the flare and the aluminum strip in one hand and the oxygen bottle in the other he was able to keep his little torch operation working.

While it seemed like the oxygen was burning, Kurt knew it was actually an oxidizer. It didn't burn. It caused other things to burn hot and fast—in this case, the aluminum and, once a little cut appeared in Joe's chain, the steel in the chain links.

The jury-rigged setup smoked and bubbled and snapped unevenly. For a moment it looked as if it would go out, but it stayed lit. After thirty seconds he pulled the torch away. The links were glowing red but not yet melted. He brought the torch to bear once again. After another fifteen seconds, Joe's hands suddenly snapped apart.

He was free.

Kurt shut off the oxygen, thinking they might need it, and moved back into the sub.

Joe was all smiles. "I'd hug you," he said, holding up his balled fists, "but I'm too damn cold."

"How long we been down here?" Kurt asked.

"Thirty minutes," Joe said.

That sounded right to Kurt. Thirty minutes at one hundred feet. They'd need at least one decompression stop. With Joe's survival bottle largely untouched and what was left in his own, along with the green oxygen tank, Kurt was certain they could make it without any problem.

He slid Joe's mask over his face and forced the swim fins on his feet. With the life raft and the ELT beacon under his arm, Kurt led Joe out of the sub.

Outside, he twisted the beacon until it began to flash, released it, and watched it shimmy toward the surface.

He looked to Joe and pointed upward. Joe nodded and began to swim, kicking slowly for the surface.

Kurt took one last look at the *Barracuda* and noticed something shiny on the ocean floor beneath the lights. The knife. The same knife once again. Another taunt from Andras.

Angrily, he reached out and grabbed it, and then he began to swim after Joe and the distant flashing light from the ELT.

THEY BROKE OUT INTO THE DAYLIGHT ten minutes later. Kurt tried to keep their ascent to one foot per second, as per the old Navy standard rules. But just to be sure, he and Joe stopped at forty feet for two minutes and then at twenty feet for three more.

Finally breaking into the sunlight was a glorious feeling. Kurt pulled the inflation cord on the raft. The CO_2 charge filled and expanded the small raft in a matter of seconds. It unfolded and stiffened with full inflation.

"Ready for passengers," Kurt said.

He helped Joe climb aboard and then pulled himself in.

Once they'd made it into the raft, lying still and flat was highly recommended. Kurt was pretty certain he could do nothing else.

He lay there breathing, aching and exhausted. He was surprised at how cold and numb he felt now compared to their time down below.

After several minutes with no sound but the slap of the water against the side of the raft, Joe spoke. "Where's the driest place on earth?"

"I don't know," Kurt said, thinking. "The Atacama Desert maybe."

"Next adventure we're going there," Joe said. "Or somewhere hot and dry."

"I'm not sure the National Underwater and Marine Agency has a lot going on where it's hot and dry," Kurt said.

Joe shook his head. "Dirk and Al spent some time in the Sahara once."

"True," Kurt said. "I'm not sure they would recommend it though."

"Hot and dry," Joe said firmly. "I won't take no for an answer."

Kurt laughed. It really didn't sound too bad right now.

He was painfully aware how close they'd come to dying. It wouldn't have taken much to tilt the scales from life to death for either of them. Kurt knew his overconfidence about what their foes were doing was half the reason for that.

He looked over at Joe, who was finally beginning to show some color in his face.

"I was wrong," he said to Joe.

Joe turned his head awkwardly. "What?"

"I was wrong about St. Julien," Kurt added. "He's a gourmet. He would never chow down at some all-you-can-eat buffet."

Joe stared at him for a moment and then started laughing and coughing all at the same time. Kurt laughed too. He knew Joe understood what he was trying to say.

"We all screw up, Kurt," he said. "You just do it bigger than the rest of us."

Kurt nodded. It sure seemed that way.

He looked out over the surface of the water. Thirty yards away he saw the emergency locator beacon, riding the swells and flashing. He hoped rescue would come soon because there was still work to be done.

The way he saw it, Andras had screwed up even bigger than he had. He'd left Kurt alive and stirred the bitter embers of vengeance in his heart.

Off the coast of Sierra Leone, June 26

DJEMMA GARAND STOOD near the edge of the helipad on the false oil platform given the number 4. This platform contained the control center of his weapon and would be his command post if he ever needed to use it.

The control center sat three stories above the helipad, the glass enclosure of its main room jutting out like the bridge on a ship. At the moment Djemma's attention lay elsewhere.

He stood, leaning up against a rail, in the shadows, his eyes hidden behind the ever-present green shield of the Ray-Bans he wore. Out in the center of the helipad, wilting under the blazing equatorial sun, stood the captured scientists from the various teams who had flocked to the lure he'd offered. The Azorean magnetic anomaly.

Djemma smiled at his own cunning. So far, all things were falling in line with his plan.

With the scientists forced to line up as if for inspection, he waited. Each time one of them tried to sit or get out of line,

Andras or one of his men would march out and threaten them with reprisals far worse than standing in the sun. At all times a few men roamed the perimeter with machine guns in their hands.

Finally, when the moaning and complaining began to lessen, Andras came over to where Djemma rested in the shade.

"Leave them out there any longer and you're going to fry their brains," Andras said. "Which, if I'm not mistaken, isn't what you brought them here for."

Djemma turned to Andras. He would not respond to the man's questions.

"There were thirty-eight experts in superconduction, particle physics, and electromagnetic energy on Santa Maria," he said. "I count only thirty-three prisoners. Explain the discrepancy."

Andras turned his head, spit over the side of the rig, and looked back at Djemma. "The French team took a core sample of the tower. It could have blown the whole operation before we made our move. I had to eliminate them. The Russian expert turned out to be a spy. She tried to escape twice. I killed her as well."

Andras did not blink as he spoke, but he did not seem to like explaining himself.

"And Mathias?" Djemma asked.

"Your little key master forgot his place," Andras said. "He questioned me in front of the others. I couldn't allow that."

For a moment Djemma was angry. He'd placed Mathias with Andras to watch him, perhaps to keep him under control. No doubt that was half the reason Andras had killed him.

Still, Djemma could not show his anger. Instead he began to laugh. "What leader could afford such insolence?"

He pushed off the rail and stepped away from Andras, walking out into the hot sun to address the assembled group.

By the time he'd reached a spot in front of them a trickle of sweat was running down the side of his face. The scientists looked as if they might soon pass out. Most were from cooler climates, America, Europe, Japan. Seeing their weakness, he took his sunglasses off. He wanted them to see his strength and the fire in his eyes.

"Welcome to Africa," he said. "You are all intelligent people, so I will dispense with the games and secrecy. I am Djemma Garand, the president of Sierra Leone. You will be working for me."

"Working on what?" one of the scientists asked. Apparently, they hadn't steamed the starch out of everyone yet.

"You will be provided with the specifications and requirements of a particle accelerator I have built," Djemma said. "You will have a single job: to make it more powerful. You will of course be paid for your work, much as I was once paid for working in the mines. For your efforts you will each receive three dollars a day."

To his right one of the scientists, a man with short gray hair and uneven teeth, scoffed.

"I'm not working for you," he said. "Not for three dollars a day or three million."

Djemma paused. An American of course. No people of the world were less used to being powerless than Americans.

"That of course is your option," he said, nodding to Andras.

Andras stepped forward and slammed a rifle butt into the man's gut. The scientist crumpled to the deck, was dragged away toward the edge of the platform, and summarily thrown off.

His scream echoed as he fell and then stopped suddenly. The water was a hundred twenty feet below.

"Check on him," Djemma said. "If he lived, renew our offer of employment."

Andras motioned to a pair of his men and they double-timed it over to the stairwell. Meanwhile, the rest of the scientists stared at the edge over which their associate had just been thrown. A few covered their mouths; one of them went to her knees.

"In the meantime," Djemma said, quite pleased that someone had been stupid enough to resist right off the bat, "I will explain our incentive program. One I know you will find most generous. You will be divided into four groups and given the same information to work with. The group that comes up with the best answer, the best way to boost the power of my system, that group will get to live."

Their eyes snapped his way.

"One member from each of the remaining groups will die," he finished.

With that, Djemma's men moved in and began to separate them.

"One more thing," Djemma said loudly enough to stop the proceedings. "You have seventy-two hours for your initial proposal. In the event I have no satisfactory answer by then, one member of each group will die, and we shall start again."

As the now thirty-two members of the world's scientific community were separated and hustled toward the waiting elevators in the center of the rig, Djemma Garand smiled. He could see the shock and fear in their faces. He knew that most, if not all, would comply.

He turned to Andras and another African man in uniform, a general in his armed forces.

"Get back to the *Onyx*," he said. "Get her into position."

Andras nodded and moved off. The general stepped up.

"It is time, old friend," Djemma said. "You may begin to take back what is rightfully ours."

The general saluted and then turned and was gone.

39

Washington, D.C., June 27

KURT AUSTIN STEPPED OFF the elevator on the eleventh floor of the NUMA headquarters building on the shore of the Potomac River in Washington, D.C. He moved slowly, his body battered, his ego suffering from the badly missed call that had taken them out to the tower of rock in the dark of night.

He was walking with noticeable pain. His face and arms were peeling from saltwater sores and eight hours waiting for rescue in the burning sun. His ribs were sore from the pipe attack, and his cheekbone, the bridge of his nose, and his lips were creased with healing scabs where Andras and his thugs had pounded him and split the skin.

Adding insult to injury were the hours sitting in the *Argo*'s tiny conference room, answering questions from the Spanish and Portuguese authorities with Joe and Captain Haynes, and then a fourteen-hour trip by plane from Santa Maria to Lisbon and over to D.C.

The least someone could have done was spring for business class.

Now fighting jet lag, exhaustion, and his wounded pride, Kurt pressed forward toward another conference room, where he and

Joe would discuss with Dirk Pitt and members of the U.S. Navy and the National Security Agency everything they'd already explained a half a dozen times. All the while, whatever trail Andras had left grew colder and faded away.

He neared the end of the hall and despite the pain and fatigue spotted a reason to smile and keep going. At the door to the conference room he saw Gamay Trout. It troubled him that she was alone.

They hugged, and he could feel that much of her usual self-assurance was missing.

"You don't look so good, Kurt. How do you feel?"

"Never better," he said.

She smiled.

"Paul?" he asked.

"He's still unconscious," she managed.

"I'm sorry."

"His EEG is improving, and a CAT scan showed no damage, but I'm scared, Kurt."

"He'll come back," Kurt said hopefully. "After all, look what he's got waiting for him."

She tried to smile, and then grabbed the door handle and pushed through.

Kurt followed her in and sat protectively beside her. Joe arrived a moment later and sat on her other side. Dirk Pitt, Hiram Yaeger, and some brass from the Navy held positions down the table from them. At the head of the table, a suit from the NSA took center stage.

Dirk Pitt stood and explained. "I know you've all been through a lot, but we're here because the situation has gone from bad to worse."

He waved toward the man in the suit. "This is Cameron Brinks from the NSA. He and Rear Admiral Farnsworth are spearheading the response to what we believe is a very present threat to international peace."

Cameron Brinks stood up. "We have to thank you men for discovering and bringing this threat to our attention. Like you, we believe a well-financed or even nationally backed group has developed a directed-energy weapon of incredible power. If the extrapolations from the data are correct, this weapon could undermine the current world socio-military balance."

Kurt wasn't sure what exactly the term *socio-military balance* meant, but it sounded like a politician's made-up parlance, and he guessed Brinks was more a politician than a man of action. That meant they were in for a long speech. *Great.*

Brinks continued. "After consulting with Mr. Yaeger, and also running our own studies, we've concluded that this weapon uses a system of particle acceleration similar to one suggested years back for the Strategic Defense Initiative's anti-missile shield."

Kurt considered what Brinks was saying, and he allowed some of his aggravation to dissipate. At least these men seemed to grasp the danger.

"To make matters worse," Brinks said, "the kidnapped scientists are precisely the kind of people one would need to improve on whatever these terrorists are already in possession of."

"Do we have any idea who they are?" Kurt asked.

Brinks nodded. "In addition to the individual you identified, we've two pieces of credible evidence suggesting their base of operations is in Africa."

"Africa?" Gamay said.

"Yes, Mrs. Trout," Brinks replied. "Early this morning a body was recovered two miles south of the spot where Kurt and Joe were rescued."

Brinks nodded to an aide, who brought photos out that were passed to Kurt and Joe.

"Recognize him?" Brinks asked.

The water had bloated the man's face, but it wasn't enough to hide his identity.

"Key master," Joe whispered.

Kurt nodded. "This guy was with Andras," he said. "What happened to him?"

"Twenty-two, Old West style," Brinks said. "Right between the eyes. Any idea why?"

"He was alive when we went down," Kurt said. He put the photo away. "Who is he?"

"He's been identified as a citizen of Sierra Leone," Brinks said. "A former major in their armed forces, perhaps even a bodyguard for the president, Djemma Garand."

"Sierra Leone," Kurt said. This was the second time that nation's name had popped up.

Brinks nodded. "As odd as it sounds, the links are starting to point to a connection with that country. We know the superconducting ore was transferred in Freetown, but until now we thought it was the work of a group of mercenaries manning the docks. Your friend Andras may have been one of them."

Kurt didn't like hearing Andras referred to as his friend, however facetiously. Beyond that, something sounded odd about this assessment. "Sierra Leone is one of the poorest countries in the world. They can barely feed and clothe their people. You're telling me they have the wherewithal to create a particle accelerator using advanced superconductors?"

"We have this man's body to prove a link," Brinks said, not looking particularly thrilled to have questions coming at him. "We have other intelligence suggesting there may be a connection, including some odd military mobilizations of late."

"Okay, so what are we doing about it?" Kurt asked, unable to take any more preamble.

Brinks retrained his gaze on Kurt. "To begin with, greater surveillance of the nation is beginning. Until now we haven't much reason to keep a close eye upon them. But we're starting to."

"What else?"

"Believe it or not," Brinks said, "we still think your initial guess is correct. These people undoubtedly have to be operating from a submarine. Portuguese divers have been all over that rock tower and they've found hidden tunnels designed to funnel the current through turbines, banks of batteries, and powerful electromagnetic coils. All designed to create the appearance of a magnetic anomaly. The construction would have required extensive use of submersibles."

Kurt felt a small amount of vindication, but he'd still been wrong in a highly costly manner.

"And?" he asked.

"And the three of you are to be assigned to a Navy task force charged with finding this submarine," Brinks said. "Mrs. Trout will work with the Navy acoustics team in trying to refine the signature left on the sonar tapes from the attack on the *Grouper*."

"And what are we going to do?" Kurt asked, growing aggravated at what looked like a giant detour.

"Because of your experience in salvage operations and construction of submersibles, you two will be assigned to ASW teams that will be sent out looking for this sub."

Kurt wasn't sure he'd heard correctly. "Looking for it?" Kurt said. "You mean wandering around the ocean, listening to hydrophones and hoping to pick up something more than whales making out?"

Neither Brinks nor Admiral Farnsworth reacted.

"Are you kidding me?" Kurt continued. "There's forty million square miles of ocean out there. And that's if these idiots are still sailing around, waiting to get caught. More likely they've parked that thing under a shed somewhere and are on to the next step in their plan."

"Our ASW teams are the best in the world, Mr. Austin," the admiral said.

"I know they are, Admiral, but how many are you going to spare?"

"Seven frigates and twenty aircraft," he said. "We'll also be using both the SOSUS line and other listening stations in the South Atlantic."

That was better than Kurt had expected, but paltry in comparison to the need. And unless Kurt had missed something, they didn't even know what they were looking for yet.

"Did we pick up anything on the SOSUS during any of the incidents?" he asked.

"No," the admiral admitted. "Nothing but the sounds of the *Kinjara Maru* breaking up on her way down and the explosions of the torpedoes during the attack on the *Grouper*."

"So all we have is the garbled tape from the *Matador*," Kurt said.

"Do you have a better idea, Mr. Austin?" Brinks asked pointedly.

"Yeah," he said. "I'm going to track down Andras. And when I find him, that'll lead us to whoever he's working for."

"CIA's been looking for him for years," Brinks said dismissively. "He never stays in one place long enough for anyone to get a line on him. What makes you think you're going to succeed where they failed?"

"Because there are certain rocks they don't like to turn over," he said bluntly. "I have no such qualms."

Brinks pursed his lips, looking disgusted. He turned back to NUMA's Director. "Mr. Pitt, would you do something, please?"

Dirk leaned back in his chair, looking as casual as could be. "Sure," he said to Brinks and then turned to Kurt. "Are you serious about this plan?"

"Yes, sir," Kurt said. "I know someone who Andras used as a contact years ago. I believe he's still active."

"Then what are you doing wasting your time with us? Get your butt moving."

Kurt smiled and stood. "Yes, sir," he said.

"This is ridiculous," Brinks said.

"And take Joe with you," Pitt added, "if he wants to go."

"Thought you'd never ask," Joe said.

Brinks ground his teeth and leaned over the table, looking at Dirk Pitt.

"One call and I'll override this," he said.

"No you won't," Pitt said confidently. "For one, Kurt's right. Sticking him and Joe on a destroyer is a waste of resources. For another, it puts all our eggs in one basket: your basket. Which I realize, having spent so much time in Washington lately, is half the point. You get the credit if we succeed and you blame them and

NUMA if you fail. Simple math. But you forgot a very important variable and that is: I don't work for you and neither do these men. And I'll be damned if I'm going to let you put the country or maritime community at risk for your own personal political agenda."

Brinks looked about like a man who'd been gored in a bullfight. Even Admiral Farnsworth seemed pleased with the outcome, no doubt wondering what he needed a couple of NUMA civilians on his boats for anyway.

The admiral chuckled and then looked over at Gamay. "We could still use you, Mrs. Trout. Our sonar teams are very friendly."

"I'll do my best to help," she said.

Kurt stepped to the door.

"One thing, Kurt," Dirk said.

Kurt looked back.

"Stay on the narrow road. This is a mission for us," Pitt reminded him, "not a sortie of revenge."

Kurt understood Dirk's concern. He could feel the conflict inside himself, and no doubt it was easy for someone like Dirk Pitt to pick up on.

He nodded to Pitt, glanced at Brinks, and then headed for the door. He opened it and ran right into one of NUMA's administrative assistants, a young woman he didn't know.

"Are you okay?" Kurt asked.

The young woman nodded. "I just came to give Mrs. Trout some news."

Kurt opened the door wider and let her in.

"Paul's awake," the woman said. "He's asking for you."

40

Freetown, Sierra Leone, June 28

DJEMMA GARAND STOOD TALL in the commander's position in the turret of an aging Russian-made battle tank. His nation had only forty of them, and as Djemma sprung his nationalization plan on the world he intended to put together a show of force in the most public way possible.

While infantry units supported by helicopters and militiamen took control of the mines out in the country, Djemma and twenty of his precious tanks rolled through downtown.

They traveled in a long column, flanked by missile-carrying transports and jeeps and armored personnel carriers. They flowed through the center of town to the sound of thunderous cheers. Tens of thousands of civilians had come out on their own after hearing Djemma promise them better jobs and higher wages once the nationalization was complete. Thousands more had been prodded to line the parade route by the subtle suggestions of Djemma's security apparatus.

As the convoy rolled past, the cheers sounded genuine, and Djemma took pride in what he was doing. His force was headed to the port in a ceremonial gesture. It was already in his hands, as was the large refinery a few miles to the north and the airport and the few factories on Sierra Leone's soil.

Riding beside him, a handpicked reporter and cameraman recorded the event.

"President Garand," the reporter said, almost yelling to be heard over the roaring tank engine and its rumbling, squeaking tracks, "I understand you've informed the IMF that Sierra Leone will no longer be making payments on its outstanding portfolio of loans. Is this correct?"

"Yes," Djemma said. "We are tired of breaking our backs just to pay interest."

"And that choice is tied to today's actions?" the reporter asked right on cue.

"Today is a day of liberty," Djemma said. "Once upon a time, we became free of colonialism. Today we are freeing ourselves from a different kind of oppression. Economic oppression."

The reporter nodded. "Are you concerned that there will be reprisals for this action?" the man said. "Surely the world will not stand by while you violate the property rights of dozens of multinational corporations."

"I am only obeying the principle of an eye for an eye," Djemma said. "For centuries they have violated the property rights of my people. They have come here and taken from us precious gems and metals and treasures and given us only pain in return. A cook in one of these companies' executive lunchrooms makes twenty times more than a miner who toils in heat and danger, risking his life every day. Not to mention the executive who does less work than the cook."

Djemma laughed as he spoke. A little good cheer went a long way.

"But the mines, the refinery, the infrastructure, these things cost billions of dollars in investment money," the reporter said.

"And my people have already paid for them," Djemma said. "In blood."

The tanks rolled on, rumbling toward the dockside cranes. A small cloud of dark smoke rose into the sky to the west of the port. It was definitely a fire, but Djemma doubted there had been any real resistance.

Perhaps someone had done something foolish. Or perhaps the black smoke had nothing to do with the events. A car or truck fire or some other industrial incident.

No matter, it made for a good visual. "Film the smoke," he said to the cameraman. "Let them know we mean business."

The cameraman turned and zoomed his lens, getting a closer shot of the rising cloud. His recording, and the video of Djemma aboard the tank, would play in endless loops on CNN, FOX, and the BBC.

In twenty-four hours people around the world would know all about him and a country most had never heard of. By then Djemma would have most of the foreign nationals rounded up and placed on flights back to their respective countries.

Their nations would bluster and bluff, and freeze Sierra Leone's all-but-nonexistent foreign assets. They'd demand he explain himself, which he would gladly, again and again if necessary. In his mind the actions were legitimate; why should he not speak of them?

And then they'd come to him, demanding all kinds of things. The negotiations would begin. They would try very hard not to offer anything at first, lest they be seen to be giving in. But it would matter little as he would not budge.

They would grow angry and pound the desk and rant and rave and threaten things. And then it would get dicey, for with the nations of the world finally interested in him Djemma would not give in but instead he would demand more.

He knew the risks. But for the first time in two thousand years an African general was in possession of a weapon that could bring down an empire.

PAUL TROUT WAS SITTING UP in his hospital bed. His wife stood nearby. She'd been hugging and kissing him and squeezing his hand non-stop for an hour. It felt good despite all the other pains in his body.

His back ached. His head hurt and his thoughts came slowly, like he'd been overmedicated or had too many glasses of red wine. Still, he felt surprisingly good, considering what Gamay was telling him.

"I don't remember any of that," he said after hearing her explanation of the escape from the *Grouper* and the fact that he'd been in a coma for the past four days.

"What do you remember?" she asked.

He reached back, clawing at the darkness in his mind. Since he'd awoken, random thoughts had been popping into his head. Like a computer rebooting itself after an unexpected shutdown, it seemed as if his mind was reorganizing things. The smell of food from the commissary brought an odd thought to the forefront.

"I remember that one Thanksgiving in Santa Fe when you burned the turkey and then admitted that I was right about how to cook it."

"What?" she said, laughing. "That's what you remember?"

"Well . . ." he said. "To actually be right about something and have you admit it all in the same day was a pretty rare experience."

She pursed her lips. "I've heard that people with head trauma sometimes come out of it with new skills they never had before. It hasn't happened with you, my love. You were never a comedian and you're still not."

He laughed this time. His head felt as if it was clearing a bit more each second.

"I remember the sun shining off the sea," he said. "And that we were getting ready to take the *Grouper* down. And I was thinking we shouldn't both go."

As it turned out they had worked together seamlessly and almost made it back to the surface. He didn't remember it, but Gamay seemed to indicate that if he hadn't been there she would have died.

"So what do we do now?" he asked.

She filled him in on the rest of the details, finishing with her next duty. "I'm flying out to an antisubmarine frigate in the Atlantic this time tomorrow. We'll be working on the sonar tapes."

Paul stared at her. He understood the call of duty and he wasn't about to interfere. But he could not shake the great sense of almost having lost her even if he couldn't recall the details.

He threw the sheet back. "I'm going with you," he said, swinging a leg over the edge.

She put a hand on him. "Paul."

"I'm out of the woods," he insisted. "The doctor said so. Besides, I've worked with sonar a lot more than you have. Specifically, the GEO sounder unit on the *Matador*."

He could tell she was against it and worried. After what had happened, who wouldn't be? But he wasn't staying behind.

He forced his way out of bed and stood, a little unsteady. He was so tall, the hospital gown looked like a miniskirt on him.

"Don't these come in long?" he said.

Gamay continued pouting.

"We'll be on a warship," he said. "Armor plating, missiles, guns, torpedoes. We couldn't be safer."

She shook her head and then exhaled sharply. "Fine," she said. "I never could talk sense into you anyway."

He laughed, pressed the buzzer for the nurse, and started looking for a robe or something to cover himself up with.

"One thing," she said seriously.

He turned.

"I'm not going back in the water," she said.

He cocked his head. "What?"

"I'm not going back in the water," she said. "Not in a submersible, not in a dive suit, or any other way. I'm not ready for that."

As long as he'd known her, Gamay had never been afraid of anything, but the fear was plain in her voice now.

"You don't remember it," she said. "In some ways I think you're lucky on that count. But it was horrible."

"We'll stay on deck," he said. "Or in our air-conditioned quarters. Hopefully, near the mess and the soft-serve ice-cream machine."

He grinned, hoping to coax a smile from her, but she didn't offer one, and Paul began to worry about her in a way he never had before.

42

Singapore, Malaysia, June 30

TWENTY-EIGHT HOURS AFTER being freed from the NSA's clutches, Kurt and Joe landed in Singapore. They'd boarded a flight at Dulles, gladly paid through the nose for first-class tickets, and literally flew to the other side of the world.

A trip to the hotel to unpack and a call to an old friend who'd helped him years back had left Kurt with nothing to do but get some sleep. As it turned out, he was too damn tired to make it off the couch and fell asleep right there.

His two-hour nap ended when the phone rang in the darkness.

Startled awake as if he'd been jabbed with a cattle prod, Kurt lunged for the phone. He grabbed it as he tumbled off the couch, picking up the receiver just in time to prevent it from going to the message system.

"The White Rajah," a voice he didn't recognize said.

"What?" Kurt asked.

"You are Kurt Austin?"

"Yes."

"I was told to call you," the voice said. "And to explain where you will find what you're looking for. The White Rajah."

"Wait," Kurt said. "What is the—"

The phone line went dead, and a dial tone soon followed. Kurt placed the receiver back on the cradle and leaned against the front of the couch.

"Where am I?" he mumbled to himself.

He remembered flying, changing planes at LAX, and then part of the next flight. He remembered checking in at the hotel. "Oh yeah," he said. "Singapore."

He looked around. The room was utterly dark except for a clock radio between the beds opposite him. The clock read *7:17 p.m.* It felt like three in the morning.

Kurt stood awkwardly and pounded on the door to the adjoining room.

"Get up," he grumbled to Joe. "Time to go to work."

The door opened seconds later. Joe stood there, clean-shaven, hair gelled, wearing an Armani shirt and white linen slacks.

Kurt stared at him dumbfounded. "Don't you sleep?"

"The night calls me," Joe said, smiling. "Who am I to refuse?"

"Yeah, well, somebody else called me," Kurt said. "So while I shower, you find out what on earth the White Rajah is. I'm guessing it's a hotel or a bar or a street."

"Is that where we're going?"

Kurt nodded. "Someone's going to meet us there," he said.

"Who?"

"That's the thing," Kurt said. "I don't have any idea."

FORTY MINUTES LATER, looking refreshed and like a more conservative version of Joe, Kurt Austin marched into the friendly confines of the White Rajah, a restaurant and bar that had once been an old

English gentlemen's club in the Victorian era, when the English had a substantial influence on the island of Malaysia.

Kurt wandered through several large rooms with exquisitely carved mahogany paneling, hand-blown glass-block skylights, and overstuffed leather chairs and couches that looked as if Churchill himself might have once sat on them.

Instead of bridge tournaments between retired members of the British East India Company and captains of industry smoking pipes and thick cigars, he saw the young and wealthy of Singapore dining on oysters and knocking back expensive drinks.

An informal count registered the crowd to be mixed about fifty-fifty: half were Western expatriates and the rest local citizens or visiting Asian businessmen.

Circling back around to the front of the house, Kurt took a seat at the main bar, which appeared to be made from a thin sheet of alabaster lit from below. It looked almost like glowing amber.

"Can I get you something?" a bartender quickly asked.

Joe smiled. Kurt knew he'd been to Singapore before. "I'll have a Tiger," he said.

"Perfect choice," the bartender said, then turned to Kurt. "And you, sir?"

Kurt was still looking around, scanning for someone, anyone he might recognize, including the contact he'd phoned upon landing. No one looked familiar.

"Sir?"

"Coffee," Kurt said. "Black."

The man nodded and hustled off.

"Coffee," Joe said, apparently surprised at Kurt's choice of beverage. "Do you have any idea what time it is?"

Above them blue light flickered through the glass blocks of the skylight; either heat lightning in the distance or an approaching thunderstorm.

"I don't even know what day it is," Kurt said. "I barely know what planet we're on."

Joe laughed. "Well, don't blame me if you're up all night."

"Somehow," Kurt said, "I have a feeling I'm going to be."

Kurt looked at the wall behind the bar. A six-foot canvas displaying a strapping Englishman in colonial garb stood front and center.

"Sir James Brooke," Kurt said, reading the inscription on the brass plate at the bottom.

The bartender returned with their drinks and seemed to notice the focus of their attention. "The White Rajah," he said.

"Really?"

"He put down a rebellion against the Sultan of Brunei in 1841 and was granted the title Rajah of Sarawak. He and his family ruled a small empire in what we now call Kuching for about a hundred years, until the Japanese invaded in 1941."

"But Sarawak is across the strait," Kurt said, knowing Sarawak and Kuching were on the neighboring island of Borneo.

"Yes," the bartender said. "But when the war ended, the family gave the territory back to the British Empire. The club here was renamed in his honor."

As the bartender shuffled off, Kurt took a sip of the rich, bold coffee, another step on the road to feeling like himself again.

Joe looked over at him. "So what are we doing in Singapore?" he asked. "Aside from getting a history lesson?"

Kurt began to explain. "Twelve years ago I did a salvage job down here," he said. "One of my last jobs for the company before joining NUMA."

Joe cocked his head. "Never heard this story."

"It's probably still classified," Kurt said. "But since it matters now, I'll give you the gist of it."

Joe pulled his chair closer and glanced around as if looking for spies. Kurt laughed a bit.

"An E-6B Prowler got into trouble and went down in the South China Sea," he said. "It was a prototype. There was all kinds of equipment on it that we didn't want the other side finding, and the other side included China, Russia, and North Korea."

"Still does, for the most part," Joe said.

Kurt nodded. "The pilot was using a new side-scan radar and running right along the edge of Chinese airspace. We had reason to believe he'd gone off course and crossed over the line."

"Ah," Joe said. "I can see why that would be a problem."

"You know the rules of salvage," Kurt said. "In the open ocean it's finders, keepers, but if that plane was even one foot inside Chinese territorial waters and they found out about it they'd park half their fleet on top of it and shoot at anyone who came within ten miles. Even if it wasn't, we knew they'd be after it."

"Yeah," Joe said. "Chance of a lifetime."

"Exactly," Kurt said. "So we concocted a story that we'd rescued the pilot and recovered the wreckage. Even faked video of him being pulled out of the sea and wing sections being hauled aboard a tender. In the meantime, my team and I rounded up a group of locals who could look for the wreck and salvage it without raising any suspicions from the Chinese.

"The guy who helped set it up was a CIA contact known as Mr. Ion. This guy is a half American, half Malaysian operator. He knew everybody and how to get pretty much anything. Still does, from what I hear. But he works the middle ground. You can usually trust him to do what he says and keep it quiet, but you can't count on him not working for the other guys once you're gone.

"Anyway, he helped us build the team, including a guy who was with us from Day One. Andras."

"Was he a problem?" Joe asked, tipping back the beer.

"Not until the very end," Kurt said. "He even sniffed out a traitor who was connected with the Chinese secret service. But after we set up the lifting rig and got ready to make our move, we caught some bad weather. Three days of sitting made me nervous. Too close to the finish line to pause like that. I decided we would lift the Prowler despite the weather. I rounded up the team, but Andras was nowhere to be found."

"What happened?"

Kurt took a slug of the coffee. "We got out to the site, and the aircraft was gone. Word was, Andras had been bought out by the Russians. They were just starting to fall in love with capitalism, and one of the things they were selling like hotcakes was MiGs. With the avionics and technology in the Prowler, they could have leapt forward a generation overnight."

"So that guy was a snake even back then," Joe said.

Kurt nodded.

"What'd you do?"

"On my first dive to the sunken jet, I'd rigged up fifty pounds of charges. My orders were to blow the plane up if we couldn't lift it or if we pulled it off the bottom and got caught by the Chinese.

The explosives were still on the plane, and they were armed and just waiting for a signal. I uplinked to the satellite and triggered them. Somewhere over Kamchatka a Russian jet exploded. Poor souls flying it probably had no idea what their cargo was."

Joe shook his head softly. "Rough business."

"Yeah," Kurt said, feeling a tinge of remorse for the poor flight crew even after all this time. "So is this. And this time when someone suffers, I'm going make sure it's Andras."

Joe looked around. "I'm with you. You think we're going to find him here?"

"Not him," Kurt said. "But someone who knows how to find him."

Kurt picked up the coffee and took another sip.

The way he saw it, Andras had beat him twice. No doubt the man had been paid when he handed the E-6B Prowler over to the Russians. The explosion was their problem. And if history was any guide, he was probably already counting the cash for delivering the kidnapped scientists to whoever they were given to. Then again . . .

Kurt looked up at the oil painting of the White Rajah. He remembered Andras insisting he'd be *a king* when this was all over. He wondered what the man was up to.

Kurt finished the coffee and motioned for another. As the bartender refilled his mug, Kurt turned around to check the room.

He assumed whoever had called him would be able to find him and then some kind of deal for the exchange of information would be crafted. But, so far, no one had approached, no note had been passed, no waiter or bartender had suggested another party was waiting to see them.

All around, the patrons dined, glasses clinked, and the occasional flash of blue lightning lit up the skylight above, but nothing out of the ordinary happened.

It was odd. At times in his past, Kurt had felt a sixth sense telling him he was under surveillance. He didn't even feel *that* here. It was more like they'd been shunted off to a siding and left there to rot, like a railcar rusting to pieces in waist-high weeds.

He began to wonder if he'd been fed bad information.

And then the double doors across from him opened and a trio of men came in. Two hulking bodyguards. With dark-tanned faces and square jaws, they looked more Samoan than Malaysian.

In front of them was a smaller man, mostly American-looking with some Malaysian features. He had soft eyes, relatively smooth skin. Short dark hair spiked with gel stood atop his large round head, one that seemed way too big for his narrow-framed body. The slightest touch of gray could be seen at his temples.

From his clothes and casual manner he might have been able to pull off mid- to late thirties, but Kurt knew him to be older, pushing late forties by now.

"Ion," Kurt said, standing.

The man turned upon hearing his voice. He focused on Kurt from a spot between his two bodyguards. Recognition took a few seconds, and then a smile washed over Ion's face.

The smile was false and forced, and it vanished almost as quickly as it had come. A sign that could mean only one thing: trouble.

IN THE SWANK CONFINES of the White Rajah, the man who called himself Ion took a step backward. His new position placed him between and behind his guards, who stiffened, and focused their attention on Kurt like a laser.

As Kurt studied them, all he could see was a World Wrestling tag team ready to start body-slamming him and Joe if either of them made any false moves.

Now feeling safe, Ion spoke. "Standards must be dropping to allow someone like you in here, Austin. I must complain to the management."

"No need for that," Kurt said. "Give me a little bit of information and I'm gone like the wind."

"Information costs," Ion said. "With inflation the way it is, the price gets higher every day. But tell me, what are you after? And how much are you willing to pay?"

"You owe me," Kurt said. "What I need will square us."

"I owe you nothing," Ion insisted.

Kurt had expected as much. "In that case, I offer you the right to keep your reputation. You'll have to decide what that's worth."

"My reputation?" Ion said. "What are you babbling about, Austin? And make it quick, I have reservations."

Kurt's chest swelled, but he made no other outward move. "I explain the consequences that will face you once I wipe the floor with your bodyguards and pound the information out of your overly large, egg-shaped skull."

He waved his hand around the room. "I can only imagine how that will damage your standing among these good people."

Ion's face showed the exact reaction Kurt had hoped for: anger, but coupled with a hint of fear and calculation. Maybe he would listen. And then again . . .

Ion took a hurried breath, puffed himself up for a few seconds, and spoke to his bodyguards.

"This man is a threat," he said. "Deal with him."

A wall of Samoan muscle flexed and began moving toward Kurt. One man pounded a fist into an open palm, and the other twisted his neck to the side, cracking it loudly and smiling. Apparently, they were ready for battle.

Kurt realized the one advantage he still had: both men were staring at him and only him. Ion had said, "*This man* is a threat," not, "*These men* . . ." He hadn't realized that Joe, in his sharp-looking clothes, had anything to do with Kurt.

Kurt's hand found the coffee mug behind him. As the big brutes reached a distance of five feet, Kurt swung it toward them.

The piping hot liquid splashed across both men's faces. The coffee was not hot enough to scald or scar, but the surprise and sting of it snapped the heads of both men to the side, eyes shut tight.

In that instant Kurt charged, lowering his shoulder and hammering it into the first guard's torso just below the sternum. It felt like crashing headlong into a tree, except the man stumbled backward as Kurt drove through him, legs pumping hard. It was a perfect tackle that would have made any linebacker in the NFL proud, and it sent both men crashing into a table and onto the floor.

Even as Kurt attacked, Joe was springing into action. He hopped to his feet, grabbed a barstool, and slammed it across the shoulders of the other guard. The man crumpled and groggily began to crawl away. Joe let him go and turned to see if Kurt needed any assistance.

Kurt had landed on top of the bodyguard he'd tackled, but the man was far from out. Eyes half opened, he shoved a hand into Kurt's face, catching him under the chin. It was a jarring blow, but Kurt shook it off and dropped an elbow hard between the man's neck and shoulder, hitting the pressure point.

The man's head tilted back in pain, offering a perfect shot at his jaw. Kurt fired a right cross with every ounce of strength and adrenaline in his body. It slammed the man in the chin, snapped his head sideways, and put him out like a light.

It all happened so fast, the patrons of the restaurant had only enough time to register shock; gawking; drawing back, and looking horrified. A couple had made it out of their chairs but still held their drinks. This wasn't the kind of club that needed bouncers, so no one appeared ready to throw Kurt and Joe out, though the bartender now held a Louisville Slugger in his hands.

Kurt stood slowly, and the crowd began to relax. Some looked upset at having missed all the fun.

Kurt turned back to Ion, actually surprised at how well it had gone.

Ion's gaze went from Kurt to Joe to each of his beaten men. He looked horrified at first, and then disappointed, and then he locked his gaze on Kurt and shrugged his shoulders as if to say "Oops."

And then, just when Kurt thought the man would give in and talk, he spun like a cat and raced out the door.

"Damn," Kurt said.

Caught off guard by Ion's flight, Kurt scrambled over the unconscious Samoan and rushed outside. Joe was right behind him.

"There," Joe said, pointing

Ion was on their right, racing down the street on foot. They took off after him, running along the empty sidewalk.

Kurt might have expected Ion to go for a car, but most likely he didn't drive himself here, the Samoans drove. And even if he had the keys, a man like Ion wouldn't self-park, he'd use the valet. And not wanting to get caught and pummeled while the kid at the valet stand went looking for his Maserati or Mercedes, Ion had no choice but to hoof it to wherever he was going.

That suited Kurt just fine. Catching Ion in a footrace didn't sound too hard. At least, that was, until it started to rain.

On the one hand, the rain cleared the sidewalks of the few remaining pedestrians; on the other hand, it reduced the visibility sharply. And when Ion cut to the right, dashing off the sidewalk and into an alley, Kurt almost missed him.

He whipped around the corner and saw Ion fifty yards ahead, passing under the veil of a streetlight. He and Joe raced on as the rain poured down harder.

"I can't believe this little guy can run so fast," Kurt shouted.

"He must know who's chasing him," Joe said.

Kurt guessed that adrenaline would play a part in it, but he doubted Ion could stay at full speed for as long as he and Joe. And all those laps, at home, in the gym, and on the *Argo*, were about to come in handy.

Ion glanced back at them and quickly turned in to another alley. Kurt and Joe chased. As Kurt made the turn, Joe slipped on the wet pavement and went down hard. He slid across the sidewalk and crashed into a large concrete planter. He bounced right back up, barely missing a step.

His shirt was torn and bloody at the elbow now, his slacks shredded at the knee, but he kept on running.

"Remember what I said about our next adventure being somewhere dry?" he shouted. "I mean it."

Kurt tried not to laugh; he needed all his breath. At the end of the alley was a fence, which Ion scaled like an acrobat, dropping to the other side. Kurt went over first, and Joe landed on his feet a second or two later.

Now that they were in a park of some kind, the visibility was even lower. Hiding might have worked for their quarry, but the rabbit continued to run, and when Kurt spotted him he sensed Ion slowing.

After racing across the wet grass and past some manicured trees, Ion hopped another fence and went back out onto a narrow side street filled with shops.

Ion stumbled, and turned right on another street.

Kurt pressed harder, summoning every ounce of extra speed his body had in it. This was their chance. But when he reached the street, Ion was nowhere to be seen.

Kurt skidded to a stop, looking around. "Where'd he go?"

"He definitely came in here," Joe said. "I saw him take the turn."

Kurt blinked away the rain and looked around. There were

crevices in this particular section of town. They came in the form of doorways and alcoves for the little row of shops. There were also a couple of parked cars, sitting stoically as the rain pelted them and made them shine. Despite a streetlight at each end of the row, the wet blacktop seemed to be absorbing all light.

"That little rat has to be hiding," Kurt said. "You take that side of the street, and I'll walk this side. Go slow. He's here somewhere."

Joe nodded and crossed the road. As he began moving down the right side of the street, Kurt began to recon the left side. He checked under cars and inside them, but he saw no one hiding in the backseats or beneath the frames.

The shops had doors recessed in alcoves. Kurt checked each niche, ready for a surprise attack, but found nothing.

From across the street Joe shook his head.

A car drove past in the wet. Its headlights brightened the street for a moment, throwing off a blinding glare. Kurt saw a woman in the driver's seat but no one else. The car had come from so far off, Ion would have needed a Jetpack to have gotten to it and hidden inside.

The lightning flashed again, and this time a slight rumble of thunder was heard. The rain was falling harder, and Kurt stepped back into the alcove behind him. He was all but ready to admit Ion had escaped when the lightning flashed again.

Looking down, he noticed wet footprints on the mostly dry concrete of the alcove's floor. His own prints were obvious, but the others swung wide and then back, in places Kurt had not stepped.

Remaining still, Kurt reached behind him. His fingers found the doorknob and closed around it, but he didn't need to turn it.

Even from that slight touch, the door moved freely.

44

A CHILL RAN UP KURT'S SPINE that had nothing to do with the soaking wet conditions. He stood forward, careful not to react. With one hand, he waved Joe over.

"You find anything?" he asked a little louder than necessary.

"Nothing," Joe said. "He's gone."

Kurt nodded his head toward the door behind him. Joe glanced at the door, which was slightly ajar. He nodded. He understood.

"All right," Kurt said, "let's get out of here."

But instead of getting out, he put his hand back on the round knob. Taking a deep breath, he shoved it open with a snap of the wrist.

There was a sudden squawking and the sound of scampering and skittering feet, but no one was there. Kurt saw a cage filled with toucans and some other brightly colored birds he didn't recognize. Behind them another cage held a huge iguana the size of a thirty-pound dog.

As the birds settled down, a few feathers floated through the air.

"So much for the element of surprise," Joe mumbled.

Kurt had to agree, but seeing more wet tracks on the floor told him for certain they were onto Ion's trail.

"Some kind of pet store," he said, although he couldn't imagine taking the giant iguana, which looked like a small dinosaur, for a walk.

He glanced back at the door. The wooden frame was broken and splintered where it had been kicked in. Ion must have pushed the door shut once he'd gone inside, but damaged the way it was, it couldn't be latched again.

Kurt's eyes moved upward. A sign read "Rare and Exotic"—apparently, it meant the animals.

There were two aisles in the long narrow store. In the center stood a row of stacked cages; on the sides were larger enclosures, some with bars, others with clear plastic walls and doors.

Kurt pointed to the right, and Joe moved toward that aisle. Kurt took the other one.

As he moved down his aisle, Kurt saw a Komodo dragon sleeping under a dim light. Lemurs and monkeys and a sloth slept in large cages in the center. A caracal, a wild cat with tawny fur and black ears, occupied a medium-sized cage beside them.

Treading softly, Kurt listened for movement. He heard noises, but they sounded like the snores and shuffles of the animals as far as he could tell. Then he heard a clink like metal on metal. Silence followed and then another metallic sound.

Footsteps came next, but not two at a time. There were four.

They stopped, and Kurt heard a low growl. Suddenly, there was a hiss and a roar and the crashing of cages.

The monkeys woke in a start and screeched and banged the bars of their enclosure, and another roar went out from some larger cat.

Kurt lunged around the corner to see Joe squashed into the thin space between the top of the monkey cage and the ceiling. A juvenile leopard swatted at him, with its teeth bared and its ears flat against its head.

Kurt grabbed what looked like a bowl of food and threw it at the leopard, hitting the animal in the shoulder. It turned his way in shock, let out another growl, and then ran the opposite way toward the front of the store. Kurt watched it until it slipped out through the gap in the open door.

"Remind me to call animal control when we're done," he said as Joe clambered down.

Before Joe could answer, a shadow moved near the back of the store. This time, it walked upright.

Kurt ran that direction. Ion had made it to the rear exit and was pulling on it with all his might, but the steel door was locked tight. And unlike the front door, it was designed for security, not looks. He pulled and then pounded on it with his shoulder, and then turned and stared at Kurt.

Desperate, he tried to race past Kurt, but Kurt grabbed him and flung him back into the door. He darted for the other aisle, saw Joe, and stopped.

In a last desperate act he pushed a fish tank off a shelf toward Kurt. It crashed to ground and exploded, sending glass, water, fish, and a flood of tiny blue pebbles across the floor.

Somewhere in the tank, Kurt guessed, there were piranhas or some other kind of tropical fish, but he didn't care at the moment. He jumped back. Avoiding the main impact, he looked up in time to see Ion making another break for the front door. This time, Kurt lowered the boom, clotheslining the elusive little man and body-slamming him to the floor.

Dazed and defeated, Ion looked up, surrounded by blue gravel and flapping fish.

"This could have been so much easier," Kurt said, grabbing him by the lapels and yanking him to his feet.

"I'm not going to give you anything," Ion said.

"You don't even know what I want," Kurt replied.

"You want Andras," Ion said. "I know you're looking for him." Maybe that's why he'd been so resistant.

"He'll kill me if I talk to you," Ion explained.

"Not if I kill him first," Kurt said.

"You'll never kill him," Ion said. "He's always been ahead of you."

"You'd better hope you're wrong about that," Kurt said. "Because you are going to tell me where he is."

"Whatever you do to me, it won't be worse than what Andras will do," Ion said.

Kurt realized that was probably true. A handicap of being a decent human meant that, barring the worst circumstances, he wouldn't stoop to the darkest levels of inhumanity. And that meant people like Ion would always be more afraid of someone like Andras than they would be of him.

Glancing at a bleeding abrasion on Joe's arm that matched the claw pattern of the leopard, Kurt suddenly had an idea. There had to be something in this "Rare and Exotic" pet store that was a little less evolved.

He grabbed Ion by the neck and dragged him across the floor.

"Where shall we put you?" he mumbled, stopping in front of one cage after another. "The monkeys are too smart for you. The sloth might mess you up, but we don't have all night."

With Ion looking at him as if he were crazy, Kurt dragged him up to the Komodo dragon's enclosure. The giant lizard had not moved a muscle despite the commotion.

"Now, this guy might do," Kurt said, putting his hand on the door and working the double-levered latch.

"What?" Ion shouted. "Are you crazy?"

As Kurt managed to get the door open, the lizard's tongue flicked out and sampled the air. A single eye opened, but it didn't move.

Ion tried to squirm out of Kurt's grasp, but Kurt grabbed a collar off of the shelf beside him. It had a long stick attached to it. It looked like some kind of animal control device that allowed the keeper to either push or pull the animal as needed, especially designed to keep a dangerous mouth away from a trainer.

In his own way, Ion had a dangerous mouth, but Kurt needed it to open.

He pulled the collar over Ion's head and onto his neck and shoved him forward with the pole, pressing Ion up against the open door.

"I don't know if this is the right choice," Joe said.

Kurt looked back at him.

"I mean, the dragon," Joe said.

"No on the dragon?" Kurt asked.

"Something about their bite," Joe said. "It's poisonous. But not like a cobra. They bite and then leave their victim to die. It takes days."

"Huh," Kurt said. "You're full of surprises, Joe. Since when do you know about lizards?"

"Worked at a zoo one summer," Joe said.

"Was there a girl involved in this story?"

"Callie Romano," Joe admitted.

"Of course."

Kurt yanked the stick collar back, and Ion was dragged across the floor and almost fell on his face. As Kurt shut the door, the Komodo dragon closed its eye and went back to sleep.

"So what do you suggest?" Kurt asked, beginning to enjoy himself.

Joe moved slowly down the row of enclosures. "How about this?"

He stopped in front of one of the largest enclosures in the small store. Eight feet deep and six feet wide, with some foliage, a small pool of water, and brown dirt on the floor. There was also a box with a grate over the top just outside it. A pair of large rats crouched inside the box.

Kurt looked into the larger enclosure. What he first thought was part of a tree moved a bit.

"Reticulated python," Joe said, looking at the notes on the front of the clear plastic door. "Nocturnal hunters. They can reach almost thirty feet in length," he added, "though this one is supposed to be only twenty-two."

"Constrictor," Kurt said, thinking aloud. "A twenty-two-foot, two-hundred-seventy-pound snake. Perfect."

"You're not going to—"

Before Ion could finish his sentence, Kurt had flipped the latch on the door, swung Ion in front of the opening and shoved him backward. He splashed down in the snake's water pit.

Kurt opened the collar, pulled it over Ion's head, and withdrew it. Joe slammed the door and pinned the latch.

"This thing's handy," Kurt said, looking at the stick collar and putting it down.

Ion got to his feet and looked around. Incredibly, the snake had already begun to move. Just its head and neck, sniffing around, nothing aggressive so far, but it seemed interested.

"I've been to a couple zoos," Kurt said. "Honestly, never even seen one of these things move before."

"Yeah," Joe said. "The pythons in zoos are fed all the time, and they get so fat and overweight that they don't do much of anything. But see how thin this one is."

Joe pointed. The snake didn't exactly look thin to Kurt, but he played along.

"He does look a little skinny," Kurt said.

"Probably been starved for months," Joe said.

By now Ion had moved toward the door.

"Why would they starve him?" Kurt asked.

"The owners of these places sell to rich collectors who want to see the snakes in action, crushing something and eating it," Joe said. "So they keep 'em hungry until a buyer comes around. That what the rats are for."

Kurt had no idea if Joe was serious or just making this stuff up, but it was a good shtick.

The snake was cooperating too, sliding down from the ledges near the back of the enclosure and beginning to stretch out.

Ion came up to the door. "Let me out of here, Austin."

Kurt ignored him, instead looking at some type of poster describing the python. He looked at Joe. "It says here these things can eat a goat."

"Oh yeah, sure," Joe said.

Kurt looked into the enclosure. "He's not much bigger than a goat. I wonder if it can get him down."

"I don't know," Joe said. "He's got a big head."

Kurt turned. "He does have a big melon. Bet his neck gets tired holding it up."

Ion went to speak and then froze. The snake had moved up behind him, its tongue had flicked out and grazed his thigh.

Kurt wondered if it would bite him first or just start coiling around him. Before it did either, Kurt decided to give Ion another shot at freedom.

"You want to tell me about Andras?" he asked, the joking nature of his voice long gone.

"I can't," Ion whispered.

"Once that snake wraps around you, there's nothing I can do but leave and try to shut the door behind me," Kurt said, "so you'd better talk quick before it's too late."

Ion was pressed against the plastic door. He seemed as if he was barely breathing. The snake slithered past his legs and began to curve back around.

"Can it sense him?" Kurt asked Joe.

"Oh yeah. That tongue senses heat."

The snake began to coil up as if it would strike.

Ion sensed it; he was shaking but he didn't speak. Then the snake lunged, knocking him down, and wrapping around him.

Kurt hadn't actually expected it to happen.

Ion screamed and struggled. Both moves were a big mistake because they expended air, and as soon as his chest cavity shrank a smidgen, the constrictor tightened.

"Austin," he managed, freeing one arm and grabbing at the snake's neck. "Austin . . ."

Ion could speak no more, and obviously he could say nothing if he was dead. Kurt opened the door and sprang into action. He looped the stick collar over the snake's head and tightened it. Moving to get leverage, he forced the snake's head and neck up and away from Ion.

Kurt pushed with all his might. He found it hard to believe how strong the snake was. It fought him and twisted and flipped, even with Ion still in its coil.

"Joe," Kurt shouted. "A little zookeeper help please?"

Joe was already there. He'd dropped down beside Ion and grabbed the snake's midsection, pulling with all his might. He arched his back and managed to create a small amount of space in its tight coil.

Thin, wet, and desperate to live, Ion squirmed free, crawled out of the pen, and collapsed on the floor.

Joe followed right behind him, and Kurt released the snake and slammed the door shut. He immediately placed the stick collar over Ion's head again. The man didn't even resist.

"Where can I find Andras?" Kurt asked.

Ion turned his eyes toward Kurt, his face drawn, his look that of a beaten man.

"I haven't seen him in over a year," Ion said.

"Bull," Kurt said. "You were his go-to guy for work. We all know that."

"He doesn't need work anymore," Ion said. "He has a permanent gig now. He hasn't looked for action in two years."

"And yet you saw him a year ago," Kurt said, tightening the collar again. "Get your story straight."

"I did see him a year ago," Ion admitted. "But he wasn't looking for a job. He was hiring."

"Hiring?"

"He needed men," Ion said. "He needed some guys who knew demolitions and ships. More than he could round up on his own."

Kurt thought about that, thought about the pirate attack on the *Kinjara Maru* and Dirk Pitt's information about the mercenary group that had loaded the superconducting material on board in Freetown. It certainly sounded like Andras had built a small army. But why?

"How do you contact him?" Kurt asked.

"By e-mail," Ion said. "You want to go beat up a server in some office tower somewhere?"

One of the problems with the modern world: people could send and receive information anywhere at any time. The days of the dark meeting and the dead drop had passed, for the most part.

Kurt looked down at Ion. He was still holding back, Kurt was sure of it. "You know something you're not telling me," Kurt said. "Otherwise, you would have told me all this without the hassle."

Ion didn't respond.

"Joe," Kurt said. "If you please, it's feeding time again."

Joe unlatched the door to the snake pen one more time. Kurt began to drag Ion over there.

"Wait . . . Wait," he said.

"Talk to me," Kurt said, "or talk to the snake."

"He lives at sea," Ion said. "Andras lives on the sea. He doesn't have a home. He goes from place to place on a ship. That's why no one can find him. That's why he can get in and out of almost any country even though he has no citizenship or passport and is wanted everywhere. He comes ashore as part of the crew or even with the cargo."

Now it made sense. Every time the CIA, FBI, or Interpol got a lead on Andras, he seemed to vanish into thin air like a ghost, only to pop up somewhere else a month later. It was like an international game of Whack-A-Mole. But no one had been able to figure out how he did it. Turned out he was like an evil version of Juan Cabrillo.

"What's the name of this ship?" Kurt asked.

"It could be any ship," Ion said.

Kurt pushed him toward the door.

"I swear," Ion said. "Do you think he would tell me?"

Kurt relaxed. He had a better idea. "When was he last in Singapore?" he asked. "The exact dates."

"The last I saw him was February fourth," Ion said. "I know because it was the day after Chinese New Year, a holiday here."

Kurt sensed that Ion was telling the truth. He glanced at Joe, who closed the door of the snake enclosure tight. The python had retreated to the back of the enclosure and coiled itself up defensively anyway.

Kurt released Ion and stood over him. "We're leaving," he said. "Don't even think about warning Andras. If you do, he'll know you ratted on him. And you're right. He'll do far worse than feed you to the snakes."

"What are you going to do?" Ion asked, looking up and rubbing at his neck where the collar had choked him.

"I told you, I'm going to kill him," Kurt said. "For your own sake, you'd better hope I succeed."

KURT AUSTIN SAT huddled over a laptop computer in his room. He and Joe had arrived back safely at the hotel and reported seeing a leopard in the shopping district to the proper authorities. And then they'd promptly gotten down to business.

For Joe that meant a hot shower and tending to his various wounds. For Kurt it meant toweling off his face and hair, changing into dry clothes, and getting on the horn to NUMA headquarters. He needed downloads of information, some which NUMA had access to, some which they had to beg Interpol, the FBI, and other agencies for.

Fortunately, NUMA had a long and positive history with these agencies, and there were enough markers to call in to still be on the right end of the balance sheet.

He'd been working at it for nearly forty-five minutes before Joe reappeared through the room's adjoining door.

"What took you so long?"

"I was cleaning the gravel out of my knee."

Kurt laughed. "That's what you get for wearing Italian shoes to foot-race in the rain."

"I didn't know we were going to be running all over town," Joe said.

Truthfully, neither did Kurt. "How's your arm?"

Joe held it out. The claw marks were bandaged but clearly visible. "That's gonna make a great story one day. Maybe even for your old girlfriend at the zoo."

Joe did not seem too amused. "Very funny," he said. "Just tell me my favorite Armani shirt didn't die in vain."

Kurt turned back to the computer. "A valiant sacrifice, my friend. And not without results."

He brought up parallel lists.

"On the right, we have official confirmed sightings of our friend Andras, courtesy of Interpol, the FBI, and someone Dirk knows at the Agency."

As Joe studied the list, Kurt read the names off. "Pyongyang eighteen months ago. Singapore five weeks later, on the exact date Ion gave us."

"Score one for snake intimidation," Joe said.

"Yeah," Kurt said. "It gives a whole new meaning to squeezing information out of a suspect."

Joe laughed, and Kurt continued.

"After Singapore, we find Andras in Kaohsiung, Taiwan. He's there for twenty-four hours, at which point he disappears for three months until a possible sighting in Yemen. Six weeks later he was confirmed in Madagascar."

"Madagascar?"

Kurt nodded. "Another possible in Cape Town, South Africa, back to Madagascar again, and then three months ago an extended stay in Lobito, Angola. Well, extended for him. Four sightings in approximately three weeks before he vanished. The next time he pops up is when I ran into him on the *Kinjara Maru*. But if Dirk's theory is right and he was part of the crew that loaded that superconducting material onto the ship, that would put him in Freetown, Sierra Leone, less than a month ago."

"Okay," Joe said. "So we know his course. How do we figure out what he's traveling on? He could be on an oceangoing yacht, a freighter, a garbage scow. Maybe the submarine we're looking for is his."

"I don't think so," Kurt said. "My encounter with him on Santa Maria occurred almost simultaneously with the attack on Paul and Gamay five hundred miles away. The submarine they're looking for has to be under someone else's command. But the rumor about Andras is, he doesn't trust anyone enough to even have a second-in-command. He works on a totally flat command structure. It's him and a bunch of pawns. That way, there's no one in a natural position to challenge or usurp him."

"Sounds paranoid," Joe said.

"Absolutely," Kurt said. "And that means if he had a submarine, he wouldn't hand the keys to someone else, especially not someone he picked up at Mr. Ion's Shop of Mercenaries."

"Good point," Joe said. "So it's a surface ship. But there are probably ten thousand ships capable of making the journeys he's made."

"Maybe more," Kurt said. "But think about it this way. Starting with Singapore and its harbormaster's records, we can substantially narrow that list down. If we assume he was there on February fourth, and that his vessel was in the harbor or nearby, we can eliminate ninety-eight percent of the vessels in the world's inventory right off the bat."

He looked at his notes. "During the days Andras was here, one hundred seventy-one oceangoing vessels were either docked here or anchored offshore and submitted papers to customs officials."

"That's not a small number, Kurt."

"No," Kurt said. "But if we cross-reference it with the other places Andras was seen and the ships docked in those places at the time, we narrow it down substantially."

"I'm guessing we don't have records for Yemen, Madagascar, or Angola," Joe said.

"No," Kurt said, "but we have satellite images of their harbors on pretty much every day of the year, including those days that Andras was reported present."

"And?"

"With the exception of South Africa, one ship has been present or in close proximity to every spot our friend Andras has been in the past year and a half. And only one."

Kurt clicked on a name from the list on the right-hand side of the screen. A photo came up, displaying a large tanker with a black-painted hull, a white main deck, and a Liberian flag flying from its mast.

"The *Onyx*," Kurt said proudly.

Joe looked impressed but skeptical. According to the stats at the bottom, the ship was a 300,000-ton supertanker. "You're telling me this guy has that kind of funding?"

"Didn't you ever read Sherlock Holmes?"

"I saw the movie," Joe said. "Does that count?"

"It's elementary, my dear Zavala," Kurt said. "Rule out the impossible, and whatever remains, however improbable, must be the truth. This ship was docked offshore in every port Andras appeared in over the last year except Cape Town. But the sighting there was

debatable. Also, she's too wide for the Suez Canal, which may explain the long route around Africa to Freetown before they pulled
their little bait and switch on the *Kinjara Maru*."

Joe began to look convinced. "Who's she registered to?"

"Some corporation out of Liberia that no one's ever heard of,"
Kurt said.

Joe stepped back, still looking concerned. "So let's tell Dirk and
Brinks we think this ship might have our suspect on it, call it a day,
and go fishing."

Kurt shook his head. They needed hard evidence. And if by any
chance Andras had the scientists on the ship, they needed the element of surprise. Otherwise the people he was interested in saving—
Katarina, in particular—would be in worse danger than ever.

"Since when has the machinery of government sprung into action because a regular Kurt or Joe *thinks* any particular thing?"

Joe looked away. "Not often."

"Exactly," Kurt said. "We need proof."

"You want to get on board that ship?" Joe guessed.

Kurt nodded.

Joe looked resigned to helping him as usual but seemed none
too happy about where this was going.

"And how exactly do you plan on boarding a hostile vessel,
crewed by terrorist thugs and killers who are undoubtedly watching for any type of advance from any quarter or direction, without
them knowing about it?"

Kurt smiled. He had a plan. It may have been even crazier than
his last plan, but that one had worked.

"The same way you remove a tiger's teeth," he said. "Very
carefully."

USS Truxton, *July 1*

PAUL TROUT SAT with a sonar operator in the air-conditioned comfort of a darkened control room on the USS *Truxton*. The space around them was given over to flat-screen monitors and computer controls. Part of it resembled a mixing studio, which was appropriate as the recorded sounds were sliced and diced and spliced back together in segments.

Part of the problem in getting any coherent information out of the signal was the nature of the *Matador*'s sonar system. It was twenty years old and had been designed to map the seafloor in broad swaths for various survey teams. In its active mode, a sound wave would be sent from a bell on the bottom of the *Matador* and bounced off the floor and collected by the system's hydrophones. In passive mode, it simply listened and picked up ambient noises.

Another limitation was that each hydrophone pointed downward, covering a thin but widening swath as it penetrated into the depths, like a cone of light beneath a streetlamp. The problem was, like the metaphorical streetlamp on an incredibly dark night, nothing outside the cone was visible.

One of the *Truxton*'s anti-submarine warfare operators, Petty Officer Collier, was with them. A wiry young man with a calm demeanor, Collier had been slicing and dicing the tapes with them for hours. While Paul found it tedious, the petty officer seemed to latch onto even the smallest thing and get enthusiastic about starting the process over.

"Okay, here we go," he said for the fiftieth time.

Paul put a hand to the soft-padded headset and pressed it into his ears. He saw Gamay click a pen into writing mode and tilt her head in anticipation. The young petty officer pressed "Play," and Paul heard the familiar sounds of the tape beginning for the umpteenth time. Each time there had been a slight difference as the ensign and his computers filtered out background noise or other sounds. This time, he'd added something.

"To better orient you with what you're actually hearing," Petty Officer Collier said, "we've synced up your voice records from communications with the surface with the tape."

This time, as the playback ticked over, Paul heard his own voice—it was he and Gamay, bantering with the *Matador* on the surface and then with each other.

It was all so surreal. It was *him*, he knew it was him, but he couldn't recall saying any of the things he was hearing. Couldn't recall what he was doing while the words were being spoken.

Gamay looked over at him. "Anything?"

"You mean memory-wise?"

She nodded.

"No."

She looked back at her notes, and the tape continued. Finally, it reached the point of the initial attack.

Paul pressed the headphones against his ears once again but kept his eyes on Gamay. Each time it reached this point she got agitated. And this run-through was no different. She'd already begun tapping her pen nervously.

"I'm taking her deeper into the ship," he heard Gamay say on the tape in reference to *Rapunzel.*

A slight change in the background noise was detected, marked by a spike in certain frequencies on the computer screen.

Several seconds later the *Matador*'s controller spoke.

"Paul, we're picking up a sonar contact."

"What kind?"

"Unknown. West of you and very faint. But moving fast."

Paul listened to the sound. It was more discernible this time, as if it had been enhanced.

He heard his own voice ask if the sound was mechanical or natural, and then, as the signal grew louder, the controller's voice changed in pitch as well, suddenly gaining half an octave.

"Mechanical or natural?"

"Unknown . . . It's small . . ."

"It's a torpedo. Two of them, heading your way."

"Stop the tape," Paul said. "Play back the last twenty seconds."

"I don't think we need to, Paul," Gamay said. "It's useless."

"No," Paul said. "I heard something. Something I didn't hear last time. Play it back."

Gamay turned from him, looking frustrated and pensive. Her

fingernails were chewed down to nothing, and she kept looking around, focusing on the door and the clock like a kid in the last class on the last day of school.

Paul guessed that listening to the tape over and over again was forcing her to relive the incident and he understood how it might be affecting her, but despite his repeated suggestions she would not leave him to do it alone.

The tape played again, and Paul listened closely.

As it finished, he asked for one more listen.

He saw Gamay gulp at an imaginary lump in her throat as the tape ran forward again.

"Paul, we're picking up a sonar contact."

"What kind?"

"Unknown. West of you and very faint. But moving fast."

"Stop!" Paul said. "Right there."

Gamay took her headset off and put it down on the table. "I have to get some air," she said.

Paul nodded and watched her leave the room. In a bizarre way his memory loss seemed to be helping them, as he had no emotional attachment to what had gone down. It was an investigation like all the others. A mystery he wanted to solve. But it dredged up no particular feelings for him.

"Can you isolate the vibration and remove the voice track?" Paul asked.

"Sure," the petty officer said.

It took a minute, and then it was ready and playing again. There was something else blocking the sound. Paul looked at the computer screen. A frequency chart showed a bunch of low-level background noises and two major vibration sources. One was on a slightly lower band than the other.

"What's this?" he asked, pointing to the spike on the chart.

"That's the *Grouper*'s motor signature," the ensign said.

"Can you pull it out?"

Collier nodded, and a few seconds later indicated that he was ready.

"Go," Paul said.

This time, as the playback went through, Paul was sure of what he was hearing. He didn't know what it meant, but it wasn't his imagination.

He pointed to the other frequency spike. "Can you eliminate all other background noise and just play this? And can you enhance it?"

"Mr. Trout," the petty officer said, "the government makes sure we have the best equipment in the world. I can make it play the 'Star-Spangled Banner,' if you want."

Paul laughed. "Just make this sound wave louder," he said, "and stretch it out a bit."

This time, as the playback came, it sounded a little like a moped speeding toward him on an empty city street. No other noise, no urgent shouts of inbound torpedoes, just a whiny vibration that grew slightly louder and then lowered its pitch, not once but twice. As if it had passed them and was turning away.

"Is that what I think it is?" Paul asked.

The petty officer played the tape one more time and nodded.

"Compression," he said. "The initial sound is compressed to high frequency because the source is coming toward the *Grouper*, and on the last three seconds of tape the sound is stretched out to lower frequency because the source is moving away from the *Grouper*."

"Like a train whistle," Paul said, "or a car passing you on the street. The vehicle is still making the same sound, but your perception is different. So it can't be the torpedoes."

"Nope," the petty officer said. "It's definitely a vehicle. From the sound of it, I'd say it's two vehicles."

Paul nodded; that's what he was thinking. "But why didn't we hear them before?"

"All the distortion," Collier said. "And the torpedoes. In fact, the signature is being picked up in almost the same frequency bands as the torpedoes."

"What does that mean?"

"To me, Mr. Trout, that means you were attacked by something small and fast. Submarines making high rpms with small propellers, much like a torpedo."

"Not one big submarine but two small ones," Paul said. He wasn't sure what that meant, but he guessed it would bring the mother ship theory back into play. At the very least, they were making progress.

Collier ran it one last time just to be sure. The sound was only audible for a couple of seconds in real time before the noise of the torpedoes drowned it out.

Collier took his headset off. "I'll inform the captain. And we'll do some more work on this."

"You want me to stick around?" Paul asked.

"I think you have some work of your own to do, Mr. Trout." He nodded upward as if to suggest Paul go topside.

"Right," Paul said. He put his headset down, got up, and made his way through the bulkhead door.

Two minutes later he stepped out onto the *Truxton*'s aft deck.

Sunshine, fresh air, and the sound of thumping helicopter blades greeted him. A stone gray SH-60B Seahawk was descending toward the helipad with a payload suspended beneath it.

He found Gamay watching it and moved up beside her.

"I think we've found something," he shouted over the noise.

She didn't respond except to acknowledge that he was there.

"I think we've isolated the acoustics of the sub that attacked us," he explained. "It was actually two subs."

"Good," she said, sounding anything but excited.

"I thought you'd be happy," he said. "We don't have to listen to the tape anymore. Why are you so upset?"

She looked at him and then nodded toward the helicopter. "What's that doing here?"

Paul looked over. The payload beneath the helicopter was being lowered to the deck in a cradle. It was now close enough that Paul could make out what it was: a small submersible. Attached to the rear of the sub was a package of mechanical equipment and a human-shaped figure made of metal. *Rapunzel.*

"Dirk sent it over," Paul said.

"You knew about this?"

"He told me this morning," Paul said. "It's only a contingency. Just in case we need it."

Gamay said nothing. She just shook her head angrily, glared at him for a second, and then pushed past him and went back inside the ship.

47

Sierra Leone, July 5

IN HIS EXECUTIVE PALACE, with its marble floors, Djemma Garand sat with Alexander Cochrane. Cochrane had spent the night reviewing the options arrived at by the ad hoc scientific guests.

"Essentially," Cochrane said, "they've all come up with the same solution. I see minor differences, no more."

Cochrane looked tired. His usual petulance had been replaced by a sense of exhaustion and perhaps fear.

"And your evaluation of their solutions?" Djemma asked, eager to get to the point.

"The fact that they all came to it independently tells me it's probably correct. I see nothing wrong with their calculations."

"And the implementation?" Djemma asked.

"In essence, we can use the particle accelerator as it stands now," Cochrane said. "We just have to generate a heavier charged particle to fire through it. It's like trading out a twenty-two shell and replacing it with a forty-five. Everything else is the same. The particles will move a little slower, not enough to affect the operation, but they'll hit with three times the power." He put his notes down. "It's rather simple, actually."

"Pity you didn't think of it months ago," Djemma said, the words sliding off his tongue with open disdain.

"This is theoretical work," Cochrane said. "Not my field."

"Yes," Djemma said. "After all, you are just a mechanic."

The intercom on Djemma's phone buzzed. "Mr. President," his secretary said, "a guest has arrived to speak with you. The American ambassador."

"Excellent," Djemma said. "Send him in."

Cochrane stood. "I need twenty-four hours to make the changes."

"Then I suggest you get to it," Djemma said. He pointed to a back door. "Leave that way."

Cochrane obliged, moving quickly out the back as the front door to Djemma's office opened and the American ambassador came in. Normally, Djemma would meet such a man halfway across the floor, but he remained in his seat, beckoning the ambassador to sit across from him in the spot Cochrane had just vacated.

"President Garand," the ambassador said in an easy Texas drawl, "I'm sure you know the sad business I'm here to ask you about."

"Whatever do mean, Mr. Ambassador?" Djemma said. "We are celebrating our Fourth of July. A day late, perhaps."

The ambassador managed a forced smile but shook his head. "What you're calling independence is nothing but naked aggression, theft, and the violation of international law. To be honest with you, I can't recall such a brazen act."

"Then you must be a poor student of history," Djemma said. "In 1950, under the threat of nationalizing *all* of Standard Oil's assets, the Saudi royal family took half the oil in Arabia. That oil has been worth three and a half trillion dollars over the last sixty years. In 2001, Hugo Chávez of Venezuela did virtually the same thing. In 1972, Chile nationalized its copper mines under Salvador Allende. In 1973, India nationalized its entire coal industry. In 1959, Fidel Castro took Havana, waiting patiently until the Havana Hilton was complete so he could use it as the Communist Party's head-quarters. He seized all foreign assets and has never relinquished them. Do you not recall any of these events, Mr. Ambassador?"

The ambassador took a deep breath. "Of course I recall them, but this is different."

"Yes," Djemma said. "And just how different you have not yet discovered. In the meantime, in strict dollar terms, my actions are relatively minor in comparison to the events I have just reminded you of. To be honest, I'm surprised to see you. I would have ex-pected the Chinese ambassador to arrive first; they stand to lose far more than you."

The last statement was a jab at the ambassador's pride, but he didn't react.

"We're here on their behalf," he said. "And on behalf of all the countries that have a grievance and a claim. Now, off the record, we're prepared to consider modifying the repayment terms of your loans, but we're not forgiving you any of the principal. And before any negotiations start, your forces must withdraw from the indus-trial institutions owned by foreign parties."

Djemma smiled. "I make you a counteroffer," he said. "I will keep what we have rightly taken. And I will ask only for twenty bil-lion a year in grants from your country."

"What?" the ambassador said.

"I would ask for new loans," Djemma said, "but considering that I didn't pay the other loans back, I fear no one will extend us credit. Therefore, it will have to be grants. Do not worry, we will be demanding the same contributions from China and Europe."

"You can't be serious," the ambassador responded curtly. "You steal the world's property and then demand that we collectively give you sixty billion dollars a year in free money?"

"It is a small amount," Djemma assured him. "You gave your own banks seven hundred billion a few years ago. You spent a trillion dollars on Iraq, twenty billion a month. What I ask for is a fraction of that, and no one has to suffer. In return, we will allow American corporations to handle many of the construction projects. You may consider it a stimulus program."

By now Djemma was smiling like a madman. For so long he had listened to the Europeans and Americans lecturing poor nations on fiscal responsibility. Hypocrites, he thought. Look what they had wrought upon themselves. Now he would throw it back in their faces.

The ambassador's face was turning red. "Your reach is stretching beyond your power to grasp, Mr. President," he blurted. "This will not stand."

"The Saudis still stand," Djemma said. "Chávez still stands. So does Castro. You will find it easier to negotiate than you are letting on. And if you don't . . . I warn you there will be consequences."

This was the first hint of a threat that Djemma had made. He needed to be subtle. By the sudden focus on the ambassador's face, he knew he hadn't been too obscure. But when the ambassador began to chuckle, Djemma felt his own ire rising.

"What is so funny?" he demanded to know.

The ambassador settled down, but a smile remained on his face. "I feel like I'm in a production of *The Mouse That Roared*," he said. "I could take over this country with a group of Boy Scouts and a few state troopers, and you think you can threaten us?"

The laughter returned, and Djemma snapped. He brought the riding crop down on the desk in a stunningly swift move. The ambassador jumped back at the sound, shocked.

"Your arrogance betrays you, Mr. Ambassador," Djemma said. He stood, drawing himself up to his full six-foot-two-inch height.

"For too long you and the other rich nations have mocked countries like mine," he said. "Whether you believe it or not, those days are about to end. The industrialized world will support us, not in dribs and drabs but in substantial amounts. You will help us stand or we will drag you down into the mire with us! Only then will you see the truth. We are not mice for you to play with. Sierra Leone is the Land of Lions. And if you are not cautious, you will feel our teeth in your soft, decadent necks."

Djemma didn't wait for a reply from the American ambassador. He pressed the intercom button, and a group of guards entered the room.

"See the ambassador to the airfield," he shouted. "He is to be deported immediately."

"This is an outrage," the ambassador shouted.

"Take him!" Djemma ordered.

The ambassador was hustled outside, and the door slammed behind him.

Djemma sat alone, fuming. He was angry with the ambassador's arrogance and disdain. He hadn't expected it so soon. But he was even angrier with himself for jumping at the bait and voicing his threat so forcefully. He hadn't planned to speak so soon. Now there would be no negotiations. Unless . . .

He had no choice. He had made a claim that the Americans would assume to be a bluff. He had to demonstrate his power, otherwise they and the world at large would only scoff and laugh with disdain as he ranted and raved: another mad dictator in a banana republic.

He would unleash his weapon in all its glorious power and leave them no choice but to treat him with respect.

48

Washington, D.C., July 6, 1330 hours

DIRK PITT HAD A FRONT-ROW SEAT in the Situation Room at the Pentagon. Cameron Brinks of the NSA was putting on a show. The President wasn't there, but his Chief of Staff, military brass from all four branches, and several members of the cabinet were present. As was the Vice President of the United States, Dirk Pitt's former boss, Admiral James D. Sandecker.

With the bizarre actions in Sierra Leone over the past few days, followed by the threats coming from its President, Brinks had totally embraced the possibility that Sierra Leone was involved in the scientific kidnappings and the creation of some type of energy weapon.

How else could they have the gall to threaten the world and America in particular? After several days of searching with his satellites, Brinks claimed to have identified the location of such a weapon, calling it a clear and present danger.

At the front of the room, on a screen that was just a fraction smaller than some Jumbotrons he'd seen, Pitt studied a satellite feed. It showed an area off the coast of Sierra Leone, a shallow bay ten miles across, home to an oil production zone known as the Quadrangle because of its dimensions and the four evenly spaced platforms. On a wide angle they showed up as four pinpoints of gray. At closer ranges, those points were easily identifiable as huge offshore oil rigs.

Other data was being overlaid on the screen, numbers and codes that Pitt wasn't familiar with. In some respects he wondered why he was even there. NUMA was peripherally involved in the search, but for the most part any action at this level would be well out of their hands.

With the participants given a few minutes to review the files in front of them, Dirk studied what he'd been given a second time. One thing that caught his attention was the fact that the entire field and the four rigs were owned by the government of Sierra Leone and always had been, unlike all the structures taken just days before in the sweeping nationalization.

Another red flag that stood out was the fact that oilmen the CIA had spoken with insisted there was no oil beneath the shelf where the Sierra Leone government was drilling. It was a boondoggle, they insisted. A waste of the money the IMF was pouring into the country.

Add to that the continued presence of construction barges and constant deliveries of equipment well after the construction of the platforms was completed, and something odd seemed to be going on.

Pitt closed the file in front of him and looked up to see Brinks and Vice President Sandecker walking his way. They stopped and chatted with the Navy's chief of staff before wandering over to where Pitt sat.

Pitt stood and shook hands with both men.

"I told you your man was off on a wild-goose chase, looking for this mercenary," Brinks said.

Pitt smiled and his green eyes showed nothing but pure joy, despite a desire to punch Brinks right in the mouth.

"I honestly hope you're right," Pitt said. "After all he's been through, Austin could use a vacation."

"Well," Brinks said confidently, "we're about to give him one."

As Brinks moved off, Sandecker took a seat next to Pitt.

"Thanks for the invite," Pitt said, sarcastically. "It's like a pool party with sharks and alligators."

"You think I wanted you here?" Sandecker joked. "Brinks dialed you up."

"Why?"

"Probably wants to gloat."

"Nothing like a sore winner," Pitt said.

Sandecker agreed. "I hear you shot him down pretty hard the other day."

"He was asking for it," Pitt said.

The VP chuckled and leaned back, focusing on the screen. "I bet he was."

Pitt appreciated Sandecker's support. Always had. "You know it's weird for me to see you without a cigar in your mouth," Pitt said.

"No smoking in the Situation Room," Sandecker replied. "Now, pipe down and you might learn something."

Up front, Cameron Brinks stood and began his presentation. After explaining what Dirk had already discovered in the file, he went on to elaborate.

"I'll make this as quick as I can," he said. "We all know the situation in Sierra Leone is spiraling. What we didn't know until now is whether there was any credence to the threats leveled against us. We now believe, based on information uncovered by various sources, that there is. As odd as it sounds, Sierra Leone, one of the poorest countries in the world, is now in possession of a weapon of incredible destructive power."

Brinks walked to the side of the room, conferring for a second with an assistant who seemed to be hooked up to NSA headquarters in Fort Meade, Maryland, where the satellite data was coming from.

"In the time since we put together the files in front of you," Brinks said, "we've conducted additional satellite passes of the area described in them. The Quadrangle. The video on the screen is a real-time scan."

Brinks looked down, waited as his assistant tapped a few keys on the computer terminal in front of him, and then raised a remote control device and pointed at the screen. With the click of a button, the colors on the screen changed. False hues illuminated the water, the land, and features that hadn't been visible in the earlier shot.

"This is an infrared scan of the Quadrangle area," Brinks said.

Pitt looked on. The area around each oil platform was bathed in a reddish color that elongated with the tide. It had to be a discharge of some kind, one that was raising the water temperature around the rigs and slowly being drawn off by the current. Pollution was his first thought, leaking oil or distillates of some kind, but then he remembered that there was no oil in the region.

"The rigs are pumping heated water," he said.

Brinks nodded. "Very good, Mr. Pitt. Each one of these platforms is shipping heated water out into the Atlantic. Hundreds of thousands of cubic feet of high-temperature water every day. There can only be one reason for that: whatever they're doing requires an immense amount of cooling."

"They're generating power," Pitt whispered to Sandecker a few seconds before Brinks confirmed it.

"The question is, why?" Brinks said. "The answer is simple: to use in a massive particle accelerator that they have turned into a weapon."

Brinks clicked his remote control, and the image changed again, adding purple to the dark blue, gray, and magenta already on the screen. The new iridescent color ran in a thin line, encircling the four oil rigs—which were, in fact, spaced miles apart—in a giant loop. Other thin fingers branched off this loop and stretched out into the Atlantic. One group went to the west and the northwest, another group north and northeast, a third group of these thin purple filaments branched back toward the African continent.

"This loop demarks an underwater structure that was identified through a combination of infrared scans and surface-penetrating radar from an Aurora spy plane. The loop is fifteen miles in diameter," Brinks said, using a laser pointer to indicate the circle. "And each of these supposed oil rigs is just a facade to throw us off. Beneath their structures are throbbing power plants, each large enough to light a small city."

"What kind of power plants?" someone asked.

"Gas turbine generators, feeding off a large natural gas pipeline that was built allegedly to bring gas out of the area. We now know the opposite is true."

"And all that power?" someone else asked.

"Used in the superconducting electromagnets that accelerate the particles," Brinks said, "and the massive cooling system required to keep the ring at operating temperature."

Brinks stood back and explained. "By our calculations, this system is generating and using twenty times the energy that CERN uses for its Large Hadron Collider. We can come up with only one explanation for such a power need. This thing is a weapon. It can probably take down satellites over Europe, the Atlantic, and Africa of course. It can threaten shipping in the Atlantic, perhaps as far as a hundred miles out. It can threaten commercial aircraft in a three-hundred-mile radius."

"The weapon can only fire three hundred miles?" Pitt asked.

"No," Brinks said. "It can probably do damage at a much farther range, perhaps even tens of thousands of miles, but it fires in a straight line like a laser. It cannot curve around the surface of the earth like a ballistic missile."

That made sense, but something else didn't.

"What about the *Kinjara Maru*?" Pitt asked. "That ship was nowhere near Sierra Leone when it was hit."

"No," Brinks admitted. "Probably they have a derivative weapon on that submarine we're looking for. But that's a tactical weapon, small potatoes. This thing is strategic and threatens an entire region. We'll deal with this first, the submarine afterward."

Brinks turned back to the group. "Our recommendation is that it be taken out in a surgical airstrike before Djemma can use it against someone."

Silence followed that statement. No one disagreed, not after Djemma Garand's actions in the days preceding and his threats, however unspecified, against the United States.

"Best recommendation as to method, Mr. Brinks?" Vice President Sandecker asked.

"Advise we take out the rigs, Mr. Vice President," Brinks said. "That'll effectively shut off the power. And without power, the particle accelerator is just a big tunnel with a lot of fancy equipment stored inside."

Though Pitt didn't like Brinks's jaunty tone, he calculated the situation similarly. A threat existed, controlled by a leader who appeared to be unstable. An airstrike would create minimal destruction, minimal casualties. The technology would be preserved for study.

Much to Pitt's dislike, he had to agree with Brinks's assessment.

"I'll relay your recommendation to the President," Sandecker said, then stood.

Meetings like this didn't often last long. And even if it was going to continue, the VP had seen enough.

But before he could leave, something odd happened to the screen at the front of the room. The colors shifted for a second and then bled, like something was interfering with the signal.

All eyes focused on it.

Brinks looked to his assistant. "What's going on?"

The assistant was tapping away at a laptop. He looked up, shaking his head.

A second later a flare of white light crossed the screen and then everything went dark. Static followed and then a blank screen. Text in the bottom right-hand corner indicated complete signal loss.

Brinks looked embarrassed. "Get on the horn and find out what happened to the feed."

"The line's clean," the assistant said. "The signal's coming through fine. It's just not carrying any data."

Pitt had been watching something odd on the screen right before it flared. He doubted anyone else had noticed as the VP was leaving. When Sandecker stood, everyone else stood, Pitt as well, but he'd never taken his eyes off the screen.

That allowed him to see a number indicating heat output from the oil platforms suddenly rising. It had climbed rapidly, like an odometer rolling over. A new area of red and magenta had appeared over one of the angled filaments. It had been visible for only a second, but Pitt was fairly certain he knew what it was.

Somewhere in Fort Meade the techs probably knew too; they just were too stunned to say so until they'd checked every other possibility.

"The problem's not the computer," Pitt announced. "It's your satellite."

All eyes turned to him.

"Really?" Brinks said. "And when did you become an expert in remote imaging diagnostics?"

"I'm not," Pitt said. "But play the last five seconds back. You'll see an energy spike right before the image flared. They fried your satellite, Brinks. It's gone."

Brinks looked over at his assistant. "We're trying to reestablish a link," he said.

"Forget it," Pitt told him. "You're calling up a dead bird."

"Switch to Keyhole Bravo," Brinks said, referencing the backup satellite that was orbiting at a different angle and higher altitude.

Brinks's assistant finished his last desperate act of tapping and looked up. There was nothing to say.

"Two satellites gone," Sandecker said. "That's a damn act of war."

Everyone in the room grew more somber at that realization.

"I figured you'd be happy," Pitt said to Brinks. "This proves your theory. Djemma Garand is dangerous, his weapon is operational, and he's not afraid to use it. Even I agree with you now. He has to be taken out."

Somewhere over the Atlantic, July 7

KURT AUSTIN AND JOE ZAVALA found themselves in the noisy cockpit of a Russian-designed IL-76 transport as it cruised at thirty-four thousand feet. They sat in the jump seats, just behind the pilots. They wore headsets and flight suits and stared through the windshield at a brilliant sunset out over the Atlantic.

After leaving Singapore, they'd spent several days rounding up the equipment Kurt felt he needed to get aboard the *Onyx*. The last piece of the puzzle had been a jet capable of a transatlantic hop, piloted by a few people that would ask no questions.

They'd chartered it out of Tangiers, through a somewhat murky chain of brokers that began with an Egyptian friend of Joe's, who knew a man from Greece, who had good contacts with a few people in Morocco.

While the chain of command worried Kurt a bit, the aging craft they were flying in was even more concerning. It shook and rattled and smelled as if it were leaking jet fuel in half a dozen places. The pilots tapped hard on the old analog-style gauges as if they weren't working, fiddled with a pair of fuses at one point, and chatted in English with an Eastern European accent, making constant references to the "worthless mechanics."

So far, the wings hadn't fallen off. Kurt considered that a small victory.

As he pondered whether their luck would hold, the copilot turned to him.

"Radio call for you," he said. "Switch to channel two on headset."

Kurt looked over at the toggle switch beside the headset jack. Cyrillic writing and the numbers 1 and 2 presented themselves. He flipped the switch to number 2.

"This is Kurt," he said.

"You're a damn hard person to find, Kurt." It was the voice of Dirk Pitt. "If it wasn't for a rather large item on your NUMA credit line regarding an aircraft charter, I wouldn't have been able to track you down."

"Um, yeah," Kurt mumbled. "I can explain that."

He tapped the copilot on the shoulder.

"Is this line secure?" Kurt asked.

The copilot nodded. "It's a proprietary channel. Scrambled until it reaches plane." He smiled, a large mustache turning up with the corners of his mouth. "All part of our service to you."

Kurt almost laughed. Not exactly the cone of silence, he thought, but it would have to do.

"I think we're onto something," he said, wishing he had been able to have this conversation after he'd confirmed the accuracy of that particular thought. "I think we've found our man."

"Where?" Dirk asked.

"On a ship in the middle of the Atlantic."

"Then why are you airborne?"

Kurt gazed out the window. The sun was about to drop below the horizon ahead of them. The moment of truth was still two hours away.

"It's the only way to get close enough," he said. "The ship we think he's on is sitting in the middle of the Atlantic, making a few knots and pretty much going nowhere. The problem is, it's a hundred miles from the nearest shipping lane in a barren spot in the middle of the ocean. Approaching it on the water would be a dead giveaway—with emphasis on the word *dead*. Our only hope is an airdrop."

Dirk went silent, perhaps evaluating his employee for bravery or maybe a Section Eight.

"I'm sure they have radar," Pitt said finally. "I take it you're not going to fly overhead and jump."

"No, sir," Kurt said.

"Okay," Dirk replied, obviously aware of what Kurt was planning. "That explains the second item on your account."

"I made sure to get receipts," Kurt insisted, as if it mattered.

"We'll talk about that later," Dirk said. "The thing is, I don't believe you need to make this jump."

"Why?"

"Let's just say we've confirmed our primary target as lying elsewhere," Dirk said. "Unfortunately, we've already sparred with them once today and we lost that round. Brinks was right, your man is nothing more than a hired hand. He delivered his hostages and took off. While there's some value in locating him, I wouldn't risk your life over it."

Kurt considered what Pitt was telling him. The brass all assumed Andras was a soldier of fortune, and why not? That's what he'd always been. It seemed they thought his part in this was over and that he was on his way to a vacation or another job.

Maybe they would pick him up later, maybe they wouldn't, but if Kurt understood what he was being told, they'd confirmed Sierra Leone was the sponsor of all this madness.

"Why don't you just sit this one out?" Dirk added.

"You know I would," Kurt said, "but something is still bothering me. Our target is not acting like a mercenary. More like it's his party. I'm not sure what it all means, but I swear there's more to this than we know."

He glanced over at Joe. "On top of that, Mr. Zavala says there's a lot about this tanker that doesn't add up. For one thing, she's forty feet wider than most tankers her length, which gives her a kind of stubby appearance even though she's twelve hundred feet long. She also has odd bulges protruding near the bow underneath the forward anchors, and a raised section amidships. We have no idea what any of it is for, but neither one of us likes it. If it's all the same with you, I'd just as soon get a closer look at her."

"You've earned the right to make this call," Pitt said. "Just be sure you're making it for the right reason."

"I'm not trying to be a hero," Kurt said. "If there's nothing interesting down there, I'll go over the side, pop the cork on my survival raft, and wait for you to send a blonde, brunette, and a redhead to pick me up. But on the odd chance Joe and I are right, better we find out now rather than later."

Pitt was quiet. "Okay," he said finally. "Don't get yourself blown up before I can yell at you for all these bills that are coming in."

Kurt laughed. "I'll try not to."

With that, Pitt signed off. Kurt gazed ahead at the orange ball of the sun just dipping below the horizon. The truth lay eight hundred miles ahead, moving slowly through the dark of night.

TWO HOURS LATER, still on the old jet, Kurt and Joe had moved from the cockpit back into main section of the fuselage. They now stood in a cavern of metal, surrounded by equipment, small containers, and tie-down straps.

Despite a pressure suit, gloves, boots, and fighter pilot–style helmets with noise-canceling headphones and forced oxygen, Kurt could feel the bite of the frigid cold at thirty-five thousand feet. He could feel every shudder of the aircraft and hear nothing but the piercing whine of the jet's narrow seventies-era engines.

Such were the accommodations in the cargo bay of a Russian transport.

Standing beside him, in a parka with fur lining around the face and a headset and oxygen mask of his own, Joe Zavala appeared to be saying something, but Kurt couldn't make out the words.

"I didn't copy," Kurt shouted.

Joe pressed his oxygen mask and its microphone tighter on his face and repeated his thought. "I said, you must be crazy," he shouted back.

Kurt didn't respond. He was beginning to think Joe might be right. Holding firmly to a strap that dangled from the side of the airframe like a man on a crowded subway, Kurt turned toward the aircraft's tail. A crack began appearing near the rear as the ramp in the tail opened.

As the ramp went down, the old jet shook worse than ever, and the wind swirled through the cargo bay, buffeting him and Joe and threatening to knock them over.

The aircraft had been depressurized thirty minutes before, so there was no rush of escaping atmosphere, but the temperature instantly dropped from just above freezing to fifteen below, and the howling of the jet's engines jumped four notches at the very least.

Kurt stared out the yawing opening into the waiting blackness of the night sky. He was sucking oxygen off a tank and wearing a specially designed parachute. And while he'd made over two hundred jumps in his lifetime, including twenty HALOs (High Altitude–Low Opening), what he was about to try was something he'd never done before, something Joe had been continuously advising him to rethink.

So far, he'd laughed off Joe's pessimism, calling him a "mother hen," but now, staring out the back of the jet, Kurt wasn't so sure.

Letting go of the strap, he stepped cautiously toward an object near the open tail ramp. It looked like a cross between an Olympic bobsled and a "photon torpedo" from the *Star Trek* series. The designers called it a Single Occupant Tactical Range Insertion Unit. The men who'd tested it out called it the LX, or Lunatic Express.

It worked like a one-man glider. Dropped from seven miles in the sky with a glide ratio of twenty to one, the Lunatic Express could transport its occupant on a one-way trip across a hundred forty miles and do it without a sound or a heat trail or a radar signature, since the whole thing was actually made of specialized plastic and covered with a radar-absorbing layer that looked and felt like soft tire rubber to Kurt.

To fly it, the occupant climbed in, lay down face-first, and grabbed a pair of handles that did not seem too far removed from the grips of an old ten-speed bicycle. He then jammed his feet into what felt like ski bindings.

The most-forward section of the device was a clear Plexiglas windshield with a basic heads-up display projected on it. It gave him speed, altitude, heading, glide ratio, and rate of descent. It also offered a visual glide-slope indicator designed to help the pilot maintain the correct angle and reach whatever destination had been targeted. In this case, that meant the tanker *Onyx*, seventy-five miles away.

Because of her odd position in the ocean, the *Onyx* had proved hard to get to. Not only was she far away from the closest shipping lane, there were no air routes anywhere close to her. To fly overhead, even at thirty-five thousand feet, would have been instantly suspicious, but there was a heavily traveled air route seventy-five miles to the south, and on radar the IL-76 would appear as just another passenger jet on the airborne highway. Kurt couldn't imagine it being worth a second look.

And even if they were watching, no system Kurt knew of would pick up the glider and its single occupant.

It was a simple setup in theory. In the simulator Kurt had felt like he was playing a video game. Somehow the real thing was slightly more intimidating.

"Come on," he said to Joe. "Get me into this thing before I chicken out."

Joe moved up to the glider. "Do you have any idea how many things could go wrong with your plan?"

"No," Kurt said. "And I don't want you to tell me."

"The launch could go bad, you could get ripped up by the jet's wake turbulence, your oxygen could fail, which means you'll pass out before you can even get down to a safe altitude . . ."

Kurt looked up. "What did I just say?"

". . . You could freeze to death," Joe continued, ignoring him. "You could be unable to release the cover or pop your chute. Your feet could get stuck. The airfoils could fail to open correctly."

Kurt climbed over the rail and into the torpedo-shaped glider, giving up on stopping Joe.

"What about you?" he asked. "You have to stay on this contraption. Did you see the corrosion near the wing root? Did you see that smoke pouring from the number three engine when they all were fired up? I can't believe this old bird even got up into the air."

"All part of the Aeroflot experience," Joe insisted. "Not that I wouldn't rather be flying American-made, but I think she's safer than what you're about to do."

Kurt wanted to disagree, but he couldn't. In truth, he believed the transport was safe, even if it shook and rattled and whined like a banshee. But if Joe was going to make him sweat, he was going to return the favor.

"And don't forget the pilots," Kurt added. "I think I saw them doing shots of sake kamikaze style right before we took off."

Joe laughed. "Yeah, in your honor, amigo."

A yellow light came on. One minute to the jump site.

Kurt locked his feet in, lay down flat, and switched on the video display. As it initialized, he gave the thumbs-up to Joe, who snapped the thin cowling over Kurt's back, covering him and his specially designed parachute.

A second yellow light came on, and a red light began to flash. Thirty seconds.

Joe moved back out of Kurt's view and toward the launch control.

A few seconds later Kurt heard Joe counting down— "*Tres . . . Dos . . . Uno*"—and then with great enthusiasm, "*¡Vámonos, mi amigo!*"

Kurt felt the glider accelerate backward as a powered conveyer belt sped him toward the back end of the plane. And then he dropped, and was slammed back even harder as the torpedo-shaped glider hit the 500-knot airstream.

Seconds later, a tiny drogue chute deployed behind the glider, and the g-forces from the deceleration hit Kurt as hard as a launch from a carrier deck, but in the opposite way.

The restraint harness crushed Kurt's shoulders as he slid forward. His arms bent, and his hands bore the rest of his weight, and all the while his eyes felt like they might pop out of his head.

It went like that for a good ten seconds before the deceleration slowed.

Once he got his body stabilized, Kurt scanned the heads-up display. "Four hundred," Kurt called out to no one but himself. A few seconds later, "Three-fifty . . ."

The glider slowed and dropped, heading toward the waters of the central Atlantic like a giant artillery shell or a manned bomb. Finally, as the speed dropped below 210 knots, Kurt released the chute.

It broke away with a resounding clang, and the descent went from a shaky violent ride to an unnervingly smooth one. The whistling wind was almost completely blocked out by his helmet, and the buffeting was all but gone.

A moment later, as the airspeed hit 190, a pair of stubby wings extended, forced outward by a powered screw jack.

This was the most dangerous moment of the flight, in Kurt's mind. Prototypes had been lost when the wings did not extend evenly, causing the glider to spin out of control and break apart.

True, he still had a parachute on if that happened, but there was no telling what it might do to his body if the vehicle began to spin out of control or came apart in midair at nearly 200 knots.

The wings locked into place, accompanied by tremendous pressure on Kurt's chest and stomach, as the glider developed lift and transformed itself from a manned missile on a downward-sloping trajectory to an aircraft pulling up and then flying almost straight and level.

Once Kurt had control, he decided to test the wings to make sure all was working well. He banked right and then left. He put the glider back into a dive and then leveled off, and used its momentum to enter a climb.

All systems were go, and despite the danger ahead and all Joe's pessimism, Kurt could not remember feeling such exhilaration. It was the closest thing he could imagine to being granted the power of flight, like a great bird.

The little glider responded instantly to his touch, and he found he could turn it by using his weight and leaning this way or that like a motorcyclist racing along an open road.

All was dark around him, save the dim illumination of the heads-up display and the pinpoint lights of the stars.

As he maneuvered, he almost wished it was daylight, to enhance the sensation, but to reach the *Onyx* unnoticed required a night approach. Recreation would have to wait for another day.

Done playing around, Kurt set himself on course, adjusted the glide slope, and settled in. He was at twenty-seven thousand feet, losing five hundred feet per minute, and cruising at 120 knots. According to the target icon, the *Onyx* was seventy miles away.

51

KATARINA LUSKAYA SAT in a chair in a small cabin on the lower level of the accommodations block of the *Onyx*. She could only guess at the time, but it seemed like evening. It didn't matter. The light never changed in her windowless cabin.

She tried to stretch but couldn't. Her hands were tied and her feet shackled. She'd only been given a minimal amount to eat or drink for the past five days.

As she tried unsuccessfully to rest, the cabin door opened. Andras came in. He was alone. He'd come every day, her only visitor, always to regale her with bad news.

The other scientists were gone, dumped in a foreign country and made slaves. She remained here because he wanted her there, but he could change his mind. No one was looking for her, he insisted. He'd told everyone she was dead.

And so it went, every day. At no time did he mention his plans for her, but from the way he leered and almost drooled she doubted they were anything less than horrible.

Normally, she greeted him with absolute silence, refusing to talk or answer questions. The day before that had ended with a slap across the face and his removal of the water bottle she'd been given.

Her throat was so parched now, her mouth devoid of saliva, she didn't know if she even could speak.

Andras stood across from her, carrying a new bottle of water with him, and she found herself staring at it. He set it down just out of her reach, much like the knife with the key tied to it that he'd offered to Kurt.

"Visiting hours already?" she said, her voice hoarse.

"Ah," he said. "At last the caged bird sings."

Defiance and silence had done nothing for her. She decided to be more aggressive. "You'll be the one in the cage soon. If someone doesn't kill you. The Americans might be interested in arresting you, but my country has a different way of dealing with aggression. We like to teach people lessons."

"Ah, yes," he said. "I'm well aware of that. You are still clinging to the notion that you are a great power. Like a child with bad self-esteem, you resort to bullying in hopes of proving your strength."

Some of what he said was true. "It doesn't make you any safer," she said. "Your people killed Major Komarov, that was one strike. Taking me will be the second. They will have no choice but to cut you to pieces or look weak, whatever you do with me."

He almost seemed moved. "Interesting that you use the word *choice*," he said, pulling up a chair, spinning it around, and taking a seat, "because we all have choices to make."

He grabbed the water bottle, twisted the top off, and took a sip. Then he put it back down, once again just out of her reach. He leaned toward her, his arms resting on the chair's back, his face uncomfortably close.

"Your friend Austin, for instance," he said. "I gave him a choice. He could choose to save himself or he could choose to die with his friend. I offer you the same choice. Live and prosper or die with those who are about to suffer."

She held silent again, not sure what he was getting at and yet finding herself thinking only of the water.

"And," he added with a flourish, "I offer your self-esteem-challenged nation an option as well. A chance at revenge against myself or . . . a way to restore its power and former prestige."

He pulled a stiletto knife from some hidden pocket and pressed the switch on its side. The blade shot out and locked in place instantly. He held it toward her face.

"I'd ask what destiny you pick for yourself, but words can be so deceptive. Let us see what your actions tell us."

He grabbed her hands, sliced the rope with the stiletto, and then stepped back.

She waited for a second or two, but her thirst was overwhelming. She reached for the water, conscious that he'd already sipped it. She took a sip and then a gulp, even though she worried that it would make her sick. It took a supreme effort not to gulp the whole thing down.

She stared up at Andras, who hadn't moved a muscle. She reached for the key. It fit the shackles on her feet. She turned it and she was free.

"You're letting me go?" she asked.

"Where will you go?" he said. "We're a thousand miles from the closest speck of land. What are you going to do? Swim for it? Steal a longboat and row yourself to Gibraltar?"

He laughed. And of course he was right. There was no escape.

"You have a choice: you can be a prisoner or a guest," he added.

"What do I have to do to be a guest?" she asked suspiciously.

His eyes traveled over her body admiringly. "You think highly of yourself. You are . . . somewhat desirable, I must admit, but I deny myself the pleasure of having you because there are more important things you can offer."

She was happy to hear that. "Like what?"

"This ship is not a tanker, as it appears to be," he said. "It's a floating weapon of incredible power. This ship can destroy ballistic missiles in flight. It can eradicate an entire naval task force in the blink of an eye. It can be used to sterilize a city without ever blowing up a single building."

He moved to a couch, put his feet up, and continued.

"The world doesn't know all this just yet," he added. "But it will soon. And once it does, I want you to contact your superiors in Russia, tell them who I am, and begin a negotiation for the sale of this weapon. I offer, for half a billion dollars in diamonds, the weapon of the future."

Her eyes narrowed. She wasn't sure what he was talking about, but she had a vague idea. "Why don't you contact them yourself? Surely you know a few people?"

"Oh yes," he said. "And they know me. But the last time I sold them something, your friend Austin snatched it from their grasp before they could really enjoy it. I'm afraid it left a bad taste in their mouths. It was their incompetence, really, and I felt no need to offer a refund or an apology. Since then, they don't trust me like they should."

He did need her help, she thought. Perhaps *need* was the wrong word, but *wanted* fit nicely. If he really intended to do what he was saying, her presence could certainly make it an easier sell. But then what? She had no desire to be part of the weapons trade and couldn't be sure she would survive the transaction once she'd done her part.

Still, there had to be a way to use it to her advantage. Perhaps if she could move around the ship, she might be able to increase her options.

"So I'm supposed to call them, tell them the story you just fed me, and ask for a truckload of diamonds in return for an old tanker hull? They don't trust me that much either," she said.

"You are an expert in advanced forms of energy production and transfer," he countered. "You have a working understanding of particle physics. I'm sure once you've had a look under the hood, you'll be able to convince them what I have is the genuine article."

He stood. This was what she'd hoped for. She had no idea what to do next, but getting out of that cabin came first.

"A tour of the ship?" she asked.

"I will show you what you're selling," he said and then smiled. "They will be very impressed with what their junior agent has discovered."

"And when it's all over?"

"You go with the ship," he said. "Taking your prize back to Murmansk like a conquering hero returning home."

She didn't believe it would end so nicely for her, but there was no sense in showing that now.

"And what about your friends, the Africans?" she asked. She'd heard the argument on the motor yacht. She knew the name Djemma. "Won't they be upset?"

He smiled. "You're sharper than I thought," he said. "Tell me, why do you think I shot that man back there on the boat and left him in the water to float away? Because he made me angry? No. Because he will lead the Americans to Djemma. He already has. An American carrier group is moving in position right now. They will force his hand. I will get my demonstration. And after that, he will be too busy with the barbarians at his gates to do anything but wave good-bye to me."

She grabbed the water bottle, took another sip, and spoke. "I'll look," she said. "And if what you say is true, then I'll tell them so. And maybe we can trade this water in for something more pleasant, like wine."

She doubted he would accept the change in her as being anything more than an obvious ploy, but she'd seen the way he looked at her. She would do whatever she could to get him off balance.

AFTER THIRTY MINUTES in the glider, Kurt was nearing the tanker.
The little green readout on the HUD had his airspeed locked in at
120 knots, and things were looking good. He could even see the
tanker in the distance lit up like a monument of white marble in a
sea of black.

Two miles out, Kurt released the cowling-like cover that Joe had
locked into place. It flew off behind him, and the smooth ride suddenly reverted to a wild one, like cruising the autobahn at top speed
in a Porsche convertible.

He slowed to 90 knots, and actually crossed over the ship at
thirty-five hundred feet. A silent blackbird in the dark of night.

He continued forward for half a mile, and flicked on a rudimentary autopilot that would keep the nose pointed forward and the
wings level. Satisfied that he was far enough out, Kurt released his
boots and hands simultaneously and was literally sucked out of the
glider.

In an instant he was free-falling and popping his chute.

The glider would fly forward for another four or five miles before splashing into the sea and disappearing from sight. A scout

with night vision binoculars wouldn't see it touch down, but if he were watching the sky he might spot Kurt Austin dropping from the heavens.

To reduce that possibility, Kurt was clad in black, and his maneuverable chute was black. At two thousand feet, swinging beneath it, Kurt turned in a wide arc and locked onto the approaching ship. He had one minute.

Thirty seconds later he was a quarter mile from the ship's bow, nine hundred feet above it, and in the process of realizing a giant flaw in his plan.

The ship's blazing lights had seemed like a boon from long distance, making it easy to spot the ship and hone in on it, but Kurt suddenly realized it could prove disastrous now.

The blazing quartz lights reflecting off the white-painted deck were almost enough to blind him. And far worse than that, he would be spotted the minute he touched down like a giant bat landing on a lighted patio in the midst of someone's outdoor dinner party.

Realizing his mistake, Kurt pulled tight on the chute's reins, slowing his descent. He drifted to his right, the port side of the ship, and continued to drop.

He could see only one way to land on the ship without being noticed. The last section of the main deck out behind the superstructure was unlit. He would have to pass up a thousand feet of flat space, circle in behind the ship, and hope to keep up enough speed to reach the last few feet of the deck there.

It seemed almost impossible. But it was either that or splash down in the ocean, call for a pickup, and float around for several hours, hoping not to attract any hungry sharks.

He drifted past the ship, four hundred feet high and wide to port. He had twenty seconds. As he passed the superstructure, he could see a figure on the bridge but no lookouts. He doubted anyone on the blazingly lit ship could see him. Their night vision would be nonexistent in all that light.

He started to turn.

Turbulence from the accommodations block caught him and threatened to spill the air from his chute. He recovered, and swooped in behind the boat.

Below him he saw the end of the deck and the churning white water of the ship's wake. Beneath that wake, a pair of twenty-foot screws would be spinning at a hundred rpms, like a monster-sized blender just waiting to dice him up.

He angled himself forward, picked up some speed, and began dropping fast. He pulled hard on the lines, but it was too late. The wind whipping around the ship blew him backward. He missed the deck, and dropped farther, headed for the white water below and a grisly death.

He tried to turn away, but the swirling wind reversed, sucking him forward like a scrap of paper swept along in the wake of a passing car. The surge of wind threw him toward the aft end of the ship. He saw a flash of huge white letters reading "ONYX," and then he was tumbling into an open space between the main deck and a deck beneath it.

The impact jarred him, and then flung him forward, as the parachute's lines caught on something around the opening. He landed flat on his back and was almost immediately yanked backward toward the rail. The turbulent air behind the ship had filled the chute again, which now threatened to drag him off the deck and back out once again.

Backward, forward, backward. Kurt had had enough.

He hit the instant release on his harness, and the parachute was sucked out over the water. It fluttered and faded and finally vanished in the gloom behind the great ship.

He was on board. Despite all risks and logic to the contrary, he'd landed safely on the *Onyx*. He thought about Joe's long list of warnings regarding what could go wrong and almost laughed. None of those things happened. But Joe had never once mentioned lighted decks, wind shear, and getting chopped up by the ship's propellers.

Looking around, Kurt had to wonder exactly what he'd landed in. The dark open space reminded him of the fantail at the aft end of an aircraft carrier, the huge area between the main deck and the hangar deck.

A few ladders descended toward the water. A pair of hatchway doors looked to be shut tight, and to his left were a few ratty deck chairs and a bucket filled with cigarette butts. Fortunately for him, no one had been sitting out there, having a smoke, as he came in for a rather ugly landing.

Fairly certain no one had noticed his arrival, Kurt pulled off his helmet and disconnected the oxygen bottle. With a hard fling, he launched both out into the night.

He heard no splash. The wind and the wake of the ship were too loud for that.

With those items gone he moved to the darkest corner of the unlit opening and dropped to one knee.

Kneeling in the dark, Kurt slipped a 9mm Beretta from a side pocket and began screwing a silencer into the barrel. His senses were on overload. He listened for movement.

He could hear little beyond the throbbing of the engines and the hum of machinery. But before he could move, the handle on one of the doors turned. The starboard hatchway opened, and Kurt pressed himself farther into the dark like a spider trying to hide in a cracked bit of concrete.

Two figures walked out illuminated by the interior light until the hatch door slammed shut.

They walked to the rail.

"I can tell that you're impressed," he heard a male voice say, a voice he immediately recognized as belonging to Andras.

Unable to believe his luck, Kurt's hand tightened on the Beretta. But then the other voice spoke, and Kurt recognized it as well. A female voice. A Russian voice. Katarina's voice.

"I don't know how you people built such a thing without the world knowing," she said. "But much as I hate to admit it, it's rather an incredible design. I suppose I should thank you for the tour, and the food and the wine."

"Now you understand why your superiors will be interested," Andras said.

"Yes," she said. "I suspect they will be fascinated with what I have to tell them."

Kurt's mind whirled as he listened to her speak. He certainly didn't blame her for using any method she could think of to earn her captor's trust and a chance at freedom, but the words she used made it sound like something bigger was in play here.

Before anything more was said, a crewman opened the hatchway door.

"Radio call for you, Andras," the man said. "Coming in from Freetown. It's urgent."

"Time to go," Andras said.

He led Katarina toward the door, guided her through first, and then followed. The swath of light widened and then narrowed and vanished as the heavy steel door clanged shut.

If there had been any doubt in Kurt's mind before, it was gone now. The Russians wouldn't be interested in a random supertanker. The ship had to be something more, which meant all the odd structures and anomalies probably had some purpose. Kurt was pretty sure it wouldn't turn out to be a benevolent one.

Getting to his feet, he moved to the bulkhead door which Andras and Katarina had gone through a minute before. Silently, he applied torque to the handle. He moved it slowly until it clicked.

He cracked the door a quarter inch and looked down the passageway. With no one in sight, Kurt opened the door wider and slipped inside.

GAMAY TROUT STOOD beside her husband Paul in the operations center of the USS *Truxton*. The activity aboard it and the other ships in the battle group had increased to a frenetic pace over the past few hours.

The ship was being readied for battle, and it wasn't alone. Helicopters had fanned out not only from the *Truxton* but from the group's flagship, the aircraft carrier USS *Abraham Lincoln*. Shortly after that, she heard the scream of jets launching and flying off in full afterburner. The sound was unmistakable even though the *Lincoln* was five miles away.

Until now she and Paul had not been officially updated, but she guessed they were about to find out what was going on.

The ship's captain, Keith Louden, stepped forward. An average-sized man, with short gray hair and sharp hawklike eyes, he was in his early fifties, fit and trim.

"As I'm sure you're aware," Louden began, "we're about to take action against a hostile enemy. An enemy that has already destroyed two of our satellites with some kind of weapon designed around a particle accelerator."

Gamay took a deep breath. "Are we safe here?" she asked,

remembering the bodies they'd seen in the *Kinjara Maru*, blackened and burned.

The captain nodded.

"According to the experts at the Pentagon, this weapon operates on a line-of-sight trajectory. That is, it fires in a straight line, something like a laser. Unlike a bullet or artillery shell, or even a ballistic missile warhead, it can't hit anything around the curvature of the earth. So we should be out of harm's way in our present position. But once a ship or plane pops up over the horizon, that's a different story."

The captain went on to explain the situation, relaying what was known about Sierra Leone, the threats Djemma Garand had made, and the military's planned response.

As the captain spoke he walked them over to a touch-screen monitor. On it they saw the section of Sierra Leone's coast where the weapon and the oil platforms were located. A curved line across the screen flashed in red.

"That's the horizon," the captain told them. "Anything that goes beyond that line, whether it's a ship or plane or missile, is likely to be incinerated within seconds."

Gamay studied the line, a circular arc at a range of approximately forty miles.

"I thought the horizon was sixteen miles," she said.

The captain turned to her. "It depends where you stand. That's one reason every soldier likes to grab the high ground, it allows you to see farther. In this case, Mrs. Trout, it depends where and how high they're firing from."

He tapped the screen and brought up a photo of one of the oil platforms.

"The main structure on those oil platforms rises about three hundred fifty feet from the surface. The particle accelerator ring has a diameter of fifteen miles. A blast from the forward platform, or the forward part of the accelerator ring, could reach a lot farther out into the Atlantic than the platform closest to the coast. In addition, the height lets them shoot downhill at us."

"Like archers in a castle's tower," Paul said.

"Exactly," the captain said. "The taller we are, the farther out they can strike us."

"For instance?" Paul asked.

"We have a pretty low profile for a destroyer," Louden said. "But we still poke up above the surface a tad over sixty feet. They could hit our superstructure at thirty miles, our radar masts at thirty-five."

"And aircraft?" Gamay asked.

"They face the same kind of danger," the captain said. "Flying on the deck still comes with some vertical component. And pilots who encounter problems are taught to pitch up immediately because that's better than flying into the deck or the ocean. But out here, that would immediately expose them to direct fire. And for aircraft flying at altitude, like civilian airliners, the danger zone might extend three hundred miles or more."

Gamay took a deep breath and looked over at Paul.

"Truth is," the captain continued, "it's something we've never dealt with before."

"What are your options," Paul asked.

"Normal procedure calls for airstrikes," the captain said. "Beginning with cruise missiles. But both Tomahawks and Harpoons fly at subsonic speeds. F-18s max out around Mach 2, and not that fast down on the deck."

He turned back to the screen and its red "Event Horizon" line.

"An accelerator like this one fires a particle stream that moves at almost the speed of light. That means our fastest missile will cover no more than one or two feet in the time it takes that beam to cover fifty miles."

An image flashed into Gamay's mind. She pictured soldiers in World War I going over trench walls in futile charges against enemies armed with machine guns. She was no war historian, but she understood why the carnage was so high and the battle lines never moved. Most of the men in those charges were cut down before they'd made it ten yards. This sounded like a similar situation.

"So if supersonic aircraft and missiles are too slow to attack this thing, how are you proposing to do it?" she asked.

The captain pointed to the circular ring.

"They obviously chose to build this system beneath the surface in order to keep anyone from spotting it. That's left them with one vulnerability: they can be attacked beneath the surface, where the water density prevents a particle beam from being an effective weapon."

"Do you have submarines standing by?" Paul asked.

The captain nodded.

"Every carrier battle group brings along a couple of unseen friends. We have two Los Angeles–class attack subs. The *Memphis* and the *Providence*. Our intention is to send them on the offensive.

"We've had the *Memphis* creep up to a position fifteen miles from the target zone. Their sonar is picking up a whole bundle of signals matching the signature your team recorded."

"A whole bunch?" Gamay said.

The captain nodded. "They have at least a dozen of these small submarines patrolling the mouth of this zone. If they're all armed, even with a couple of torpedoes each, that's a big issue."

"Surely two Los Angeles–class subs can deal with them," Paul said.

"We can get in there and mix it up," the captain said, "but our subs are designed to hunt large Russian and Chinese subs in the deep dark parts of the sea. This weapon is situated on a shallow stretch of the continental shelf. The depth at the Quadrangle site averages no more than sixty feet. At two miles, it drops a little, and you even get this tiny cut of a canyon here . . ."

He pointed to a thin line that widened and deepened into a gash in the ocean floor as it moved away from the target zone.

". . . But aside from that ravine, the depth never exceeds two hundred feet until you've passed beyond ten miles. That limits the maneuverability of our boats, and it gives them the advantage."

The captain stood back and took a breath, pulled his hat off, smoothed his short hair, and tucked the hat snugly back on his head.

"Part of a commander's job is not to commit his units to indefensible ground or to send them into battle on missions they are not suited for. The other part is to know when he has to violate that principle. If these guys have some way—any way—to threaten the U.S. mainland, then we have no choice but to take the risk here."

"I get the sense you're telling us this for a reason," Gamay said.

The captain nodded. "We may need your help."

Her eyes grew wide. "Our help?"

Paul seemed just as surprised. "What can we do that the U.S. Navy can't?" he asked.

"With your small submersible, you can get deep into that canyon—it runs to four thousand feet—and you can sneak up on them from the blind side."

Gamay had to fight not to lose it. Her head swam dizzily. Her stomach felt sick.

Paul spoke up for her. "Why can't you get one of the attack submarines into the canyon?"

"It's too tight," the captain said. "Near the top it's just a fissure, no more than twenty feet wide. Even deeper down there are sections no large submarine could maneuver through."

Paul looked at Gamay. She was trembling and shaking her head "no." She and Paul were only here to listen to tapes; they were civilians.

"I can't order you," Louden said. "But I'm asking. None of my men are rated to pilot that submersible, and even if they could be trained on the quick the real key is your *Rapunzel*."

Paul shook his head. He was the man she loved. Her protector.

"I'm sorry, Captain," he said. "I'm sure you know what we just went through. I promised my wife when we agreed to come aboard that we wouldn't be at any risk if we joined you. Honestly, I couldn't have imagined these circumstances, but, as my old man used to say, 'You don't give your word if you're not going to keep it.'"

The captain looked disappointed.

"I understand why you're asking us," Paul continued. "But, I'm sorry, I won't break my vow to her."

The captain took a breath, looking pained, but he seemed to understand.

"Then I'll inform the—"

"Wait," Gamay said.

The captain looked her way.

"How many men are on those submarines?" she asked.

"Two hundred sixty-one."

Two hundred sixty-one men, she thought. She wondered how many had families. Wives or husbands or children. If they were going to risk everything, how could she not? It was her country too.

She looked at Paul. He knew what she was thinking. He nodded. "What would we have to do?" he asked.

"While we try to draw their fire," the captain began, "you maneuver through the fissure and release your robot. We're going to attach two hundred fifty pounds of high explosives to her frame. You guide her along the accelerator ring and look for a weak spot, anywhere that power might be delivered or where the tunnel slopes up toward the surface, as it must in order to fire. You cozy her up to it and hit the detonator."

"And then?" Gamay asked.

"We'll take it from there," the captain said.

Gamay took a deep breath. She couldn't imagine getting back into a submersible. It literally made her weak in the knees. But she would do it because it had to be done.

WITH HIS BERETTA out in front of him, Kurt Austin crept through a narrow corridor that ran for forty feet before terminating in a stairwell.

One flight led up, the other down.

Glancing over the railing, he couldn't tell how far in either direction the stairs climbed or descended, but it was a long way. Probably all the way up to the top of the ship's accommodations block, maybe even out onto the roof where the various antennas and radar emitters were. Ten stories up.

And down . . .

Maybe all the way to the bottom of the hull. To the bilge. He guessed Katarina and Andras had gone up. Despite a nagging desire to find and confront Andras, Kurt looked downward.

Whatever the *Onyx* really was, the truth would not be found in the ship's offices and living quarters or even on its bridge. It would lie below, where the oil tanks and the pumps and the guts of the ship were supposed to be.

Two levels down, he found a dormant pump room. He snuck inside.

Tankers the size of the *Onyx* had massive pump rooms; a ship that could hold millions of barrels of oil had to be able to load and unload or even transfer it around rapidly. Kurt had spent time on a few tankers whose pump rooms were as large as their engine rooms. This was no different, except . . .

Kurt moved closer to the main pipes. A layer of frost clung to them and spread across the bulkhead wall. He tapped a pipe with his fingers. It was incredibly cold.

They certainly weren't pumping oil.

He found a bank of controls and a computer screen. The read-out said:

```
System slaved to bridge
Interrupt y/n? _____
Password: _____
```

Whatever was going on down there, it was being controlled from up above. He didn't dare mess with it. He probably couldn't get in anyway, and just trying would almost certainly alert the bridge crew to his presence.

He moved back to the door and put his ear against it. Hearing nothing other than the hum of the engine and various generators, he opened it.

He made his way back to the stairwell and headed deeper. He decided to skip a few levels and literally get to the bottom of things.

He'd climbed down two flights when a clanking sound stopped him in his tracks.

A quick glance over the railing showed a hand two flights below, sliding along the railing and coming up. He heard voices, and feet lazily pounding the stairs.

". . . All I know is, he wants full power brought up and maintained," one man was saying.

"But there isn't even another ship nearby," a second voice said.

"Don't ask me," the first man said, "but something's going on. We've never gone to a hundred percent before."

Kurt wanted to hear more, but he couldn't wait around. He moved to the landing closest to him and went through the door, closing it behind him as quickly and quietly as he could.

The machinery was louder on this deck, and Kurt reckoned he was right above the engine room. He pressed himself against the wall, one eye on the door to his right, one eye on the hallway to his left.

The footsteps continued up toward his level. He could still hear that the men were talking but could no longer make out the words. He felt relieved when the footsteps rounded the corner and went higher.

Then suddenly the door swung open and stayed that way.

"Hey, don't say anything," the man holding the door shouted back to his friend, who was continuing up the stairs, "but I'm ready to get off this tub the next time we dock."

The man continuing up the stairs laughed. "At least until you blow all your money, right?"

Kurt stared at the door.

The man was standing in the doorway, hand on the open door and his back to Kurt, as he continued his conversation with the man on the stairs. Kurt needed him to go back out or come on in. But standing there was anything but ideal.

Laughing at his friend's joke, the man turned, stepped into the hall, and came face-to-face with the business end of Kurt's Beretta and its silencer.

"Don't even blink," Kurt whispered. He waved the man in.

The crewman was a thin Caucasian with a Mediterranean look about him. He had short curly hair and a tanned and lined face from too much sun over the years, though he couldn't have been more than thirty-five.

The man did as Kurt ordered and shut the door behind him.

"Who are you?" he asked.

"I'm a gremlin," Kurt said. "Haven't you ever met one before?"

"A gremlin?"

"Yeah, we sneak around, screw things up. Generally make a nuisance of ourselves."

The man gulped nervously. "Are you going to kill me?"

"Not unless you make me," Kurt said. "Come on." Kurt nodded down the hall. "Let's find you a nice place to rest."

The man moved in front of Kurt and walked slowly. He made no false moves, but Kurt knew that could change at any second. At the end of the hall another door beckoned.

"Open it," Kurt said.

The man did as he was told and then stepped inside. Kurt followed and then stopped. He was standing in a huge open room with a ceiling at least forty feet high.

The heat from steam pipes radiated through the space, and Kurt felt the humidity soak his body almost immediately. An odd harmonic hum issued from a bank of generators as they vibrated in a low octave. Large white pipes ran in one direction while blue-painted ones crossed them, shielding electrical conduits. The blue pipes continued alongside a catwalk and twisted up and around a pale green cylindrical structure three stories tall that dominated the center of the room.

Kurt walked forward, pushing the Mediterranean man in front of him. On the side of the huge green cylinder he saw stamped lettering. A number and the Russian word *Akula* confirmed his fears.

"This is a reactor?" Kurt asked.

The crewman nodded.

As if to confirm, a sign, written in English, French, and Spanish, also carried the international three-triangle symbol for radioactivity.

Kurt looked past the huge structure and saw an identical one, perhaps two hundred feet away. "The missing Typhoon," he said to himself.

All the evidence had pointed to someone buying it and making it disappear. It turned out he was right about what happened, even if he was wrong about the purpose. The sub had indeed gone missing, and Andras and whoever he was in league with were in fact the new owners, but apparently they'd been more interested in the reactors than the hull.

Why? Kurt wondered. What on earth did an oil tanker that was doing only 7 knots need with a pair of nuclear reactors? She was venting diesel smoke, he'd smelled it on his approach, so if they weren't using the reactors to push the props what were they using them for?

"What's this for?" he asked.

"I don't know what they do," the crewman said.

Kurt bashed the man across the face with the butt of the pistol and then aimed it at his eye. "Don't lie to me," he said.

"For the accelerator," the man said meekly.

"A particle accelerator? Here on the ship?"

The man remained quiet.

"Come on," Kurt demanded, cocking the hammer of the Beretta. "I heard you tell your friend someone wanted more power. That's why you got off on this floor. By the look of your clothes, you're an engineer, not a deckhand. You know what's going on here. Now, you're either going to tell me or you're going to take your secrets to the grave, immediately."

The man stared at the pistol in Kurt's hands. He ran his tongue over his lips and then spoke.

"They use the reactors to power the accelerator," he said. "The energy is channeled out through the front of the ship. It can incapacitate a vessel."

"It can do more than that," Kurt said. "I've seen the bodies of men burned alive and their brains fried in their skulls from your little toy."

"I just run the reactors," the man pleaded.

"Great excuse," he said. "Where were you headed?"

"The control room," the man said.

"Take me there," Kurt demanded.

The man glanced at the pistol in Kurt's hand once again and then nodded. He moved to the catwalk and began climbing it. Kurt followed as the catwalk curled around the reactor's containment wall.

AT THE TOP OF THE CLIMB, the catwalk bent away from the reactor. There, a small offset area enclosed with steel walls and plate glass windows overlooked the entire setup.

The crewman grabbed a handle and opened the door. Kurt shoved him inside and raced in behind him.

Two other men waited there, dressed in white, studying a monitor screen. One wore coveralls and looked like an engineer. The other, he guessed, was a technician, based on the coat he wore.

Kurt soon had all three backed up against the wall.

The question now was what to do.

He inched forward to the screen the men had been studying. The monitor displayed a side view of the ship.

"Schematic?" he asked.

One of the technicians nodded. "Power conduits," he said.

Kurt looked more closely. Colored icons had different text next to them. Beside a yellow block was "Primary Electrical." He figured that was the ship's standard electrical system. A blue-colored icon read "High Voltage." Its lines ran down toward the bottom of the ship and then looped in a circle and rose up near the bow and came back to a section amidships. Based on the photos he and Joe had seen, he could tell the raised-up sections coincided with the odd protrusions Joe had noticed near her anchor lines and the bulging section in the ship's center.

"Is this the accelerator's path?" he asked.

The men nodded in perfect synchronization. "It runs around the ship and exits near the bow," the engineer said.

"Of course," Kurt mumbled. Kurt could not believe he hadn't seen the connection sooner.

The *Onyx* had been in Sierra Leone when Andras was seen there, and Kurt knew this coincided with the loading of the YBCO material onto the *Kinjara Maru*, but he'd never taken it a step further and made the leap of realization that the *Onyx* contained the weapon that fried the *Kinjara* in the first place.

Now it seemed so obvious, but one thing puzzled him. Where was the *Onyx* the morning he and the *Argo* had happened on the stricken freighter? They'd performed a pretty good search after Andras had fled and faked his death by destroying the speedboat. They'd found nothing visually or even on radar.

That meant there still had to be a submarine.

Kurt guessed that Andras and his men had gone overboard just before the explosion. He guessed they swam down to a small submarine, perhaps twenty or thirty feet below the surface, and entered through an air lock of some kind.

Meanwhile, Kurt and the rest of the *Argo*'s crew had been transfixed by the explosion.

But if the Typhoon was laying in a scrapyard somewhere, then what were the thugs using?

"You have a submarine?" he asked.

The technician nodded. "There are three here."

"Any of them big enough to haul cargo?"

"The Bus," the engineer said. "It's one hundred ten feet long. Mostly empty space."

Unless it's filled with tons of YBCO, Kurt thought.

If Kurt was right, the *Onyx* had fried the *Kinjara Maru* and moved on. Andras must have taken the YBCO off the *Kinjara* during the night, loading it aboard the Bus and sending the sub to haul it to wherever the *Onyx* was, somewhere long over the horizon. But he couldn't get the ship to sink fast enough, and that led to Kurt's spotting the smoke trail in the morning.

But it didn't answer a more pressing question. If the *Onyx* was the ship killer, why was Andras demanding full power from the reactors? If Kurt'd heard correctly, there was no ship in range to fry with the particle accelerator.

He tapped the screen to zoom out. His eyes fell on the huge bundle of high-voltage lines in the dead center of the ship, where the tanks would have been had the *Onyx* actually been a crude carrier.

"What's this?" he asked, pointing to the central section of the ship. "All this mess, what is it?"

The men hesitated.

"Come on," Kurt snapped, gun held steady. "I don't have all day."

"It's the Fulcrum," the engineer said finally.

"Fulcrum?" Kurt said. "What does it do?"

The engineer reached over and tapped the screen, zooming in on the array. Kurt's eyes went to the screen a little too intensely. It made him vulnerable. Something he realized too late.

The engineer lunged for him, grabbing his gun arm with both hands. Kurt yanked it free, slammed an elbow into the man's gut, and then knocked him sideways with a forearm to the face. But the crewman had grabbed some type of wrench off the floor. He swung it at Kurt, missing his face by inches as Kurt pulled back.

Kurt triggered the Beretta with two quick pulls, and it spat two shells into the crewman's chest, the sound muffled by the silencer. The man fell back, dropped the wrench noisily, and crumpled to the deck.

Kurt snapped the weapon around to his right. But it was too late.

The technician had punched some kind of alarm button. Klaxons began sounding and lights flashing.

Kurt jammed the gun into the man's face, thought of killing him, and then relented. For all he knew, this guy was the only one who knew how to shut down the reactor.

Guessing he had little time, Kurt kneed the man's solar plexus and sent him sprawling. Then he turned, ducked out the door, and began racing down the catwalk. His feet clanked on the open metal loud enough to be heard over the humming generators, but he didn't have time for stealth.

Halfway down the catwalk's stairs, shots rang out.

He saw a ricochet first and then a group of men near the door he'd come in through. He fired back, forced them to take cover, and leapt over the railing. Landing on his feet, Kurt took off running. He sprinted past the reactor units and raced deeper into the ship.

He came to a door, grabbed the handle, and wrenched it open. To his surprise, a blast of cold air greeted him.

He sprinted inside only to find himself racing beneath a giant lattice of huge interlocking arms, folded up in a way that reminded him of stacked lawn chairs or a monstrous jungle gym that hadn't been assembled.

Hundreds of gray blocks lined each one of the arms. High-voltage power conduits and a network of pipes and hoses covered in frost ran between the blocks.

The whole compartment was the size of a small stadium, ten stories high, four hundred feet long, and stretching the entire breadth of the *Onyx*. As he raced along the metal floor he spotted giant hydraulic pistons connected to the folded array of hinged arms.

He guessed this was the Fulcrum. But what that meant, he had no idea.

The design gave him the impression that it could open up, spreading apart like a giant handheld fan. A diagram on the wall warning the crew to keep clear of the hinges seemed to indicate the same thing. He'd assumed the particle accelerator that ran around the hull and exited near the front was the ship's weapon. So what the hell did this thing do?

Whatever it was, it seemed more important to the engineers than the particle accelerator, and that worried Kurt.

Before he could learn any more, Kurt heard footsteps and another door opening at the far side of the cavernous room. He realized he was being surrounded. He looked up. Another catwalk beckoned thirty feet above.

Cautiously, he climbed up the hydraulic actuator and pulled himself onto the array. It was like scaling the world's largest set of monkey bars. He was almost there when he accidentally touched one of the coolant pipes.

He pulled his arm back with lighting speed and somehow managed not to lose his balance or curse in pain. Gritting his teeth, he looked at his hand. The skin was peeling off as if it had been burned, but he knew better: it had frozen instantly.

He looked at the pipe. Writing barely visible beneath the frost read "LN_2," a common abbreviation for liquid nitrogen. From what he'd learned, superconducting magnets had to be chilled to ridiculous temperatures in order to activate their superconducting properties. He guessed the pipe's insulated surface was at close to 70 degrees below zero. The liquid inside would be pressurized and pumping through at an incredible 321 degrees below zero.

Kurt began climbing again.

Don't touch the pipes, he mouthed to himself, as if his freezer-burned skin wasn't enough to remind him.

By the time he reached the catwalk he could see the men pursuing him. Three of them approached from one side, five more from the other, spread out along the floor.

As quietly as he could, Kurt climbed onto the catwalk. After sitting still for a second, he began creeping along it.

He remained virtually silent, but the vibration caused by his movement caused a chunk of frost to break off of the bottom. It dropped like an icicle from a power line and made a sound like shattering glass as it hit the ground.

"Up there!" someone shouted.

Kurt took off, running. He heard a single shot and then nothing.

Had he managed to look back, he would have seen the leader of the pursuers grabbing the shooter and all but choking him for firing a stray shot in this room. But Kurt never looked back. He made it to the door on the far side of the Fulcrum's vast bay and pushed through it, closing it behind him.

He raced forward, desperately looking for a place to hide and a way to send a message.

Something was about to happen, this ship was about to take some type of action, he was certain of that. And whatever it might be, he was pretty certain the rest of the world would not like what was coming.

56

Moscow, Russia

THE BALD MAN FROM THE STATE, a ranking member of the FSB, held
court in a windowless room in the Lubyanka, the huge monolithic
headquarters building of the Russian Federal Security Service.

In the room with him were several members of the Politburo
and a representative from the Russian Navy and a general in the
Red Army.

He'd just finished listening to a radio call from Katarina Luskaya,
claiming she was aboard a ship with a man named Andras who
wanted to sell them a superweapon, one that would put them years
ahead of the Americans and the Chinese.

After listening to the explanation, one of the politicians could
not contain his scorn. "Strange that we have not heard anything of
this weapon," he said, "and now we are to believe your most junior
operative has uncovered it."

"She was captured by Andras," the Bald Man said. "It is fortunate that he has kept her with him. It is he who brings the offer to
us. We have a history with him."

"It is not a good one," the general noted.

"No, it is not," the Bald Man admitted.

"And he demands an outrageous amount," the Politburo member said.

The Bald Man waved him off. "Of course we would not pay what he asks. A fraction, perhaps ten percent. Even then, only if it was decided that we should."

"Your agent sounded as if she was under duress," the general said.

"Yes," the Bald Man replied. She had used a code word designed to alert only them to the fact that she was being held against her will. But, to her credit, she had chosen the less harsh of the two codes, which meant she thought the situation might be manageable. He was rather impressed with the young former Olympian.

The lone naval representative in the group spoke up. "It would be nice to get a look at that ship," he said. "If it turns out to be of interest, we can start negotiations. If it turns out to be a lie, we simply write Ms. Luskaya off."

The Bald Man cut his eyes to the naval representative. This younger generation understood little. It concerned him. "All of you are missing the bigger point. According to Andras, they will demonstrate the weapon against the American capitol in less than thirty minutes. That makes the question of the ship irrelevant. What we must decide—now that we have been informed—is whether to tell the Americans."

The room went silent. No one wanted to speak.

"It is a very delicate situation," the Bald Man said. "If the threat turns out to be real and it should come out that we knew about it in advance . . ."

There was no need to elaborate.

The Politburo member spoke. "What do you recommend?"

The Bald Man wrung his hands. Every instinct in his body told him it was an American problem. To some extent, he wouldn't have minded seeing a disaster sprung on his old adversary. But the repercussions could be enormous. The law of unintended consequences could not be discounted.

"Inform the Americans of the threat," he said finally. "Do not speak of the ship, and make sure you forget that we had this conversation."

He looked around the room. All present were men of power, but they feared him, as they should.

"What happens after that is up to them," he added.

"And the ship?"

"If the opportunity should arise," the Bald Man replied, "we take it when it's offered. Perhaps we pay, perhaps we barter. Those are mere details to be considered later."

FIVE THOUSAND MILES AWAY, in the middle of the Atlantic, Andras stood over Katarina, who remained at the radio console. Finally, a call came through. It was the Bald Man.

"Tell Andras we are not interested in damaged goods this time," he said.

She looked up. Whatever the message meant, Andras understood. He nodded.

"He understands," she said, keying the microphone.

"*Da,*" the Bald Man said. "Well done, Ms. Luskaya. We await your return."

She didn't feel as if she'd done well. All she'd done was cower before a thug who'd kidnapped her, threatened her, and killed others, including Major Komarov and Kurt, who had tried to save her from this very fate. And now she was part of an incident that would take countless lives in his country.

She could see no way to stop it.

Suddenly, Klaxons began to sound. Andras reacted, and the door opened seconds later.

"What the hell is going on?" Andras demanded.

A breathless crewman stood there. "Problem in the reactor compartment."

"A leak?" he asked.

"No," the man said. "We have an intruder."

Andras laughed. "An intruder? Are you sure? We're twelve hundred miles from the nearest land."

"I know," the man said. "I can't say how it happened. No ships or boats have come close to us. Sonar has detected no undersea craft. Maybe a stowaway," he guessed finally.

"Also unlikely," Andras said with supreme confidence. "More probable, someone's drunk and making a very big mistake."

Katarina could hear the anger in his voice. She wouldn't want to be the crewman who might be making that mistake.

"All the crew are accounted for," the man said. "One of the engineers is dead, another was beaten up by an American commando with silver hair."

Katarina's face lit up.

"Silver hair?" Andras said, suddenly tensing.

The crewman nodded.

"Austin," Andras muttered slowly.

Katarina hoped so. She couldn't figure out how it was possible, but she hoped it was true.

Andras saw it.

"Look at your eyes," he said sarcastically. "All full of hope. You won't make much of an agent if that's the best you can hide your feelings."

"I'm not an agent," she said.

"Clearly." He sounded disgusted.

"We're looking for him now," the crewman said, interrupting. "But he ran through the Fulcrum bay and vanished."

"This is a ship," Andras said. "There are only so many places to go. Keep searching. I'll be on the bridge. Post guards at all entrances to the Fulcrum and near the reactors. Shoot anything that approaches either."

The crewman nodded, and Andras looked at his watch. "We have nineteen minutes. Keep him at bay that long, and I'll hunt him down myself."

The crewman left. Andras grabbed Katarina by the wrist and dragged her into the hall. Two doors down, he opened her cabin, threw her in the chair, and tied her up once again. Hands first, behind the back of the chair, and then her feet.

"I'd hoped to have more fun with you," he said, "but it'll have to wait. Don't worry, you won't need to pretend that you're interested anymore. I don't care."

With that, he stormed out, slamming and locking the door.

If ever there was a time to escape, she thought, now was it.

She pulled and twisted and tried desperately to slip the ropes, but they only grew tighter. She looked around the room. Nothing sharp presented itself; no knives, no letter opener, no scissors. But that didn't mean she would give up.

She rocked the chair back and forth until it fell over. Now on the floor, she dragged it, moving along like an inchworm with a stone on its back and making about as much progress. Finally, she had inched her way over to the small desk.

Sitting on top were two wineglasses and the bottle that she and Andras had shared, each of them hoping to impair the other's judgment.

Lying at the base of the desk, she began banging into it with her shoulder. It rocked back and forth slowly until one of the glasses fell and shattered.

She squirmed around, trying to reach one of the pieces. She felt a few shards digging into her arm. She didn't care. All that mattered was getting a larger curved one and using it on the rope.

Finally, she touched one. Grabbing it awkwardly, she felt it cut her palm, but she managed to hold it in a position where she could work it against the rope. She began to move it back and forth, pressing it against the rope as best she could.

She hoped it was cutting into the rope that bound her because with each movement she felt it slicing into her hand, and her palm and fingers were growing slick with blood.

It hurt like crazy, but she wouldn't give up until every drop of blood had drained from her body.

Still working on the rope, she heard a soft thump on the door. Almost like someone had bumped against it.

The sound of the door opening came next. She couldn't see it;

she had her back to it. She feared what Andras would do if he discovered her. Maybe he'd just let her lie there and bleed to death.

The door shut, and something heavy thumped onto the ground beside her. She felt hands on her, not cold and threatening but caring.

She turned.

Instead of Andras's face, she saw kind blue eyes and silvery hair.

"Kurt," she gasped.

He held a finger to his lips. "Don't move," he said, "you're bleeding badly."

He untied her, grabbed a rag, and wrapped her palm tightly.

Behind Kurt a crewman lay dead on the floor, blood trickling from a bullet hole in his chest. She guessed he'd been the guard at her door.

"I thought you were dead," she whispered.

"Seeing you on the floor with blood all over your wrists, I thought the same thing about you," he said.

He helped her to sit up.

"They're going to use this ship to harm your country," she said. "They're going to attack Washington, D.C., in less than fifteen minutes."

"How?" he asked.

"They've built a colossal particle accelerator off the coast of Sierra Leone. They intend to send a massive beam of charged particles at Washington. It will sweep back and forth like the scanning beam on a computer screen. It will destroy every electrical device in the city limits and set fire to anything that burns. Gas mains will explode. Cars. Trucks. Aircraft. People will spontaneously combust as they walk down the street. It will kill and maim hundreds of thousands."

"I've seen some of that already," he said. "But how can they do it from so far off?"

"This ship is fitted with a powerful electromagnetic array," she said.

"The Fulcrum," he said. "I saw it. What does it do? Does the beam come from there?"

"No," she said. "The beam comes from Sierra Leone. But it passes over us, and with all the power they're generating and running through the Fulcrum, they'll be able to bend the course of the particle beam. Instead of continuing off into space in a straight line, it will reach an apogee of sorts, miles above this ship, and then it'll be bowed by the magnetic forces and directed back down onto your capital."

"Like a bank shot in pool," Kurt said. "So that's why they call it the Fulcrum."

She nodded in agreement.

"They must be insane," he said. "They're inviting all-out war."

That they had to be stopped went without saying. Kurt stood, popped the clip out of his gun, and switched it for a full one. "I have to get to that array," he said.

She stood up beside him. "They're waiting for you there. They know you'll go for it. They have the reactors covered too. "

He looked aggravated. "Tell me you have a suggestion?"

She racked her brain. It was fuzzy from the lack of sleep and the half bottle of wine, but finally something came to mind.

"The coolant," she said.

"Liquid nitrogen," he said.

She nodded. "If we shut off the nitrogen, the magnets will rapidly warm above their operating temperature. Their supercon- ducting properties will fail, and the array will lose power. Hopefully, enough to keep it from doing the job."

Katarina noticed Kurt's face tighten with determination. Then he turned slightly at a sound she also heard.

The door to the cabin opened with a rush. A crewman stood there. "I told you to stand guard out—"

They were the last words he ever said as Kurt drilled him with two shots from the Beretta. Kurt ran for the door, but it was too late, the man had fallen back out into the hall.

He crumpled in the passageway. By the time Kurt reached him, shouts were raining out from down the hall.

Kurt fired, first in one direction and then the other.

"Come on," he shouted to Katarina.

She ran out and cut to the right as he fired down the hall to the left.

Kurt ran after her, and in a moment they were scampering down a ladder.

"I know where to go," Kurt said, grabbing her hand and pulling her along. "Let's just hope we can get there in time."

PAUL TROUT SAT in the command seat of the new submersible, cramped like a basketball player in a compact car. Even though this sub was smaller than the *Grouper*, it was designed with a taller profile, one that at least allowed him to sit up. There was also enough space for Gamay to do her virtual reality thing without having to lie down.

Currently she sat in her getup, unmoving and staring out the small portholes in front of them. The view was surreal. They were speeding along at 140 knots a mere ten feet above the surface, suspended beneath the SH-60 Seahawk on a swaying group of cables.

Though it was night, the whitecaps were visible as they raced by.

The plan was for them to be air-dropped to the south, as close to the Event Horizon line as possible. From there they would dive into the canyon and work their way up, carrying their little robotic bomber with them.

In twenty minutes the first wave of air attacks would commence. While no one expected it to go well, the hope was that waves of missiles and feints by the *Lincoln*'s fighter squadrons would distract

Djemma Garand's forces and allow Paul and Gamay's insertions to go unnoticed.

"One minute to drop point," the helicopter's pilot told them.

"Roger," Paul said. There was nothing for him to do. The sub was all buttoned up and ready to go. When the pilot decided to drop them, they'd drop. He hoped it wouldn't be at a hundred miles an hour.

"I brought along some supplies," he said to Gamay.

"Like what?" she asked. "This isn't a picnic."

He pointed behind them. Diving gear secured with bungee cords. "In case we have to repeat our miraculous escape. This time, we can do it a little more leisurely."

She smiled, just enough to let him know he'd reached her. Then her eyes grew suspicious. "Do you remember?"

"Climbing into this thing brought it all back," he said.

She looked sad. "Too bad."

"Why?" he replied.

"It was horrible," she said.

"It was scary, but we survived. I like to think it was one of our shining moments."

He hoped they wouldn't have to do anything like it again, but the tanks, masks, and fins would help if they did.

"Thirty seconds to drop," the pilot's voice said.

"Let's do this," she said bravely. "Many will die if we fail."

"Ten seconds," the pilot said.

He saw Gamay take a deep breath.

The sub swayed back and forth as they slowed almost to a complete stop. And then a sudden feeling of weightlessness hit, followed a second later by a sharp deceleration and the sloshing feeling of the sub in water. They were already configured for a dive, and in seconds the waves had closed over them.

Paul gunned the throttle, kicked the right rudder, and brought the sub onto course. "We'll be in that canyon in five minutes," he said. "From there, it's a Sunday drive. Fifteen minutes to the top and then it's all *Rapunzel*."

Twenty minutes total. It didn't seem bad at all, but somehow Paul knew they would be the longest twenty minutes of his life.

DJEMMA GARAND STOOD in the control room of his grand project, fifteen stories above the sea. He was well aware that his game of brinksmanship with the Americans had reached a critical point. He had already destroyed two of their satellites and declared the space over Africa off-limits to the spy craft of any nation, but the latest news from his military commanders suggested the game would be played without limits.

"There is an American carrier fleet two hundred miles off our shore," one of them told him. "Our main radar has detected at least twenty-four aircraft inbound."

"What about submarines?" he asked.

"Nothing yet," the commander of his naval forces replied. "The Americans are known to be very quiet, but once they enter the shallows we will hear them and we will pounce."

This was as he'd expected.

"Raise the torpedo nets," he said. "And surface the emitter."

Beneath the platform, his patrol boats started their noisy engines and raced outward toward the mouth of the bay. Meanwhile, his helicopters, loaded with antisubmarine missiles, rose from the platforms of the Quadrangle.

It was good to see, but they'd be nothing but target practice for the Americans if the energy weapon itself didn't work.

A mile in front of platform number 4, a long sloping ramp began to rise out of the water like a massive serpent come to life. It climbed until it stood three hundred feet above the waves, the telescoping towers locking into place like stanchions beneath a bridge.

A long tube lay cradled in the center of the ramp, and at its head was a half circle filled with his superconductors that could direct the particle stream in any direction.

"Emitter online, power levels ninety-four percent," one of his technicians called out.

Nearby, Cochrane studied the readout. He nodded his agreement. "All indicators online."

"Missiles inbound," his radar operator reported. "Six from the south, ten coming from due west. Eight from the northwest."

"Engage the particle beam," he said. "Destroy them."

Switches were thrown, and a computer coding program initiated. The powerful radar systems he'd bought were online, picking up the American missiles, tracking and targeting them. The fire control system went on automatic.

The battle was joined at last.

Djemma knew the odds were long. To win he would have to beat back the American attack and then hit them hard on their own land. To succeed he would have to accomplish what no country had managed to achieve in almost two hundred fifty years: he would have to force the Americans to back down.

As he considered this multiple explosions lit the dark horizon, and Djemma Garand knew he had drawn first blood.

SEVERAL THOUSAND MILES AWAY in the Pentagon's Situation Room, the same group that had gathered twelve hours before watched and waited as the attack on Sierra Leone unfolded in real time.

Dirk Pitt couldn't remember a feeling so tense, perhaps because the events were beyond his control at this point, perhaps because at least two of his people, Paul and Gamay, were out there in it.

After two flights of Tomahawks had been destroyed and a radar-jamming aircraft had been destroyed as soon as it got into position, a second wave of attacks had been initiated.

On-screen, Pitt watched as icons representing a squadron of F-18 Hornets approached the coast of Sierra Leone from different directions. The aircraft were converging on an imaginary line, the Event Horizon. It was believed the particle beam weapon could incinerate anything that crossed beyond that line, but they couldn't grant Djemma free reign without testing it first.

A few miles from the line, the Hornets released a flight of Harpoon missiles, the Navy's fastest nonballistic weapon. By attacking from different angles at the same time, they hoped to overwhelm the system's capacity to respond, but as one missile after another stopped reporting telemetry Pitt began to sense the failure of step two.

At the bottom of the large screen, video from an onboard camera recorded the flight of a missile approaching from the south. Three other missiles were ahead of it by various distances, all of them deliberately traveling on slightly different courses.

In the distance an explosion appeared well to the left of the missile. It began as a flash, and then a cloud, and then a burning arc of rocket fuel igniting spread across the frame. Seconds later, two similar explosions followed, ahead and to the right this time. And then a flare in the lens and nothing but static and a black screen.

"What happened?" Brinks demanded, though everyone certainly knew.

"The missiles are gone," one of the telemetry operators said.

Radio calls in the background confirmed that the pilots were seeing the same thing. And then all of a sudden one pilot radioed with trouble.

"Experiencing control failure—"

The signal cut.

A second pilot reported something similar, and then his signal went dead.

"Large explosions, bearing one-five-five," a third pilot said. *"We have two, maybe three aircraft down—"*

The squadron commander cut in. *"Drop to the deck, pull back."*

Before his orders could be followed, two more signals were lost. And moments later he confirmed five aircraft down.

"Apparently, we drew the damn line in the wrong place," he said.

With a red face, and veins popping out on his neck, Brinks looked as if his head might explode. A sense of unease crept over everyone else in the room as well.

The submarines would move next, along with an end run attempted by Dirk's two civilians. But this attack would happen in slow motion.

As they waited an aide came into the room and spoke with Vice President Sandecker. He passed a note.

Sandecker looked up, concerned anew.

"What is it?" Brinks asked.

"Contact from Moscow," Sandecker said.

"Moscow?" Pitt asked.

Sandecker nodded. "They're claiming to have just uncovered information suggesting that Washington, D.C., is about to be attacked. The threat comes in the form of a particle beam weapon. Apparently, the same one we've just failed to destroy. They insist that the intelligence is highly credible and that the threat is valid. They urge we do everything possible to defend or evacuate."

"What in the name of . . ." Brinks began.

Sandecker looked up. "If the information's accurate, the attack will come within the next ten minutes."

"Ten minutes?"

"Nice of them to get us a warning so early," someone else grumbled.

"We can't evacuate the city in ten minutes," someone said. "We couldn't do it in ten hours."

"Emergency Broadcast System," someone else said. "Urge everyone into shelter. Basements, underground garages, the Metro. If this is true, people will be safer in those places."

Brinks shook his head. *"If this is true,"* he said sarcastically. "This is a joke. And if we start crying that the sky is falling, a thousand people will die in the panic for nothing. Which is probably just what they want, along with our citizens worrying whether we can protect them or not."

"What if we can't protect them?" Pitt asked. "Are we just going to let them die in their happy ignorance?"

Brinks squirmed. "Look," he said. "Garand may have taken this round, but there's no way they can hit us here. Every one of our experts concludes that. Their weapon fires in a line of sight. It simply cannot hit anything over the horizon. Even the F-18s were safe, once they dropped back a few miles."

The Vice President looked around. "Anyone have anything to add? Now's the time if you do."

There was silence for a moment, and then another staffer from the NSA spoke up, a slight man with frameless glasses. "There is one possibility," he said.

"Spit it out," Sandecker ordered.

"Particle beams are aimed and directed through the use of magnets," the man explained. "One study concluded that an extremely powerful magnetic field placed along the target line could bend a particle stream, redirecting it onto a new target. In essence, giving it the ability to shoot around corners."

Pitt didn't like the sound of that. He stepped forward, though it wasn't really his place. "What would it take to hit us here?"

The man straightened his glasses and cleared his throat. "The power output of a small city channeled into a vigorous magnetic array of some type."

"Where would this magnetic array have to be?" Pitt asked.

The man didn't hesitate. "It would have to be located roughly halfway between the weapons emitter and the target."

That made the threat seem less likely. There weren't any islands out there, certainly no place big enough to generate the kind of power this man was talking about. Then again . . .

Pitt turned to the Pentagon staffer who was operating the tactical display. "Widen the screen to show the entire Atlantic," he demanded.

No one objected, and the task was accomplished in two quick strokes of the keyboard.

On the big screen the familiar profile of the American East Coast appeared on the left-hand side. Africa and Western Europe took their places on the right.

The battle group and the Quadrangle continued to be marked by a series of tiny icons in the lower right-hand side, just under the bulge of West Africa.

"Show me the location of the Liberian tanker *Onyx*," Pitt said. "Based on Kurt Austin's last report."

It took a few seconds and then a new icon appeared in a blue tint, one so pale it looked almost white. A tiny flag next to it read "Onyx: Liberia."

Dirk Pitt stared at the icon along with everyone else in the Situation Room.

It sat almost dead center of the screen, exactly halfway between the Quadrangle off the coast of Sierra Leone and the city of Washington, D.C.

"My God," Sandecker said. "When do our submarines attack?"

The Navy's attaché answered. "Thirty minutes just to get in range. They won't be able to stop it."

With that, Sandecker sprung into action, grabbing the aide.

"Get the President to the bunker," he said. "Order an immediate alert on the Emergency Broadcast System. Contact all law enforcement and emergency services personnel and the power companies. Tell them to have their people take cover and be ready for an emergency shutdown. We're going to need them to get this place back up and running if this happens."

As Sandecker spoke to the aide, a brigadier general from the Air Force was on a phone to Andrews, passing the word and ordering a scramble. Other people around the room were giving similar commands, in person or over phone lines. The normally quiet Situation Room suddenly resembled a busy telemarketing center or a Wall Street trading pit.

Pitt grabbed his own cell phone and sent an emergency text that would reach all NUMA personnel in the vicinity. He called the office to follow up.

For his part, Brinks looked stricken, fumbling with a cell phone, trying to call his wife. Dirk understood that; he was thankful that his wife, Loren, and his children, Summer and Dirk Jr., were on the West Coast this week or he'd have been doing the same frantic dance.

Brinks hung up and wandered unsteadily over to Pitt, of all people.

"Voice mail," he said as if in a trance. "What a time to get voice mail."

"Keep trying," Pitt told him. "Ring that phone off the hook."

Brinks nodded but continued to act as if he'd been drugged. The shock had stunned him into inaction.

He looked at Pitt through starry eyes. "Did your man get on that ship?" he asked quietly.

Pitt nodded. "As far as I know."

Brinks swallowed, perhaps his pride. "I guess he's our only hope now."

Dirk nodded. One man on a tanker in the middle of the Atlantic now held the fate of thousands, if not hundreds of thousands, in his hands.

59

ABOARD THE *ONYX*, Kurt ran and fired and ran again. He emptied his second magazine, loaded another, and kept moving, pushing Katarina ahead of him.

Clear of pursuers for a second, they ducked into an alcove between two of the ship's storerooms and listened.

Some kind of strange alarm had begun sounding. It almost resembled the *Whoop, Whoop* heard on a submarine before it was about to dive.

"What's that?" Katarina asked.

"I don't know," he said.

Seconds later a recorded voice came over the ship's loudspeaker. *"Fulcrum deploying. Stand clear of midships array. Repeat. Stand clear of midships array."*

"We're running out of time," Katarina said. "Can't be more than a couple minutes left."

"And we're going the wrong way," Kurt said.

They'd had no choice, each pack of crewmen they'd run into had forced a detour. Since they'd left the cabin, they'd actually moved farther forward instead of aft.

In their favor, the ship was mammoth yet crewed by no more

than a hundred or so. Some of those had to be at duty stations to pull off whatever Andras was doing with this Fulcrum array. And at least six were now dead.

Working against them was the ship's architecture. The Fulcrum compartment was between them and the coolant room at the aft end of the ship. Since the Fulcrum took up the top half of the ship, and ran from beam to beam, the only way to get past it was to go deep into the ship and use one of the bottom decks to cross under it.

The alarm and recording continued, and Kurt imagined the giant fan-shaped array, larger than a football field, emerging through huge doors on the top of the *Onyx's* hull.

"Let's go," he said, pulling Katarina up and getting on the move once again.

She was struggling to keep up but had yet to make the slightest complaint.

Kurt found a ladder that dropped through a hole in the deck. He took it, sliding down with his feet on the outside rails.

"Come on," he said. As Katarina came down the ladder he noticed the rag around her hand was soaked right through in red.

He went to look at it.

"I'm fine," she said. "Keep going."

Another ladder dropped them down a few feet to one more deck. And this time, Kurt stopped. He could hear machinery throbbing in an odd pattern, on, off, and back on.

It gave him an idea.

"Wait here," he said.

Kurt crept forward. Markings on a pair of closed hatchway doors read "Thruster Unit."

Behind him, Katarina leaned against the wall and slid down it in slow motion.

"I'm okay," she said as he started back toward her. "Just . . . taking . . . a little rest."

She wasn't going to make it much farther. At least not running through the ship at breakneck speed. And they were running out of time anyway.

The *Whoop, Whoop* alarm stopped, and even down in the bowels of the ship the hull shuddered slightly as something big locked into place.

"How much time?" he asked.

"A minute," she said through her exhaustion. "Maybe less."

She slumped onto her side, the blood-soaked rag over her hand smearing blood across the metal deck.

He couldn't help her now. He had to do something about the Fulcrum before it was too late. With a fire ax he pulled from a bracket on the wall, he broke open the lock on the door in front of him. The sound of throbbing machinery echoed throughout the room.

He stepped inside. Down below were the powerful electric motors of the bow thrusters. By the way the system was acting, it was struggling to keep the ship in some kind of perfect alignment.

Kurt guessed that redirecting a particle beam would require exact precision. If he could stop the thrusters, or throw them off, that might ruin either the beam's cohesiveness or its aim.

OFF THE COAST OF SIERRA LEONE, Djemma Garand studied the field of battle from his vantage point in the control room of platform number 4. He had forced the Americans back. Twice he had repelled their assaults. Now he would strike with a vengeance.

"Bring all units back to full power!"

Cochrane was beside him, looking nothing like a man who was about to become infamous for all eternity. He looked like a rodent who would rather have scurried under a bush and hid than a man ready to claim his place in history. But he did as he was told, and he had trained Djemma's other engineers well enough to operate the machinery if he balked.

"All units at a hundred one percent design load," Cochrane said. "Magnetic tunnels are energized and reading green. The heavy particle mix is stable."

He looked over at one more screen, a telemetry display from the *Onyx*. "The Fulcrum array is locked in position," he said. "You may fire when ready."

Djemma savored the moment. The Americans had attacked him with missiles and aircraft, and now his sonar readings detected two of their submarines entering the shallows. They were breaking themselves on his strength, and now, as he promised, they would feel his bite.

Once he gave the order, the system would energize. It would take fifteen seconds for the charge to build up in the tunnels of his massive accelerator, and a quarter of a second later the energy burst would race forth, cross over the *Onyx*, and be directed down onto Washington, D.C.

For a full minute it would spread across the American capital, panning back and forth and wreaking havoc and destruction.

He looked over at Cochrane. "Initiate and fire," he said calmly.

———

IN THE THRUSTER ROOM of the *Onyx*, Kurt found what he needed: the thick high-voltage lines he'd seen in the reactor room. The blue lines, he thought, remembering the schematic. They were routed through the accelerator and then back to the Fulcrum.

That was his only shot. He stepped toward them, swinging the ax and releasing it at the last instant to avoid being electrocuted when it cut into the cables.

The blade hit, and released a massive shower of sparks. A blinding flash of electricity snapped across the gap like man-made lightning, and the entire ship was plunged into darkness.

Kurt was thrown to the deck by the blast. His face felt burnt. For several seconds the compartment was in absolute darkness. The motors of the bow thrusters rattled loudly and began winding down. Finally, the emergency lights came on, but, to Kurt's great joy, nothing else seemed to have power.

He hoped it was enough. He hoped it had been done in time.

UP ON THE SHIP'S BRIDGE, Andras stared. The ship had gone black, and in the dark of the night it seemed as if the world had vanished. Seconds later the emergency lights had come on.

At first he feared the array had somehow overloaded the system. He reached forward, tapping at the Fulcrum's controls and flicking the toggle switch on the side of the unit. He got no response, not even a standby light.

A second later some of the basic systems came back online, and Andras looked around hopefully.

"It's just the one-twenty line," one of the engineers said. "The high voltage is still down." The man was flicking a few switches of his own to no effect. "I have no thrusters, no power to the array. No power to the accelerator."

Andras leaned forward to check the Fulcrum array visually. It stood there, spread out like the canopy of a giant tree that had somehow sprouted from the center of the ship, but it was dead. Not even the blinking red warning lights were illuminated anymore.

He grabbed the joystick that had raised it into position and fiddled with it for a second, then flung the controller aside with great bitterness.

"Damn you, Austin!" he shouted.

After a moment to reflect he realized that power could be restored. He just needed to make sure Austin wasn't around to cut it a second time. He grabbed his rifle and checked the safety.

"Get somebody down there to reroute the high-voltage lines," he ordered. "We'll try again, once it's up and running."

The engineer nodded.

Another man looked over at Andras from the far corner of the bridge. "What do we tell Garand if he calls?"

"Tell him . . . he missed."

With that, Andras stormed out of the bridge, a single thought burning his mind: Austin must be destroyed.

60

THE TENSION in the Pentagon's Situation Room had grown as tight as a drum. The proverbial pin dropping would have sounded like a cannon shot.

One of the staffers, with a hand to the earphone of the headset he wore, relayed a message.

"We're confirming a discharge from the Quadrangle site," he said. "Continuous discharge . . . Duration at least sixty seconds."

No one moved. They all stared at the screen and waited for the inevitable. Unlike ballistic missiles with their seventeen-minute approach time, it should have taken only a blink.

Ten seconds later the lights were still on, the computers still running.

Everyone began to look around.

"Well?" Vice President Sandecker asked.

A female staffer spoke up. "The networks are still broadcasting live," she said. "No sign of impact or damage."

Brinks's face began to fill with color again. He turned to Dirk Pitt. "Your man did it," he said hopefully.

"His name's Austin," Pitt said.

"Well, you give him my thanks along with the country's," Brinks said. "Along with my apology for being a bigmouthed idiot."

Pitt nodded, guessing that Kurt Austin would enjoy all three. He turned to the Navy brass in the room. "He's going to need a way off that ship."

"Already on it," one of them replied, smiling.

That pleased Pitt. But they weren't out of the woods yet.

Up on the monitor the icons that represented the USS *Memphis* and the USS *Providence* were flashing. A new ship's status was being reported. They were going into battle.

THE USS *MEMPHIS* had come up from the depths, just beyond the edge of the continental shelf. Holding station there, it had begun pinging away madly with the powerful sonar in its bow.

This was not normal operating procedure, as it gave away the ship's position, but the plan was to draw Garand's fleet of small subs out from its bay and allow the Trouts and *Rapunzel* to sneak in behind them.

A further effect of the violent sonar emissions would likely be confusion and even terror on the part of the enemy.

Inside the sub's control room the sonar operator could see the plan working almost too well.

"Five targets approaching," he called out. "Labeled bravo one through bravo five."

"Do we have firing solutions?" the sub's skipper asked.

The fire control officer hesitated. His computer kept flashing green for yes and then red for no.

"The subs are so small, and continually changing direction, the computer can't create a solution."

"Then fire on acoustic mode," the captain ordered. "On my mark."

"Ready, sir."

"Fire from all tubes."

Over a period of five seconds compressed air launched six Mark 48 torpedoes from the *Memphis*'s midships tubes.

Seconds later the sonar man heard a different sound. "Incoming torpedoes," he called out. "Bearing zero-four-three and three-five-five. At least four fish."

There were torpedoes approaching from the right front quadrant and the left. It took away their ability to maneuver.

"Hard to starboard," the captain shouted. "Full revolutions, bow planes full up. Deploy countermeasures."

The ship turned, accelerated, and rose toward the surface. The countermeasures designed to draw off the approaching torpedoes were dumped in the water behind them.

Submarine battles were slow-motion versions of aerial dogfights. And the wait as a torpedo tracked inbound could be interminable.

Ten seconds passed and then twenty.

"Come on, go," the skipper grunted.

The sub rose fast.

"One miss," the sonar man reported. Then seconds later, "We're clear."

They'd managed to avoid the incoming weapons. But the *Memphis* wasn't as nimble as the small craft it was fighting. Like a bear tangling with a pack of wolves, she wouldn't last long. As if to prove it, the sonar man called out again.

"New targets, bearing zero-nine-zero."

"Full down angle," the captain ordered.

In the distance a series of explosions rocked the depths as two of the torpedoes from the *Memphis* found their marks in quick succession. But there was no celebration; their own troubles were too close.

"Bottom coming up fast, skipper," the helmsman reported.

"Level off," the captain said. "More countermeasures."

The bow angle eased. Another explosion rocked them from far off, but the sonar man looked stricken.

He turned to the captain, shaking his head. "No good."

An instant later the *Memphis* was hit. Anyone not seated and belted in was thrown to the floor. The main lights went down. The sound of alarms wailed throughout the ship.

The captain got to his feet, managed a quick look at the damage board. "Emergency surface," he ordered.

The *Memphis* blew all tanks and began to rise.

MILES AWAY, Paul and Gamay Trout couldn't see any screen or hear any radio calls describing the action. But the ocean carried sound much more effectively than the air, and echoes from the booming explosions reached them one after another like the sound of distant thunder.

Neither of them spoke, except as necessary for navigation.

Finally, Paul slowed the craft. They'd dropped from the Navy helicopter, descended into the far end of the canyon, and wound their way back toward the platforms.

"We're at two hundred feet and holding," Paul said. "If the inertial system is right, the platforms are less than a mile away."

Gamay was already activating *Rapunzel*'s program. She wanted to get this over with as quickly as possible.

"Detaching umbilical," she said.

She felt herself sweating once again despite the cold. And then she felt Paul's hand on her shoulder, massaging it softly.

Another series of explosions rumbled through the depths, these far bigger, closer, and more menacing than any that had come before.

"Do you think that was one of ours?" she asked.

"I don't know," he said. "Don't think about it. Just do what you have to do."

She tried to block it out, even as another, smaller boom reached them, but there was nothing to see through her visor except darkness.

Seconds passed.

"How far?" she asked.

"You should be almost there," Paul said.

Something was wrong. "She's not moving," Gamay said.

"What?"

Gamay studied the data feed from the little robot. "Her motor is operating, but she's not moving. She's stuck."

"How is that possible?" Paul asked.

Gamay, with a flip of her right hand, switched on *Rapunzel*'s exterior light. The answer to Paul's question came through instantly.

"She's stuck in a net."

Gamay put *Rapunzel* in reverse and pulled her back a few yards. The net was no fluke; it was draped from above.

"Antitorpedo nets," Paul said. "We must be right beside the platform."

Gamay switched on *Rapunzel*'s cutting tool. "I'm cutting through it."

———————

THE *MEMPHIS* had broken the surface but was taking on water fast. The order to abandon ship was given, and men were scrambling from the hatches and into boats or just into the sea itself.

But the survivors were well inside the Event Horizon line. If their enemy wanted to, he could fry them all with a single burst from his weapon.

ON THE *ONYX*, Kurt noticed the lighting returning to normal. He was thankful that the bow thrusters hadn't come back to life. He hoped that meant the high voltage was still out and the Fulcrum array was still off-line.

He moved back to where Katarina sat in the hall. "Ready for one more run?" he asked.

"I don't think I can," she said.

He studied her hand. The blood flow had slowed, the wound was finally clotting.

"Come on," he said. "You're a champion. Prove it to me."

She looked into his eyes and clenched her jaw. He helped her up, and they began to move.

"Do you still want to get to the coolant room?" she asked.

He nodded. "They'll get this power back on soon enough. We have to permanently disable this thing."

"I know another way to get there," she said. "They'll never expect us to use it."

She led him forward until they came to another hatch. This one was sealed tight.

Kurt dropped beside it and grabbed the wheel.

After two full rotations it spun easily. He opened it to see a ladder dropping down through a shaft. Dim red lights lit the rungs, and glacial air wafted up toward him. Kurt suddenly thought of Dante's *Inferno*, which depicted some of Hell's outer layers as frigid, Arctic-like zones.

"What's down there?" he asked.

"The accelerator tunnels," she said.

That didn't sound like a safe place to be, but the sound of feet pounding on the metal deck above changed his mind.

He helped her onto the ladder, climbed down behind her, and shut the hatch. At the bottom they dropped into a tunnel.

It reminded Kurt of standing on a subway platform, like the Washington Metro, only narrower. The familiar high-voltage lines and liquid nitrogen conduits raced down each wall and also along the ceiling and floor. Rows of the shiny gray rectangles that Kurt knew to be the superconducting magnets traveled off into the distance, curving slightly at the limit of his vision.

Kurt exhaled a cloud of ice crystals. He was already chilled to the bone. It reminded him of the Fulcrum's compartment only colder.

"If we go this way," she said, "we can pop up through the rear access hatch. One level down from the coolant room."

Kurt began walking, with Katarina leaning heavily on his shoulder. It was a great plan. The crew would never search for them down there, he was sure of it.

"What if they turn this thing on?" he asked.

"Then we'll be dead before we even know what's happened."

"All the more reason to hurry," he said.

BY NOW DJEMMA GARAND could feel the danger clawing at his own throat. Washington, D.C., stood untouched by his weapon. Andras would not answer and the crew of the *Onyx* reported commandos aboard.

Swirling around him, the American military showed no signs of backing off, no matter how hard he pounded them.

"Where's Andras?" he demanded into the radio.

"He is looking for the American," came the reply.

"What about the array?"

"It's still down. We have no power."

The crewman from the *Onyx* sounded panicked, though he could not be facing what Djemma was facing.

He put the headset down. It would end in failure. He could see that now.

He looked out over the waves. One of their submarines had been destroyed and forced to surface. The other continued to fight, firing from deeper waters.

Through a pair of huge binoculars, he saw the crew of the American submarine bobbing in their orange life rafts.

"Target their position," he said calmly.

Cochrane hesitated.

"We are going to die, Mr. Cochrane," he said. "All we can do now is take as many of them with us as possible."

Cochrane stood back from the controls. "Forget it," he said. "You want to go down in flames, that's your business. I'm not dying here."

Djemma had been waiting for this moment. He pulled out his old sidearm and blasted three holes in Cochrane.

Cochrane fell back in an unmoving heap. Djemma fired a few more shots into his worthless hide just for the sheer pleasure of it.

"And you are proved wrong yet again, Mr. Cochrane," he said.

He stepped to the controls, glaring at the engineers. "Target the life rafts and fire!"

GAMAY TROUT had finished cutting through the net and had eased *Rapunzel* and her harness of explosives through. Since then, she'd been looking for what the *Truxton*'s captain had described.

"Head two-nine-zero," Paul said.

She turned *Rapunzel* onto the course and got her moving again. She considered shutting off the floodlight, but she didn't want to run into any more obstacles. Besides, they were almost there—up ahead she could see the base of some large structure.

A large tube ran up to it, like a city's oversized sewer pipe. She guessed this was part of the accelerator.

"That's it," she said. "It's got to be."

"I think you're right," Paul said, excitedly. "Find the base where it connects to the seafloor.

Gamay looked around, shining *Rapunzel*'s light in the darkness. Then she directed her to the base of the huge pipe.

"What do you think?" she asked.

"Wedge her in there between the bottom and the pipe where it starts to angle out of the water," Paul said. "It'll give the explosion more force."

Gamay did as he suggested. "That's as far as she'll go."

Paul grabbed the detonator, flipped the safety cap up.

"Do it," Gamay said.

He pressed the switch.

"Good-bye, *Rapunzel*," she said, thankful for the little machine and sorry to see her go.

The feed to Gamay's visor cut out, and she lifted it up. Two seconds later the concussion wave reached them. It hit with a shuddering rumble, shaking the sub for a moment and then fading away.

UP ON THE PLATFORM Djemma saw all the indicators on his weapon turn red. He saw a great eruption of water and silt just behind the emitter. A moment later the raised portion of the accelerator tunnel collapsed into the sea.

How? he wondered. How had they done it?

At almost the same moment, one of his men called from the radar console. "More missiles inbound. One minute to impact."

Djemma ignored him. He walked out of the control room, moving forward onto the platform. The wind buffeted him. The darkness of the night swirled, and the water churned where his weapon had been breached.

He looked up to the horizon. He could see the tiny dots of fire approaching: the tail end of the Harpoon missiles that were zeroing in on him. There was no escape.

"And so I shall fall," he whispered to himself. "Like Hannibal before me."

The missiles hit to his left and right almost simultaneously. The explosions merged together, vaporizing him into a fireball that could be seen for miles.

KURT AND KATARINA continued toward the aft end of the *Onyx*. Kurt kept one arm around her waist and held her close beside him because she was weakening and barely able to keep up with his pace.

The tunnel itself was filling up with a dense white fog and a cold that chilled them to the bone. With the high voltage off-line, the liquid nitrogen was beginning to warm and expand. It would boil off as soon as it got above negative 321 degrees. Kurt guessed a system like that would have relief valves that might vent the gas into the tunnel.

They pushed forward, feeling their way through the frigid cloud. At times, visibility in the tunnel was no more than three feet. They moved slowly, looking for the aft-most hatch.

Finally, Kurt's hand fell on a curved seam. He recognized the recessed handle and the shape of an access hatch.

"Our way out of here," he said, reaching up and turning the wheel that sealed the hatch shut.

After pulling it open, he helped Katarina onto the ladder. She began to crawl up the rungs. Kurt was ready to join her when a familiar voice cut through the dense mist like a knife.

"Kurt Austin."

Katarina stopped on the ladder.

"Go," Kurt whispered. "And don't wait for me."

She pushed off, moving upward, and Kurt held still.

"Do you realize you're quite possibly the most aggravating man alive," Andras said, still hidden in the vapors.

Certain the killer was setting up to spray the tunnel with automatic weapons fire, Kurt dropped flat to the deck and pointed the barrel of his nine millimeter into the white blanket of mist.

Andras wasted no time sending a volley of gunfire into the passageway. The shots rang like thunder on a warm drizzly night. The shells thudded against the steel bulkheads and ricocheted like a flight of deadly wasps.

As Kurt hoped, the bullets all passed above him, but he let out a groan and spoke as if he were in agony. "It doesn't matter what you do to me," he grunted. "You've lost."

He waited for a reply but none came.

Kurt could hear the catwalk creaking underneath him. He surmised that Andras was taking a new position and zeroing in on the sound of Kurt's voice. Kurt needed to get him talking so he could do the same thing, since it didn't take a wizard to predict that Andras was not standing in the middle of the tunnel but was either lying on the deck like Kurt or pressed up against the bulkhead on one side or the other.

Breathing heavily for effect, Kurt spoke again. "If I was you . . . I'd be . . . getting out . . . of here."

He was counting on Andras having enough of an ego to feel he had mortally wounded his prey. But, so far, the man had made no mistakes.

"Give me your weapon," Andras said, his voice coming from the shroud of gas like an unseen evil ghost.

Austin lay there with the cold seeping in his skin. His face was so numb, he could hardly feel anything. He held the Beretta in hands nearly frozen, his elbows placed on the deck.

"Let the girl go," he said, cupping a hand to one ear like a radar directional finder and waiting for a response.

"Of course," Andras said, his words echoing in the tunnel. "Everyone goes free. I'll send them all off with roses, and mints on their pillows. Now, slide over your weapon!"

"I'll . . . try," Kurt muttered brokenly.

Kurt inched to his left, thumped his pistol onto the metal walkway as if he had dropped it and scraped it along the deck, to make it seem as if it were sliding over metal before stopping.

With that, Kurt rolled quickly to the other side of the tunnel. A burst of three shots rang out, pinging off the deck where he'd just been.

"Sorry, Mr. Austin," Andras said as if he were bored. "I don't trust you any farther than I can throw this ship."

And then several more bursts shook the tunnel. The muzzle flash lit the fog like lightning in a cloud. The glare was too diffused to give Andras's position away, but Kurt spotted something else. He couldn't see the bullets themselves fly, but he noticed they created tiny shock waves in the thick, frigid mist.

He fired back, unleashing an eight-shot salvo that blasted through the fog. When he finished, the slide of his gun locked in the open position. His clip was empty.

The silence that followed was haunting. Kurt stared into the fog, wondering, hoping, he'd made a killing shot.

Andras had not fallen or Kurt would have heard it. Nor had he fired back.

Beginning to worry, Kurt checked what remained of his ammo. Only one bullet remained in another clip that he hadn't emptied.

He pulled back the receiver, slid the round into the breach, and thumbed the slide release. The weapon locked, his last shot in the chamber.

Finally, he heard movement through the icy shroud. It came like a drunk shuffling along a sidewalk. A vague, ghostly form slowly appeared: Andras, limping, dragging his leg.

He held an assault rifle, the stock pushed into one armpit, the muzzle pointed at an awkward angle toward the deck and Kurt Austin. Blood seeped from his mouth, indicating a shot to one lung. His face was stained crimson as blood flowed from a deep crease on the top of his scalp. For a second Kurt thought he would fall, but he didn't.

The eyes, Kurt noticed, burned with an intensity beyond all madness. It was the picture of a man shocked at finding out he was vulnerable to any other man. He pulled himself to a stop six feet from where Kurt lay. He stared at Kurt through his bloody mask, appearing amazed that, after all his fire, Kurt had survived without a scratch.

Kurt had his own dilemma. With one 9mm shell left, he wasn't sure he could finish Andras off, not without a head shot. And as soon as he fired, Andras would open up with his rifle, shredding Kurt at such close range.

It had become a standoff.

Kurt eased off the deck and stood. They were only yards apart, aiming their weapons at each other. Kurt's right hand held the Beretta, his left had found a knife in his pocket. The same knife he and Andras had traded back and forth three times already. He couldn't open it, but he still could use it.

He flipped the knife at Andras, who caught it deftly and smiled as he stared at it.

"Out of ammunition, Mr. Austin? Pity you didn't open the knife before you threw it." Now confident, Andras moved slowly. He raised the assault rifle in preparation to fire.

Kurt beat him to the draw, took an instant to aim, and fired at the liquid nitrogen pipe just above Andras. The liquid burst out under high pressure, dousing Andras heavily on the right side of his body, washing over his arm and the assault rifle he held.

The rifle fell and broke open as it struck the deck. Andras stumbled and hit the tunnel's wall. He watched uncomprehending as his arm, hand, and fingers shattered into a thousand fragments like a crystal vase crashing from a top shelf to the floor. A scream of agony froze in his throat.

In seconds the nitrogen began filling the tunnel. It blanketed Andras, his body already frozen like a block of ice. It swept down the hall toward Kurt as he raced to the hatch and pulled himself up the ladder.

The frigid mist followed him like a wave in the surf, but Kurt climbed as fast as his hands and feet could take him and made it out through the top of the passage.

He slammed the upper hatch shut. Feeling it lock into place, he lay on his back and relaxed for the first time in more hours than he could calculate.

After one minute, and one minute only, he rose to his feet and searched for Katarina. He found her sitting by a stairwell as if she was waiting for a miracle.

"How are you doing?" he asked.

She turned and looked at him, her face lighting up like a cloud under the sun. "Oh, Kurt," she said. "How many times did I think you were dead?"

"Luckily, it's Andras who is dead."

Her smile widened in a mixture of doubt and joy. "Are you sure?"

Kurt nodded. "I watched him fall to pieces with my own eyes."

KURT AND KATARINA arrived at the same stairwell Kurt had come down hours before. He looked up. There was no way Katarina could climb eight flights of stairs.

"Is there another way out?" he asked.

She nodded.

"This way," she said, leading him past the stairwell.

Twenty yards on, another door beckoned. Kurt opened it. Sitting in a pool, secured to the edges of a metal dock, were three submersibles. Two of them looked suspiciously like the XP-4 he had rescued a week ago. The larger one dwarfed them, and he assumed this was the Bus.

He noticed that the XP-4-looking craft had torpedoes mounted on either side, like pontoons.

Beside them was the 60-foot motor yacht that Katarina had been prisoner on.

"This is where I came in," she said.

Kurt looked for the door controls. "Are we above the waterline?" he asked.

She nodded.

He pressed a switch but nothing happened. The high voltage

was still down. He found a manual release and threw the lever over. A capstan-like wheel began to spin as the door fell with the force of gravity.

Seconds later he and Katarina were in one of the XP-4s, moving out into the darkness of the night.

With Andras dead, the high voltage disabled, and the liquid nitrogen blasting out into the particle accelerator tunnel, Kurt figured he'd lived up to his claim of being a gremlin, but he had one last act up his sleeve.

He turned the small sub around and circled to the very aft end of the ship.

He fired both torpedoes into the ship's propellers and rudder assembly.

The explosion was blinding. Almost immediately Kurt could see that the ship's wake was turning to mush. The props were damaged or gone, and seawater was likely flooding the bottom deck.

The ship itself wouldn't go down. The torpedoes were relatively small, and a vessel the size of the *Onyx* could take on massive amounts of water before she foundered. With all the damage near the tail end, that wasn't going to happen, but she wouldn't be going anywhere either. Not to Russia or China or any other unfriendly nations.

With that done, Kurt turned the submersible away from the *Onyx* and began to put some distance between them. Both he and Katarina would struggle to keep awake for the next three hours, but shortly after dawn a U.S. Navy helicopter spotted them, swooped down, and picked them up.

Kurt asked for news.

The medic told him of the panic in Washington but that nothing had happened. He asked about Sierra Leone and was told that an engagement off the coast of Sierra Leone had been completed. Lives had definitely been lost, but the threat had been eliminated. Kurt asked if there had been any mysterious crashes of old Russian cargo jets and was thankful to hear a firm negative to that question.

He went to ask about the missing scientists when the medic held up a hand.

"You're going to be all right," the medic said, "but you need to stop talking now."

Kurt understood.

He watched over Katarina as they flew past the smoking hull of the *Onyx*, now swarming with U.S. Marines. From there they turned west and began a ninety-minute journey that would bring them to the guided missile frigate from which the helicopter had been launched.

With the news he'd been told, Kurt felt a sense of peace he hadn't known in weeks. That feeling, his exhaustion, and the rhythmic thumping of the helicopter blades, everything around him seemed determined to soothe him and lull him to sleep. He closed his eyes and went with it.

EPILOGUE

IN THE DAYS AFTER THE INCIDENT the world seemed to spin a little slower. The situation in Sierra Leone had stabilized with the help of a UN peacekeeping force and troops from the African Union. Many political prisoners had been freed, including Djemma Garand's brother, who was now being asked to help build a coalition government.

The missing scientists had been found and returned to their respective countries. Several were injured, but only one had died. The U.S. attack force had suffered the brunt of the losses. Thirty-one men and women from the *Memphis* were dead or missing. Eleven naval aviators—pilots and radar officers—had been killed. But their sacrifices, and the efforts of the NUMA civilians, had prevented a catastrophic incident from occurring.

Not a single death was recorded in the last-minute emergency in Washington. Dozens of car crashes, hundreds of injuries, but people had remained remarkably calm in their efforts to reach safety.

Kurt, back in the States, recuperated. He watched a lot of news and was regaled with visits from Joe Zavala, the Trouts, and Dirk Pitt.

Joe spent hours telling him stories of his adventures with the crew of the IL-76, back in Tangiers. Paul and Gamay had their own stories, not as lighthearted, but the kind that filled people with pride. He noticed they never stopped holding hands.

Dirk Pitt congratulated them all on a job well done and then began adding up the tab. The *Barracuda*, the ultralights, damage to a soccer field, legal issues with the White Rajah Club in Singapore, and something about a missing leopard.

"I don't even want to know why we're paying for the capture of a juvenile spotted leopard," Dirk said.

Kurt opened his mouth in an attempt to explain but then shut it. What was the use?

The IL-76 charter was next on the list, the expended Lunatic Express, and multinational cleanup issues regarding oil leaked from the *Onyx* as a result of his torpedo attack.

When Dirk finished going through the list, he smiled. "As I've gotten older I've learned a few things," he said. "One of them is: you get what you pay for. You and Joe are like one of my cars. Expensive, bad for the environment, and often a pain in the backside. But you're worth every penny."

As soon as he was able, Kurt made contact with Katarina, arranging to meet her back on Santa Maria.

After all that had transpired, the U.S. and Russian governments had agreed that items aboard the Constellation rightly belonged to the Russian people. Both sides agreed that it would be appropriate if Kurt and Katarina supervised the dives to retrieve them.

Katarina beamed when she saw him, and she kissed him long and hard as soon as they met up despite the presence of a small audience.

A few days later they were out on a chartered dive boat with representatives from the Russian and U.S. governments on board keeping an eye on the proceedings.

After one dive as a run-through, they went down to retrieve the stainless steel trunks. Using torches to free them from the Constellation's floor reminded Kurt of Joe's narrow escape.

He realized they wouldn't have survived had this old wrecked aircraft and its oxygen bottle not been here. After moving the cases outside the aircraft and attaching them to floats, which were inflated with air from their tanks, Kurt went back inside and swam up to the cockpit.

He reached for the copilot's dog tags, which still dangled around the man's skeletal neck. He gently pulled them free and then swam from the plane.

Surfacing, he climbed aboard the dive boat. Katarina was already working on cutting the lock off one of the stainless steel cases.

It broke and fell to the deck. Katarina opened the trunk.

Despite the tight seal, all these years on the bottom had allowed sediment and water to seep inside. At first all they saw was murky water, but Katarina dipped her hand into it and pulled out a necklace of large white pearls.

She placed the necklace on the deck and reached in again carefully. This time, she retrieved a tiara that looked as if it were encrusted with diamonds.

A representative from the Russian historical society stood by. Seeing this, he stepped forward. With careful precision he took the tiara and began to smile.

"Exquisite," the bespectacled man said. "And almost unbelievable. But it is certain now."

He held up the tiara. "This was worn by Anastasia, daughter of Tsar Nicholas the Second," he said. "She was photographed in it in 1915. It disappeared, along with many other jewels, when the Tsar fell to the revolution."

Kurt looked over at him. "I thought all the Tsar's treasures had been found."

"Yes and no," he said. "The treasures they were known to possess were discovered long ago. Indeed, many jewels were sewn into their clothing to hide them from the guards. Both Anastasia and her sisters were shot and stabbed to no effect because their clothing was so stuffed with precious stones that they were all but bulletproof."

"I figure you have those," Kurt said. "So where did these come from?"

"The Tsar's fortunes were so vast, the extent of his wealth was never really cataloged," the man said. "For political reasons, the Soviets insisted that all the wealth had been collected and placed in trust for the people. The Russian government that succeeded the Soviet one continued this charade, but many photographs from that era display treasures that were never discovered. It was long assumed they had been lost to history. Who would have thought that both your government and mine knew where some of them were?"

Kurt considered what the man was saying. It didn't bother him that the jewels would be going back to Russia, he just wondered how they'd left Moscow in the first place.

"How'd they end up here?" he asked.

"I can tell you that," a wavering voice said.

Kurt turned. While he and Katarina were down below on the dive, a new arrival had come aboard. Kurt knew who he was and had requested he be found and offered the chance to be present.

Kurt stepped up and shook the man's hand.

"Katarina," Kurt said, "members of the Russian government, meet Hudson Wallace."

Wallace stepped forward, moving slowly. He had to be almost ninety, though he still looked like the kind of guy who could thump you if you got out of line. He wore a bright red Hawaiian shirt, tan cargo shorts, and boat shoes with ankle socks.

He fixed his eyes on Katarina and smiled from ear to ear.

"My copilot and I picked up a fellow in Sarajevo," he said. "A political refugee named Tarasov."

"He was a criminal," the Russian man said, "who took the jewels after burying them with three other soldiers years before."

"Sure, sure," Wallace said. "One man's criminal is another man's freedom fighter. Anyway, we whisked him out of there and brought him to Santa Maria, where we were supposed to fuel up and hop across the pond. But we got grounded by a storm, and some of their agents found us."

He shook his head sadly. "Tarasov was shot in the back. My copilot, Charlie Simpkins, was killed as well. I was wounded. I managed to take off, but an electrical storm, a couple engine failures, and loss of blood brought me down. I lost control of the plane and hit the sea. To this day I don't remember how I got out."

"You know," Kurt said, "that story was part of the reason we believed in this hoax."

Wallace laughed, and his face crinkled up. "In those days things like that happened all the time. Instruments iced up, gauges froze, you couldn't tell up from down."

"But what about the engine failure?" Katarina asked.

"I had a hard time figuring that myself," Wallace said. "We kept those babies in prime condition. Then it hit me. It rained there for three solid days. We fueled the Connie from their ground tanks. I think we sucked up a bunch of water when we took on five hundred gallons of the stuff the day before we left. Damn bad luck, if you ask me."

Kurt nodded as Hudson looked down at the tiara and the necklace.

"For sixty years I always wondered what was in those boxes," he said. "I guess they're filled to the top."

Katarina smiled at him kindly. "You'll be able to see them in a museum, I'm sure," she said.

"No thanks, miss," he replied. "I came for something much more valuable." He turned to Kurt. "Were you able to get 'em?"

Kurt reached into his pocket and retrieved the dog tags he'd pulled off the copilot. Wallace looked at them with reverence as if they were made of the purest gold.

"A Navy team is coming out tomorrow," Kurt said. "Charlie will be buried in Arlington next week. I'll be there."

"You?"

"You lost a friend here," Kurt said. "But in a way you and your copilot saved a friend of mine. We'll both be there. We owe you that much and more."

"A long time to come home," Wallace said.

Kurt nodded. Yes, it was.

"I'll see you there," Wallace said. He smiled at Katarina, thumbed his nose at the Russian expert, and walked back to the boat he'd motored in on. It took a moment for him to climb aboard. Once there, Wallace grabbed a wreath and held it out. Then, with a gentle toss, he laid it out on the water.

THREE DAYS LATER, after finishing the recovery and spending forty-eight hours with Katarina that actually qualified as R & R, Kurt was back in the States.

Katarina denied it, but he had a sneaking suspicion she'd enjoyed her time as a spy of sorts. They promised to meet again someday, and Kurt wondered if it would happen first from careful planning or at random in some out-of-the-way place with a swirl of international intrigue unfolding. Either way, he looked forward to it.

He wandered by the NUMA headquarters and found the place empty for the weekend. A message from Joe told him to go home.

Heading the advice, he made his way back to his boathouse on the Potomac.

Suspiciously, he detected the scent of marinated steaks grilling on a barbecue emanating from his own deck. He walked around to the back of the boathouse.

Joe and Paul were standing on the deck above the river. Gamay sat nearby on a chaise longue. Paul appeared to have commandeered Kurt's gas grill, and what looked like rib-eye steaks for the four of them were sizzling away on it.

Joe was scribbling something on a Dry Erase Board, and a bottle of merlot sat on his corner table along with a cooler of beer and some travel brochures.

Gamay hugged him. "Welcome home."

"You guys know this is my home," he said, "not a dormitory."

They laughed, and Kurt leafed through the brochures, noticing a theme.

Joe handed him an ice-cold Bohemia, just like the one he'd liberated from the captain's stash on the *Argo*.

The Trouts sipped the wine.

"What's going on?" Kurt asked, feeling as if he'd stumbled upon a secret gathering.

"We're planning a trip," Joe announced.

"Haven't we spent enough time together?" Kurt said, kidding, and well aware that he was standing amid family.

"This will be a vacation," Gamay said. "No running, no shooting, no explosions."

"Really?" Kurt said, taking a sip of the beer. "Where are we going?"

"Glad you asked," Joe said. He walked over to the Dry Erase Board on which three names had been written. Each had a single check mark on it.

"We've all voted once," Paul said, "but we have only white smoke to send up the chimney."

"So I'm the tiebreaker," Kurt guessed.

"*Correcto,*" Joe said. "And don't let all the times I've saved your life influence you."

Kurt stepped closer to the board, cutting a sideways glance at Joe. "Or all the times you've caused me trouble."

He studied the choices.

"Eight-Day Moroccan Camel Safari," he said, reading choice number one. It had Paul's name next to it. "Have you ever been on a camel, Paul?"

"No, but . . ."

"Eight minutes might be fun, but eight days . . ." Kurt shook his head.

Paul looked hurt. Gamay and Joe smiled.

"Death Valley Hiking Trip," he said, looking at the next line. Gamay's choice. He looked at her. "Death Valley?" he said. "Nope, that's a little grim, don't you think?"

"Oh come on," Gamay protested. "It's beautiful there."

"Yes," Joe said. He raised his arms as if he'd won.

"Hold on there, partner," Kurt said. "I'm not sure the Gobi Desert even counts as a vacation spot."

"Sure it does," Joe said. "I saw a commercial. They even have a slogan. 'Go be in the Gobi.'"

Kurt laughed. "They might want to keep working on that."

"It's dry there," Joe said. "No chance of drowning or freezing or ruining your best Armani shirt."

Kurt laughed again. He could just about imagine Joe wearing Armani in the middle of the desert. He sighed, guessing they weren't really serious, but there was one dry, sunny place he'd always wanted to go.

"I vote for the Australian Outback," Kurt said. "Ayers Rock, rustlin' roos, and Foster's."

They looked at him for a second, stunned.

"Rustlin' roos?" Gamay said. And they broke into a cacophony of noes and long-winded reasons why Australia would never work. By the time they were done Paul was flipping the steaks and Kurt had finished his beer.

"Okay," Paul said. "Let's try again."

Joe erased the board and scribbled "Round 2" at the top. Meanwhile, Kurt sat down in the other chaise, grabbed another beer, and gazed out over the peaceful river as the nominations came in.

As the names of various hot and dry places were called out, Kurt couldn't help but smile. He had a feeling this might go on for a while. And sitting there, surrounded by his friends and soaking up the sun, he kind of hoped it would. In fact, for the moment, he could think of nowhere else he'd rather be.